Mckinley

D J Etchell

Burghwallis Books

Mckinley

Also by D J Etchell

Sonnets from the Iliad
Sonnets from the Odyssey
The Lych-gate
Not to be read by your Wife or Servants

For
John, Alice and Bert
and Mick Bownes

Contents

Introduction

"We may as well face the fact that several million men in England will—unless another war breaks out—never have a real job this side of the grave." This is George Orwell's assessment of the situation in England as described in *The Road to Wigan Pier*, which he published in 1937. The situation did improve for a few decades after that but now we are pretty much back to square one, especially if you add in the legions who are in the make-work schemes and hundreds of thousands of other non-jobs, to the millions who are semi-permanently unemployed and on invalidity benefits.

Mckinley starts in this bleak situation that Orwell described and moves through World War II, and into the long period of relative prosperity for mining communities, which continued until the 1984 miners' strike. Eric Blair's viewpoint is the horrified one of a socialist, old Etonian. Though it is well-observed, it perhaps misses some of the importance of family life, and from my perspective is too stark and rather over-idealised.

I will leave the accounts of what happened in and after the '84 strike to others, but will make a few relevant observations. The first is the fact that during the twentieth century about sixty-four-thousand miners were killed in the course of their work, with thousands more dying of lung diseases and various injuries after finishing work. The numbers of those seriously injured during the century runs into hundreds of thousands.

Coal provided the bedrock upon which Britain achieved industrial greatness and I for one feel that a debt of honour is owed to the miners and their families for their contribution to this country, a debt that was dishonourably and conveniently ignored by Thatcher and her cronies, who used the strike as an excuse to get rid of the pits.

The pits have now gone and the vibrant mining communities which served them are in massive decline. This story is an attempt by someone who lived in those communities and who worked as a scientist in the mining industry to preserve some inkling of that culture and life in mining during the last century.

The central thread of the story is woven around my uncle John Mckinley. Much of it is factual and based on anecdotes from the mines and mining villages and on memories of my own family. In part, it is fictional and what I would have liked to have seen happen to a very remarkable man.

D.J.E.

1

Mckinley and Education

'Mckinley—' A voice echoed down the corridor. 'Mckinley—' The classes had just started, somewhat reluctantly, to come in after the late break. It was a fine July afternoon in the last week of the summer term and the austere chapel-like school buildings, looked almost attractive.

Mr West looked round from where he had been supervising entry to his classroom: 'It sounds like Miss Styring. You had better get down there and find out what she wants. I hope you've not been up to anything silly?' he said, smilingly, knowing full well that young John Mckinley was the least likely of any of his pupils to get up to the sort of tomfoolery which would require a visit to the Head.

John walked unhurriedly down the pale workhouse-green corridor towards the Head's office. The paint scheme was standard in the West Riding and was matched perfectly by the yellowing white of the window frames. The combination exuded an air of supreme weariness, of utility, and of a necessary and yet unenthusiastic provision of educational premises for the lower orders.

He reached the school secretary's door and knocked. She opened it and emerged carrying a ledger. 'Oh, Mckinley,' she said in a sad voice, which reflected spinsterly world-weariness and inner loneliness. 'Mr Sharp wants to see you urgently; he has to leave the school early for a meeting.' She took him across the corridor and knocked at a door on which was mounted a small brass plaque with the embossed words: Mr. G. Sharp B.A.

'Come in!' said a voice, identifiably northern in accent, but with a correctness of pronunciation and a smoothing of the vowel sounds which rendered any attempt to define its origins impossible. John thought the accent alien to Doncaster but knew it must have started out somewhere in the broad swathe of industrial towns and cities which covered South and West Yorkshire.

Miss Styring poked her head round the door and said, 'Mckinley's here to see you, sir,' and then ushered him in.

The Head looked up from the document he was writing with an old and treasured tortoise-shell fountain pen. 'Thank you Miss Styring, there will be nothing else,' he murmured. She turned and left, closing the door quietly as she did so.

Sharp was unfailingly courteous and unfailingly formal. He always addressed everyone, including the school cleaners, by their full title, managing at the same time to give an impression of authoritative concern. Everyone respected him. From the professionals at the local education authority down to the school's part-time groundsman, all held Sharp in very high esteem. This was perhaps as much due to his appearance as his manner. He was unusually tall for those days at over six feet, slim and with pale blond hair. In summer, he dressed in a charcoal grey suit, although this was now showing some signs of age, with a little wear at the cuffs. He was always smart with well-pressed trousers and an impeccably knotted regimental tie. In winter, he wore a suit of heavy dark blue serge, always with the same tie or its twin, and accompanied by a white shirt on which the collar stood rigidly to attention due to the heavy starching that Mrs Sharp administered to it.

The headmaster was a serious man. He regarded education, especially education within the hard and poverty infested mining villages, as a sacred vocation. His diligence in trying to get the utmost from and for each of his charges was well known in the area. His ideas were progressive. He frowned on physical punishment and had got rid of one female member of staff who seemed excessively keen on administering it. She had protested that it was the only way that she could keep control in class. Sharp knew that it was not and that a quiet or a severe word when necessary was almost always as effective. He was very well aware, when it came to administering corporal punishment, that some in teaching liked it and he was having none of it.

In his own eyes his family life was idyllic. He had two bright and healthy daughters and a young wife. He idolised all three. Most of his own life was centred around his home and the church. The only luxury he allowed himself was the occasional round of golf, mainly during the school holidays. In summer he always departed to the beautiful and mostly deserted beaches near Holy Island in Northumberland.

His sister had married a local borough treasurer and the four always spent a fortnight with them in their spacious house in the small township of Bamburgh. The house was typical of many middle-class homes of that period. A cleaner came in three mornings a week and a cook and part-time gardener were also employed. Whilst the women and children of the two families enjoyed the beaches, he and his brother-in-law always made time for a morning round, trying to improve their handicaps on the local links. It was now near the end of the summer term and Sharp was starting to think about his treasured holiday.

However, at this moment young Mckinley stood before the Headmaster's desk. He had never been into the inner sanctum before. His eyes roved over the bookshelves, which stood out not due to the quantity of books but by virtue of their quality in respect of binding and scholarly titles. For some reason one in particular caught his eye. The spine was gold lined with an embossed title that read: *Shakespeare, his Mind and Art* by Edward Dowden. The book was published by Paul, Trench, Trübner and Co. Ltd. He noticed that the u in Trübner had a double full stop over it and wondered what that signified. He also noted that the spine said 'eleventh edition'. This led him to believe that the book must be of extreme interest or importance.

Sharp put his pen down and looked straight at John and said, 'I won't waste time and I know in your case that there is no need to.' John knew exactly what he meant. For reasons that escaped him, some of the other kids needed telling three or four times and then pretty often did not quite grasp what was required of them. With him, the message sank in first time every time and the Head appreciated that. John looked at the adult, waiting for what was to be imparted to him.

Sharp told him that he had been looking at the school's end of year results. He went on: 'This is a very unusual state of affairs; we have had bright pupils here before but not like you. You had very high marks in the scholarship exam, apparently the highest ever at your Junior School. Your work there was exemplary; your former headmaster recommended that you start here in our second year. At half-term you were moved up into the top form, coming top of that class in the end of year exams. You actually came first in all subjects apart from art.

'Thus, John, you have completed your secondary education. I could ask you to repeat this for the next two years,' he said, looking up and straight at John, 'but there would be no point. What I propose is that you sit in the library, which is usually quiet, and read. By read, I mean read useful publications. There is a set of encyclopaedias and many of the English classics and many other interesting and useful books. I will keep an eye on what you are doing and once a week I can schedule a short session to keep track of your work and answer any questions. I know that Mr West is also keen to help; you might like to ask him about mathematics and science, and Mr McChrystal will be useful. My own field is English literature and the Classics. Ahem,' he said, clearing his throat, 'by that I mean the classical literature of ancient Greece and Rome, but you probably know that without me having to tell you. Many people assume that when I mention the Classics I am talking about Jane Austen or the Brontes.'

John was somewhat taken aback, not because of the Head's plan, which he thought was eminently sensible, but because he had actually addressed him by his first name. This was the first time he had heard Sharp being anything other than rigidly formal to anyone.

The Headmaster said: 'I will explain what is happening to the staff and I have already talked it over with the chairman of our governors, who is rather pleased and interested in participating in a novel educational experiment in the West Riding. Do you have any questions?' he asked.

John said, 'No, sir,' though his mind was racing at this unexpected and yet pleasing turn of events.

Sharp smiled, which was also a highly unusual happening, and continued: 'I knew you would understand. Miss Styring has a note for your parents. If your father is in any way unhappy about what I propose please tell him to come and see me.'

Mckinley replied, 'It's my step-dad—my proper dad was killed, sir.' His tone was matter of fact and unemotional about the event that had occurred in 1915, which also happened to be the year of his birth.

The Head paused, reflected briefly and then said, 'Ah! Sorry Mckinley, it had slipped from my memory. It was during the war, wasn't it?'

'Dardanelles, sir,' was the rejoinder.

Sharp was quiet for a moment, thinking about the recent conflict in which he also had seen service. 'Yes John, my sympathies; it was and still is a great sacrifice for many of our families.'

At that moment, Miss Styring knocked and entered the office and said, 'The Chairman is here, sir.'

'Thank you,' said the head. 'Please give Mckinley the note for his parents. I must get off to my meeting.'

John was ushered out and given the letter which was sealed in a brown manila envelope upon which was printed, just above the tip of the flap, the legend WRCC, signifying that the school came under the aegis of the redoubtable West Riding County Council, Education Authority. He made his way, unhurriedly, back towards Mr West's classroom; he knocked and entered. His teacher smiled at him in a knowing sort of way and he was told to sit down.

The chairman of governors was the local Church of England rector, Dr Whyte. He entered the school slowly, needing to use a walking stick because of troublesome arthritis in his left knee joint. The Head waved and hurried down the corridor to meet him. They shook hands. 'Good to see you, sir,' said Sharp.

As they left the school, the rector said, 'Would you mind driving, old chap? It's the knee, you know.'

Sharp replied: 'Delighted to, sir.'

The motor had been left running as the car was a quite elderly Cherwell and was somewhat difficult to start. It was a model that had briefly been manufactured in Doncaster and had been named after a minor tributary of the River Don.

Whyte was an old style Liberal. He had voted for the party all his life and was sad to see its present decline, which he hoped was temporary. He was liberal and generous in temperament also, shepherding his small flock through the difficulties and challenges of life and death with humour and compassion. His church duties were not onerous and thus he could devote time to community work and to his reading and those studies which had made him an expert in the field of children's literature. In his sermons, he was just as likely to make reference to *Toad of Toad Hall* or to *Tom Sawyer* as to St Paul or St Luke.

Sharp saw the older man into his seat and then climbed into the driver's side and slowly set off for their meeting at the local offices of Adwick-le-Street Urban District Council. The four-mile drive in those days was leisurely, partly due to the twenty mile an hour speed limit, which though still in force was becoming increasingly disregarded due in part to the fact that the latest cars could do far more than this. Secondly, although motorised road traffic was light, the roads were still narrow and horse drawn vehicles of various sorts were often encountered on them.

'Do you know what it's all about?' said Dr Whyte. 'Is it to do with the Hadow scheme?'

'Yes,' replied Sharp. 'We are fairly progressive in the West Riding and moving towards separate schools where possible. Due to the nature of the existing structures, it will be easy to establish two secondary schools, one in Woodlands and one in Skellow. The proposal is that the infants will occupy parts of those two buildings, which are more or less separate structures in any case. The juniors will be removed entirely and attend two new schools, one in Carcroft and one in Adwick. Most pupils live reasonably close to the schools and none should need to walk more than a mile and a half to get to them.'

Whyte asked what Sharp thought about Hadow's proposal to raise the leaving age to fifteen. Sharp said, 'A good idea in principle, but how will it be funded? And, after the fairly recent increase from twelve to fourteen and the ructions that caused, I am not overly optimistic.'

The rector said: 'Yes, that's rather what I was getting at.'

Sharp went on: 'The problem is two-fold, of course. We have the hurdle of finance on the one hand and the opposition on the other, which will come from parents denied a year's income from a son who would be working at the pit. In addition, many of the girls from these villages go away to the big industrial cities to work in service until they get married. This lifts the burden of the cost of a daughter's upkeep from the parents.'

'I understand,' said Whyte. 'It's a great pity.'

'In a few cases especially so,' Sharpe replied.

'What do you mean?' said the rector.

Sharp explained about Mckinley: 'He is exceptionally bright and if he was from a better background he would have undoubtedly gone to the Grammar School, and thoughts of progress to university would very certainly have been appropriate in his case.'

Whyte continued: 'It was a minor public school as far as I was concerned, but I am well aware of the advantages which education confer and of the injustices which the random lottery of birth impose. We both know that each year several of the pupils in the top class at junior school pass the scholarship exam, which entitles them to go to a Grammar School. We also know it is a very rare event if they do so.'

Sharp was all too aware of the depressing waste of talent which this entailed.

'I suppose it is the cost,' said Whyte.

'Oh yes,' said Sharp. 'The annual fee to attend is fourteen guineas. This plus the cost of summer and winter uniforms, sports equipment, stationary and books puts it beyond reach for almost all. The sum equates to several week's wages for most of the fathers. Money is far too tight in most families to allow the luxury of Grammar School and there is also the problem of two years' loss of earnings if the boy leaves at sixteen rather than fourteen. There are, of course, in practice, social barriers. The bulk of the pupils at the school are from middle class families, with fathers in the professions. Most of the rest have sufficient income from parents who farm or keep shops to afford them the luxury of attendance.'

Whyte said: 'Yes, it is very sad; there was a similar case to that of Mckinley at the Woodlands School. There, one pupil stood head and shoulders above the rest, name of Gravil. Everyone thought it such a pity, Mr Bardill the Head had been very impressed with the boy and went to extraordinary lengths and wrote several letters in order to try to get him the sort of employment in which he could start to exercise his talents. But the boy, like most of his class mates, went to work at the pit; the stigma of being from a mining family is hard to overcome in some people's minds.'

'How did he get on?' asked Sharp.

'Apparently he was keen,' said the rector, 'and wanted to

prove himself to his father and workmates and progress to a coal face as soon as possible. He did that at nineteen but soon afterwards got buried up to his neck after a roof fall.'

'Oh!' said Sharp. 'Was he badly injured?'

'Oh no,' said the rector. 'The problem was mental! The accident induced a nervous condition and he had to come out of the pit. He finally managed to get employment with the local council as a dustman.'

After that exchange, there was a period of silence as they drove up the lane to the cluster of Council offices. Sharp mused to himself on the ironies of the situation: 'The brightest of our working-class pupils; and all that they can expect out of life is to become a dustman!'

2

Mckinley and Empire

The year of 1928 gave way to '29 and then to 1930. At Skellow Secondary School, Mckinley was completing his formal education. At almost every level in that establishment, the British Empire intruded prominently. It was present as a huge red welt, slapped across the face of the world on the large maps that were hung in each class. His majesty King George the Fifth was King. His marriage to Princess Victoria Mary Augusta Louise Olga Pauline Claudine Agnes of Teck ensured that the progeny of the royal house continued to be, by lineage, one hundred percent German. Its name though had been changed from Saxe-Coburg to that of Windsor in 1917. This in order to deflect any anti-German sentiment resulting from the huge losses of the Great War away from the royal family. Other branches of that family took similar steps to disguise their links to the detested Hun—the Battenbergs, for example, becoming the Mountbattens.

In most quarters 'the Royals' were spoken of in very respectful and even reverential tones. The King was, after all, Emperor of India, King of the dominions of Canada, Australia and New Zealand, and the rulers of more than forty other countries owed fealty to the British Crown. He was related to most of the other royals of Europe. His shortcomings were well known within the inner circle of families who then ruled the United Kingdom. The fact that he was rather a dull man intellectually, who wore his trousers creased at the

13

sides rather than front and back to disguise rather bowed legs, was never mentioned to outsiders. Amongst the lower orders, only extreme deference was expected towards those personages who embodied the pomp and power of a great empire.

The British Navy was the largest in the World, holding sway over the seas and oceans upon which the Empire depended for its trade. There was a large proportion of the Army stationed abroad, mainly in India, with some units in Africa and Asia. This was in order to maintain stability and good order in the many lands that served Britain's commercial interests. Germany had recently been defeated and another major war in Europe was considered to be almost impossible. Strategic planning for such an eventuality was therefore almost nonexistent. Location of forces and development of armaments largely depended on how forcefully senior officers advanced arguments in favour of their personal theories. Success in the advancement of these theories, of course, usually resulted in the further promotion of the person advancing them.

Cosmo Gordon Lang presided over the Church of England as its Archbishop of Canterbury. Although all churches were in decline, the C of E still had almost three million regularly practising Anglicans, and through its place as the established church, with twenty-four of its Bishops sitting in the House of Lords, it still spoke with a powerful voice in national affairs.

John became aware, through his reading of the *Harmsworth Self Educator* and other tomes from the school's library, of the late Victorian and Edwardian view of the superiority of the British, and especially of the English, who stood at the peak of the pyramid that comprised the various types of humanity. He read that they were amongst the tallest of the world's races along with their northern European kin. This was of course to be expected, as Germanic and Viking blood was common to all of them. The worthy Victorians and their successors had expended much effort in measuring the differences between skulls and facial features of all nations, and in rigorously classifying their racial types they knew that western culture and civilisation was superior to all others and had expended significant and somewhat biased efforts in proving it.

He learned that skulls could be classified according to the proportion of the face that extended in front of the cranium. In some animals, such as apes, this extension was very prominent. He read that this was also a characteristic of the 'lower' races of mankind such as the Negros and Australian aborigines. This reinforced the 'self-evident' fact that they were inferior to the white races; this could clearly be seen in their primitive dwellings, weapons, agriculture, dress, lack of religion, etc. What passed for religion among these primitives was classed as a low form of fetish worship that depended on evil spirits and sacrifices. The absence of the idea of a supreme being among these peoples had obviously inhibited them from developing those modern methods of warfare possessed by the superior nations, which could now efficiently slay millions.

It was thus clearly established, by 'meticulous' scientific study, that the Europeans were the highest type of living men, with the strong inference that the English were at the pinnacle of this resplendent mountain of humankind. Harmsworth stated, with unchallenged authority, that, 'In the Europeans the whole contour of the face is regarded as expressing the highest nobility of character to be found in mankind.' In respect of individual facial features, John noticed with wry amusement that only the English, Scots, Basques, and for some unknown reason, Parisians, were blessed with the advantage of leptorhine, or narrow, nostrils. Thus John, though pretty near the bottom of the pile in terms of the English class system, could console himself with the fact that at least the pile that he was part of was placed above all of the others.

Britain was a democracy; any of its adult citizens apart from members of the House of Lords and lunatics had the right to stand for parliament. There were some worrying features of this process, in that the working classes since the turn

15

of the century had increasingly insisted on exercising these rights, through a Labour Party that was largely financed by the Trade Union movement. It was a source of some consternation in certain quarters that these people had managed to form a government, albeit a minority one, in 1924 and again in 1929. These concerns were somewhat assuaged by the fact that Ramsay MacDonald's first cabinet of nineteen men included: the Viscounts Haldane and Chelmsford, and the Lords Parmoor, Olivier and Thomson. His second contained four peers of the realm and a knight.

However, the strange ideas held by the socialists were highlighted for many by the fact that the cabinet included a certain Margaret Bondfield, the first woman ever to serve in that exclusively male club. Young Mckinley had overheard part of a conversation just after the 1929 election; it was between two of the local landed gentry who were passing by astride their horses on the way to the hunt. The comments that were made going along the lines of: 'My God, they'll be wanting women vicars next!' With the reply, 'Oh, don't worry old boy, that will never happen, that really will be going far too far!'

The last two years at school were happy ones. The staff trusted John, and West, McChrystal and Sharp were keen to help him when they had the time. He was aware of the pressures on staff at the school—they were frequently occupied with playground or dinner supervision in addition to their teaching duties. For this reason, he always held his questions in reserve until an opportune moment presented itself, and was always careful not to labour the point and take up too much valuable time when he made his enquiry. He found that as he read more he needed to ask less. The school library contained most of the works of Charles Dickens, which John read avidly. *Our Mutual Friend* and *The Mystery of Edwin Drood* were the missing volumes. John asked the Head about them, and he was told of the first: 'Not one of his best, a difficult read,' and of the second: 'He didn't complete that one—they only printed it out of respect for him.'

Only sixty years had passed since Dickens died. John's own world seemed similar to that author's, especially in respect of domestic circumstances and food. He related to the many illustrations within those novels of people at the bottom end of society. They were portrayed as oddly dressed, in ill-fitting clothes and battered hats and somewhat fantastical appearances and not at all like the wealthy who appeared to him to be unnaturally clean, extravagantly dressed and unusually well fed, often to the extent they frequently looked exceedingly corpulent.

The poor were usually depicted as thin faced and with a half-starved or wild-eyed look, which he could sympathise with through occasionally seeing that look on the faces of people at the end of their tether in Skellow. The depictions were also very real due to his own experiences of times when the food in the house was insufficient to fill the bellies of himself and his siblings. Although John had never starved, he had been hungry; most of those he knew had experienced the severe privations that had to be endured during the various miner's strikes. The hardship of the six-month long strike of twenty-six was still vivid in his mind. With its memories of only bread and thinly scraped margarine or dripping to eat, or dinners of nothing more than mashed potatoes or turnips with gravy or even just boiled cabbage with a little brown sauce.

John loved Dickens' choices of names for his characters. The idea of being called a Newman Noggs or Mrs Squeers set up an expectation that was usually fulfilled as the author fleshed out his characters in rich and imaginative detail. The library also contained a reasonable selection of other classics such as Don Quixote, through which he drank in insights into Spanish culture via the text and copious footnotes which he thought were often written in a somewhat tongue in cheek manner.

John was also particularly fond of Sir Walter Scott, with *Waverly*, *Rob Roy* and *Ivanhoe* in particular gripping his imagination with their insights into the times of the crusades and the chivalric code of the knights, and of Scotland just after the rebellion. Wilfred of Ivanhoe battling for the honour of fair maidens, usually against unfair odds and often while fainting due to loss of blood from his wounds, filled his mind with thoughts of those far-off days. He was unimpressed with the grasping Isaac of York and wondered, after later encountering Shylock, if all Jews were like that.

He had never met a Jew, and apart from the frequently used expression 'to be Jewed out of something' and dark or unflattering references in his religious instruction lessons, he knew nothing of them. His opinion of that alien race was thus destined to be low. The view he held was pretty commonplace in the West Riding townships until after the war, when events in the concentration camps caused a radical rethink and an alteration in opinions.

His reading ranged widely using the school resources and the newly opened public library, which was situated next to the Miners Welfare Hall, which was a few hundred yards from where he lived. That particular institution was founded on a high-minded notion that its readership should aspire to better things. Just what these things were or how they were to be achieved by the readers had not yet been worked out, but aspiration was encouraged by the rule that although two books could be taken from the library at any time one of them must be from the non-fiction section of the institution. Thus, military history was absorbed, the *Odyssey* and the *Iliad* and works by other poets such as Milton, Pope and Lord Macaulay.

Young Mckinley particularly enjoyed Macaulay's 'Horatius'. He and the noble lord were about as far apart in education and background that it was possible to go in England, and although he knew little of the Classics or of the history of ancient Rome, something within the poem struck a chord deep inside him. He particularly enjoyed the bloodthirsty stanzas containing lines describing how the hero with his two companions withstood the onslaught on the narrow bridge leading to the city, repulsing attack after attack until the citizens could demolish the foundations and send it crashing into the Tiber.

> *Stout Lartius hurled down Aunus*
> *Into the stream beneath:*
> *Herminius struck Seius,*
> *And clove him to the teeth!*

His favourite was the one describing the approach of Lars Porsena's hordes. He liked its descriptive and rhythmic qualities. He admired the skilful way that Macaulay had achieved this by using an unusual rhyme scheme containing two groups of three lines, each one with a similarly rhyming end word. He realised that this must be responsible for the sustained feel of the piece. He often went through it, recalling the magic of the poem to himself in quiet moments:

> *And nearer fast and nearer*
> *Doth the red whirlwind come;*
> *And louder still and still more loud*
> *From underneath that rolling cloud*
> *Is heard the trumpet's war-note proud,*
> *The trampling and the hum.*
> *And plainly and more plainly*
> *Now through the gloom appears,*
> *Far to the left and far to right,*
> *In broken gleams of dark-blue light,*
> *The long array of helmets bright,*
> *The long array of spears.*

Sharp had explained that the poem's author, Thomas Babington Macaulay, was a noted politician, historian, poet and essayist writing mainly during the first half of the nineteenth century. The head was particularly useful in opening up poetry to John as he had a keen interest in it himself. He explained various technical aspects of metre, which vastly increased Mckinley's ability to analyse what was set out before him. He explained terms such as lyrical saying: 'Lyre-ical! The pre-Christian Greeks spoke the poems to the regular beat or strum of a lyre. Try to look out Bacchylides, he wrote victory odes and various types of songs. I would recommend that you look Sappho up, she was undoubtedly the greatest of the Greek lyric poets but we have almost nothing of what she wrote apart from fragments.'

The Head could also quote huge chunks from poems such as Tennyson's 'The Revenge — A Ballad of the Fleet', or Kipling's 'The Ballad of East and West' as well as innumerable stirring, shorter poems such as Hawker's 'The Song of the Western Men', and needed very little encouragement to do so. In absorbing all these wonders, Mckinley's prodigious memory undoubtedly helped, but even without it he felt it would have been difficult to forget verses such as:

And have they fixed a where and when?
And shall Trelawney die?
Here's twenty thousand Cornish men
Will know the reason why!

Sharp's experiences during the Great War had led him to be far from jingoistic. However, he had been brought up in an age where considerable numbers of poems had undoubtedly been written to further the needs of the great British Empire. These poems enabled vicarious enjoyment of war without having to experience the blood, the smell of fear and the terrible injuries and deaths. John thought that some of the poems such as Allan Cunningham's 'Sea Song' and Wolfe's 'The Burial of Sir John Moore' were exceptionally good, whilst others such as Felicia Hemans' 'Casabianca' were so heavily loaded with artificiality and bathos that he could not read them with a straight face. Many were so blatantly jingoistic that they had a similar effect on him.

He felt that he could do without the sort of encouragement that he read about in Newbolt's 'Vitaï Lampada', which was heavy with public school references that were alien to his own experiences. Although he could see a situation such as:

The Gatling's jammed and the Colonel dead,
And the regiment blind with dust and smoke.

Try as he might he just could not envisage:

— the voice of a schoolboy rallies the ranks
— play up! Play up! And play the game!

In addition to much poetry, he absorbed information about inventions, motor cars, aircraft, ships, engineering and industry. Mckinley noted with interest that the British were the leaders or amongst the leaders in all of these areas of endeavour. The youthful student also devoured the lives of notable Britons and its sporting heroes avidly.

John delighted in Kipling, Robert Louis Stephenson, Dumas and many others. He was amused and educated by *Essays of Elia*, discovering that Charles Lamb, the work's venerable author, differed somewhat from Hutchinson in his classification of the races of men. Lamb's classification was simpler, less scientific, and considerably more intuitive than that put forward by the learned Doctor Leighton in the *Self Educator*. Lamb stated that, 'the human species, according to the best theory I can form of it, is composed of two distinct races, *the men who borrow, and the men who lend.*'

After a few humorous pages traducing the motivation of those such as Sir John Falstaff, who had made it their life's work to subsist by borrowing, he turned his attack to the real villains, such as his acquaintance Comberbatch, who committed the unpardonable sin of borrowing his books and never returning them.

John was also highly entertained by *The Ingoldsby Legends*, loving the rough and rollicking nature of the unsophisticated rhyming couplets or ballade metre, in which many of the lays had been written, and the illustrations of the strange goings on which they described. Shelley or Tennyson it certainty was not, but the tales of Old Nick, obese and corrupt clergy, roistering knights, and young ladies getting into difficult situations, gripped his young imagination. The mixture of strange and fanciful tales, and poems such as 'The Witches Frolic' and 'The Jackdaw of Rheims', harked back to an older age. He always made mental note of the unexplained references in these books, such as 'Anatomy of Melancholy' or 'alembic' or 'compline' for future searches into their origins and meaning as he did of the liberal sprinkling of Latin phrases and those of other languages within the texts.

The Ingoldsby Legends often contained descriptions of feasts and feasting which left him licking his lips and feeling somewhat envious. He was not sure exactly what 'barbecued sucking-pigs crisped to a turn' were, or 'fat stubble-goose swims in gravy and juice' but they sounded delicious compared to the scrag end of neck of lamb or the liver and onions or ham hock or corned beef or fatty bacon, which he usually got, if he got meat at all.

The Legends abounded in guidance usually in the form of a *moral* or *morals* set at the ends of the various chapters. They were quite often in an extended form such as, '*pay the debts that you owe,—keep your word to your friends,—*but DON'T SET YOUR CANDLES ALIGHT AT BOTH ENDS!!' Or—'There's many a slip 'twixt cup and the lip!' Be this excellent proverb then well understood, and DON'T HALLOO BEFORE YOU'RE QUITE OUT OF THE WOOD! John absorbed all the excellent advice that was liberally scattered through the entire volume.

He very much enjoyed the irreverent take on *The Merchant of Venice* that appeared in 'A Legend of Italy'. The legend purported to have originated from two ancient manuscripts and said in the foreword that: '*Readers in general are not at all aware of the nonsense they have in many cases been accustomed to receive as the genuine text of Shakespeare!'*

The lay falls considerably short of the Bard in its use of verse. That poet's brilliant iambic pentameter construction being replaced by more mundane lines such as those that start the tale:

I believe there a few
But have heard of a Jew
Named Shylock, of Venice, as arrant a 'screw'
In money transactions as ever you knew;
An exorbitant miser who never yet lent
A ducat at less than three hundred percent.

The story ends with Antonio, having been made a Count by the Doge, moving to England and bringing the now Christian, Shylock with him. The latter, who substituted the letters 'er' for the 'y' in his name, is then rumoured to have been made a Bishop.

Mckinley had become acquainted in the previous year with *The Merchant of Venice* as it had been performed in a truncated form by a troop of travelling actors at the village hall. These occasional cultural activities were encouraged by the sister of the local MP, a Miss Daisy Markham, who had a most progressive and socialistic outlook on what existence should offer in the pit villages. Feeling that occasional exposure to classical music or the higher arts could perhaps teach the inhabitants that there was more to life than beer, football, and pigeon racing.

The vast bulk of the residents remained unmoved by her efforts but young John had been taken to see the play by his grandmother. The old lady was not typical of those in the village. As a young girl from a comfortable middle class family she had been privately educated. However, her husband, whose name was Edwards, had been gullible enough to be persuaded that he might have title to a choice piece of land on which Wall Street had been built. The solicitor involved had pointed out to him that, if title could be proved, he would be a millionaire many times over. The hook once inserted drew him further and further in. With a limited expenditure of £100 pounds suggested initially, in order to pay for searches, and then, as things developed, with assurances that things were going well, very well indeed, he was gulled into agreeing to expenditure with no upper limit in order to successfully complete the final lap.

The land which has a current value of about two trillion dollars was certainly given to an Edwards, namely Robert Edwards, a Welsh-born buccaneer. He received 77 acres of that now invaluable real estate which comprises a big chunk of Manhattan from Queen Anne for his service in disrupting Spanish sea lanes. Edwards gave the land over to the Cruger brothers on a ninety-nine year lease, on the understanding that it would revert to his heirs after that—but it never did! Since that time and up to the present day various people of the multitude who share that name have tried to establish their ownership.

The lawyer eventually reported that, unfortunately, despite strenuous efforts and much expenditure, his agents had not been able to establish that final, tenuous link, which would have made John's grandfather a very rich man. He was then presented with a bill for several thousand pounds, which ruined him. The result of all this was a trip to the local colliery to seek employment. The manager, on seeing the fine copperplate hand on the application letter said, 'He will be wasted down the pit, get him a job in the office with 'the clerks'. Thereafter John's grandparents lived with his mother and her second husband. A substantial proportion of the family's wealth had come from his grandmother and she hated her husband until the day he died for losing it.

John's grandmother had been named Margaret Williams before her marriage. The family had owned land and property in North Wales. One of her brothers was a notable Methodist minister in the Merthyr Tydfil area and Margaret herself spoke fluent Welsh, which she had been taught at home. Welsh was frowned on by the English authorities at this time who discouraged its use. However, her grandfather was a poet and an authority on the Welsh bards and had thus insisted that the knowledge of this ancient language was preserved within his family. She had learned French while she was at school and helped John, educationally, whenever she could. The visit to see *The Merchant of Venice* was one example of this assistance. She told him all about the play before they went, explaining Portia's speech and how the play had been constructed as a poetic drama written in blank verse.

Margaret still held notions of superiority deriving from her former background rather than from her present circumstances which were those of relative poverty in a mineworker's cottage. The family had settled on Crossfield Lane, which was near to the village school. Just over the road was an old stone lodge, which had been one of the gatehouses to the Owston estate. It was now lived in by the widow of one of the estate workers. Everyone knew her as Nelly and the small gatehouse, even long after she had died and it had started to fall into ruins, was always known as 'Nelly's Lodge.' The lodge had an earthen floor with a little kitchen containing an ancient black fireplace with an oven next to it and a small parlour with old wooden chairs and dining table. Above them were two small bedrooms. A primitive toilet stood in a lean-to at the rear of the property. After using it, a shovel full of ashes was used to cover the result and keep down the smell. The closet was emptied from time to time by one of the estate workers.

Nelly was small and brown skinned due to her always being out of doors tending her chickens, her small vegetable plot and apple, pear and plum trees. She had been young when Prince Albert had been alive and whenever she referred to 'the Queen' it was always to Victoria and not to Queen Mary. She had rhubarb, strawberries, and gooseberries, or goosegogs as they were known locally, growing round her plot at the borders of the wood that surrounded her small dwelling.

She and her niece gathered kindling and firewood from the wood during the drier autumn days to use during the winter and to cook with during the rest of the year. The cooking was always done in the late afternoon, this having the dual effect of providing a late meal and giving some warmth to the house especially in the winter and the chilly spring evenings. They bought a bag of coal occasionally, but it was held in reserve and used frugally. If coal spilled from one of the coal merchant's carts as it turned the sharp corner by the Lodge, Nelly would be out quick as a flash with her shovel in order to scoop the few precious pieces up and add them to her meagre store.

Nelly had tried to be friendly to John's sisters and to his mother and grandmother but was always dismissed by the latter as 'a—country woman, country woman' almost as though this was the equivalent of being a gypsy or beggar. John could not understand the reasons behind the prejudice and he was uneasy about it but he respected his grandmother's judgement.

The Nelly lived well into her eighties, getting more and more stooped and wrinkled with each passing year. She had become ill after Christmas, during one particularly cold winter, and as the turn of the year had approached this turned to pneumonia. Late on New Year's Eve, she had asked her niece to help her into an old upright armchair so that she could breathe more easily. The niece did this, wrapping her in a woollen shawl and a quilt. A fire had been lit in the old fireplace in the bedroom for all of the previous week, something which had not been done for as long as the niece could remember.

'It will be nice to see the New Year come in,' Nelly said, looking out over the frosty fields and wood. They could hear the church bell in the distance toll the midnight bell for the start of the New Year. Her niece said, 'I will get a little elderberry wine and we will toast its coming and hope it is a happy one.' 'Oh yes,' said Nelly, 'very happy, dear.' The niece departed for the kitchen and returned after a short while with two small and ancient glasses containing the wine, but Nelly had departed from life, sat looking out over the fields into the future with the light gone from her twinkling brown eyes.

After the funeral, which was so well-attended that the congregation spilled out into the graveyard beyond the porch of the church, the niece left the Lodge and obtained employment as a housekeeper for a local doctor. The Lodge was left unoccupied and slowly started to decay and fall into ruin. Nowadays all that is left are the occasional overgrown and neglected foundation stones, which are recognised only by those who know exactly where to look for them.

3

Mckinley and Religion

It was the year of 'Our Lord,' nineteen hundred and twenty-eight. Those years were actually years of Our Lord because well-attended churches and chapels abounded in the area. There were three ancient limestone Church of England places of worship situated in the similarly ancient villages of Owston, Burghwallis, and Adwick-le-Street. All of these had been mentioned in the Doomsday Book and were sleepy hamlets with populations of a few dozen families in each. They had been there when the feudal 'three field system' was in operation. The populace had been largely dependent on agriculture for their livelihoods but the populations had burgeoned into many thousands that now mainly depended on the two mines for their existence.

There was a huge, new, red brick monument to the established church, sited at the centre of the newly built mining village of Woodlands. This was consecrated in 1913 and was largely financed by a donation of £10000 given by the local landowner, Charles Thellusson. There were also numerous Baptist and Methodist chapels of various sizes, which were always much more humbly built than those belonging to the established church. One Methodist chapel, built about a mile from the huge new C of E building, was erected in 1912 for the modest sum of £394. Due to an influx of some Irish men to the mines, there was now even a small Roman Catholic Church, which had been built in 1928 at the edge of the latest of the mining village extensions.

The oldest of the splendid old limestone churches was St Helen's in Burghwallis; this certainly had signs of Saxon construction in parts of its walls. The faithful believed that St Helen had visited the site on her way to witness the coronation of her son Constantine the Great as Roman Emperor in York in 306AD. A local, amateur, historian, had pointed out that a Roman fort had been in existence about a mile from the church since about 100AD. He said that because it had mainly been manned by pagan troops from the far flung auxiliary regiments of the Roman provinces, a spring erupted nearby, and the area had for centuries prior to the Roman occupation been settled by the savage tattooed pre-Christian tribe known as the Brigantes, the name was far more likely to have been derived from Ellen, a pagan goddess of water, rather than St Helen!

His views were largely ignored, of course. The mass of the population adhered to the huge pillar of entrenched belief. This, then as now, being far more powerful in supporting irrationality than the slender rod of analysis and logical argument was in supporting rationality. The historian also suffered from the disadvantage of being a known socialist and for this reason was considered by most to be inherently untrustworthy and probably making it all up as part of some Red plot.

This was the age of the Zinoviev letter and of anti-communist paranoia deriving from the very recent Russian revolution and the execution of a Czar and his family, who were closely related to the British royals. The letter was claimed to have been sent by the president of the Communist International to the British Communist party in order to incite revolution. The letter was 'helpfully' published by the Daily Mail just before the 1924 general election. The letter was later proved a forgery, but mud sticks.

It was widely believed at the time that socialists were subversives and fellow travellers with the Communists, who probably secretly received instructions from Moscow on how to undermine church and state and defeat capitalism.

During these years, the delusion of the 'Red Peril' persisted. In 1925 the Home Secretary of the time, a Mr Joynson-Hicks, was so concerned about communists hiding under every bed that he instigated a prosecution against twelve leading communists under the incitement to mutiny act of 1797. Although no mutinies had been incited, the twelve were found guilty and sent to prison. Not for anything they had done, of course, but merely for the political opinions they held and which they were constitutionally entitled to hold. The case was embellished with the ludicrousness which it richly deserved by an absurd offer by the judge to the twelve: to let them off with a caution if they renounced their political opinions! Suspicions about socialists were given further credence and impetus by the General Strike of 1926. Their credibility at that time was about on a par with that of the bearded, rope sandal wearing, CND supporting, nut cutlet eating types of today.

Interestingly, in mining areas, publication of the letter had no effect whatsoever. The very bitter strike of 1926 started after the nation's mineworkers had been locked out of their pits for refusing to take a cut in pay. They stuck it out for a further six months after the General Strike had faded away. Thus, memories of being starved back to work were bitter and the families of the mining villages voted Labour with a solidity that is only now fading.

Thus, this was the state of affairs in the late 1920s. The churches were strong with reasonable congregations, though even then all were in slow and almost imperceptible decline. However, with active Sunday schools and other community-based activities such as harvest festivals and carol services, they were still reasonably full at the major Christian celebrations, and for weddings, christenings and burials of course. In the rural areas, it was difficult to escape attendance if you were an agricultural labourer, as the squire or farmer would notice your absence. Though this had meant workers losing their employment and tied cottages in the past, now it was the lingering fear that a job could be lost, combined with a slowly rising unemployment rate, which maintained the labourers in the semi-feudal mindset in which they had lived for centuries.

In the mining villages the situation was different: alienation from the Church of England, in particular, had been given impetus by the Great War. Though some wives and widows still attended, the colliers themselves mostly preferred to spend their Sundays on their allotments or tending their pigeons or just by having a lie-in after a boozy Saturday night. Sunday was the only full free day that the workers had to themselves as the working week consisted of five and three quarters shifts, due to the marvellous concession by the coal owners of a twelve o'clock finish on a Saturday—following a six o'clock start, of course.

John's family did not attend church or chapel. The lead in this came from John's stepfather, Cuthbert Errington. Cuthbert, or Cud, as he was known by his mates, would walk, stony faced, straight past any Church of England clergyman he came upon, refusing any sort of acknowledgement even if he was spoken to. Strangely, though by no means a Roman Catholic, he always had time for any Catholic priest he came across. John did not understand Cud's reasons, which were never spoken about, yet he accepted his actions without question.

He knew his stepfather's attitude to the C of E had its roots somewhere in the Great War. His understanding of the sort of thing which must have happened was increased much later when he came upon a copy of the recently published *Goodbye to All That*. In it Robert Graves, in addition to being very forthright about the lies told by politicians and about army incompetence during the war, had the following to say about the established church: 'For Anglican Chaplains we had little respect. If they had shown one tenth of the courage, endurance, and other human qualities that the regimental doctors showed, we agreed, the British Expeditionary Force might well have started a religious revival.' Apparently, the chaplains had orders not to become mixed up in the fighting. Soldiers could hardly be expected to respect clergymen who obeyed these orders.

Graves, with heavy sarcasm, went on to say, 'occasion-ally, *on a quiet day in a quiet sector,* the chaplain would make a *daring* afternoon visit to the support line and distribute a few cigarettes, before hurrying back.—Sometimes the colo-nel would summon him to come up with the rations and bury the day's dead; he would arrive, speak his lines, and shoot off again as soon as possible.' The situation was very differ-ent with the Roman Catholic chaplains. Although respect for the cloth was ingrained in most officers because religion massively permeated the public school system, on occasion a senior officer could become so fed up with what he saw that he actually did something about it. The colonel in question apparently got rid of four Anglican chaplains in four months and then applied for an RC chaplain citing a change of faith in the men under his command as the reason for doing so. The difference between the two churches on the western front was huge. The Catholic chaplains were not only permitted to visit dangerous posts, but were positively enjoined to be wherever the fighting was happening so that they could give extreme unction to the dying. Graves says that they never heard of one who failed to do all that was expected of him and more. He described the incident where father Gleeson, a jovial priest serving on the front line with the Munster regiment at the first battle of Ypres, stripped off his black badges of office and took command of the regiment after all the other officers had been killed or wounded. His courageous action contributed to the Munsters holding the line during the battle.

All of this enabled John to understand the roots of his stepfather's animosity to the Church of England, although he never found out the exact detail of Cud's own experiences. At twelve years of age, Mckinley treated any churchman he met with certain wariness. He was, naturally, polite to Dr Whyte; he could see that the Headmaster respected him. John in turn respected Sharp and thus followed his lead.

The period between twelve and fifteen is one of pubescent turmoil, with intellectual faculties developing at the same time that the body is changing. Although in the 1920s poor diet combined with childhood diseases, which were generally not protected against by vaccination, and the absence of antibiotics, frequently led to a very late onset of puberty. Menstruation frequently did not start until a girl was seventeen or eighteen.

John was fortunate in that he had gone through the period of measles, mumps, chicken pox and scarlet fever relatively easily. He had inherited the genes that had given his father and uncles their considerable physical strength and the almost eidetic memory that had enabled his maternal grandmother to recount the details of her own life in such ferociously clear detail. He had learned the virtue of being taciturn, realising that a few direct and well-chosen words were very effective in communicating his intentions to others and in achieving from them his expected response.

The period was one of growth and exploration. John carefully observed people and situations; he listened and often came to conclusions that were very different to the fanciful and superstitious or hysterical nonsense that seemed to satisfy others. He was interested in clergymen and those involved with the various chapels and churches, but purely as an outsider.

He knew that the Baptists were simple people led by lay preachers who were uncomplicated, both in their beliefs and lives. He talked to some of the kids at the school who attended these nonconformist institutions. The impression he got was that most of them were somewhat reluctant captives to the religious upbringings of their parents and grandparents.

He could see that the Methodists were more organised than most of this group. They had a mix of lay preachers and professional ministers who seemed to lead rather Spartan lives because they actually believed in the precepts as laid down by the founder and thus lived Christian life-styles that modelled his! He could also see that the flocks at these institutions seemed to be in a more rapid decline than those of the established church. John could not yet work out why this was, as his frame of reference did not yet have the sort of depth that would have enabled that sort of analysis to be made. However, it was abundantly clear to him that religious belief was slowly waning.

The War, socialism and increasing opportunity for education were slowly hammering the nails of slow and inevitable demise into the coffin of religion in England. Although it would obviously be many decades before the coffin was finally lowered into the ground, he thought that the Methodists and Baptists would lead the way. These churches were founded on the twin pillars of belief and powerful preaching, and for this reason were the first to feel the effects of belief starting to evaporate as other distractions such as the cinema, radio and the popular press led an increasingly literate population away from Christ and towards secularism.

Mckinley also observed tensions. The Catholics, who were largely of Irish descent, were seen almost as subversives who kept themselves to themselves and were not widely trusted. He saw that the Church of England clergy, with the exception of Dr Whyte, were, from his perspective, a rather odd lot. They seemed to have comfortable lifestyles and be heavily involved with the middle classes. The working classes seemed to be something of a puzzle to them, neither speaking with the same accents or using the same language as themselves, nor living according to the same codes of 'civilised' behaviour. If conversation needed to be engaged in with the 'lower orders', it tended to be perfunctory or in a sharp authoritarian tone; or worst of all it was patronising. It seemed to John that it was almost as though the clergyman or his wife were addressing a benighted savage in some jungle clearing in a place where 'civilisation' had barely reached.

He listened keenly to the chatter of the adults, particularly to that of the men in those unguarded moments after they had consumed a few pints. It became clear that the local vicars were generally held in low esteem. Although most miners were rather generous in spirit and would reciprocate if shown generosity, health warnings were widely issued in respect of three of the local C of E clergy. The least, worst offender was Canon Playfair. He had the habit of hovering at the end of a bar in that posh room called 'the lounge' of a local hotel. If approached by some unwary soul and asked if he would like a drink, the Canon would invariably reply, 'Really, that is most kind of you; I will have a triple rum!' The second offender was reputedly one of the sons of minor nobility or landed gentry. He was obviously ex-public school and Oxford and very, very posh. He was also a notorious drunk. One of the colliers said of him: 'He has an unpaid slate as long as your arm at every pub in the area.'

The most objectionable of the three was of cultured Irish extraction. The man had chosen the Church of England rather than the church of his native land purely as a career choice. Church of England clergy could marry and had rather good pensions in addition to the other perquisites that were to be had if you could get a good parish. He had not realised when he signed up that obtaining a good parish usually depended on having family connections in the area in which it was located. As an Irishman, cultured though he was, he stood no chance. He thus had to make do with a church in a mining area.

He was slight in stature and grey of hair. He smoked Player's cigarettes, drawing heavily on each of the thirty or so a day that he got through. He was dismissive or patronising when speaking to any of the local villagers. He was exceedingly civil to the local doctors, colliery managers, or headmasters and their families. He also took great care to cultivate those wives of local tradesmen who were prone to give the occasional gift to the church.

Mckinley first ran into him at the christening of one of his cousin's offspring. After the baptism, which had been performed in a perfunctory manner and with little warmth, the vicar gave a waspish lecture on the high cost of the upkeep of his church, ending with the stern injunction that there were collection plates at the rear of the church 'for your use as you leave!' John liked neither the tone nor the manner of the man but thought that this appeal for funds was fair enough considering the relative splendour of the ecclesiastical premises that he administered. Some years later, however, it was explained to him that one of the colliery officials, a keen racing man who had made a motorbike trip to the rather out of the way racetrack in Beverly, had seen the vicar in question bet one of the old white fivers on each race. A fiver in 1930 represented much more than a week's wage for most of the men living in the village.

The lounge bar at which Canon Playfair was a regular attendee was generally frequented by those who thought themselves somewhat better than the common herd. This was usually by virtue of owning or renting a shop or because they were Deputies or other supervisors at the pit. The beer was always a halfpenny a pint dearer in the lounge than in the bar. Colliers were not encouraged to enter its hallowed portals because of the prices charged and by being ignored if they dared to do so or by being glared at by those wives who accompanied their husbands to the pub on Saturday evenings.

Obviously, the Deputy's wives were better than the wives of common colliers, or so they thought. They had developed the petty snobbery of the lower middle classes to a fine art. Nothing was missed and nothing was forgiven; no opportunity was lost to demonstrate that they were better than workmen and their wives. The senior management also discouraged fraternisation between deputies and the colliers. Deputies organised the work at the coalface and in the headings that advanced the roadways that ran either side of the face. They also marked out the areas to be worked by the individual colliers and therefore determined how much each was paid. For these reasons, it would not have done for the two classes of workers to become too matey.

The only other significant frequenters of the lounge were

the occasional bookmakers or similar types on their way back from one of the race meetings in Doncaster. Sometimes, young and attractive women accompanied them. This invariably became the source of much salacious and speculative gossip in the subsequent week. 'Yes, far too familiar to be his daughter, and much too young for a wife,' gives the general tone of these remarks. The gossipers, indulging in the vicarious thrill of knowing about the possible occurrence of illicit sex, let their imaginations give spice to the otherwise dull, frustrated, or unimaginative sex lives that they enjoyed.

In 1928, sex was never mentioned in the context of actually indulging in it, but the undercurrents surrounding the activity were always present. A mighty conflict raged, especially in the young. This was produced by the hormonal need that impelled them towards indulgence in the 'pleasures of the flesh' as they were quaintly known in those days. Need, of course, was held in check by the fear of pregnancy. If a girl became pregnant, the shame was almost overwhelming. Almost invariably, the culprit would be sent away when she came close to delivery, to one of the institutions that always seemed to be run by one of the churches. These specialised in dealing with 'bad girls' and in taking them in in return for an agreement that they would place the child for adoption. The mother, from the point of birth, was prevented from having any further contact with, or access to, her 'bastard' child.

John also noted that religion was riddled with a mysterious language. He came upon terms such as catechism, Eucharist and transubstantiation. It was almost as though the priests and their acolytes belonged to some sort of secret society from which he was excluded. John always made a point of finding out what these obscure words meant. This was often done with difficulty, via the various encyclopaedias and dictionaries that were available at school and in the local library. Occasionally one of his teachers helped him clarify the definitions that he had laboured to understand. Old 'Snuffy' McChrystal, his teacher, helped him in this. Snuffy was nicknamed after the McChrystal's snuff which he shared a name with and not from any predisposition to colds.

The old Scot was in his sixties and had started out in youth as an ardent Calvinist. In old age, he was a disillusioned communist. This was something he kept to himself of course. He had attended a religious training college as a young man with the intention of becoming a minister but he had started to question his religion and had drifted away from it. Whilst he was there, though, he had learned biblical Greek with the intention of reading the Bible in the language it had been written in.

This had led to a lifelong passion for the language. He had graduated to classical Greek and this became his overriding interest. He had read the Histories of Herodotus and most of the great plays left to us by Euripides, Aeschylus and Aristophanes, worked through most of Plutarch's lives of Ancient Greeks and Romans, and been thrilled by the marvellous military adventure described in the Anabasis. He was not too fond of the philosophers but had read most of the poets and was seduced by the wonderful poetry and stories in the *Odyssey* and *Iliad*. He had read both several times in the archaic and difficult Greek of Homer, teasing out the meaning of obscure words, using a battered old copy of Liddell and Scott, that massive, nineteenth century, Greek-English lexicon that had been compiled by the two Oxford dons from whose surnames its title is derived.

He had explained the Greek alphabet to John and how to pronounce simple words built from it. He ensured that his pupil grasped the difference between the large *o* or *o mega* and the small *o* or *o-micron* and the long and short *e* letters. He showed him how to use an etymological dictionary, so that he could make a good attempt at pronouncing words derived from classical Greek correctly. He constantly stressed the simplicity of it once you had grasped the basics. He had explained to John that the word *Eucharist* was made up of two words, *eu* meaning well and *charizesthai* that meant to show favour and was in turn derived from the word *charis* or grace.

'Nothing difficult about that is there?' he said, looking at John over the top of his old-fashioned glasses. Though he was very careful never to propagandize about his political beliefs, in respect of the Eucharist he could not resist the dry comment: 'Some people believe that the act is symbolic, but others believe that when a priest says the correct words over the wafers and wine they miraculously turn into the body and blood of Christ.'

'All I can say,' he said, acidly, 'is that whenever I tried it the blood tasted exactly like wine, and the flesh just like wafer biscuit. Maybe I have something wrong with my taste buds!'

At first, John found the process of understanding to be oddly disconnected, but as his knowledge grew the various pieces of the jigsaw puzzle slowly slotted into place. His reading in the school library helped him in his quest.

One particularly useful set of books was the full set of the *Harmsworth Self Educator*. These were printed in 1906 and were several thousand pages long. The title page had the motto: 'Every door is barr'd with gold and opens but to golden keys' and further down was the modest claim: 'A Golden Key to Success in Life.'

In these dryly written volumes he explored subjects as mundane as 'the statistics of cost and wear of materials used for footpaths' and meandered through the basics of chemistry, physics and biology, natural history, mathematics, geography, engineering, etc, etc, as far as brief notes on advanced violin practice. He found the sections on languages fascinating and stored these basics in his retentive and capacious memory for future possible use. He was amused by the section on 'one hundred useful travel phrases in six languages', the six being, English, French, German, Spanish, Italian and Esperanto. Thereafter, he carried in his head such useful phrases as *Tiu ci viando estas tiel mamola, ke mi ne povas gin mangi*, which in Esperanto translates as, 'this meat is so tough that I cannot eat it.'

John had a natural aptitude for mathematics, thus the

algebra and associated equations in the various branches of engineering described in Hutchinson came easily to him. Though he had access to maths textbooks in the library it seemed to him that they were written in such a way that they were difficult to understand and that certain key elements were either missing or not fully explained. Recourse to Mr West usually immediately solved any difficulty, but John failed to understand why they were not written in a clear manner with a logical and linear explanation of the complete mathematical process required, set out in a clear sequence on the page. After mastering quadratic equations and those of probability, with West's help he was encouraged to look at the Calculus. West told him that this was the key to higher mathematics and said he was sure it would become of increasing importance as it was the only way he could see of solving the problems associated with acceleration as planes got faster and faster. 'Some of 'em are approaching two hundred miles an hour now,' he said. 'Amazing!'

West, who was interested in the history of mathematics, had the great advantage of actually understanding the origins of the Calculus unlike some maths teachers of that era, who taught the subject by rote and with only a hazy idea of the subject's origins and possible applications. Usually the arcane arts of differentiation and integration were reserved for sixth form maths students. West explained that in the seventeenth century great difficulties had been encountered in developing equations which would accurately describe motion. He said that the roots of that problem lay in the algebra of the time, which had its own roots in classical geometry.

He went on enthusiastically to describe the efforts of the two geniuses, Leibnitz and Newton, in overcoming these difficulties and arriving at the new algebraic methods on which the subject was founded. He taught John some of the basic methods for determining the slope of a curve, at any point on the curve, using the algebraic process known as differentiation, and those of integration, which seemed to John to be pretty much differentiation in reverse, for calculating the area enclosed under any portion of a curve. West was delighted at John's facility in grasping mathematical ideas that often defeated seventeen- or eighteen-year-olds in the sixth at the Grammar school. He reinforced his pupil's grasp of the subject by giving him an old book on elementary calculus. The book was, very usefully, heavily annotated in West's handwriting.

Mckinley's mind not only absorbed the facts but also seemed to discern an underlying pattern in the various branches of knowledge he encountered. For example, his biological and anthropological readings seemed to suggest with varying degrees of subtlety that the English had been placed on earth as the natural leaders of the other races and nations, whose denizens did not have the advantage of being born in the British Isles.

It seemed to be subtly implied in all these learned tomes that the noble British had taken up the task of leading the rest of the world towards the paths of truth and enlightenment, or even of having that task thrust upon them by the supreme-being. Amid this enlightened literature, it seemed to be suggested that, although they were Britons, those born in Scotland, Wales and most particularly in Ireland were at something of a disadvantage to the English.

Amid all of this, the Church of England and the almost sacred English Monarchy laboured under the heavy burden of duty of leading the British peoples and all those under their sway in the right direction; a direction that coincidentally brought significant material benefits to the Church and to the royals and nobility. The young Mckinley observed that most of these benefits seemed to linger amongst the upper classes. Some crumbs percolated down as far as the masses but this seemed to be accidental rather than part of any great scheme to equitably redistribute the wealth which was being produced in large part by the efforts of those lower orders.

Above all else, John was curious! He absorbed knowledge and fitted it into his own worldview. He had the annoying habit of asking very perceptive questions. One occasion after a cousin's wedding, he asked about the letters I.N.R.I. that he had seen fixed to the large cross at the front of the church on which was nailed an effigy of Christ. People he knew, who had attended the church for most of their lives, met his question with blank stares. John could not understand how someone could go to a place week after week and look at an inscription with unquestioning acceptance and never be interested enough to ask what it meant.

McChrystal rapidly sorted the problem out for him, explaining that they were the initial letters of the Latin words *Iesus Nazarenus, Rex Iudoeorum.* Going on to tell him that they translated as Jesus of Nazareth, King of the Jews. He went on to explain that in the absence of a J in the Latin alphabet an I was always substituted to represent it. Old Snuffy, late in life, had become more and more atheistic, yet he retained the comprehensive knowledge of religion that had been drummed into him as a child and young man. He also retained a considerable fascination for the conundrum which religion presented.

The old Scot explained the Greek and Latin roots of the bible to Mckinley and explained the structures of the languages. John said: 'When you read about things like declensions and conjugations in books like *Tom Brown's School Days*, everyone seems to know what they are but they never explain it, and each chapter starts with a bit of Greek but there is no key to it or translation anywhere in the book.' Snuffy smiled and explained that in those days the educated classes would have been taught Latin and Greek at prep school from the age of eight, and they would be able to read the stuff and know all about how the languages were constructed. He went on to explain that in some languages such as Latin and Greek the words such as you, he, or I, when they were used with verbs, were incorporated into the verb, rather than being separated from them as in English.

Snuffy said, 'Are you grasping this, John?'

Mckinley said that he was and that it seemed perfectly straightforward, and asked, 'But why do they call this linking of stem and ending a conjugation?'

Snuffy smiled. 'It sounds very complicated, doesn't it?' he said. 'But it is simplicity itself. The word conjugation is made from the Latin word *coniugo* which means "to yoke." The verb stems and the various endings are yoked together like a horse to a cart.'

John murmured, 'I see.'

The old teacher said, 'When we are talking about declensions, we are talking about things such as nouns, pronouns and adjectives. There are three main declensions in Latin. Once again, they have endings which differ, but with these the ending indicates who is doing something or having it done to them. Declensions always start in what is called the "nominative case", which applies to the doer of an action. It then falls away or "declines" through the other cases which are listed in order of importance or usage.'

McChrystal went on, 'It is a lot to take in at one time but if you are interested I will get you a copy of some old notes of mine which lay out the whole thing in an understandable form and with examples.'

He was as good as his word and about a fortnight later gave Mckinley two double sided sheets of foolscap on which he had laid out the basics of Latin grammatical constructions. He said, 'I couldn't recommend that you learn Latin or Greek John; both are in decline.' He smiled at his own joke and went on, 'You will never, bright as you are, get up to the standard of public school types. But it's nice to know about it. Never let yourself be overawed by someone who can decline nouns or conjugate verbs in Latin or Greek; it doesn't require a lot of brains but it does require a lot of learning by rote.

'In addition, it is important to remember that over half the words in the English language are derived from Latin either directly or indirectly through other languages such as Norman French. Thus, if you learn Latin it will give you insights into English which would otherwise be lost to you. If you do educational courses after you leave this school, take my advice and stick to engineering, science and mathematics. These are the things that will be useful during this century, not long dead languages like these.'

The dry old Scot had little time for the establishment and detested the privilege represented by the public school system. Although he knew he could do little to smash the system, and he had little or no hope of violent revolution, which had changed things so radically in Russia, and prior to that in France. But he did his best to undermine it whenever he could. Young Mckinley was fertile ground and McChrystal did not hesitate to sow the seeds, which he hoped would encourage the youngster to think independently. With the hope, of course, that he would come to similar conclusions to those which he himself had arrived at.

On John's last day at school he sought him out and said, 'I would like to give you a leaving present; you may not agree with what it says but read it and come to your own conclusions. The political analysis it contains was arrived at by a German Jew who spent about twenty years sat in the reading rooms of the British Museum reading reports compiled by the factory inspectorate in the first half of the nineteenth century. Apparently, he got awful boils on his bum as a result. As you might imagine the reports provided dismal reading as they were compiled in the days before most of the factory acts which improved conditions, and all that other legislation which got rid of child labour.

'It can't hurt me to give the book to you now. If I was a young teacher it could have resulted in disciplinary action against me if anyone found out. However, I will be retiring at the end of next year and going back up to Scotland, but even so, can we keep it as our little secret? Don't go waving it about or showing it to others!' Snuffy passed him a small envelope. He said, 'Don't worry too much about the introductions, they were written for workers in different countries in different

45

situations. I should start at page forty-one. One important point there though. The first sentence there is often quoted out of context and has thereby been misused. Make certain that you remember the second sentence, which reads: "All the powers of Europe have entered into a holy alliance to exorcise this spectre: Pope and Czar, Metternich and Guizot, French radicals and German police spies." Enjoy the book, and finally let me say, John, that all my very best wishes go with you for your future; what you make of it is up to you.'

John thanked his teacher profusely and sincerely, and with some sadness. Of all the teachers at the school, the dry old Scot had been closest to being a mentor to him. He secreted the envelope in his school bag. Later that afternoon, when alone after his tea, he opened it. The volume it contained was slim. In gold letters at the top of the faded buff cover were the words K. MARX and F. ENGELS and below that in bold red letters: THE MANIFESTO OF THE COMMUNIST PARTY. On the back cover he could see some lettering, which he thought was Russian. There was enough similarity between the Cyrillic and the English alphabets for him to be sure that they repeated the legend in bold red on the front cover.

Later that evening he glanced through the prefaces, which had been written at different times for the proletariats of Germany, Russia, England, Poland and Italy. Then, as McChrystal had advised, he turned to page forty-one. His attention was immediately seized by the riveting first sentence of the manifesto.

"A spectre is haunting Europe—the spectre of communism!"

4

Mckinley and the Law

For most of the inhabitants of the West Riding of Yorkshire, the only contact they had with the law was the occasional sight of the village bobby. He was observed either on his ancient black bicycle or on the beat, usually in the late evening. As almost no crime occurred in the villages the bobby's task was not onerous. Theft or burglary were almost unheard of, for the simple reason that almost no one had anything worth stealing. Houses were frequently left unlocked at night, as the few sticks of furniture and ornaments that they contained were not worth the effort of purloining. In addition, as any thief would have had to be operating on foot or at best on a bicycle, they must have been from the same locality and as such would have been easily identified and subsequently ostracised by their community.

If a drunken fight occurred on a Saturday night at the pub or Working Men's clubs, the protagonists were usually rapidly separated by friends or relatives and made to shake hands. The attitude among the miners was that if fisticuffs occurred the law had better keep out of it, and the matter was their own affair. If arrests were made for drunkenness these usually occurred in the nearby town of Doncaster, which had a much larger population, a fair proportion of it itinerant, with casual labourers, commercial travellers or lorry drivers on their way through the town, staying at the pubs or boarding houses or doss houses near the town centre. Having no family or friends around them, these isolated individuals would usually spend their evenings drinking, sometimes becoming aggressive or becoming incapable due to overconsumption.

Long distance lorry drivers often came into the town, delivered their loads, and then stayed overnight. They often came from the ports of Hull or Liverpool. The local medical services could usually trace cases of syphilis, which very occasionally occurred amongst the town's good time girls, to lorry drivers who had picked it up in the dock areas of those ports from one of the common prostitutes there; these in turn had usually contracted it from sailors who had briefly berthed there. The common prostitutes were cheap and serviced a clientele garnered from locals and the substantial passing trade. The higher-grade prostitutes rarely presented with any symptoms due to their almost universal use of sheaths, or 'rubber Johnnies' as they were then known, and other careful hygiene measures such as the douche containing weak permanganate solutions.

Doncaster had a large cattle market and frequent race meetings and thus supported a good number of good time girls. The clientele at the higher end of the business consisted mainly of punters who had managed a good day at the races and wanted to finish it off with a hearty meal and a drink, rounded off by illicit sex. Alternatively, the clients could be ruddy-cheeked farmers who had sold beasts at the market and wanted to celebrate with a good meal and a drink, and then enjoy the late afternoon company of an exotic and naughty woman.

Fistfights had been common out in the villages but had declined since the abolition of the 'Butty System' in 1912. Prior to that, the mines operated on piecework, with those at the faces being paid based on tonnage extracted. The colliery management posted price lists, which gave the rate at which men were paid for each job. The money was paid out in a lump sum to the four or five men who supervised the dangerous work at the coalfaces.

The day men, who were involved in tasks such as moving the coal away from the face in the small pony-hauled tubs, or moving props down to it, were paid out by the Butty men according to the price lists. For adults, this usually worked out at about thirty-five shillings per man each week. After the payments were made, the Butty men frequently departed with five or six pounds each. If the share out was disputed, the matter would not infrequently come to blows. Occasionally, a haulage lad who normally would be paid about fifteen shillings a week was tipped if he had been particularly smart in delivering the tubs to the face; this had the desired effect of making all the lads keen.

Domestic disputes sometimes resulted in police involvement but the policeman attending usually settled these. Sometimes it was with a dire warning that next time a summons would be issued, but more often than not with a telling off and statement that he didn't like wasting his time with this sort of nonsense and that they ought to have more sense and behave like grown-ups. The only other significant problems were thefts from meters, suicides and poaching. In the case of the first the crime was almost invariably committed by one of the adult occupants of a house. They all shared the characteristic of being stupid because the criminal was always identified, committing the crimes because they were skint but had to have the money for beer and fags. A fine for the first offence was usually followed by seven or fourteen days in prison for a second.

As the pit villages were surrounded by farmland and the estates of the local landowners, poaching for rabbits was an accepted activity. The rabbits would eat valuable crops, thus the police and the local gamekeepers paid little attention to it. The activity which was really frowned on was any attempt to take the pheasants, which were raised every year to provide shooting for the gentry and friends.

Suicides, usually caused by despair, were not infrequent in the villages. When they occurred, they were always spoken of in hushed tones, especially if children were left behind. Occasionally this was done by hanging, with someone tying a rope to the banister and then standing on a chair and kicking it away. Some would swallow bleach. This would produce an agonising death over a period of several hours. The most favoured manner was by gassing. The suicide would put his or her head in a gas oven and turn it on. The domestic gas of those days contained about eight percent (80,000 parts per million) of the deadly carbon monoxide. Only 500 parts per million of the gas could cause death. Thus, those trying this method of escape found that release came rapidly after only two or three minutes. Suicide was a criminal offence and remained one until the 1960s. When it ceased to be illegal, one hard-bitten police sergeant said: 'Suicide: the only crime with a hundred percent clear up rate, and they took it off the statutes!'

Young John knew that the police in the area, though not generally liked, were respected. They were seen as the guardians of property and as the representatives of the gaffers if a pit was on strike. If a youngster was caught doing mischief he was liable to get a clip round the ear by the constable who caught him and then sent straight home with an 'I'll be round to see your parents later, so you'd better tell them what happened.' The threat was almost never followed up but if the father did hear about the incident it resulted in another whack from the displeased parent's thick leather pit belt after the sorry tale had been told.

The local bobby was called Jim Young. He was a beefy ex-guardsman whose imposing stature was exaggerated by the ten inches of helmet perched on top of his red and massive face. Young was a creature of habit; anyone with intelligence knew where he would be at any time of day or evening. He varied his day beat a little to take the lawless hordes by surprise. He ambled down the village streets at the leisurely regulation pace of two and a half miles an hour, his stately progress obvious to all. The brighter mischief-makers would thus stand around innocently until he had passed by. Occasionally he would double back surreptitiously but only the wild or stupid were caught by this craftiness.

What Young did not want was an arrest. This would mean a trip back to the station, followed by notebook entries and form filling if charges were to be laid. What he did want was smooth progress towards retirement, which in his case would be in seven years, with a clean sheet and his pension intact. What Young also wanted was a quiet life. He had been in the police force before the Great War. He volunteered for the Guards after his eldest brother was killed at the Somme and returned to the force after the conflict.

He had been married but his wife had tired of the boredom of a solitary existence with a husband at the front, and had decamped with the son of a local fruit merchant. Rumours were that they had left for Australia or Canada. In fact, they got as far as Brixham in Devon and set up as the proprietors of a small boarding house there.

Young still lived in the small police house situated just off the main road at a point central to the villages that made up the Adwick-le-Street Urban District. His married daughter lived nearby and did his cleaning and washing. She was glad to receive the few shillings a week he gave her for doing it. Young also had some meals with her but had organised his life so that fry-ups at the station, fish and chips, pork or meat pies from the local butchers, or visits to the kitchens of the houses of the local gentry, adequately satisfied his needs. Bread and cheese, corned-beef, or the use of the stew pot at home filled in any culinary gaps.

As the local representative of law and order, Young saw to it that the local public houses had the full benefit of his guardianship. Although he did not abuse their hospitality, he frequently called at the various pubs just after closing to enquire if everything was all right. Any remaining locals would usually drink up and leave rapidly. After they had gone, the landlord would usually invite the concerned constable to 'have one with me'. They would chat and sometimes-useful information would be forthcoming about people who, for example, seemed to have a little too much money. This could occasionally be linked to petty thefts of coal or the like.

Another problem in the area was 'pitch and toss,' a peripatetic gambling game run by local gangs on waste land. Coins were thrown in the air, money changed hands based on bets on the number of heads and tails shown after the coins had landed. The odds of course favoured those taking the bets and complaints were frequently received from wives and mothers about the money lost to households due to this activity. Because of this, the police mounted organised raids against the gangs from time to time

One notable success chalked up by Young involved one of the locals, a certain Cyril Sumption, better known as Slygo Sumption and sometimes as Con Sumption due to his rather cadaverous appearance. He had been pretty much in fulltime unemployment since the war. The man did not seem incapacitated in any way but had drawn the meagre benefits available to him for many years. He did a little glass or bottle collecting and worked as a part time cellar man for the steward of one of the working men's clubs. He received no wages for this but was recompensed in beer for his efforts.

It was noticed that he had managed to buy a nearly new bicycle and seemed more than usually flush with money. For several months before that, some enterprising individual had been sawing off the thick lead waste pipes which ran into the outside drains from the kitchens and bathrooms of the local mining and council properties, although each weighed several pounds. It was only when the thief turned his attention to the lead pipes running from shops, pubs, chapels and school buildings that the law became interested.

Young lay in wait for several nights, concealed near Slygo's cottage, and this was rewarded late one evening when he saw him depart from his house just after midnight.

He did not follow him but waited there. After a couple of

hours Sumption returned carrying a couple of sacks, which were obviously heavy. The constable stepped from concealment just as his suspect walked past, saying: 'Now then Slygo, what do we have here!'

The thief, for so he proved to be, nearly jumped out of his skin. The sacks revealed several cut off ends of lead piping and a hacksaw. Young arrested the man and escorted him up to the police station, which was about a mile away. He made Sly carry the sacks to the station and then locked his prize away for the night. On arrival, the culprit was sweating heavily due to a mixture of exertion and apprehension. This was not due to fear of what the law would do to him but to his concern at what would happen when his neighbours in the villages found out that he was the one who had been stealing their lead waste pipes.

Searches of Sumption's cottage revealed several-dozen more lengths of lead and other enquiries revealed that more than two hundred had been stolen in total. A shed at the bottom of the captive's garden revealed about sixty lead soldiers and the moulds from which they had been manufactured. Some of them had been painted with the bright red infantry jackets and white belting with the black busbies of the guards, or headgear of the hussars, in readiness for sale.

On interview, Slygo said, 'You can get a lot more money out of lead like that; if you sell it for scrap you get next to nowt.' PC Young had to admire the man's enterprise, but the officer charged him with the offence and he was subsequently sent before the bench. The three elderly worthies sitting that day did not appear to be massively concerned about the thefts from the council and pit houses but were very annoyed that thefts had occurred from various privately owned properties. So much so that they awarded the chagrined Sly a term of three months in prison.

He emerged from the institution a changed man both physically and mentally. He had lost about two stone in weight and now seemed afflicted with some sort of nervous condition, which constantly had him looking over his shoulder, and a reluctance to be seen out of the house during the hours of daylight. After a few months, he left the area having obtained a job as a night porter at one of the less salubrious hotels in Leeds and disappeared forever from village life.

For Young, the affair could not have worked out better. He had had a couple of good arrests of poachers that year, and also of a gypsy who had stolen a horse which the policeman recognised as belonging to one of the local farmers. Although he had passed the sergeant's exam many years previously he had little hope of any promotion. The lack of finance, due to the depression which had resulted in a five percent cut in police pay being announced in Chamberlain's 1932 budget, had removed all prospect of moving up the ranks.

However, with the unexpected retirement of two sergeants due to ill health and the population increase, which had risen because of new seams being opened at both Brodsworth and Bullcroft collieries, it was considered that an experienced man from the area needed to be appointed to one of the vacant posts. Jim Young fitted the bill perfectly; though not massively talented as a police officer, he did have the great talent of not upsetting anyone in the area. When his name was circulated, senior officers, the local landowners and other notables all showed no disapproval and thus he was promoted.

John's first direct experience of the law was at eight years of age when police arrived in a car and took away a man who had come to stay with his sister who lived in that street. Afterwards, she was very tight-lipped about the affair. She explained to her best friend under the strictest injunction not to tell anyone else that the arrest had been for maintenance arrears and that her brother had been 'moving about to avoid arrest' until he could sort matters out. The best friend of course told her mother, again in the strictest confidence; unfortunately telling her mother was about on a par with having the item on the nine o'clock news.

John absorbed the strange sight of two burly policemen escorting the protesting brother into the car. He asked his stepfather what was happening. Cud was intrigued but none the wiser at that stage. He explained later that the man owed money, which had mounted up, and that when men left or deserted their wives the court said they had to pay a certain amount each week for the wife and any children. John was told: 'Some can't and others won't!'

'What happens then?' said John.

Cud replied: 'They go on the assistance. We pay it out of rates or taxes; that's why they chase 'em and try to get the money out of them.'

John could see the logic but still felt sorry for the man he had seen escorted away. There was a look of harried hopelessness on his face, which John never forgot.

His second experience was late one summer's evening. He and Quiller Jones, his best pal, were walking home down the bridle path which led from fields to the pit village. A man burst through the hedge in front of them and threw a bag he had been carrying over the opposite hedge and then legged it at high speed down the path. A couple of minutes later a policeman and gamekeeper burst through the hedge. They looked around, and then set off in the direction they thought that the fugitive had taken. John and Quiller continued to walk homewards down the path.

A few minutes later the PC and the gamekeeper returned; both were sweating profusely. John realised the man they had been chasing had escaped. The two were bent low as they approached, looking for something in the hedge bottoms. The gamekeeper came up to them and said, nastily, 'You two, did you see who it was, did you see if he threw anything into the hedge?'

John was thirteen then, and said, 'My pal was looking at a bird's nest—he didn't see anything.' He knew that Quiller might get scared or confused and say something which might get somebody into trouble. By now, he knew that poaching could result in jail and that this could have a disastrous effect if a family was involved. He continued: 'All I saw was a bloke jump through the hedge and then you two followed him. You startled us.' And then, very truthfully: 'I didn't see him throw anything into the hedge.'

'Are you sure?' said the PC. 'You can get into trouble if we find out you are lying to us.'

'He didn't throw anything into the hedge,' said John. 'Scouts honour.'

He had seen the man, who he knew was one of the colliers from 'the village', throw the bag over the hedge and not into it. Thus, he was speaking the absolute truth and with conviction. The pair of pursuers turned to leave. As they did so the game-keeper said sourly: 'OK, you two. I know who you are. If you hear anything tell the police. If you do not you will be sorry.' The two then retraced their steps through the hedge and John could see them later walking back over the fields towards the woods, which surrounded the old hall.

Quiller said: 'Do you think he knows us, John?'

'No, I've never run into him close to. I know he's one of the gamekeepers up at the Major's place and I would remember.' He looked at Quiller, who invariably took John's lead, and said, 'We don't say anything about this, don't tell your mam or dad, or anyone else. If somebody finds we were out here just say you saw somebody being chased but it was all so fast you didn't take much in.'

The third occasion was a year later. Mckinley had an acute awareness of the juvenile culture in the village and knew that certain of the youths from it were just wrong'uns. They were almost always from a certain type of family with single parents, or fathers with large families who wouldn't work and who spent as much of their assistance money on beer as they could get away with.

A large family of eight might get forty shillings dole a week. In those days, there were twenty shillings to a pound and twelve pennies to a shilling. Beer at a Working Men's Club could be had for as little as two and a half pence. If the father kept two half-crowns, i.e. five shillings of the assistance money, he would have enough for twenty-four pints a week. If he could get a part time job collecting glasses or moving crates, paid in beer, he could easily increase this with a little scrounging to half a dozen pints a night.

John disliked the type. His own step dad was a hard worker who got every shift in he could get, working on the coalface. His pleasures were a pipe in the evenings and three or four half pint bottles of Mackeson stout down at the club on a Saturday evening.

John knew that one of the great causes of crime amongst this type was their desire for cigarettes or sweets. Thefts from slot machines happened occasionally, usually by someone filing bits of metal until they were of a size that activated the machine. The farthing was a favourite as it was almost the size of a sixpence and required little work to alter it to activate a sixpenny slot.

In the summer during which John was due to leave the school, a police car arrived and disgorged a police inspector who went to see the Head. Apparently, a local brass foundry had sold a large consignment of metal as scrap. Unfortunately, it included about sixteen hundred brass tokens, which were exactly the size of a shilling. The founders were guilty of carelessness and the tokens should have been melted down. Instead, they were discovered by juveniles in the scrap yard and then used to empty half of the slot machines in Doncaster and its surrounds. The schools in the area were asked to keep a look out for any pupil with cigarettes or large quantities of chocolate. Sharp passed the information to all the staff and asked John to keep an eye out.

A couple of days later he saw Syd Croot, one of the local layabouts. Syd was a year older than John and was always known by the nickname of Snekker, due do his very large and prominently curved nose. John did not like Croot and he in turn was very wary of John. On this occasion, though, he clumsily engaged in conversation with Mckinley, saying that he had seen the car arrive and wondered why the police should visit the school. John said, 'I would watch yourself, Snekker! It's about slot machines. They've brought the C.I.D. in and they've got fingerprints. It'll be Scotland Yard next!'

John kept a straight face and was rewarded by seeing Croot turn very pale, and look almost physically sick. The youth hurried off and John heard later that a group of young men including Snekker had been arrested. All had been sentenced to be birched due to the large scale of losses from the machines with the ringleader also sent off for a period in an approved school.

John was aware that birching could have two effects: one was to cause resentment and make the recipient an even worse criminal who was determined to hit back at those who had caused them that pain and indignity. The other was to instil such fear of receiving this treatment again that they never repeated their actions. Croot was one of the latter, and although he spent the rest of his life in and out of employment, he never fell afoul of the law again. In his case, his revenge consisted of moaning about the police and the inequities of the judicial system. His complaints usually fell on the ears of his layabout cronies, and so the words were pretty much wasted because all of them had shared Snekker's experience of the law in one way or another.

Mckinley was far too intelligent to listen to or be swayed in any way by types like Syd. He was well aware that the police were tolerated in the mining communities as a necessary evil. Most miners or wives would not socialise with policemen or their wives and they were always kept at a distance. Some of the older pupils treated even the children of police officers with coolness in the school system.

As he got older, he sought the opinions of his stepfather and the invaluable McChrystal. Cud was very taciturn about the constabulary: 'Best kept clear of,' he said. 'Never involve them in anything; sort your own problems out.' His teacher was much more helpful, explaining the history and necessity of a police force. He said, 'Some people seem to see the police as an artisan class whose major job is the protection of private property. They are certainly paid about the same wages as a skilled artisan such as a brick-layer. They are also usually chosen for their height and build; you never see a short or thin constable, do you John?'

He went on: 'Times are changing, though, and policing is getting more scientific. This demands brains, amongst some of the constabulary at least.' He added: 'Lots of miners don't like 'em due to the fact that during strikes they are seen as being on the same side as the coal owners, in that they protect colliery premises while the men are out. Nevertheless, John, ask yourself who else could do it? Do you want the troops brought in as they were before the war? Remember, soldiers carry guns! Miners and dockers ended up getting shot in those strikes before 1914. I am as unhappy as the next man about some things in Britain but the great advantage of using the police is that they only carry a truncheon. Also, they and their families live locally and if they were too heavy handed they would come up against a wall of non-cooperation or sanctions in the villages, which would make their jobs impossible.'

John said, 'What about the courts? Lots of people say there's one law for the rich and one for the poor.'

McChrystal smiled. He went over to his shelf in the classroom and pulled out a volume of history. It was the latest of the Oxford History of England series to be published. Sir Robert Ensor had compiled it. The old teacher said: 'Two things, John. This contains a lot of facts. I wouldn't dispute any of them. You should read it sometime but remember who wrote it. He is a noted historian who had radical and socialist leanings and the book is written in a very learned and gentlemanly manner, but some entries are subtly shaded by omission, in my opinion, to favour the class he comes from. Some events are missing the names of the people responsible or the event is described in general and not in specific terms. Which class do you think he is from, Mckinley?' he asked with a smile. 'How many miners or trade unionists do you know with a 'Sir' in front of their names? What sort of volume do you think it would have been if Kier Hardy had written it?' Young John smiled and took the point.

Snuffy then pulled out a yellowing cutting from between the pages of the book and told John to read it. 'It's about a couple of court cases heard in 1892—the people involved were locals.'

The first case involved a dispute in which one man attacked another with an iron bar in an argument over some chickens. The assailant had been fined and bound over to keep the peace because the recipient had only sustained mild concussion, cuts and severe bruising.

The second case described the owner of Skellow Hall, who had fastened a bottle of champagne in the waters of the stream which flowed at the edge of his property in order to cool the wine before drinking it. A local post boy had spotted the bottle whilst on his rounds, and rescued it from the stream with gratitude. With little thought about ownership, he had taken the Champagne home and then drank it. The penalty for this 'crime', which of course transgressed against the property rights of one of the local gentry, was four months in prison for the poor post boy.

'Are you getting the picture, Mckinley?' asked Snuffy. 'Do you perhaps now think that there is a 'class' bias in the way that justice is meted out?' John smiled and nodded. The old Scot went on, 'You can't blame the magistrates, and it's the system. You can't blame 'the haves' wanting to hang on to what they have. Before the 1888 local government act, benches included none but country gentlemen or the owners of local mills, mines or factories. Although things have changed somewhat since the act became law and now some Labour justices are appointed, the middle and upper classes still form the overwhelming majority of those who fulfil this duty. It is rare to find a Labour justice acting as the chairman of a bench.' He explained, 'Magistrates sit in threes, usually with a senior magistrate as chairman.'

'What about the local mayor?' asked John. 'He's Labour?'

'Aye,' said the Scot. 'You are very sharp for a young lad. A few mayors are appointed to the bench by virtue of their office, just for their year in office—that is *ex-officio* in Latin. You've heard it used?' John nodded. 'Because they are the Mayor, by virtue of the dignity of that office they take the chair of their bench whilst it is sitting. Many people think it's not a good idea, as they have little or no experience of the way a court works and they can be sat with two very experienced JPs, which puts them at a significant disadvantage in holding authority over them.

'I understand that the clerk of the court who sits at the front of them keeps them out of trouble. He is the paid professional in a magistrate's court. In higher courts, everyone is legally qualified, apart from the ushers. The Judges are usually senior barristers who are appointed because of considerable experience. Barristers are specialist lawyers who are legally trained in court procedures and in advocacy. The other main lot of lawyers are called solicitors. Think of it like this: they get, or solicit, work for the barristers, and they do other work, of course, like the legal side of selling houses. They may not speak in the higher courts themselves.'

He went on: 'The law in England is very interesting. It has differences to Scottish law, because until the act of union Scotland was a separate country. In different circumstances you would have made a good barrister; you are very quick thinking and have an exceptional memory. Lots of English law actually has its roots in what the Romans did. They were very good on property law and inheritance. They were very smart. Why do you think the Roman Empire lasted a thousand years? How long do you think the British Empire will last? It's been going about two hundred years; do you think it will make it to three hundred?'

John looked at McChrystal quizzically, knowing that a shrewd gem was about to be imparted. 'The head priest in Rome, or *Pontifex Maximus* as he was called, was effectively the head of the college that made the laws. This meant that if you broke a law in Rome you were not only committing a criminal act but also an act of impiety!' Snuffy looked at John over the top of his specs. 'Clever, eh!' Mckinley was impressed.

Snuffy said, 'I could go on. There was a case last year when the Major up at the hall veered across the road and knocked a cyclist off his bike. He was charged with careless driving. In court, he maintained that he had been driving carefully and that the cyclist had appeared from nowhere and there had been an "unfortunate" accident. His barrister asked the bench to come to the "usual" conclusion. They did so, of course, and found him not guilty. In all probability the old duffer nodded off at the wheel. It's a good job the cyclist suffered no more than a few bruises. Anyway, I think I've said enough. You think about it and observe for yourself how the law works. One last piece of advice though, never be frightened of 'em, but keep clear—police, lawyers, judges, the whole parcel of them. If you ever do get involved, say nothing or as little as possible!'

John thanked his old teacher once again for that invaluable advice which he adhered to for the rest of his life. He came to realise that falling foul of the law usually depended on one of two things, the first being deliberate criminal intent. In such cases, he had no sympathy for the perpetrators. The other reason, he came to realise, was stupidity of various sorts. The most obvious of these being drunkenness, which usually led to a fine. This would usually deprive the rueful recipient of the means of repeating the offence for a few days. He also realised that life was not just, in terms of the rewards and ills it meted out, and that only a fool would expect the law to be so.

5

Mckinley at school's end.

John lay in bed. He had just turned twenty, and he occupied one of the two ex-army, iron, single beds in the smallest of the two bedrooms in the house; his younger brother occupied the other bed. Two of the three girls slept in one of the two ancient double beds in the largest of the three bedrooms in the house with his grandmother in the other. His parents slept in the middle bedroom containing a rather splendid Victorian brass bedstead. His younger sister Alice, who was aged six, also occupied the room. Her bed was a makeshift bunk arrangement situated in the alcove formed by the chimney-breast and the outside wall.

For John, Sunday morning was a time for thought and for reflection on his own and his family's situation. He thought back to the day he had his first employment. He left school in the summer of 1930 and immediately had a job at the local colliery. He had said his goodbyes to Sharp, McChrystal and other members of staff at the school early on the Friday afternoon and had then walked straight down to Bullcroft Colliery, which was about a mile away. He had had his plan of action ready for some time. He knew other lads would be down there on Saturday or on the Monday morning trying for work.

On entering the pit gates, he asked at the wages office for Mr Burkinshaw the Colliery Undermanager. He was directed through the foreboding and grimy maze of workshops to the company offices. The older man sat in his ancient swivel chair, still covered in full pit muck, writing a report. The door was open but John knocked and waited on the threshold. The older man looked up, put his pipe in his mouth and took a long slow puff at it. John recognised the aroma of the black twist tobacco favoured by many of the miners. Sitting back into the cracked green leather of the chair he looked up and said, 'Come in!' John entered. The under-manager said, 'Now then lad, what does tha' want?'

John said, 'Any chance of a job, gaffer? I've just left school this afternoon.'

Burkinshaw was well known to be very clever; he was also very shrewd and the two characteristics are not always found in the same person. Some 'clever' people can be of the very silliest sort, and others can have a sort of animalistic shrewdness without much intelligence, but the senior official had both. He knew of John through gossip at the mine and recognised elements of himself in the boy. He also knew that his step-dad was a good and regular worker who never missed a shift if he could help it. He knew that work patterns tended to be the same amongst families. One of Burkinshaw's tasks at the mine was hiring and firing, and as his own position depended, in part, on having the right sort of blokes at the pit, he was careful to exercise his skills judiciously. He knew that Mckinley would be a good 'un. The Undermanager stretched back in his chair and said, 'Aye lad, tha's got theesen a job. Be here at six on Monday and I'll tek thee down.'

The man was fifty-four years of age, but in those days, having worked since he was twelve and in mining since he was fourteen, with the physical stress and the pressures of management, it had all combined to make him seem at least ten years older than he was. He had been at the pit almost since it had been sunk and before that at a neighbouring colliery.

Before the pit his first job had seen him do two years as a butcher's delivery boy in his home village. His main task had been to deliver orders of meat, mainly to the larger houses on the fringe of the estates. He did this on a large black Victorian boneshaker of a bicycle. The bike was almost too large for the small and wiry boy to hold upright, especially when the iron basket built into its front was full of carefully wrapped cuts of meat, chops, pork pies and sausages. Although Jack Hope, the local butcher, had tried to encourage him to stay as a butcher's apprentice with the inducement dangled before him of eventually owning his own shop, he had left to get work at the pit as soon as he could.

The Burkinshaws had come from the Barnsley area and he had never lost the very broad Yorkshire accent, which characterises those who originate from the Dearne Valley. Even today, you only need to hear someone say booit rather than boot, or hee-ad, instead of head, in order to be able to identify their place of origin immediately. His dad, Joe, had helped to sink shafts at various collieries, until he had been killed at one when a coupling had come loose on a kibble, or large bucket, which was used to transport men and materials down the shaft as it was excavated.

He had been thrown from the kibble as it had dropped down and had fallen over two hundred feet to his death. Attitudes to death at the mines were always hard with the thought at the back of the minds of many being, thank god it wasn't me. One old sweat had grimly said afterwards, 'It's a bloody good job no one was working in the shaft bottom or he might have killed them as well.' The other occupant had been on the other side of the contraption and had just been able to catch hold of a suspension chain attached to the steel tub as it gave way. He had clung to the side of the apparatus, holding on in the darkness, slowly feeling his strength drain as the kibble was raised. He was sent home suffering from shock after being examined by the doctor who had been called out to examine the badly smashed up body of his workmate. It was generously agreed by the manager that although they had just been lowered into the shaft at the start of the day, Joe and he would receive payment for a full shift.

It transpired later that the coupling had become damaged

sometime earlier by smashing into a girder as materials had been lowered down the shaft. The wire rope to which the kibble had been attached had become fouled and then freed by reversing the winding engine several times. Unfortunately, this had resulted in about thirty feet of slack cable. When the bucket had worked free, it dropped thirty feet before smashing into the protruding steel. The mines and quarries acts, such as they were in those days, apportioned no blame and recorded the death as an unfortunate accident. A footnote appended to the report stated that is was strongly recommended that in future any damaged coupling, chain or shackle, should be changed as soon as possible, and that if hazard to life was suspected the change should be effected immediately, 'even at the cost of loss of production.'

Burkinshaw had gone to work in mining because of the money. His mother had been left with him, three younger sisters, and his brother Oscar who was a babe in arms. She had started to take in washing as the only means of keeping the family together and he could see that she was working herself to death with the effort required to earn the pittance which laundry work paid.

The work was, of course, done by hand, with clothes boiled with soap flakes in a big copper in the kitchen, or pounded and spun with a dolly or tumbly-peg in a large zinc tub. The dolly was like a small stool with pegs protruding at the bottom but with a large broom like handle inserted in the middle of the stool 'seat', this enabled a pounding or rotational motion to be imparted to the heavy mass of washing within the tub. Collars and the like received his mother's attention on a rubbing board, which was a ribbed, zinc plated board against which soaped collars and cuffs were rubbed in order to loosen the ingrained dirt. The kids helped where they could, with sisters looking after the baby and himself pounding the washing or turning it through the huge cast iron mangle in the outhouse after the washing was done.

The youngster also helped by using fine evenings or

weekends to get up on the pit tip and glean coal. In those days, coal was sorted by hand in what were called screens. The screeners being women, boys, or men who were too old or injured to continue working underground. The coal passed over vibrating sieves and along conveyors and the pieces which contained too much muck were picked out and discarded. Occasionally a whack with a sledgehammer would dislodge the good coal from the dirt but mostly no one bothered due to the fact that labour, and thus the product of that labour, was so cheap.

The coal, although it would soon be buried by other spoil and become lost to everyone, belonged to the colliery company, which in common with all the others had a policy of instituting an occasional prosecution. This usually meant a fine of five shillings at that time and served to remind the locals that the coal, although discarded, was still the property of the company.

The youngster became one of the dozens who regularly scoured the waste dumped by the tubs down the side of the ever-growing colliery spoil heap. When he had filled a couple of those small sacks, which he could just about carry home without too many stops, he would bear them as his gift to supplement his mother's efforts to ensure that the family survived. At other times, he would scour the woods for kindling or, in autumn, for blackberries.

Any errand would be willingly undertaken in exchange for the odd penny or occasional three-penny bit. In late summer, when the peas were ready, he was always first in the fields with the raggle-taggle mob of impoverished children and women who would pick them. He always returned home with pea pods stuffed down his shirt and filling his pockets. Later in the year he would assist with the spud harvest. He would do anything he could for that precious penny which had the effect of lifting the horrible look of worn out stress from his mother's face. He also collected jam jars and pop bottles and returned them to the grocer in exchange for small coin.

Young Burkinshaw had learned how to set a snare and

would go into the woods and field edges at night to set them and then retrieve the precious rabbit for the pot. In the woods and fields, he would pick mushrooms. He would always eat that fruit which was surplus to the quantity he could carry home. Blackberries which started to become available from about mid-September were his favourite; depending on the location of the brambles and how much sun they got, they could still be found in October. He would eat the soggy mulberries which grew on the old gnarled trees in St Helen's church yard, chew the rather bitter elderberries, and in late autumn use the rather mushy rose hips to take the edge off his hunger. He would secretively take a late turnip from the farmer's field, cut it with his penknife, eat it raw, then pull a couple more, and take them home to be boiled for dinner.

As the barley and wheat ripened in the summer, he would walk warily down the field edges, pulling the occasional ear from its stalk and then rubbing it in his hands to separate the grain from the chaff. He would pocket the grains and nibble them as he did his rounds to the secret places which he knew might provide food. He knew at home that his mother would sacrifice her portion and expect him to take more than the girls. He was aware that having some country gleaned food inside him before their evening meal would take the edge off his appetite and restrain his urge to take a bigger share than the rest of the family.

Burkinshaw had been in the pits since the 1890s. He was a survivor. His hard childhood had prepared him excellently for the privations of mine work. By virtue of his intelligence and the accumulation of years of knowledge underground, he knew just about everything there was to know about the industry. He had started as a lad in the pit bottom progressing stage by stage, as he proved himself, to the more difficult and dangerous jobs. By dint of long effort in the evenings he had acquired the certificates of competency which had qualified him to become a Pit Deputy and then a Colliery Over-man; finally progressing to the exalted rank of Undermanager.

Although he had long held the 'First Class manager's ticket' which would have enabled him to become a Colliery Manager, he held back from it. He had seen the workload and stress demanded by that position and seen various members of that class go under due to strokes, heart attacks or mental problems. At Bullcroft Colliery, he was totally on top of his job and nothing escaped his notice. No problem or difficulty could be presented to him by the manager or directors to which he did not have a very cogent answer. Thus, he was generally left-alone and his services were valued as being very productive. If difficulties did arise and the directors were asking awkward questions or if one of His Majesty's Inspectors of Mines had visited a face and found something wanting, Sam Commons, the pit manager, would bawl out one of the deputies or overmen. Burkinshaw was never in the firing line.

He had his sights set on reaching the far-off year of 1941 and then spending a few years tending his roses in happy retirement with Winifred,, his soul mate. They complemented each other exactly. Winifred was of a Methodist background and did not drink or smoke. She was fond of needlework at which she was very accomplished. Besides that, her two great pleasures were their annual week's holiday in the Esplanade Hotel, which was situated on the sea front at Scarborough, and after that, the wireless.

In the North of England in those days, it was unusual to be able to afford a week's holiday. The old undermanager chose carefully. He knew that during the Collieries' annual break, a few of the higher paid colliers managed a holiday in the various boarding houses dotted through the east coast resorts such as Bridlington and Scarborough. He was no snob, but knew that at the reasonably highly priced Esplanade Hotel he was very unlikely to encounter anyone who originated from his village.

He wanted above all else to relax, to read, to stroll along the sea front or around the town's Italian gardens, to sit watching the sea either from his bedroom or from one of the numerous benches which were situated throughout the resort. What he did not want was the tension of the social strains which would occur if he ran into anyone from work. What he also did not want at any price was conversation about the problems on such and such a face or anything else to do with mining.

He doubly ensured that this would be the case by always taking his holiday during what was described in Doncaster as 'Race Week'. This usually occurred after the first week in September. All the Doncaster pits and most of the factories closed for that race meeting, which culminated in the running of the country's oldest 'Classic' race, the St Leger. The week was always accompanied by a massive funfair, which was held on an area of town known as Dockin Hill. The site was an area of wasteland, down past the cattle market but within easy reach of the town centre.

The miners converged on the racetrack during the four days of the race meeting, with tens of thousands in attendance from Doncaster and its surroundings on the Saturday when the Leger was run. Many attended who were not all that interested in racing; wives and girlfriends were taken to the event and watched what they could of it from the 'free course' which was a flat common on the side of the track opposite the stands. The dry comment often made about attending the racing there was: 'It's free if tha' dunt bet.'

Mckinley had been going there with the local gang of lads since he was thirteen. He had no interest in gambling. He had been down to the free course where the excited masses stood twenty deep waiting for the Leger entries to pass and had been mightily disappointed when it happened. It was all over in a flurry of thudding hooves and cheering in what appeared to be a few seconds.

Walking away from the course, he expressed his disappointment at what he had seen. 'It's a lot more interesting if tha's stood up there,' said one of the older lads, pointing to the stands. 'Tha can see the horses all the way round the course.

The trouble is, it costs, and tha can't get in unless tha's smartly dressed.' He said: 'If tha pays tha can get into the ring where they parade the horses round before a race, and they tell me tha gets better odds wi' t' bookies that are in that part.'

Despite the disappointment of the actual race, what did fascinate John were the characters who were attracted into Doncaster during the week. The tipsters, the flashily dressed bookies, the fortune-tellers, the fruit and sweet sellers and the dodgy characters who were working the three-card trick. Cud had run into it during his service in the trenches. One conscript, of very non-salubrious antecedents, had shown him how it was done. He told Cud: 'They do a couple easy so you can find the lady, then they fool the punters with sleight of hand. There are always mugs there who fall for it, despite the fact that it must be clear to everybody that money is taken off 'em every time.'

John was always interested in the wary looking showmen who ran the various rides and stalls at the funfair. He could remember one old timer saying, 'Make sure things are well locked up; all the scum of the earth gets into Doncaster during race-week.' John thought that the showmen always looked as if they were half expecting trouble, and were ready for it. This could come from some drunk or due to a complaint of being short-changed or that the coconuts were glued in place, or from dozens of other sources.

John found the interactions between the various groups and individuals fascinating, and they were a source of much later thought and conjecture. He realised that there was something different about crowds, and that they sometimes behaved in strange ways that could be irrational or even dangerous, especially if whipped up by some loudmouth. He could see in the showmen that here was a class who lived on the edge, who were not part of a normal settled community. He thought that this may be a source of that strange untrusting and almost scornful look with which they viewed the punters.

Mckinley realised that the most important function of race week and its fair was to provide a bright spot in a year which was mostly full of dullness, drudgery and back breaking hard work at the various mines and factories round Doncaster.

6

Mckinley and the Mine

Mckinley got back home from school after his last day. As he walked into the kitchen through the back door, which had been left open due to the sultry heat of that particular Friday, together with that thrown out by the cooking fire and oven, his mother looked up and said, 'You're a bit later than I expected. I thought they let the leavers out early?'

John replied in a very measured, almost nonchalant tone: 'I walked down to the pit and got a job.'

Margaret's eyes glinted with a mixture of pride and pleasure. Both mother and son knew what it meant to have a lad working. How much difference the additional fifteen shillings or so that she would have would make to the family budget. She called through to the parlour: 'Cud! — Cud! Come into the kitchen!'

John's stepdad had been fiddling with an old 1920s radio, trying to persuade it to work. He came in lighting his pipe as he did so. 'Well?' he said.

'John's got a job at the pit!' she announced.

The reaction from Cud was very different to that of Margaret. He greeted the news with animated excitement. 'We'll go down to the shops tomorrow and get you some boots, a pit belt and a snap tin and a Dudley.' The old man was delighted and showed it by acknowledging the advent of John's adulthood: 'You'll soon be coming down to the club for a pint with the rest of us.'

In the mines in Yorkshire, food was carried underground in a stout container called a 'snap tin', and the food it contained was referred to as Snap. The tin was suspended from the pit belt. It had a rounded end to prevent damage to thighs when they encountered the tin when crawling through the narrow and low spaces underground. The Dudley was a large, round, tin-plated water container. The favourite size was that which contained a gallon of water. The name came from the proud legend stamped on each of the containers: 'Made in Dudley'.

John found out later why so much water was needed. Those working in the tunnels or roadways leading to the faces or in the pit bottom would frequently not fill their Dudleys completely as the workings could be cool or even cold in places, due to the way that the air from the huge fan which pulled it down the Downcast Shaft flowed in those areas. However, by the time the airflow got out to the faces, which could often be three or four miles from the pit bottom, it had often faltered to a weak and sluggish flow. This, coupled with the fact that the natural heat from coal seams, which were now being worked at depths of up to a thousand yards, combined with the humidity produced by water from the strata and dozens of sweating bodies, meant that men were frequently working in temperatures which were in the nineties on the old Fahrenheit scale. They also worked in almost one hundred percent humidity.

Visitors underground were usually invited to put their hands on the coal or rock of the tunnel wall. Invariably this produces a comment indicating surprise at the warmth of it. Work done by the redoubtable 'Haldane' and other scientists showed that it was possible for a face worker to experience up to a stone and a half in weight loss during a shift due to these conditions. The loss was almost entirely due to fluid sweated out of the body. Thus, a gallon of water was easily consumed on a coalface, not only to replenish fluid lost but also to ease the dryness of mouth caused by breathing in the mixture of coal and rock dust produced during mining. Even a full Dudley was frequently not sufficient. Miners, emerging from the mine at the shift end, frequently did so with a raging thirst—one which was gratefully slaked by Messrs John and Sam Smith and others of the brewing fraternity in the hugely profitable boozers which lay in close proximity to the various pits.

In the early days of the mine, quart bottles of home brewed ginger beer had been sold at the Brodsworth Colliery entrance by a one-legged veteran of the Great War called Squinty Logan who augmented his meagre war pension by selling the beverage. Miners emerging from the mine would buy a quart of the brew, down it, and then hand the bottle back to Squinty for refilling. More determined individuals would decline that refreshing beverage and would march down the lane, often with their tongues sticking to the roof of their mouths, until they got to the saloon bar of the Swinger or the ex-servicemen's club, known locally as 'The Bomb'. There they would quench their thirsts at the bar whilst still in full pit-muck. When asked why they did it, the answer, almost invariably, was, 'There is nothing on earth that tastes as good as that first pint when you are that thirsty.'

John heard the old alarm clock in his parent's bedroom go off at four-fifteen. He got out of bed and started to get dressed. No point in washing, or shaving for that matter, before a shift, he had been told. 'Tha'll soon be as black as the ace of spades.' He rose and dressed efficiently, putting on the old clothes which would become his pit clothes, the unfamiliar heavy socks, and the heavy, steel toe-capped, hobnailed boots. He had been told to walk about in these over the weekend to 'break 'em in'. Cud also told him to get them a bit scuffed and knock the shine off. John knew of the mineworker's superstition about 'New Boots'. They were considered unlucky because, as with any newcomers to dangerous occupations, the accident rate was always higher among the new boys due to their inexperience with machinery and the way that the transport and other systems operated within the mine.

The older miners were aware that the cull of any new intake tended to be amongst the less bright of those starting underground. John had been given reams of advice by Cud and others, but his stepdad knew that in the end it would only be John's own experiences and sharpness of mind that would save him from dangerous situations.

Margaret was downstairs already, operating the large frying pan over the single gas ring. Breakfast consisted of fried bread and a bit of streaky bacon, with beans, which had been fried in the residual bacon fat and lard. Though it was unusually early for him to eat, he did so, but without much appetite and deep in thought. The meal was finished with a pint mug of sweet tea and just after five Cud and John donned the cloth caps, which almost formed part of the collier's uniform in those days, and set off into the early light of that July morning.

The pit was about a twenty minute walk from the house. The two turned out of Briar Road and joined the main road, which led to the mine. John could see several others walking in the same direction but the two kept their distance almost until they reached the colliery gates. At this point, the trickle of men who had been approaching the gates from various directions joined as they flooded in. Some were filling up on nicotine from a last cigarette or pipe as they entered. Matches and tobacco were classed as contraband. Anyone found with these underground could be sacked on the spot due to the danger presented by a naked flame in the mine.

This ruling did not apply to all collieries. Those in Yorkshire produced high quality bituminous coal, which was excellent as both house coal and as coking coal. The nature of this type of product meant that it and the surrounding rocks were saturated with methane and thus the prohibition was vital. As Humphrey Davy had discovered, in certain concentrations the mix of gas and air becomes explosive. However, the ignition needs a naked flame or a certain type of spark.

This had been prevented by Davy's invention of the famous lamp that bears his name, which had its flame burning behind a steel gauze. It had been observed that methane could ignite within the lamp but the gauze dissipated the heat. Thus, by this ingenious device the type of explosion which in the past had killed thousands of miners was now largely avoided.

At a later date, John occasionally saw colliers, who were sat in the club having a pint, put a cigarette in their mouths and then absent-mindedly take their cloth caps off and move them towards the cigarette as though to light it. They would then usually curse and put the cap back on their heads, usually to the amusement of the rest of the group. John was told that these men had moved down from pits in Scotland, which were gas free due to the nature of the hard anthracitic coal which was mined there.

In these pits, shot firing was done with black powder and smoking was permitted. The miners at these pits used carbide lamps mounted on their caps. In these, an unprotected naked flame was produced by slowly dropping water onto calcium carbide. This built up pressure within the lamp, which was slowly released through a valve to feed the flame. When the flame started to dim, more water was introduced. The carbide was unstable and reacted with the water to give acetylene gas, which produced a bright light on ignition. If one of the men wanted to light a cigarette underground, they would take their cap off and use the flame from their lamp.

Another advantage of using this relatively bright light as compared to the dim glow given off by the Davy lamp was the notable absence of the eye disease known as Nystagmus amongst these men. Nystagmus, which led to termination of employment underground, was produced by working in very poor lighting. If this was done over a period of years, eventually it could cause the eyeballs to start to spasm in an involuntary manner. It was thought that the eyes jerking involuntarily in search of the small amounts of light available, initiated the condition.

John knew a bloke in the next village who had contracted

the disease. He had not gone blind as had some of the others who had the disease, but he could not see very far. 'Down the passage and about as far as the back door,' was his limit, he jokingly told people. He had come out of the pit and had been put on the company's disability pension of twenty-seven shillings a week for a few months and then reassessed by the company doctor. Unusually, he had not been reassessed as fit for light work. In that case, he would have dropped down to a part pension of fifteen shillings. His good luck in this matter depended in part on Dr Lawrie, a new young doctor in the area who was of Calvinistic and socialistic inclinations and who interpreted the medical criteria strictly, without leaning in the direction of the employers. The young idealist did notice, though, that after two or three years the company stopped asking him to make the assessments.

The bloke in question was a short barrel of a man with the unusual name of Micklethwaite, or Mick for short. He had a shock of blond hair, which formed naturally tight curls about his head, and the other colliers referred to their compatriot, usually behind his back, as 'the blond nigger.' At work, he must have been very physically powerful, but now lack of work and lack of opportunity to walk very much due to his eyes had pushed his weight up to nearly twenty stone. In order to supplement his pension, he had taken up the breeding of bulldogs. He said, 'I suppose I am lucky in a way. I am out of the pit and on a pension! On the other hand I might ha' had a spot of bad luck because of the name.' The lads looked blank, but Mick chuckled sardonically and said: 'Thirteen letters in Micklethwaite tha knows!'

Arthur Howarth, who was Mckinley's other main pal in the village, was a distant relative and had taken John to see a new litter of pups; John had thus met the old collier and had seen the devastating effects of nystagmus at first hand.

John rapidly absorbed 'the Lore of the Mine'. This was the accumulated wisdom of men who had seen and who had been in dangerous situations and who had survived them. The Lore was never written down. It was always transmitted verbally and usually when at work.

John was first taken to the lamp room and Cud took down two lamps, one for himself and one for John. Both took a pair of numbered metal discs, called checks, which both had the same number on them. John was instructed that one was left at the shaft side on descending and the other was left after ascending. Any discrepancy between the two, after they were tallied up at the shift end, would result in efforts to find the missing disc. If a match could not be made, search parties would be sent into the district that the man had been working in, to ensure that death or injury had not occurred in some unused tunnel or other part of the mine, especially if the man had been working in isolation.

Cud then turned, intending to take John to Burkinshaw's office, but the undermanager at that moment entered the lamp room already fully equipped to go underground. 'Is tha ready?' he said looking at John, and John nodded. 'We'll get off then and catch the first draw.'

The men were transported underground in a large metal cage, which could hold about forty people if they were crammed in tight. Depending on shift patterns, sometimes several draws were needed to get all the colliers underground. The three walked to the shaft side. Little Billy, 'the Banksman', who supervised entry and exit to the mine said: 'Morning Mr Burkinshaw.' None of the men or deputies would use his first name. This was partly tradition and partly due to the very high respect all at the pit held him in.

'Morning Billy,' the Undermanager replied. While they were waiting, he took out a block of tobacco and cut off a couple of plugs. 'Want a chaw Billy?' he said. Billy said: 'Yes, thank you gaffer, I don't mind if I do,' and each took a piece of the tobacco and started to chew. The use of chewing tobacco or snuff was common among miners and served to ease the pangs of nicotine withdrawal, which the smokers would start to suffer during their eight hours underground. Chewing tobacco also had the useful side effect of keeping the mouth moist.

John could see the cables, which were as thick as his arm, moving rapidly above the shaft entrance—one moving down into the depths and the other to the headgear pulley wheel high above them. After a couple of minutes, he could see that they were slowing, and just after that the top of the cage came into view. The cage halted with its bottom surface about nine inches below the shaft side. Billy held out a box and Burkinshaw put his check in, followed by Cud and John. 'Only one,' Cud cautioned, but this was unnecessary as John was well aware of how the system worked and far too sharp to put both or neither in the box. The rest of the men crammed in and the Banks-man signalled his opposite number, the 'On-Setter', down in the pit bottom. The electric bells signalled ready, all clear or wait. Billy got the all clear and pushed the lever, which initiated descent.

The descent of the cage was controlled by an ingenious cam system of Victorian design. As the gradient on the cam decreased, the winding speed increased. The system was made so that the greatest gradients occurred on the cam when the cage was at the top and bottom of the shaft. This had the desirable effect of slowing the cage at these critical positions. The fine-tuning needed was done by the banks-man who slowly applied the brake as the cage neared the shaft bottom. The hope was that the base of the cage and the exit and entry decking were level when the cage stopped. Just occasionally, a two foot scramble up or down was needed by those getting in or out, usually accompanied by much abuse directed at the brake operator.

The descent was unlike anything John had ever experienced; he had travelled up and down between the four floors of the local Co-op in Doncaster in its lift, but this descent was nothing like that. For a few tens of feet movement was at a gentle pace and then it seemed as though the steel floor, which they stood on, had given way and they dropped almost as though the cage had become detached from its supporting cable. After a few hundred feet he realised that the cage was slowing rapidly. It finally came to rest at the pit bottom and John noticed a slight up and down oscillation, which he learned later was due to the elastic stretching which always occurred in the hundreds of yards of cable from which the cage was suspended.

The On-Setter opened the steel mesh shutter, which had sealed the men in the cage for its descent, and they hurriedly emerged. The undermanager, Cud and John had been first in and thus were last to leave.

Cud said questioningly, 'He'll be alright with you, Mr Burkinshaw?'

'Aye Cud!' came the reply.

John's step dad said, 'I'll see you later,' and hurried off with the rest of his shift to the distant coalface.

John walked along with his senior, saying nothing but absorbing the strangeness of it all. They got to a steel door in the wall. His leader slid a small panel set into the door open and there was a sudden rush of air. When the pressures had equalised he pulled a larger lever and swung the door open. John and he stepped through it. Burkinshaw closed the door once more, and John felt a pressure build up in his ears. 'This is called an "air door" young 'un,' the older man said. 'We need to control air flows round the mine, the pressure near the down-cast shaft is always greater than at the up-cast shaft we've just come down, we need to release it and then make sure we close the doors when we have got through. Make sure you remember, because soon enough, tha'll have to do it on thee own.'

They made their way to an area that was well lit by electric lights. They rounded the corner and John could hear voices. He was then assailed by an odour, which reminded him of a farmyard. They had reached the place where the pit ponies were kept. There were over thirty of those patient and likeable beasts in purpose built brick stables. The place was warm and dry. The roofing was made of large steel girders and thus there was no danger of a roof fall. A group of lads were getting the ponies out and harnessing them to the low steel pit tubs which were used to transport props and other equipment down the various roadways and out to the faces. Once emptied, the tubs could then be used to bring coal out of the mine.

John was struck repeatedly by the alien nature of it all: the sensation of the descent, the ear-popping pressure changes, and the smells. Not just the present organic smell of the stables, but also the stale odour of the mine air itself. This was totally new to John, with an odd dry and dusty fustiness, which needs to be experienced to be understood, and which words can only in part convey to someone who has never been down a pit.

Burkinshaw said: 'Well John, tha'd better get theesen a pony.' He went over to the senior lad and said, 'New lad for thee Terry. This is John. Get him fixed up wi' a pony and show him the ropes. He is a quick learner, but make sure he has an easy shift or two until he gets into it. I'll check on him later.' With that, he turned on his heel and walked off down the main tunnel, or roadway as it is known. John could see the light of the Garforth lamp, which swung from the Underman-ager's belt, growing fainter and fainter as he made his steady progress down the long decline on his way to the face.

John was shown how to harness a pony and then given instructions on how to get it to stop and start. 'It's a good idea if you keep them on your side,' said Terry. 'If you bring 'em a lump of sugar they will be your pal. Always try to get the same one, then you will get used to working together as a team. They've all got names.'

John learned later that some of the lads went to extraor-dinary lengths to look after their animals, making sure that injuries were avoided if possible and that those which were sustained were rapidly treated. Some even went to the length of sharing their snap with their pony. After that, John always made sure he had a piece of broken biscuit or a sugar lump to give to his pony at the start and end of each shift, and a slice of bread to give to his willing partner in the servitude of the mine at snap time. Mckinley was given one called Pete. 'Pete the pit pony,' said Terry, laughing at his own joke.

The rest of the pony lads had set off in convoy towards the face. Terry said, 'Follow me!' Terry's pony was called Nobby. He gave it the gee-up command and the beast willingly set off. John did the same, and Pete set off after Terry and his animal. They came to a fork in the roadway and Terry said, 'That one leads down to the face.' John followed his leader, still drinking in the strangeness of it all—the steel girders overhead, and the occasional sharp chunk of protruding rock. They passed a steel door set in the side of the roadway. The surrounds at the entrance were made of brick and the construction looked substantial. Terry said, 'It's a snap cabin. The Deputies and Over-men use it to keep the work books and safety and accident reports in. They all have a key; they probably use it to kip in on nights if they can get away with it!' John knew that the remark was made jokingly because sleeping underground was a sacking offence, but knowing human nature, he could also see that the remark might have some truth in it.

They arrived at what appeared to be another tunnel, but John could see that it only extended for about twenty or thirty yards before terminating in a brick wall. Terry told him that it was the end of a roadway which led to old workings which had been sealed off years before.

The tunnel section was full of wooden pit props, which were about nine inches in diameter and about five feet in length. Terry said, 'We'll load up and get these down the roadway to the end of the face.' They took their snap tins off the belts and put the Dudleys down. Then he showed John how the two of them could easily lift and then stack the props in the tubs. He said, 'When tha gets a bit bigger tha'll be able to do that on thee own, but there's two of us so there's no need to kill us-sens.' The ponies stood patiently during the loading.

When both tubs were full, Terry said, 'Time for a swag.' He lifted the Dudley and took a long drink. John followed suit. Both were perspiring slightly but the rapid airflow soon evaporated the perspiration. 'Best set off,' said Terry, 'or we might cool down too much.'

They put the snap tins and Dudleys in the tubs and set the ponies in motion. John was surprised at how responsive Pete was and they made good progress in the dim light. Terry said, 'The face end is only about a half a mile off. These are new workings.' Eventually they could see light far off down the tunnel and made towards it. They arrived to find the face deputy and a couple of older colliers. He was giving instructions about packing the side of the roadway, which had collapsed.

John found out rapidly that the constant weight of the overburden of several hundred yards of rock above caused the strata to move slowly, with the roofs of the tunnels tending to move down and the floors tending to move up. Because of this, constant repairs were needed, with replacement roof supports very occasionally being required and the floor of the tunnels frequently being dug out as they bulged upwards. This process was known as 'dinting'. The need for tunnel maintenance was considered a nuisance as it was not a productive use of labour, but it was a necessity as without it the coal could not easily be got away from the face.

The dinting delayed things due to the narrow-gauge track having to be lifted and then re-laid as the work was completed. Occasional sidewall collapses such as the one he had come across also occurred. The cavities were filled with carefully piled rock arranged almost as if it was dry stone walling. Cud later told John that the rock was very good under a compressive load from above and that if the pack had been built properly it would stand until the colliers withdrew from that part of the mine.

The Deputy walked past. 'Alright, Terry?' he said.

'Fine, Mester Stott,' Terry replied. 'Ready for me snap.'

'Couple of hours yet, lad,' came the rejoinder. 'You'll really be ready for it by then.' The Deputy walked off, frequently pausing and prodding at the roof or side wall with his yard stick as he moved along. Occasionally he held his lamp up to the roof on the end of his stick and looked at the flame.

'What's he doing?' said John.

Terry said, 'He's testing for gas. If there's fire damp about it alters the flame. A skilled man can tell how much there is, to a quarter percent.'

John said, 'How much of it do they find?'

Terry told him that he understood that in gassy workings the methane built up in the airflow as it passed round the face. He said, 'It could be over one percent by the time it reached the up-cast shaft, which is the one the stale air is expelled through from the mine'. He smiled and said, 'Don't worry, they tell me it doesn't make an explosive mixture with the air until it gets to be much higher than that.'

John learned later that the mine 'breathed', responding to the external atmospheric pressure. When the pressure was low on the surface, gases could be drawn out of old workings. This was a time for particular vigilance amongst the staff responsible for maintaining ventilation and amongst the face Deputies. Gas samples were taken daily and analysed by the colliery chemist who had a small lab next to the first aid room in the pit offices. If methane levels exceeded certain limits the colliers could, in theory, be withdrawn from the face; in practice this almost never happened due to possible production losses, although the Deputies did what they could to increase air flow and send further samples of the mine atmosphere for analysis to constantly monitor the methane concentration. All of them knew, though, that as the trough of low pressure passed the problem would solve itself.

The two youths unloaded the props and returned to the pit bottom, loaded up again and made the journey back to the face end. After unloading they could see that the two packers had sat down and were starting to eat. 'It must be snap time,' Terry said. He reached into the side of the tub and pulled out a pair of nosebags, which he put on the noses of the ponies. The two started to munch contentedly. John and he sat on a couple of rail sleepers, which had been dumped at the side of the roadway. They opened the snap tins and began to eat.

'What's tha got?' said Terry.

'Cheese,' said John.

'Lucky,' said Terry. 'Mine's bloater paste.'

Both ate hungrily; it was John's first experience of the disciplines of hard physical work and it had made him very hungry.

Terry said, 'Save a crust'. John did so but could have gladly devoured the whole of his provisions himself. Terry showed him how to hold the crust flat on his hand and let his pony take it. John noticed that after that the large eyes of the animal seemed to look at him with a mixture of gratitude and recognition.

They finished their snap with a large swag from the Dudleys and then resumed work. 'We're allowed twenty minutes for snap,' Terry said. 'Don't let any of the gaffers find you taking any longer. If they do they will fine thee, though you might just get a bollocking the first time.'

As they set off for the pit bottom once more, Terry said, 'How did tha find it, thee snap; did tha like the taste?' John considered the question. He had been so hungry that he had not thought about it, but now he realised that the food had tasted odd. Terry laughed and said, 'Yes! Nowt tastes the same down the pit. Some people can't stand to bring sardine sandwiches down or fish paste because they taste so foul. One bloke could only eat cooking chocolate melted on his bread by his missus when she puts his snap up. Others will only eat biscuits or cream crackers and a lump of cheese.' He explained the dust and the stale mine air changed the taste and smell of everything down there. Terry grinned and said, 'Even a fart doesn't smell the same down here.' John smiled at that one and they set off once more to complete their task of supplying the wooden props for the face.

Towards the end of the shift, Terry set them back on the

journey towards the underground stables. 'We have to see to the ponies before we go. We see they are comfortable and with plenty of hay and water and then we can leave. We usually get the last draw out of the pit.' At the stables, he gave John a lump of sugar to give to Pete. He did likewise with his own pony. 'Make sure you always do this,' Terry said. 'It's worth its weight in gold if you want the buggers to cooperate and not be awkward.'

They made their way towards the shaft side, and cage, which offered egress from the foulness and the dark. At the surface, John stepped out of the cage, gave up his check, and walked out into the sunshine of a fine July afternoon. He suddenly realised what wonderful commodities those previously taken-for-granted things, fresh air and sunshine, were.

As he rounded the corner at the bottom of the headgear, he saw Cud standing near the pit offices. His stepdad said: 'I waited for thee, seeing as it was your first day, but from now on go straight home when you get out of the pit; I might be out before you, or after if there's a bit of overtime.'

They trudged along in their flat caps and pit boots. Cud said, 'How was your first shift lad?'

'All right,' said John. 'A bit tiring, and I'm ready for me dinner.' Cud smiled as they walked the last few yards down Briar Road to number thirty-nine.

When they got in, Margaret had dinner ready. They sat down to eat in their pit muck in the kitchen, and by now both were ravenous. The dinner was stew and dumplings with lots of carrots and potatoes in the gravy to thicken it and make the meal substantial. Both devoured a large plate and then wiped their plates clean with a thick slice of bread.

After the meal, his mother filled up the tin bath with pails of hot water from the copper, which had been lit a couple of hours earlier. John bathed first, being quick, as instructed. Cud went in second with more hot water poured into the tub before he got in. She lathered Cud's back and shoulders and then left him to it. After they had dried themselves and got themselves changed into their other clothes, they sat back in the warm kitchen, each with a pint mug of hot sweet tea.

Cud took out his pipe and cleaned the stem with a metal spike on the end of his penknife. He then cut off a plug of black twist and began to smoke, reflectively. He said: 'I told Maggie to get us a bath ready. Don't expect one every day. We usually just get a good wash on the top half and have a bath on Saturdays. I thought with this being tha first day tha might be a bit stiff and a hot tub will take that off; after a few days tha won't get stiff. Tha legs and back will be getting used to the work.'

He went on, 'Any questions about today?' John had many but said 'no', preferring to think about what had occurred. He was sure that answers would come over the ensuing weeks. He would ask how the mine operated and about the dangers of firedamp and of blackdamp and what the functions of the various officials were. Cud said, 'Listen to the old hands, they have lots of pit-sense.' By this, he meant the accumulated experience of situations, which they had encountered and learned to be wary of, and avoid. 'And don't be smart,' he said. 'There's nothing worse than an old head on young shoulders.'

With his first week over, John collected his first pay packet; it contained seventeen shillings and four pence. He went home and proudly handed it over to his mother. She gave him half a crown in return. This was standard for all the haulage lads and he was delighted to get it. Two shillings and sixpence, and all of it to spend on himself. He had never been so wealthy.

The second week went by and on the Friday as they were waiting to come out of the pit a stretcher party approached; as it got close, John could see a small shape covered in a blanket. Young Charlie Spencer's dad accompanied the party; he was ashen faced as he followed the stretcher party into the cage. 'We'll have to wait for the next draw,' said Cud, and they stood aside. One of the colliers who had followed the stretcher was asked who it was. 'Young Charlie,' he said. 'Crushed—haulage accident!'

Charlie was one of those from Skellow Secondary Modern who had started at the pit on the same day as John. He was from the lower class in the school, not over-bright and a bit of a runt, but he was always cheerful and everyone at school liked him. Because of his small stature, some of the girls used to mother him. All those there had worked on the haulage when they started at the pit and knew very well that if you weren't careful you could easily lose a limb or suffer serious injury or even death as the unforgiving steel tubs were coupled and uncoupled to the various haulage cables which drew them out of the mine. Sometimes they could run away down a gradient if the brakes had not been properly applied. In those cases, it was a case of diving into a manhole or flattening yourself against a wall and hoping for the best as they whizzed past. The worst place to be was where they eventually derailed and piled up. Sometimes that did not happen due to them slowing down without derailing as they met and went up an incline.

Cud did not speak as they walked home apart from telling John not to tell his mother, as she would worry. Later, in the club, Cud heard one collier say, 'Bit of a bugger, and dead at fourteen.' The older man shook his head at the sad waste of it; but that was mining! A few days later, the funeral was held and all of Charlie's former classmates attended the service along with his former teacher, Mr Crellin. The interment was done in the old graveyard at Owston Church. Many of the pit lads fringed the large party of those who witnessed that mournful occasion.

On the way to work in the early hours of the Monday morning after the accident, Cud said to John: 'I know tha dun't need telling, but be careful with them bloody tubs. Your mind needs to be on the job all the time when tha's in between 'em when tha's coupling up or de-coupling.' Mckinley knew that no reply was needed. They walked on, picked up their lamps, and descended into the pit in silence. The mood of all the colliers who descended with them on that morning seemed to be generally subdued. John learned over the years that it was always like that after a fatality at the pit.

7

Mckinley and Politics

John had vivid memories of the election in 1924 for the simple reason that it was greeted with such great excitement in the house. He had picked up from his reading of the daily paper that a General Election was to occur and votes were to be cast for Conservative, Liberal and Labour candidates. His enquiring mind had elicited the basic facts from Cud that they would be voting for the Labour Party, because it represented the workers, and that they would not be voting for the Conservatives or 'Tories' as they were known. 'Irish for robber,' Cud explained gleefully, puffing his pipe with great gusto as he said it.

John had tried to elicit some information about his families' reasons for voting from his mother, but Margaret was not prepared to enter into discussion about it. She merely shrieked at John, 'We vote Labour, we never vote Tory and that's that.' The daily newspaper, which came into the house, was the newly established *Daily Herald*. Its introduction had been the subject of one of the domestic battles which erupted occasionally between Margaret and Cud; it was notable in being one of the few of those battles that he had actually won. Margaret preferred the Tory supporting *Daily Mail*, which she found far more entertaining, with its mixture of gossip, light news stories and entertainment features. The *Herald* was often worthy and aspirational in its tone and with socialist motivations attempted to raise the horizons of its readership with occasional educational features and pieces on science and the arts.

Margaret wanted none of that, nor did most of the other women in the village; what they did want was to be lifted from the drudgery of day to day life in a poorly furnished miner's cottage by a little of the fantasy world of the Royals and film and radio stars, which were avidly reported in the Mail. The discovery of a new planet called Pluto in 1930 had vastly less impact on her than what Jean Harlow was wearing in her latest film. Even the adverts, with their mouth-watering descriptions of 'the latest thing in radio' for 'just' fifteen guineas, served to elevate her out of her mundane existence.

When she was asked: 'Could she imagine a vivid and unusual holiday with flocks of egrets winging their way majestically across the dawn, the blaze of poinsettias and the date palms waving their feather duster crests?' Well, she could, but she wasn't quite sure what egrets or poinsettias were and thought it perhaps best not to apply 'at once' to the Egyptian tourist development association for 'full information'.

The 1924 election stood out particularly vividly in John's mind. His mother dressed in her very best clothes and set off with Cud to vote, after he had returned from the pit and been fed and had bathed. They set out with an air of excitement and expectation to vote for their man, 'the Labour party candidate.'

Though women had been given the vote in 1918, this was the first election at which she could vote; previously Margaret had been in her twenties and, thus, too young. The changes in franchise had made huge differences to the electorate, which now stood at about twenty million compared to the seven million before the Great War. Women had been rewarded for their contribution to the war effort by being given the vote, however it had been done cautiously. There was some concern that with almost a million men killed in the war that women voters might outnumber the men. Thus, although men could vote from the age of twenty-one, women only qualified if they were over thirty.

As the two made their way to the polling station at the local primary school, which had been closed especially for that day, they could see other individuals, pairs, and small groups moving in the same direction as themselves, drifting down the various streets and lanes which led to the polling station. It was almost as though they were streamlets, which were gradually merging into a small river, which flowed into the school entrance.

They were met just inside the building by representatives of the Liberal and Labour parties, who noted their names on lists of electors. Support for the Conservatives in the area was so abysmal that even in the 1920s they just did not bother to canvass or to attempt to get their vote out in the mining areas, preferring instead to concentrate their party workers in the much more marginal Doncaster seat.

One red-faced man refused to show his polling card, snarling: 'It's none of your damned business.' After he had entered the separate room that contained the ballot boxes, one of the Labour Party workers said, 'That's old Garwood. He lives in the private houses at the top end of Crossfield Lane. We are wasting our time with him; he's a bank clerk in Doncaster and has always been a Tory.' The party representatives knew that they had no right to see the polling cards but most people entering the school thought that the party members sitting near the entrance were part of the official apparatus of the election and happily showed their cards.

In the polling station itself, Margaret could see booths made of plywood. Cud said: 'That's where you vote; the booth is so no one can see where you put your cross.' Cud approached a table at which sat two elderly, bespectacled, and official looking personages. He recognised one of them and knew he worked in the rent office at the council buildings in Adwick. He handed the polling card to the officer in charge who proceeded to check down his list. 'Mr Cuthbert Errington,' he said. 'Yes' said Cud. 'Of 39 Briar Road?' Cud nodded. He was handed his voting slip and waited for

Margaret who was waiting to hand her card over. The senior of the two clerks scrutinised the document carefully, and much more deliberately than he had done with her husband's. 'Mrs Margaret Errington,' he said, in a very dubious tone. In common with many of his generation, he disapproved of this nonsensical idea of women being given the vote. He knew that they were prone to hysteria and science had shown that they had smaller brains than men. Thus, they could not possibly be entrusted with the great decisions that were made at elections. After all, the fate of the entire great British Empire hung in the balance here. He thought it had been far safer in the hands of the seven million or so male voters who had been responsible for safeguarding that noble enterprise with their votes, prior to the Great War.

Margaret confirmed her name and address and the polling clerk reluctantly and patronisingly handed the slip over. Margaret, who had a naturally fiery temperament, was seething with impatience by now and almost snatched it out of his hand. She walked over to where Cud was waiting. 'You know to put a cross in the box,' Cud said. She stared at him in annoyance. 'Yes, I do,' she snapped, 'and I know who to vote for as well!' They made their way to the booths. Inside was a shelf upon which several pencils had been placed. Most of them were blunt but Margaret found one that was reasonably sharp and used it to inscribe her cross inside the box next to the name: Mr Thomas Williams, The Labour Party candidate.

Margaret returned home from the election with an air of triumph: she had voted! This meant something. She now had the status of a first-class citizen; she was an elector! She was now able to help to decide who was going to represent her in Parliament and she had enjoyed the experience. It was highly satisfactory for her to find out later that the Labour Party had managed to win one hundred and fifty-one seats and that the MP for Don Valley was one of them. Though John was only eight at the time, he noticed the excitement which permeated the atmosphere of the house both before and after the event.

After that, when various aspects of politics were discussed, he took a keen interest. However, when at school he learned little of politics. After starting work he came to find that the Labour Party was largely funded by the trade union movement and promised the working class social reform.

For John, it was an evolving picture. Though he could see that the interests of his family were broadly served by supporting Labour, he never got involved in union or party activities himself as he came to have doubts about some of the individuals involved in those activities.

At the pit he had joined the National Union of Mineworkers and in his early days there had attended some of the branch meetings. He could see that some of the leadership were driven by an almost messianic fervour, which had usually originated in personal or family hardships in the past. He had no quarrel with this but thought that the long litany of dire deeds by harsh and grasping gaffers was hard to square with the obviously paternalistic and enlightened attitudes of people like Sir Arthur Markham, who had been instrumental in building the Bourneville-like model village for his workforce at Brodsworth Colliery. He realised that the mine owners were like the rest of the human race, a mixed bunch, some good, some grasping, some bad, others indifferent.

Markham was so forward-looking that he had suggested to the local NUM branch that the miners might be allowed to buy their cottages on easy terms for about £200 each. The branch reacted to this proposal with the same reactionary attitude with which all proposals from the gaffers were greeted, and it was turned down out of hand.

John learned that one coal owner in particular, called William Garforth, eventually to be Sir William, had been particularly good for the miners. He had pioneered early breathing apparatus and training for the mines rescue teams, and had invented the Garforth lamp that was now the approved model for testing for methane underground. He had also instituted research into the causes of underground explosions. John read how he had interviewed men who had been involved in explosions and had been struck by two facts: first, that the explosion sometimes seemed to stop for no obvious reason rather than continuing down the whole length of a tunnel, and second that the roaring mass of flame, which was described by the survivors, appeared to be either orange in colour or at other times a dark and hellish red.

It was well known that certain mixtures of methane and air would explode and could be ignited by a spark. Several explosions had been originated by naked sparks, caused for example by the electric bells used for signalling underground. These were especially dangerous in the notoriously gassy collieries of South Wales. Methane blowouts occurred frequently at these pits due to roof falls, and the air in the return airways always contained significant amounts of the gas. Thus, the problem was difficult to deal with and elimination of the causes of ignition seemed to be the way to avoid explosions.

Garforth concluded that the problem was exacerbated by the presence of coal dust. Significant quantities of this were responsible for the dark red flame fronts that had been observed underground. What is more, this problem could easily be solved by the use of water sprays or by scattering stone dust on the floors of the roadways and on any ledges where the dust might accumulate. The stone dust was usually powdered dolomite or limestone and though it was cheap, it represented an additional cost to the mine owners. Thus, many of them resisted any notion that coal dust could be implicated in underground explosions. Experiments were conducted and the evidence slowly mounted, making it impossible to ignore. Stone dusting was a regular feature of underground working by the time John arrived at the mine.

John was keen to learn but kept his own counsel. He knew that there was a thuggish element amongst the NUM branch membership who had the attitude of supporting the union right or wrong. He agreed with almost all of the decisions the union made, but he had the annoying habit of wanting to have the full argument for those actions explained to him. He realised that some of the denser NUM acolytes were incapable of setting out some of the arguments or even of understanding them. Some actions, of course, such as strike action in the face of a threatened pay cut, needed no explanation.

One of the freethinking and intelligent spirits at the mine was Ewan Williams; everyone called him Taffy for some reason. John was never sure where he got his information from or if he worked things out for himself, but he put an interesting slant on some of the arguments for and against strikes. On one occasion he explained that coal prices were determined by 'the market' and when coal was in high demand such as during the war, when it had been needed to power the Navy, the railways, the armaments factories and steel works, its price went up. However, after the war demand slackened and the price went down. It was then that the coal-owners tried to reduce wages or increase hours as had happened during the infamous lock out of 1921.

He asked John, 'Why doesn't the government fix the price of coal and subsidise it when prices fall and take the subsidy back from profits when prices rise?' Mckinley was somewhat nonplussed at the question and replied that, 'it wouldn't be practical,' though he could not quite articulate why. Taffy laughed. 'I'll let you think about it,' he said. 'It's not just that, though. We are caught between the union and the owners; I don't have much time for either.' John asked what he meant, and Taffy laughed and said: "Our union leaders won't compromise. They are not sensible negotiators. I won't bore you with the details but J.H. Thomas and Ernie Bevin got bloody good deals for the railwaymen and dockworkers after the war. Do you know how? By bloody skilful negotiation, that's how! Our lot decide what they want and then just won't move an inch. It is not sensible. You know what Lord Birkenhead said about our leadership?'

'Tell me,' said John.

'After meeting them, he said, "I should call them the

stupidest men in England if I had not previously had to deal with the mine owners." You see, we can't win either way!'

John wondered if Taffy was a communist and later he asked him. Taffy said, 'No, I'm not, but I've read the manifesto of course. Have you?' he said, searchingly.

John said, 'Yes, when I was fourteen.'

Taffy said: 'You know how Marx came up with his ideas? He read the factory reports produced before and during the early and middle part of Victoria's reign, and pretty horrendous they were in terms of working conditions and the treatment of workers. The big flaw in his analysis is that it applied to then and not to now; things have moved on, things are never static. Clever trade unionists have shown that they can get improvements by negotiation and the ruling classes now need an educated labouring class.

'Marx was far too black and white; all that nonsense about capitalism is theft! If the inventors didn't spend money on experiments and the capitalists didn't take risks with their capital we would still be living in wooden huts. Don't forget investment in new enterprises can fail, and frequently does so. Capitalists can go bankrupt.' The perspicacity and vehemence of Williams' outburst took John aback. He usually threw in a touch of humour or jokingly left a question hanging in the air for John to think about, but there was none of that on this occasion. A very deep nerve had obviously been touched regarding Taffy's feelings, both for Marxism and for the NUM leadership.

John wondered about Williams. He was obviously intelligent and independent-minded, but Ewan never said anything about his background, and John never asked.

Williams had grown up in a village in the Mining Valleys of South Wales. His father was the station master at the small railway station which served the community. His older sister had shown considerable talent at school and his parents had scrimped and saved and financed her education at the girl's high school and then at college, where she had trained as an

English teacher. Ewan was almost as clever as his sister but was six years her junior and had been told that the family finances made it impossible for him to have the same opportunities.

His father was a pious, narrow-minded lay preacher; the bible was hammered into the boy both on Sundays and during the week. Williams senior had explained that as the son of a rail employee he would easily find employment with the railway company. Williams senior explained that if he worked hard he could progress, possibly to the exalted rank of train driver. The son was extremely unenthusiastic about this prospect and about a life bound by the confines of chapel and the narrow-minded community he lived in. To his father's disapproval he had gained employment at a local coal-merchants as a junior clerk, the pay there being seven and sixpence per week more than in the railway offices.

The father had a somewhat bombastic temperament and had tried to browbeat his son into conformity. The lad had a stubborn and rebellious streak which had led to ill feeling. The young man started to miss chapel on Sundays and had dared to question some of his father's fundamentalist ideas, for example pointing out that science indicated that the earth must be millions of years old and not the biblically calculated six thousand or so. Ewan usually bit his lip and put up with the sarcasm and diatribes from his father. A few days after his sixteenth birthday a furious row developed. The older man told his son that he was an irreligious disgrace to the family. Ewan retorted that he would far sooner be that than a narrow-minded bigot.

As a result, his father told him to get out of the house. The young man said goodbye to his tearful mother, grabbed his top coat and did so on the spot. He took the small amount of money he had saved from his post office account and caught a train to Cardiff and signed on as a junior deck hand on one of the liners bound for Cape Town. After a couple of years at sea and after experiencing three hurricanes, he returned to England having had quite enough of the rolling main.

After a few months as a jobbing gardener at one of the big houses near London, he was let go and like many others of that era had difficulty getting employment. He went on the road and ended up in Doncaster where the new coal field was just opening up. He had readily been employed by the colliery company as a labourer and had slowly progressed until he had become a face worker.

He had never married and lived as a lodger with the widow of one of the colliers. His only contact with home was an occasional letter to his sister and mother. He had nothing to do with religion or politics and never enquired about his father. He was comfortable at widow Atkin's establishment. He did not drink and his entertainment consisted of long country walks on Sundays and reading by the kitchen fire. Ewan thought a lot, liked his own company, and somehow felt free, having thrown off the shackles of his background and upbringing.

As John grew up, he had gleaned fragments of information about how the local council worked and who was on it. It was an Urban District Council, which served about twelve thousand households. It was one down in size and importance from Doncaster, which had been made a County Borough in 1926 and which, as a result, had a Borough Council serving about seventy thousand households. Doncaster elected its own MP who was, then, invariably a Conservative. The mining districts surrounding Doncaster elected an MP for the Don Valley Constituency and this MP was always elected from within the Labour Party ranks.

The NUM hierarchy were heavily involved in local politics, dominated the local council, and had members on the West Riding County Council. John heard them speak occasionally at union meetings and realised that at the top end they were shrewd operators. They had all left school at twelve or thirteen but had managed to self-educate via libraries and trade union or Workers Educational Association courses. At the lower levels, he found that the Ward Councillors were often somewhat dense. The UDC comprised seven wards each electing three councillors. These were not paid; if they got anything out of it, it was maybe a bit of status by virtue of being called Councillor and the odd sandwich or piece of pork pie if the council or local board of school governors and managers, on which many of them served, arranged some sort of function. John realised that they were mostly there as union loyalists, there to put their hands up when told to, and that actually most of them were deeply conservative in their attitudes.

In his younger days, he had chatted to various Councillors and even asked questions at the occasional meeting. He realised that the regular members of Adwick-le-Street UDC lacked any real grasp of socialist theory. A unifying factor was their hatred of the Conservative party and 'the gaffers'. Sir Arthur Markham and one or two others were given grudging exception from their ire. He also came to realise that the driving force within the local Labour set up was a small, intelligent, and driven caucus of socialist idealists. These had all suffered hardships and privations in childhood or youth from the vagaries of the capitalist system, and resented the lack of opportunity which it had held out for them personally. Memories of semi starvation and lack of educational opportunity drove them to try to make things better for their children. At meetings, he observed the exceptional chairmanship skills of one rough diamond who had just been elected to the County Council. He admired his minimalist technique of quelling stupid or irrelevant questions, either with a withering look or just two or three words heavily laced with sarcasm. He had spotted a couple of others who stood out well above the rest.

John had rapidly been spotted as someone of unusual talent and he was approached with respect to becoming active in the union or joining the party. For some reason, which he couldn't quite rationalise, he kept clear of both; usually with a stonewalling response such as 'maybe when I get a bit more experience,' or 'I'll have to think about it.'

John thought that some of the aims of the local labour leadership were first rate. Jimmy Lane, who was the leader of the Brodsworth branch of the NUM and a County Councillor, constantly used that position to push for increased library facilities and better schools. His pet project though was the establishment of a state Grammar School in the locality.

Those pupils who passed the scholarship exam and who had the necessary financial support from their families would go to either Doncaster Grammar School, which had been established in 1350, or the Kings School in Pontefract, which was the name of the Grammar School that served that town. Lane preached that the journeys entailed in getting to these schools, which could be anything from a five to twenty mile journey by bus and train, were further discouragements to the small group of pupils from his area who actually qualified to attend these ancient and august institutions. He wanted a grammar school in the Don Valley Constituency, and if he had anything to do with it, it would be sited in his home ward of Adwick-le-Street.

On one occasion he heard some of the Labour Party deadwood complaining about the idea. The conversation went along the usual lines: 'What do we want a Grammar School here for, it'll put the rates up. I don't want my lad at school till he is sixteen when he could be working!' The possibility of a girl staying at school till she was sixteen was so far beyond the pale of their imaginings that the topic never came up.

John came to expect this small minded and unimaginative viewpoint from a certain section of the union or Labour Party. It was this section who opposed everything: the possibility of buying their own homes, a grammar school, introduction of machinery onto coalfaces. Later in the decade, they would oppose the building of pithead baths and the locker system, which would have the miners changing into their dirty pit clothes at the colliery before they went underground, and changing into their clean clothes after showering and going home fresh. The huge advantage of this in terms of saving in time, especially if a father and several brothers were to be bathed at home, and the savings in labour for wives and sisters in the boiling and bringing the hot water to the tin bath and the effort needed in emptying it, seemed to be totally outside the power of their minds to grasp. He heard one such moaner being told to shut his gob about grammar schools and that his lad was so thick that there was no chance of passing the scholarship anyway.

John was also well aware of the tradition of the black-back miner. Some of the old colliers thought that bathing had the effect of weakening the back, thus they never did so and as a result developed a hard black carapace due to years of not bathing and the effects of ingrained coal dust on the skin. If they went out to the pub, of course they would wash and shave, but their cleanliness ended at the neck.

Thus, in dribs and drabs, Mckinley formed his own and somewhat low opinion of politics and politicians. Though he realised it was not an activity which attracted him, he was conscious that the County Councils and Borough Councils had a lot of power. He was also aware that in areas controlled by Labour, some of this power was, for the first time, being exercised for the benefit of ordinary men and women and not for the benefit of the landed or moneyed classes. He knew that in Russia a revolution had occurred and that the landed gentry and nobility had fled or been slaughtered and their property taken.

He could see what had impelled this course of action in a country that was ruled in an autocratic and almost medieval manner. He could also see that slowly, inch by inch, the British working classes were moving to a position where they would be able to have a much greater share of the national cake. Would it be a 'fair' share? Perhaps! He thought. At least things were moving in the right direction without the need of a revolution in which hundreds of thousands would probably be killed and in which huge damage would be done to the towns and cities.

John also came to the conclusion that a realisation of the full fruits of the labour of the working classes, as described in the manifesto of the Communist Party, were more likely not to come about because of the small-mindedness of some of that class rather than the grasping determination of the gaffer's class to hold on to their 'ill-gotten capitalist gains'.

A picture was emerging in John's mind of how the various elements which made up British society melded together to form a whole. The roles of the law of education, industry, farming; of property ownership and political systems; of the class structure, the monarchy, media, commerce, and science and medicine and everything else. He was beginning to think of it as almost an organic entity. He realised that education was all important and decided to get as much of it as possible via the Workers Educational Association classes, his own reading, and via conversations with invaluable mentors such as old McChrystal and Taffy Williams.

He devoured anecdotes by some of the old hands at the pit. He noted their tales of past dangers and how to avoid difficulties in the mine; for example, by always being aware of the airflow direction underground. The advice was that if you heard an explosion you were to walk away from it into the direction of airflow if possible. He also received taciturn advice about the army and warfare from Cud and some of the other old sweats who had served in the Great War and even in the Boer War, about the sounds of different shells or what to do in a gas attack. He received opinions about various types of officers and NCOs, about the naive, young ones, and the hard-bitten cynical older ones; about the wastrels and cowards, about the careerists and the brave and the lucky ones. There was one old soldier who had done more than twenty years and who had gone across to France with the Old Contemptible in 1914, and who had managed to survive the war without a scratch. His considered opinion was that the British Army contained the finest men, the finest NCOs and the silliest officers of any army in the world.

Although John solidly voted Labour and always abided by union decisions, he despaired of the aspirations of a large number of his fellows. Certain rules applied: 'the rules of the herd'—the principal one being that it was not permissible to be different to the rest in any way. You could not 'get on' or be seen to be getting on; that was absolutely verboten! Buying your own house was out of the question. If you got married, you had to get a cottage in the mining village, preferably in the same street as your parents and sisters so that you had ready access to the support which was needed in the case of illness or injury, and so that your kids could have some elements of collective looking after.

It was permitted to earn a lot but you were also expected to drink a lot and to socialise with the rest of your shift. John found that to be no hardship but he also decided that he would plough his own furrow in respect of his earnings. Early on in his life, he could see the traps which society set to part the unwary from their hard-earned coin.

John was well aware that lots of his fellows drank a lot of beer—he could condone that and even join in. After all, mining was thirsty work and beer was a type of food and mine workers gained many of the necessary calories which they would burn underground from its consumption.

However, he could also see that many colliers were increasingly turning to cigarettes, and though on the face of it smoking was cheap, with the top quality cigarettes like Players costing one shilling for twenty, by the time the users had got up to thirty or forty a day they were spending ten or fifteen shillings a week on the things. John thought that that sort of money made a big and unnecessary hole in a take home wage of two to three pounds a week. He could also remember talking to one of the neighbour's girls called May Rummings, who had been told that she should stop smoking by the doctor. For some reason the doctor thought that the new tablets she was being given for her epilepsy would be more effective if nicotine was avoided.

May went on at length about how hard it was to give up. She had started when she was seventeen because many of the girls at the electrical factory she worked at smoked. After a couple of months, she had found herself unable to do without them and she had continued smoking until she was twenty. She had now been three weeks without a cigarette and thought that she had beaten the craving. John asked her if she had noticed any difference in herself. She replied, 'Oh yes, I can walk upstairs now without getting out of breath!' John had thought at the time, 'Jesus Christ! Smoking for four years and you can't walk upstairs without getting out of breath!' For these and other reasons, he had never started a habit, which was increasingly seen as being absolutely normal. Some women were starting to smoke in public but consumption of cigarettes amongst them was still low compared to men.

He knew that some of the older miners thought that pipe smoking helped to get the coal dust up off their chests. When he emerged from the mine he could see that very often his nostrils and mouth were thick with the stuff. John was also well aware that occasionally colliers developed a disease called miner's lung because of a lifetime inhaling coal dust, the medical name for the condition being *pneumoconiosis*. John had first heard the word at a union meeting, had asked about it later, and was told it was the Sunday name for miner's lung. He came to realise that one of the ways that the top men in the union held sway was by use of language. They always made a point of using the correct terminology in respect of mining law and related medical or safety matters at the larger meetings whilst only in the smaller informal gatherings did they lapse into the colloquialisms used by everyone else.

Mckinley had been fortunate enough to have been guided by McChrystal into reading a book about ancient Greek civilisation. The book, called *The Glory that was Greece*, was written by J.C. Stobart and published in 1911. The subject matter was so alien to John's own culture and circumstances that he may well not have bothered with the book, with its huge interlacing of scholarly classical references. However, a passage in the preface of the book gripped his attention and because of it, he persevered. The lines read: 'Real students are now like miners working underground each in his own shaft, buried far away from sight or earshot of the public, so that they even begin to lose touch with one another.' John was amused at Stobart's obvious ignorance of the practicalities of mining but at the same time interested and even flattered that his occupation had rated a mention. He thus worked through the book becoming seduced by its philosophical insights and marvellous anecdotes of those long-lost times of gods and heroes. As he progressed, he made lists of names and places that were to be looked up subsequently in order to fill the gaps in his understanding.

John could recall passages about the power of oratory from Stobart such as, 'we have noted how, even in Homer, persuasion by the power of speech was a God-given attribute of kings and elders.' He saw what was happening at union meetings and realised that the same techniques were still being employed by his own union's elders. Whether this was done by instinct or because of formal knowledge of the ancient skills of persuasion, he had no means of knowing. However, being exposed to the knowledge that these techniques existed gave him insights, and eventually he developed the ability of being able to see right through arguments being presented, and to separate the relevant facts from the rhetoric. He was then able to judge their validity in an analytical and independent manner.

John also developed an almost Socratic knack of asking the awkward question. He made a point of never challenging the union's position directly but usually wanted to know where a course of action would lead them, often several months hence. This in turn had the effect of making those who advanced arguments for industrial action try to think things through and not just try to call the men out on strike as an immediate reaction to events. John was well aware of the value of strike action. Yet, he thought that the threat of it alone should almost always be used prior to an actual strike, with a fair probability that the threat would produce a compromise, which would avoid a stoppage. He also came to realise that during the boom years the coal-owners were desperate for profits in order to recoup the investments they had made in sinking the colliery and therefore they wanted to avoid strikes. However, during those lean years in which production quotas were imposed by government, the weapon had significantly lost its edge.

He also ran into a few hard-line Communists and noted, with interest, that they always wanted a strike. It became clear to him that they were working to a separate agenda from that of the union. Their principal aim was a desire to undermine and wreck capitalism by rendering capitalistic enterprises unprofitable. His union had the much more modest objectives of trying to improve the pay and conditions of their members.

He listened, usually during snap breaks down the pit or in the bar of the Working Men's club, and usually without comment, to the evangelical zeal of various Communist tub-thumpers. He concluded that they were either deluded or suffering from some sort of messianic condition. He had seen the occasional 'hell fire' Baptist or Methodist preacher in action and came to realise that Communist and Christian zealots had little or nothing to choose between them; they were just working from different scripts! The result led him to distrust not only Communists but also anyone who argued from a dogmatic position, which was by definition totally inflexible by virtue of the way it had been constructed.

John also became aware of the pointlessness of arguing with such people. They were 'dogma locked' within their own belief system and no matter how cogent the arguments presented against their beliefs there appeared to be no way out for them. Thus, he categorised this class of being as 'to be avoided' and did so as soon as he became aware that he was in the presence of one of them or had previously found them to be of this nature.

Mckinley evaluated, analysed, and then cheerfully decided to plough his own furrow through life's varied and extensive pastures. He realised his own situation was a result of the vagaries of fate, and thus did not proceed through envy of those who had been luckier by birth. He knew times were hard and even as late as the 1930s there were still reports of the occasional poor soul starving to death in England. He also knew that in some parts of the world large-scale starvation and disease were destroying hundreds of thousands. He thought that things were improving, and would continue to improve. He hoped that his own kids would have things better than they had been for him.

He was aware that some miners had set out on an almost noble quest to see that their offspring got on. He was aware of one who had restricted his personal expenditure to the cost of one razor blade per month in order to finance his daughter's passage through Grammar School and then for a further two years through teacher training. There were others with similar aspirations but they were pretty much a rarity. He could also see that other colliers had set out to climb the greasy pole of promotion within the mining industry. Some became managers and Undermanagers, and others surveyors or engineers.

John had thought long about taking this route but eventually concluded that the effort, in terms of evening classes four or five nights a week, was not sufficiently recompensed by the rewards. He was well aware of some who had obtained their manager or undermanager tickets but who had not been able to get into management. There was also the great difficulty of managing to secure a job on 'days regular,' as it was called, in order to embark on the educational ladder. He could also see that one of the motivations for this was that it provided an escape route from the daily difficulties and dangers of working on coalfaces.

Only one thing depressed him. This was the small-minded short sightedness of many of his fellows. Their lack of aspiration for themselves and their kids appalled him. He could see that a fair few men in the district operated on a fairly brutish level, being quick with their fists when it came to dealing with their wives and kids and even quicker to see that their own beer and other 'necessaries' were provided in advance of anything which was obtained for their families.

He could also see that one section of the populace suffered from that incurable disease, known as stupidity. In their situations, money was sometimes in plentiful supply and sometimes not. Whichever was the case it seemed that they were always very easily parted from their incomes; they always seemed puzzled when for some reason they had not managed to have food at the end of the week or a few shillings to deal with an emergency, like providing a new pair of boots for one of the kids. It was almost as though they felt that the responsibility for their circumstances was down to someone other than themselves.

Years later he came upon a poem by Louis MacNeice called 'Bagpipe Music', and he thought that this summed up his despairing attitude beautifully. Often when he ran into the obdurate stupidity of his fellows he found lines from the poem springing into his consciousness, always causing a wry smile and a mock despairing shaking of his head, for example:

It's no go the Herring Board, it's no go the Bible,
All we want is a packet of fags when our hands are idle.

He thought these very well summed up the aspirations of this group. He also liked the last verse with its intimations of the powerlessness of the individual to change things in any significant manner:

The glass is falling hour by hour, the glass will fall for ever,
But if you break the bloody glass you won't hold up the weather.

8

Mckinley and Web of Venus

During his teens, Mckinley had experiences of sex that were both enlightening and formative in terms of his view of the female of the species. Though not tall, ending up at about five feet eight, he had that brooding look of the bruiser that led some women to compare him to the actor Clark Gable. His first experience of the opposite sex was at nineteen, when Mona Osbourne invited him back to her parental home.

Her dad ran a large and successful barber shop in Doncaster; her mother had decamped when she was three with a commercial traveller. Mona was unusual for those days in that she was well-fed, well-stacked and had a very high sex drive. She had made it her business to find out about sex and had read the revolutionary book called *Married Love*, written by Marie Stopes. She had obtained the book from a female cousin who was a radical socialist, had gone to work in London, and had something to do with something called the Fabian Society.

The cousin was about fifteen years older than Mona; she was unmarried and daringly smoked cigarettes in public. This was a rarity because in 1930 women only accounted for about five per cent of cigarette sales. The cousin believed in votes for women, equal pay in jobs such as teaching where they did equivalent work to the male, and in something called free love. She had explained to her young cousin that this had nothing to do with moral laxity but was to do with free choice, unhampered by the shackles of marriage and childbirth.

Thus, Mona, unusually for someone in the 1930s, had come to realise early in life that the intense pleasure of the sex act could be indulged, without the risk or terrible stigma of pregnancy out of wedlock, by using a rather interesting device known as a French Letter. In addition, she had access to this interesting and erotic commodity. Her father kept much of his stock of hair cream, razor blades, shaving soaps, and French Letters, in a small outbuilding attached to his house, which was situated with the other private houses just off the lane that led up to the A1.

For some reason the two outlets for these rubber prophylactics, which had become readily available after the First World War, were barber and chemist shops. Most men preferred to buy them at the barbers, and code phrases such as 'Anything for the weekend, sir?' became the stuff of comic legend. The outhouse was kept locked, but Mona knew where the spare key was and had 'borrowed' a three pack of the erotic sheaths and experimented with them, learning how to roll them on to the erect member using a large carrot in the absence of the real thing. *Married Love* completed her education. She had the means, she had the material and she had the victim in her sights. All that she now needed was the opportunity to seduce that rather broodingly attractive and intelligent youth called John Mckinley.

By now, he had undergone considerable physical development because of his work underground, and he had the sort of broad shoulders and narrow hips, which, for some reason, women find interesting. John had chatted to Mona at the monthly dances in the village hall and thought that she was lively and quick-witted. Nothing made him run the other way more rapidly than having to deal with her thicker sisters. He found that these not only tended to talk repetitively about trivialities, but were also prone to bouts of shrieking or other attention seeking devices, which he disliked intensely. He also avoided the quiet and demure girls, and the obviously religious types. He thought they were all motivated by a single thought, that thought being: 'How the hell do I get myself a husband, and on my terms?'

The last thing he wanted at this stage in his life was a wife and a kid or kids. He was painfully aware that a couple of the members of his school cohort had already been picked off in the never-ending battle of the sexes. These had fallen into the timeless trap, which waits for those who just cannot restrain the wild sexual urges of their teens. The result of this was a rapid 'shotgun marriage', as it was described, with the unfortunate youth ending up living with the girl's parents, usually in a single room along with the fruits of their unrestrained lust. Another unfortunate side effect of this arrangement was that these libidinous young men always had absolutely no money. Thus, they were excluded from the pleasant pastime of having a good drink with the lads on a Saturday night.

John rapidly became aware of the rules of the game by observing older teenagers and the sons and daughters of various friends and relatives in the village. 'The rules' were never articulated and the game was usually played in a restrained and furtive manner and was heavily dependent on body language and subtle innuendo in conversation. This was inevitable in a race like the English of the 1930s, which had social rules structured in such a way that one of their major corner stones was sexual repression. This, of course, did not apply to the ruling classes, who enjoyed sexual freedom and indulged themselves in its pleasures pretty much as they liked; these pleasures were of course denied to the lower orders.

Rule one of 'the game' was absolutely no sex before marriage! At least, not full sexual intercourse. The words *fuck* or *fucking* were never used in mixed company; they were reserved for low muttering in the saloon bar or for fraught, 'men only' situations at work, and even then were only heard in exceptional circumstances. As things loosened somewhat after the war some couples took the risk of starting to experience the sublime sensations of copulation just prior to marriage; hoping that pregnancy would not occur, but reassured that if it did, imminent marriage would disguise the fact that the two had taken an early bite out of that forbidden fruit.

He also started to amass an internal database on sex and sexual practices. This ranged from dark female mutterings along the lines of: 'He's always at her!' which was applied to those men who seemed to repeatedly impregnate their wives, year after year, to the story he was told of one couple who got married and had sex on honeymoon. After the two got back home and settled down into marital bliss, the wife explained to the husband that she enjoyed all aspects of domestic married life. She loved cooking, liked cleaning, found washing and ironing a joy. The one thing in their relationship which she decidedly did not like, was 'that, sweaty, messy and quite disgusting thing known as intercourse.' Thus, she put the proposition to her rather taken aback and mild-mannered spouse that she should continue with her enjoyments and that he should make 'other arrangements' to continue with his. Apparently, this was done and the two proceeded for many years in what seemed to all to be a very happy marriage, with her never questioning his occasional need for an overnight or weekend absence.

John came to realise that there was a propaganda war going on between the sexes, with the male usually portrayed as the lusting and predatory villain and the female as innocent and unfortunate victim. Conversations with some of the old hands in the village, especially those who had seen service in the various colonies, soon made him realise that this was far from the case. One hard bitten old veteran, who had served for many years in India and Egypt, dryly referred him to the poem by Rudyard Kipling which was entitled 'The Ladies.' This contained many very memorable lines that he relished and often retold when asked for advice on that great mystery known as woman.

The poem, John thought, was written in a humorous manner but with an underlying vein of deadly seriousness. It told the story of a trooper's exploits with the various women that he encountered during his postings in foreign parts. In these days, it would probably have the modern feminist frothing at the mouth because of its wry and politically incorrect observations.

John could quote the whole poem but he usually used certain favourite portions of it, which he thought would be illuminating. The following excerpts give the general flavour of the poem, which starts:

I've taken my fun where I've found it:
I've rogued an' I've ranged in my time;

It goes on to give accounts of the trooper's various conquests:

Older than me, but my first un—
More like a mother she were
Showed me the way to promotion an' pay

An' I learned about women from 'er!...

An' the end of it's sittin' and thinkin',
An dreamin' Hell-fires to see;
So be warned by my lot (which I know you will not),

An' learn about women from me!
An' learn about women from me!

The poem ends with this cynical yet insightful observation, and implied warning, that in tangling with the opposite sex the poor benighted male is always dealing with those seductive Sirens who just cannot help themselves, in that they are all the daughters of Eve:

For the Colonel's Lady an' Judy O'Grady
Are sisters under their skins!

The old veteran finished his discourse about the poem with the remarks, 'That about sums 'em up; you won't do much better than that for guidance about the buggers. If tha does get involved, just be wary!'

John took the remarks on board but realised that this was just one facet of the spectrum of male experiences and that there were many others. He came to realise that there was no standard model for male/female relationships. He was aware that the church and state exerted huge pressure, at least on the lower orders and middle classes, for conformity. He later learned that 'the godly' had been responsible for preventing or overturning much of the very sensible proposed legislation, which had been put forward in order to curb the spread of the venereal diseases. These diseases had plagued the armed forces in particular and had rendered huge numbers unfit for service during the Great War. One early and very ardent feminist had pointed out that sensible and effective methods of preventing or reducing the diseases were available. However, a parliamentary bill, which had sought to have this information published, had been opposed by the Bishops in the House of Lords. Consequently, it was now still illegal to disseminate such information.

Within the spectrum of relationships possible, John found that bachelorhood was frowned on within his own class and was in fact fairly uncommon amongst those men he knew. Things were different among the middle and upper classes, with the avuncular and usually pipe smoking 'confirmed bachelors' occurring much more frequently. The more he learned, the more tolerant he became, finding the hypocritical intolerance of the Victorians regarding sexual matters more and more repugnant. Theirs was the age of 'the wages of sin' and heavy sexual repression. The facts were very difficult to find, but he gathered that during the reign of the late Queen the veneer of surface respectability was underpinned by a huge number of prostitutes, with an estimated fifty thousand operating in London in 1840.

Many years later, whilst on holiday, John came across a group of Australians and grew to like both their capacity for beer and their refreshingly uninhibited attitude to sex. He absorbed their banter and found their irreverence refreshing and their stories hilarious. They seemed to have an innate optimism and cheerfulness. He wondered if this was due to the huge amount of sunshine which was to be had down under, compared to the cold grimness or grey misery of much of the English year.

At nineteen years of age, Mckinley, in common with most of his fellows, was still a virgin. His sexual experiences had been restricted to the usual burst of enthusiastic masturbatory fantasies, which had started soon after puberty and which were initiated after the usual back of the bike sheds explanation of the mechanics of the process. These were accompanied by much sniggering, and deprecatory remarks about the capability or capacity of certain individuals who engaged in this activity. John had experimented, as all, or most, post pubescent boys do, and he came to realise three things about 'wanking'.

Primarily, he found the process extremely pleasurable!

Secondly, with his usual analytical mindset, and although he knew next to nothing about the physiology involved, he realised that the intense sensation that he was experiencing during orgasm must be a modified pain reflex. That ecstasy being experienced was placed by the mind on just the right side of that knife-edge which produced agony if you slipped over to the wrong side. He read an article many years later by one of the Huxleys, who elegantly described the sensations experienced in the sentence: 'When I was thirteen I first discovered masturbation and the excruciating pleasure of the orgasm!'

Finally, he realised that it was a natural process and nothing to be ashamed of. His wide reading had included various manuals for the instruction of youth, with *Scouting for Boys* by Baden Powell being typical of the genre. In that august tome, Powell referred to masturbation, as did most others then, as 'self-abuse'. John knew from conversations with those youths in the village who had the misfortune by virtue of family circumstances to be saturated in religion, that the activity caused a deep sense of guilt and was viewed as shameful and unnatural.

He had run into some early ideas on evolution and had worked out pretty early on that humans of both sexes had been designed to find sex extremely pleasurable in order to encourage procreation and the continuance of the species. He placed those who did not choose to engage in the process into his growing database. He could see that those few men who chose not to marry had very often worked out the economics of the commitment, and had therefore made a hard-headed decision that beer, cigarettes and the occasional visit to the bookies would be their preferences in life.

He knew of a few who had found themselves landladies, who were almost invariably widows, and had moved in on a cordial room and board basis. He could see that those relationships were kept within strict bounds with the landlady always being referred to by her full married name of Mrs —, and never by her first name. He could also see that Catholic Priests usually had similar arrangements, although in their cases John had certain reservations due to the 'theoretical' commitment which they had made to abstain from all sexual activity. John shrewdly conjectured that, apart from those with low sex drives due to hormonal deficiencies, total abstinence was pretty near impossible.

He decided as usual to follow the path which seemed sensible to him and enjoy all aspects of sex without inhibition or guilt, and to let those who chose 'the hell' of sexual repression to get on with it and enjoy that experience. He was well aware of the dangers of impregnation and this was a major factor in maintaining his virginity until his nineteenth year. However, Mona, who was about eighteen months older than John, had other plans for him.

Their relationship developed, not quite into that of a besotted courting couple who saw each other as often as possible, but they did see each other very frequently and liked each other tremendously. On one weekday afternoon during a colliery shutdown, she arranged to meet him to go for a walk down the local bridle paths to experience the glories of the late spring. They eventually found themselves walking down the very quiet lane towards her father's house. She lightly made an excuse and invited him in, saying that she had something urgent to see to. John was doubtful; with the prurient attitudes which prevailed in the village, if he was seen entering the house with Mona, tongues would wag.

She realised what was worrying him and said: 'Don't worry, we will slip in through the side door into the walled garden; nobody will see us and I'll just be a couple of minutes and then we will be on our way!' John looked both ways down the deserted lane and then somewhat sheepishly followed her through the side door into the garden and then through the back door into the house. She invited him into the parlour at the rear of the place and persuaded him to sit on the rather large and comfortable sofa next to the door. She said, 'Read a magazine or something. I won't be long. I've just got to change into something more comfortable.'

Mona disappeared upstairs and John sat on the edge of the sofa looking at the titles of various books in the small bookcase opposite him; the light was rather dim due to the northerly aspect of the room and the net curtains. Squinting slightly, he noted that there were many volumes by (Enoch) Arnold Bennett. These sprang to his attention because he remembered seeing his obituary in one of the papers; the author had died in 1931 from typhoid and had left a large fortune.

John had seen some of the titles, such as *Hilda Lessways* and *Anna of the Five Towns* at the local library. Here there were others, such as *Mr Prohack* and *The Grim Smile of the Five Towns*, which he had not previously encountered. He had occasionally been tempted to take a Bennett out on loan but had been put off by the fact that his readership seemed to be predominantly those of the opposite sex.

He avoided what he thought were women's books due to an early encounter with Jane Austen. He had been told that *Pride and Prejudice* was her masterpiece and although he had appreciated the wit of its opening lines that propounded that: 'It is a truth universally acknowledged, that a single man in possession of a good fortune, must be in want of a wife.' The over ornate-ness, as he saw it, of the prose was too much for a fifteen-year old with a mining family background. The latter also meant he had little sympathy with the privileged scenario within which the novels were set.

John's mind wandered, speculating on the relationship between the books and Bennett's large accumulation of wealth, when he heard the sound of shoes slowly descending the stairs. The parlour door was immediately adjacent to the bottom of the stairs. John stood up and started to say, 'I hope you're ready...' but stopped halfway through the sentence as Mona came into the room. The door opened slowly and she entered. Her lips had been newly reddened with bright lip-stick and she wore a pair of black high-heeled shoes. Apart from that she was naked!

The effect in terms of stimulus on Mckinley was similar to that of someone who on having a quiet Sunday nap suddenly found himself at the centre of a salvo of eighteen-inch shells. His mouth dropped open in amazement and then the male hormones took over and produced an instant erection as he gazed at Mona's large and shapely breasts and at the fine bush of dark hair set invitingly above the entrance to her moist, and aching to be penetrated, pussy. She stepped close to John and planted a wet kiss on his lips whilst feeling in the area of his crotch. She let out a low giggle on encountering the erect penis, saying: 'Oh, you are interested then!' Mckinley knew what was required of him and reached eagerly for the moistness between her legs—a little too eagerly as it turned out. Her restraining hand and the word 'gently' set him on the route which she desired.

His fingers explored, penetrating the juicy opening and moving over the small erect thimble which he later found out was called the clitoris. He observed that Mona stiffened and had started to moan with especial pleasure when he stroked this area. Mona loosened his belt and his trousers dropped to the floor. John stepped out of the wide legs and urgently moved her towards the sofa. Mona said: 'Wait a second, sit down.' He did so and she revealed a French letter which she had been clutching tightly in her left hand.

She knelt and rolled the strange device over his pulsating member. She then reversed their positions, reclining back on the sofa and pulling her eager victim on top of her. John moved to enter her and she guided him past her swollen and moist labial lips, deep into her wet and waiting vagina. He saw her eyes roll back in pleasure. She gave an involuntary shudder and gasped as the first sensations of coition raced through her arching body. After that, the primal instincts which have impelled desire since the dawn of time took over and she grasped him to herself wildly as he engaged in an increasingly eager sequence of vigorous thrusts.

His excitement grew and he was drawn into more and more fevered action, both by Mona's gasps of delight and his wide-eyed realisation of the pleasure which was resulting from what was, both John's and Mona's, first fuck. Ejaculation came fairly rapidly, but not too rapidly. Mona had first gone off into a sequence of wild hip thrusting, gasping, orgasms, and thus lay back well satiated after John found he could no longer continue due to the sharp intensity of his own ejaculatory experience.

Mona would have liked to have engaged in the joys of sexual pleasuring all afternoon but realised that due to the possibility of discovery the few minutes that they had stolen from the gods of sex would have to suffice for now. She got up, bending over her lover to give him a kiss, which in this case conveyed gratitude and satisfaction rather than burning desire. She clumsily reached for the durex, which slipped easily from his now flaccid penis. She laughed with an assurance which could have come from a girl who was well versed in those arts and which could have led him to think that this sort of thing was a regular occurrence for her. He knew very well that it wasn't, and liked Mona's spirit all the more for her attitude to having sex.

There wasn't any guilt or embarrassment there, just the feeling that the two had indulged in an activity that was perfectly natural and normal. She said, 'I'll just get rid of this and then we will go for our walk.' Mona disappeared upstairs. John heard the lavatory cistern empty and he presumed that the sound represented a farewell to the sheath. Mona reappeared shortly afterwards, dressed and wearing a pair of 'sensible' walking shoes and looking rather flushed and very attractive. She then led him surreptitiously to the back gate so that they could continue their stroll.

Mckinley, as was his usual practice, thought deeply about the experience over the following months. It had been an experience that was repeated at much too infrequent intervals, as far as they both were concerned, and especially so in the case of Mona. John had noted that certain of his actions during their sexual encounters had more effect than others when it came to provoking a response of the highest intensity from his partner. He realised that stroking the clitoris was a particularly potent weapon if he wanted Mona to experience the prolonged and repeated sequences of orgasms, which her physical and psychological make up had permitted her to enjoy. He found that varying the rhythm and depth of his thrusts into her were also rewarded with the eye-widening and moaning delight with which she showed her appreciation of his attentions.

John, being John, wanted to know more. He felt inhibited about asking Cud or immediate relatives, and thus gleaned snippets from old hands and youthful fellow conspirators from the village. Mona had loaned him *Married Love* to read. He thought the tome useful for its description of contraceptive devices and methodology but thought that the doctor's style of writing was rather too gushing for his tastes. Bit by bit he managed to put together an accurate and comprehensive picture of what was happening to them during that impelling need to engage in the pleasurable paroxysms of lovemaking. He pieced the picture together by following up references and delving into various encyclopaedias, which contained dry and clinical snippets of information about sex and its consequences.

He managed to track down a copy of Krafft-Ebing's *Psychopathia Sexualis* in Doncaster's central reference library. It was brought out from the dry and dusty shelves of a hidden room at the rear of the reference section by a young librarian. The young man was inclined towards socialism and free-thinking. He said, 'Yes, I've read the thing. It was published in 1876, but let me tell you, you are wasting your time—the dirty bits are in Latin!' Mckinley had the advantage of a near photographic memory especially for things that had extreme interest for him. Using his gift and an old Latin dictionary, he slowly pieced together the incredible tale of the various sexual perversions, which Krafft-Ebing described. He learned about impotence and frigidity, finding with some surprise that some women and considerably fewer men did not, or could not, experience orgasm.

John found that his conversations with the youth of the village were next to useless in terms of gaining or imparting information as their knowledge of the actualities of sexual intercourse seemed to be based on myth, hearsay, ignorance and fantasy. On one occasion, he had explained the biology of impregnation and then became annoyed at the stupid and repeated insistence by two of the group that: 'tha can only get 'em pregnant if tha both comes at the same time!' He decided to discontinue further attempts to enlighten those youths and departed, saying as he left: 'That's OK then. Make sure that

you come before or after her the next time you get her knickers down—you don't want to be having to get married and
have loads of squawking kids, do you?' He left smiling, thinking, 'You'll find out pretty soon if you are right or wrong.'

He had now worked out the basic mechanics of the forces
which drove sexual need and knew about the menstrual cycle.
He had learned that at or around ovulation the female was
particularly keen to engage in sex. She was less restrained at
these times and more prone to indulge and take the risk of
possible pregnancy. John knew that these heightened periods of sexual desire occur at or around the fourteenth day
after the end of a period and that this was when there was the
greatest danger of pregnancy occurring. Thus, as far as he was
concerned, this was the time when it was vital for him to have
a Durex when in Mona's eager and inviting presence.

He absorbed other strands of information about sex and
about its dangers in terms of the various venereal diseases.
He discovered that there were two main types of infection
and that gonorrhoea was fairly widespread, painful, and usually relatively moderate in terms of the damage that it caused.
The only treatment up until 1935 was by mercury. Effectively
by mercury poisoning, which the gonococcus bacterium
was, fortunately, more susceptible to than the human organ-
ism. Many years later he read an account of Edward Prince
of Wales' fondness for high class Parisian brothels, and his
subsequent need for treatment with mercury, with some
amusement and a wry realisation that he shared some of the
same needs as royalty. Later in the decade, John noted with
interest that a new class of drugs called the sulphonamides
had been produced, which provided a much more comfortable cure for a dose of the clap.

The other main type of VD was syphilis; this occurred
much less frequently than gonorrhoea. It was slow developing and could have mild or almost unnoticeable symptoms
during its early stages. Though its progress was slow it was
insidious, and many years after it had been contracted the

result of its progress could be severe nervous damage, which could result in insanity or death.

He thought that he would be unlikely to contract that particular disease, as it was strongly associated with certain types of sexual lifestyles, which he did not intend to engage in. Nevertheless, he was grateful that a methodical German scientist called Paul Ehrlich had discovered an arsenic derivative, which he called Salversan 606, which would almost magically cure the condition. The number 606 refers to the fact that it was the six hundredth and sixth of the compounds which had been tested by that German chemist for effectiveness against the syphilis spirochetes and was the first to be found to be effective without poisoning the recipient.

Mckinley made his mind up early on that a monogamous, preferably life-long relationship with Mona, would be the one for him. He continued to wonder at the general ignorance of his fellows about sex and sexual matters and birth control. He noted also how incredibly long it took for the Victorian attitudes to birth control to die out. Much later on, after reading an account of an exchange in the House of Commons, he was left shaking his head in despair. A question from the Labour opposition to the Minister of Health had enquired: 'Is it not a ridiculous position, that even where family planning clinics are held in local authority premises it is illegal to advertise them or publicise them in any way?' The minister failed to see anything wrong with the prohibition; it would be left merely to the local authorities to inform doctors of their existence and refer women as they saw fit. The year was 1962.

John felt that there was a weirdness here, which he had encountered in other areas of British life, such as access to information which would enable people to protect themselves against venereal diseases; he could not quite fathom the root of it. Here was a problem involving an aspect of sex with an obvious solution that for some reason was not being made available to those who needed it!

9

Mckinley and 'Unnatural' Urges

A few months after his first highly pleasurable sexual encounter with Mona, John experienced the second of those early experiences of sex which were formative and helpful in conditioning his subsequent understanding of the subject. They involved a local choirmaster called Cedric Plunkett-Green. Cedric hated his Christian name and his acquaintances found his double-barrelled surname a bit of a mouthful. Most had settled on the compromise of calling him PG. Cedric was more than happy with this. It made him sound like some important manager of a shipping firm or a director of one of the railway companies. In fact, PG worked as a moderately competent clerk in a moderately successful solicitor's office in Doncaster.

PG was twenty-six and just tending towards plumpness. His hair was fine, fair, receding slightly, and was always neatly parted on the left side. He was of medium height, standing at about five feet six in his stockinged feet, pale of complexion and with pink cheeks that looked as though they had never seen the edge of a razor. PG was excessively mild mannered and exuded a sort of smarmy politeness which caused almost all of those who encountered him to form an instant dislike of the man.

PG was heavily involved with local choirs and especially with that of a church located in a pleasant country village about six miles from the mining townships. Cedric was an only child and had been born into a Catholic family. His father was a pillar of the church and voted Conservative. Cedric's birth had nearly killed his mother, and her gynaecologist had advised them both that: 'production of further offspring would almost certainly kill her.'

PG senior was fortunate in that he was the manager of the local branch of Marks and Spencer, and by virtue of his occupation he was in receipt of a considerable salary. Through his contact with a cousin who was a surgeon at Leeds general infirmary, he had the connections needed to make the necessary arrangements regarding the dangers to his wife.

The PGs had previously discussed the matter with their own doctor, who was also Catholic, to no avail. That practitioner was unhappy about admitting that such a thing as contraception even existed. Cedric's mother was eventually fitted with a diaphragm in Leeds and given strict advice about its use in conjunction with spermicidal creams, and reassured that it was very effective.

PG senior moved in the circles inhabited by the Catholic middle classes. It had been suggested to him that he might be considered for membership of the Catenian Association, or the Knights of St Columba, which as far as he could discover were the Catholic equivalents of the Freemasons or the Rotarians. All these organisations had a laudable charitable component and a well-structured program of social activities, which made prospective membership attractive to him. Although the PGs had attended Masonic Ladies Nights at the invitation of a close friend who was a member of one of the lodges near Doncaster and had found those events highly enjoyable, he himself as a Catholic was forbidden from joining the Masons by canon law.

PG was a keen cricketer and golfer, and in his youth had been a county level Rugby Union player. Because of these sports, his resulting good physical condition, and a naturally high testosterone level, he was still rather keen on sex. He was delighted that the diaphragm enabled intercourse with no reduction in sensation. Thus, after his wife had fully recovered from the physical effects of birth the pair had embarked on a program of very frequent and highly enjoyable sex. PG senior had tried using French letters during his courtship of the lady who was to become Mrs PG. He found them unsatisfactory because of the loss of the extremely pleasurable skin-to-skin sensation experienced during unprotected lovemaking.

Although he was aware that he was committing a sin in the eyes of the church, he knew the sin was venial and not mortal. As a history graduate from Sheffield University, PG had specialised in a study of Western society in the pre- and early Christian period and he was well acquainted with the doctrines of the early church as set forth by figures such as St Paul and St Augustine. These venerated founders of the church saw marriage as a concession to human weakness and sex within marriage as being permissible only in order to bring about procreation; it was certainly not to be indulged in for the purpose of enjoyment.

The various early religions he had studied had tended to condemn sexual practices with varying degrees of severity. Adultery was always the most serious offence. Moderate condemnation was usually applied to abortion, homosexuality or sex with animals. Infanticide and contraception were only rarely condemned. Masturbation always seemed to have been perfectly acceptable as a natural activity to all of the pre-Christian religions. This was not the case within the early Christian Church; this institution had condemned all sexual activities out of hand!

PG senior also knew that the early Popes had married and that some of the medieval and renaissance Popes had fathered numerous bastard children, often with different mistresses. He was also well aware that marriage had only become a sacrament in the twelfth century and that priests had also married and had children until about the eleventh century. Certain anti-Catholic, and thus, obviously godless, academics, alleged the compelling reason for the foisting of celibacy on the clergy was to prevent priests handing on church property and wealth to their sons rather than to the church itself. He noted that around this time the sin of simony, which involved buying or selling church property, benefices or other emoluments, appeared to have acquired much greater approbation than it had done previously.

He thought that this was well illustrated by Dante's *Divine Comedy* which was written in the early 1300s and thus not too long after the church had changed its policy in respect of clergy marrying. In the wonderful section on the damned he noted that those guilty of that sin dwelt in the third gulf of the eighth circle of Hell with their bodies trapped in cavities in the rocks with the soles of their feet forever on fire. PG thought that Dante was marvellous, almost on a par with Homer. However, he noted with amused cynicism that the very worse punishments in Hell seemed to be reserved for those who defied the established line of the holy mother church. He was unsurprised that heretics and schismatics seemed to top the list in terms of the severity of torments received, occupying the ninth circle of Hell next to Satan himself. Because of his extensive readings, PG senior, privately, came to believe that the church was perhaps overly censorious of human activity in many respects and certainly somewhat inconsistent in its various doctrines governing the marital state.

Though PG senior was, by 1930s standards, liberal in his views, he took the advice of the church he had been brought up in with gratitude and humility; after all, he had been inculcated from an early age with those doctrines, which were central to the carefully worked out, and internally self-consistent traditions of the organisation. However, in respect of his personal needs, his knowledge tended to outweigh the strictures of dogma, and thus common sense regarding matters of a sexual nature always held sway in his own marital bed.

An incident about eighteen months after the birth of little Cedric was to have life changing consequences for him and his family. PG senior was in a senior salaried occupation, and thus the local priest, a certain Father O'Keefe, called round soon after the first of each month for tea and piece of cake and to collect the routinely expected pound note. This was the Plunkett-Green's generous contribution to the running of the Parish. The money was given without any sort of receipt or book-keeping entry which would note where it came from or how the Father spent it.

O'Keefe had a liking for cigarettes and whisky and it was known that he attended the St Leger, The Lincoln, The Ebor Handicap, and The Grand National. One of his flock had joked after seeing him queuing at one of the expensive, stand side, bookmakers of the York Racecourse, saying, 'Trying to win a new church, father!' This remark had been greeted acidly. His parishioner was told: 'Yes Brennan, I'll have to include a piece on criticism of the cloth by the laity the next time you attend Mass. I do hope it will be sooner rather than later!'

Though it was well known that O'Keefe attended the major classic race meetings and that the priest made no secret of the fact, he was not prepared to tolerate criticism from one of the faithful, even in jest. He knew that the Church must have unquestioned authority in all matters pertaining to the priesthood and its flock and as far as he was concerned in respect of all other matters. His remarks held an underlying yet deadly seriousness in its determination to maintain that authority.

Brennan, suitably chagrined, turned up at the parochial dwelling later that week bearing a bottle of malt whiskey for the priest, saying: 'Sorry for my little joke at the race track, father. I intended no offence, I hope you took none.' The priest, though having not the slightest formal knowledge of psychology, was an excellent and instinctive practitioner of those arts of persuasion and manipulation whose roots were beginning to be explored and described in universities.

A less worldly priest might have dressed Brennan down and had him depart with his tail between his legs. O'Keefe knew there was no need of it and that the point had been well made and suitably taken. He also knew that the word would

get around the parish like wildfire and thus suitably rein-
force the sort of boundaries which he felt must be maintained
between himself and the members of his congregation. After
all, at the end of the day the discipline imposed by his actions
were for the good of the church!

Thus, he said to the apprehensive Brennan, 'Think nothing
of it, Patrick. If we can't have a little joke now and then between
ourselves where would we be? We would be like the Protes-
tants!' He went on, turning rapidly to enquire solicitously about
his numerous offspring and Mrs Brennan, taking care to use
her first name. 'How is Carmel? Fine girl, I knew her father well,
God rest his soul, a fine Catholic and a fine man, a credit to the
parish.' He went on with a conspiratorial wink: 'Let's open the
malt and have a drink to the dear departed's memory. After all
the O'Keefes and Brennans must have been drinking together
since whiskey was invented!' He took down two glasses and
poured out two measures of the golden liquid, a large one for
himself and a smaller one for the gift bearer; after all, he could
not encourage over indulgence in his flock.

All this had exactly the effect that the cynical old O'Keefe
wished it to have. He had started his afternoon with a large
glass of very fine Glenmorangie, a Spey-side Whisky which he
was particularly fond of, and had caused Brennan to depart in
a much-cheered mood. He had no doubt that later on the man
would be telling the rest of his family and friends what a fine
and understanding man the wily old priest was; and he knew
very well that this would pay excellent dividends in the parish.

In respect of the whisky itself, it was well known that the
father liked a drop of scotch—'the good stuff'. Others liked
quantity and not quality, but not he. Others might like more
than a drop of the hard stuff, but he was a man of relative mod-
eration. Over a long life, he had gained considerable knowledge
of the single malts and the much more numerous blended
whiskies. He kept a list of those he had sampled with his personal rating and a score awarded of between one and ten.

He thought that grain whiskies were much of a muchness

and should be awarded a two on his personal preference scale. In his opinion, they had a harsh and unpleasant taste and needed soda to make them palatable. This was far from the case with single malts, which just needed a few drops of water to release their aromatics and maximise their magnificent and very varied flavours. His interest was so great that he had cultivated contacts with priests in the Islands and Highlands and had used them during his much-needed summer breaks to fulfil his need for 'spirit'-ual refreshment.

He had visited many distilleries in both Islay and the Speyside areas. Although the priest's Irish antecedents should have required that he support Jameson's Irish Whiskey, which was produced south of the border, he was not fond of it, finding that it was a rather unsubtle distillation; to his palate, it suffered from the disadvantage of not being a single malt. He was obviously prohibited by sectarian considerations from even thinking about the excellent triple distilled whisky produced at the Bushmills distillery in the Protestant County of Antrim.

He kept a bottle of 'the Jameson's' in his sideboard as he was well aware that if he did offer the golden nectar to visitors, that occasionally, one of them would ask, if given the choice, for a drop of the Irish. He put this down either to tribal loyalties or a lack of awareness of the true magnificence of the many single malt Scotches.

Apart from these indulgences, which were unquestionably accepted and even expected by his flock, the priest was pretty much a hardliner, especially in the area of the need of the females of his church to submit to the needs of their husbands. He would frequently explain to women-only gatherings within the church that any form of contraception was a very serious sin. Any attempt to prevent conception would put their immortal souls at risk of damnation. Their only path, if they found the need to indulge in 'the pleasures of the flesh' to be irresistible, as all of them usually did, was to give way to it; but they must bear the fruits of their lust as a long series of additions to the numbers of the faithful.

Though it was never stated openly, the subtext of his message made clear that he expected the mothers of 'the true faith' to outbreed their protestant counterparts. PG senior knew that the strategic objectives of the Roman Catholic Church had been thought out in a very long term manner and that these plans would unfold over several centuries. Though he had obviously not been privy to the discussions, which must have taken place in the Vatican, and elsewhere, he had no doubt that eventually Rome would wish to welcome the English Church back into its fold. The more little Catholics that were produced, the sooner this would occur, thereby re-establishing the authority of the one true church in a country which had been wrested from its ministering grasp by the ruthless actions of the unspeakable Henry, in pursuit of his own, damnable, carnal pleasures.

Therefore, the reaction of PG Senior to the final visit of Father O'Keefe to the pleasant and spacious detached home of Cedric's parents, resulted in a considerable shock for the old priest. On his arrival he was, as was usual, welcomed into the lounge most cordially. He could see the customary pound note waiting for him on the mantelpiece. PG senior poured him a large whisky and the two engaged in the usual chitchat about parochial matters, the state of the country, PGs garden and so forth.

Eventually, and with a more serious air, O'Keefe enquired how long it had been since Cedric had been born. PG senior said, 'Oh, it must be nearly two years now, Father, but you know the situation.' The priest was obdurate. His conversation went along lines which expressed his concern that Cedric had not yet been joined with a brother or sister. He aired his views on contraception and made it clear that in the view of the church this practice would lead to damnation. He went on to say that if the pair wished to continue to have a sexual relationship it must be on the basis that children were hazarded as a result. He was insistent that this was the will of the almighty as expressed by the holy mother church and the PGs should trust in god and obey his divine will. Cedric's father became exasperated at this and said: 'But Father, if we do, it will kill her!'

The priest made tut-tutting noises and started to cast doubts on the expertise of the consultant who had given the advice on the likely outcome of a further pregnancy, saying: 'Was he a Catholic?' PG senior said, 'No, but I don't see what that's got to do with it. He is very eminent in his field.' O'Keefe persisted: 'If we all believed everything that protestant doctors told us we would have failing congregations. That's probably what they want. It's your duty to the church; it's been more than eighteen months now since your last was christened.'

At this lurch into irrationality and with the obvious disregard for his wife's welfare, PG senior saw red. He said, 'Are you seriously daring to instruct me to try to murder my wife in order to increase your congregation!' The priest reacted angrily at this challenge to his authority and a furious row erupted. PG finally exploded with the words: 'Get out of my house and get out now.'

The priest, who had never before been talked to by anyone in this way, responded in equal anger: 'How dare you challenge me in these matters, I am your Priest!' PG senior was so angry by now that he almost struck the man but just managed to restrain himself and instead vented his rage by taking him by the scruff of the neck and the back of his cassock and ejecting him bodily and with considerable force from his house. O'Keefe stumbled and almost fell as he was thrown across the threshold; he was numb with shock that one of the faithful had dared to lay hands on him. He tottered down the path muttering, 'Assaulting an ordained priest, you will burn in Hell!'

PG senior shouted after him: 'Don't you ever dare come back into this house, you foul old man. Who do you think you are? Murderer!' The vehemence of the words ensured that the priest never did return.

The priest expected that the need for communion with

Rome would ensure an eventual return to the Church by his assailant, but it never occurred. In the first few months of PGs absence the priest expected that he would see Cedric's father, looking suitably chastened, standing in penitence at the back of his church. He intended to see that any punishment in the form of prayerful and monetary recompense for the colossal and almost unbelievable insult that he had suffered was as harsh and a large as he could possibly make it.

However, he was denied that privilege, and as the seasons slipped by his expectations faded. Although he hoped to see PG senior in church someday, his thoughts of a just vengeance were eventually spoiled when he learned that his former stalwart had severed his contact with all the Catholic institutions to which he had previously been linked and had joined the Conservative Party and become active in it. O'Keefe realised that any possibility of reconciliation was out of the question when he subsequently learned that PG senior had dared to join the abominated Freemasons.

The irony of all this was that many years later, on his deathbed, PG senior imparted a final gem of advice to his nephew. It concerned joining and being active in any sort of institution which strove to change and direct human affairs. The old man said to the young man, 'I spent thirty years with the church and then forty years with politics, *don't make the same mistake!*'

Cedric had thus been brought up as an occasional attendee at the local Church of England. The nonconformists and especially the Presbyterians have the notion of a 'good protestant'. PG senior had found that this did not apply in the C of E and his choice of church was very deliberate. The last thing that he wanted was another rigid, inflexible and dogmatic religious institution to interfere in his life and possibly endanger the life of his dear wife. He came to think of the more severe Protestant churches as a sort of steeped-in-misery Catholicism but without the incense.

After his departure from the Roman Church, as PG senior

136

went through life, he made a point of noting peoples experiences with the multitude of Christian institutions in the area, resulting in a list of anecdotes, which were derogatory to all of them. Although he very occasionally met individuals who appeared to be shining examples of their faith, in respect of the various Christian institutions in general, he became more and more jaundiced with each passing year. Those shining exemplars that he did meet, gave him the impression that they were following the simple message of human kindness and brotherly love as propounded by the Saviour and he admired them for it. Sadly, he realised that these were in a very small minority and that the power politics, factionalism, manipulation and backstabbing, which seemed to characterise every other human institution which he had encountered, were also writ very large in the churches.

PG senior, although he did not attend regularly, rather liked the Church of England. It had a sort of easy-going daftness, which seemed to tolerate all strands of belief ranging from authoritarian hard liners, who were to his mind almost indistinguishable from the Jesuits, to those with the vaguest of beliefs, which bordered on and even occasionally strayed into atheism. Although he avoided the hard liners like the plague, he had time for some of the others. He particularly liked Canon Reynolds who lived in the small mining village of Great Houghton about ten miles from Doncaster.

He had run into the man on various Conservative Party committees and liked him for his very progressive and liberal views on education. The Canon abhorred corporal punishment, which he had seen un-judiciously and viciously applied by the prefects at his public school. He also believed in scholarships into the sixth forms for the very brightest of the working classes and that the general school leaving age should be raised to sixteen, even for girls!

PG senior was good friends with the colliery manager in Great Houghton as they had played rugby together at grammar school and subsequently at university. The manager was called Granville Spooner and was unusual in that he had obtained a degree in mining engineering before entering the coal industry as a managerial trainee. In the thirties, almost all colliery managers had come up through the ranks. These men had usually left school at twelve or thirteen and starting as haulage lads, progressing on the basis of raw talent up the ranks.

At a dinner party PG senior was told a story about the manager's son Philip. He thought that the tale epitomised all that he liked about the C of E. Coming up to marriage the son and his bride-to-be had gone to see the old Canon about the banns and to set a date for the big event. In those days, the only figures of note who commanded automatic respect in the village were the Canon, the local doctor, and the colliery manager. They were the only three university graduates for miles around and greeted each other socially on first name terms.

A teacher lived in the village, but as he had only done two years at a teacher-training establishment and thus was decidedly a second division player in the salaried ranks in that small community, he was never addressed on familiar terms under any circumstances by any of the three university men.

On arriving at the old rectory, the old Canon greeted the news of the forthcoming wedding with considerable delight. Philip was, after all, the son of the colliery manager.

Reynolds said to Philip, 'My dear boy, I am so pleased to hear your good news and to meet your charming bride to be. I must put a short program of talks on for you both on the Christian meaning of Marriage in the Church of England.' Phil was rather nonplussed at the suggestion but he agreed to attend, as he rather liked the old boy and wanted to make sure that the wedding proceeded with maximum goodwill and cooperation from all who would be involved in it. He was taken aback when he found that there would be eight talks, each of about half an hour's length. The talks would take place after the Sunday Morning services, which Phil and his bride would be expected to attend. Although he would sooner have been out in the countryside with his new motor bike, he did so with goodwill and found that he quite enjoyed the talks.

After one of the lectures and appreciating the fact that they had disturbed the clergyman's normal Sunday routine, and while they were drinking the obligatory cup of tea afterwards, Phil asked the good Canon how he usually spent his Sundays. Reynolds said, 'Pretty much the same as everyone else I suppose. I attend church for a brief early morning service with spoken mass for those who have urgent business during the day. Then, after a hearty breakfast, I hold the morning service and then remain at church for a while to sort out Sunday school and any problems that the vergers might have. We then have a traditional Sunday lunch followed by a family bible reading and prayers. I hold evensong at six and after it, we have family activities and listen to the wireless. We have supper at nine, evening prayers, and then retire. *We spend the day like most other people; it's a perfectly normal Sunday!'* Young Philip hadn't the heart to tell him that it wasn't!

Granville had said to PG senior after telling him the tale: 'It says a lot about how people's minds work. Here we are, all in our own little goldfish bowls, thinking that what happens in ours applies to everyone else.'

PG senior said: 'Yes, I suppose in darkest Africa the tribesmen think it's normal to dance around the totem pole whilst boiling a missionary in the pot and then go home and dine on hyena and ostrich eggs on their day of worship.'

The PGs' only offspring had displayed early musical talent at the piano, had gone on to learn the organ, and became involved in choral music. PG senior was a muscular type who needed to shave twice a day and exuded a very masculine air which women still seemed to pick up on even when he was well into his fifties. He had hoped that his son would share his interest in and prowess at sport. However, an eye defect made cricket impossible for the boy and he showed no interest in rugby or golf, or in any other sport for that matter.

Cedric spent his weekdays in the solicitor's offices. He worked alone apart from his files and a shared office junior and typist. He produced weekly and monthly reports on various legal matters and case summaries, and had as little to do with the other employees as possible. As a non-gregarious type, he had lots of time to do his work well and efficiently. He was a model employee; he did not drink, smoke or gamble. He appeared to have no interest whatsoever in politics, sport, trade unionism, motor cars, good-time girls, or in girls generally. His mother lived in hope, and occasionally made helpful remarks about courtship, marriage, and the joys of children, and especially of grandchildren. All these hints were of no avail. The boy seemed to have only one passion and that was directed solely in the direction of various choral composers.

On the face of it PG junior seemed to be about as boring and uninteresting as it was possible for a young man to be. However, Cedric had a secret. 'CEDRIC BURNED IN HELL.' He knew he was damned and that there was nothing he could do about it. He was helpless to resist the dark vortex of pleasure that had sucked him into its depths and held him there without any hope of escape.

At fourteen years of age, one of the senior choristers in his Church choir had seduced Cedric. Far from being repulsed by the act, the pink-cheeked victim found that not only did he enjoy the various pleasures that he was made to endure but that he had to have them.

The senior chorister was enthusiastic but fairly basic in his needs, which consisted of making his junior submit to his desire to undress him and explore his tight little anus with the fingers of one hand whilst masturbating frantically with the other.

Cedric, of course, knew nothing of the modern body of research that has slowly dragged homosexuality from its dark ages to a place where its practitioners are not thought to be abnormal in any way by most intelligent people. What he did know was that in his time the act was a mortal sin and a crime, which had been viewed so seriously that until 1861 it had carried the death penalty in England. Cedric lived in dread of being found out, but he also lived in the full knowledge that he was incapable of resisting his uncontrollable urge to indulge in this sin-drenched activity as often as possible.

The young man had graduated in his degree of sexual sophistication at the hands of various partners until he had finally fallen under the sway of a local solicitor who had taught him the pleasures of pain and bondage coupled with violent intercourse. This pillar of the establishment was well connected and the cousin of a local squire. One of Cedric's previous partners had revealed PGs sexual predilections to him in confidence. Thus, a carefully planned seduction took place at the solicitor's home, with Cedric, almost before he knew what was happening, rapidly tied, caned and then rampantly sodomised, and then caned again. He had experienced pleasure before but never as overwhelming as he did now. The experience left him a pulsating and quivering lump of jelly who had experienced total and complete sexual satisfaction for the first time in his life.

The solicitor, whose office door was decorated with a brass plate, upon which the words 'G.P.T.W. Brewster L.lb.' were inscribed, had judged things almost to perfection. He could see that his actions had achieved almost exactly the sort of effect that he had hoped and expected. He explained to his new conquest that he now regarded Cedric as his slave and that Cedric must obey him. The pink-cheeked slave acquiesced to those demands with abject and unrestrained gratitude.

Subsequently the two met on a weekly basis on Sunday afternoons at the lawyer's residence, which was situated in wooded isolation in the countryside in between the two mining villages. The man of the law was known throughout the district as a confirmed bachelor. His household consisted of a gardener, and a woman who cleaned and saw to the laundry, and a cook who prepared his breakfasts and evening meals. All were part-time employees and had Sundays off, with the solicitor making his own dining arrangements on that day. During the longed-for interludes of intense lovemaking and punishment, his lover refined his technique in such a way that the chains of pleasure tightened ever more closely around the willing slave, who came to realise that it was impossible to break free even if he had wanted to.

Mckinley had seen PG on several occasions from a vantage point in an old oak tree which he periodically climbed to enjoy both the view and the solitude it provided by being close to nature. This regular event involved Cedric entering the solicitor's garden and then his conservatory. John thought that there was a certain furtiveness about the young man's actions and thus decided to investigate. On one particularly hot and lazy afternoon with almost no one about, he watched Cedric approach and enter the house. He climbed down from the tree and entered the garden down the side of a garage; the route was carefully chosen in order not to be seen. John made his way round to the rear of the house, staying very close to the walls and stooping low to pass underneath the windows. He eventually came to a French window with the curtains drawn. But a small gap had been left in the solicitor's haste to receive his slave.

What he saw left him wide-eyed in surprise. The two were situated side on to him and both were naked. Cedric appeared to have his arms bound to his sides with a thick leather strap. He had a thick collar made of the same material around his neck to which was attached a leash and he was bent over the padded end of a Chesterfield chair. Brewster's face was suffused with blood and his penis was very, very erect. John heard the words, 'Do you want it boy?' 'Oooh, yes sir,' moaned the slave. 'Yes please!' Brewster brought the cane down hard on the young man's quivering fleshy buttocks, several times. Cedric was soon writhing in pleasure and at that moment, Brewster mounted him, thrusting his large and swollen penis deep into the well-lubricated anus. The barrister then proceeded to fuck his slave very hard for several minutes until with a loud gasp he ejaculated and slumped over his mindless, moaning and willing victim.

John had seen enough and retired silently, retracing his steps. The matter gave him considerable food for thought. He was almost alone among the youth of the village in being adventurous enough in those days to enter a private garden. Almost anyone else would have retold the story, which would have gone round the area and undoubtedly been muttered darkly and with some amusement to the detriment of the gay partnership. John decided to keep his own council, adding it to the number of chapters regarding sex and sexuality that were being logged in his retentive mind. He thought it was a strange situation. Initially he had found the sight shocking and somewhat repugnant to him. However, he was not prepared to condemn the pair until he had found out much, much more about what he had seen.

Later that afternoon, Mckinley and a preoccupied Cedric passed each other in the road. The suitably satisfied slave drifted past Mckinley in a sort of dream with a peculiar look on his face. John gave Cedric the slightest of nods but Cedric wandered on oblivious to all around him. His thoughts were fixed on those thin weals, which he could still feel on his still slightly pulsating buttocks, and of the delectable experience that he had just been forced to endure.

The tides of pleasure, which always ran through him after his weekly trysts, were mingled with dark squalls of guilt and fear. Those researches which would show that he was one of the individuals who had not received the vital burst of testosterone from their mothers that would have programmed their brains as male whilst at a critical stage of foetal development, lay far in the future. His psyche was feminine and that was all there was to it; he could never change.

The web of pleasure and pain, guilt and fear, would always be with him. Brewster had discussed the matter with him on several occasions and the two were very careful. Brewster also knew the law very exactly and pointed out that though prosecutions for homosexuality were rare due to the difficulty of obtaining hard evidence, a much more pressing concern was that of blackmail. The 1885 act which had introduced a penalty of two years with or without hard labour for the commission of the act, had provided a blackmailers' charter. He had explained the ins and outs of the law on the matter to his boy and had cautioned him that if he was ever arrested he was to say nothing and contact him urgently. He had cold-bloodedly explained that: 'The damage which can be done by it is proportional to a man's station in society; as a solicitor I would be very badly hurt by it and you might lose your position. Fortunately, in my case, I have sufficient capital to enable my retirement to the country, or abroad.'

Brewster was as keen as Cedric for their relationship to continue, because although he had explored the world of domination and submission with various partners he had found in Cedric an almost perfect match for his needs. Those feelings were reciprocated by his protégé; the young man found it difficult to imagine an experience which could be more satisfying and fulfilling. The lawyer went on to reassure him. He was very well acquainted with the Oscar Wilde case and others of a similar nature; he had made it his business to do so as a part of his legal studies. He told young PG that Wilde had been an ostentatious fool who had thought that his fame had rendered him immune from prosecution. He said: 'We are perfectly safe as long as we take care to be very discrete, and even if someone did get wind of what was going on he would be very strongly discouraged from saying anything under the threat of a lawsuit for libel or slander.'

The older and much more experienced man had attempted to reassure Cedric by telling him about Lytton Strachey and the Cambridge University group known as the Apostles. He said, 'Strachey was a homosexual pacifist. He did not like what he saw in society and set out to undermine it with a mixture of wit, satire and iconoclasm in his famous work *Eminent Victorians*. In it, he debunks the images of four pillars of Victorian society.' Brewster told PG that Strachey's sexual predilections were widely known—he did not try to hide them and he never suffered as a result. On one famous occasion whilst in court during the Great War due to his refusal to fight, he was asked by the prosecution: 'What would you do if you found a German soldier raping your sister?' Strachey had given the immortally camp reply: 'I would try to interpose myself in between them.' The younger man had seen the joke, which was more than could be said of the judge. However, PG junior could not ever see himself in the same situation as the eminent writer. He knew that secrecy was essential both for his own sake and for that of his master, and he was well aware that any exposure of his sexuality would be immensely hurtful to his parents.

All these considerations whirled within Cedric's brain, especially after those wonderful Sunday afternoons with his very dominant lover. Despite assurances, the situation left him in a perpetually nervous state. He had spent sleepless nights thinking about it, and suffered from bouts of irrational apprehension if he ever saw policemen approaching, or if he thought that he was being observed by strangers. He knew very well that nothing, absolutely nothing, could or would break the bond between the two; he was captured, enraptured, enslaved and totally at the service of his understanding and dominant master. In the final analysis, he had absolutely no choice but to give way to his feelings and suffer the sublime rewards, which are often reaped by those who give way to the need to explore the very enjoyable depths of what others might think of as sin and depravity.

10

Mckinley and the Mining Disaster

Mckinley very rapidly learned the ways of the mine through his own experiences of it and through chatting to the other pony lads and the older miners during 'snap' times. He took the opportunity offered by lulls in work pressure, when everything came to a standstill due to a haulage foul up or accident or roof fall or something similar, to explore old workings and tunnels, some of which were collapsing and barely accessible. He developed a keen sense of his location underground and within his mind he kept a picture of alternative routes of egress from the district should the worst happen. He was thought to be keen and useful and because of it he soon started to move up the ladder, which would take him to the highest paid job underground, that of a face worker.

John had worked in the main tunnels, or 'roadways' as they are known, and on the various aspects of haulage which involved moving materials into the mine and coal out of it. He always seemed to have the knack of speeding jobs up by finding a better way of loading or adopting some other improved way of getting things done. Old Burkinshaw kept a discreet eye on the lad and as he grew bigger and stronger moved him onto more demanding and better-paid work.

He had worked with the repair teams needed to keep the roadways open and never ceased to be amazed at the huge reservoirs of strength that often lay concealed in the spare and wiry bodies of the older men. He had seen them manhandle the strong steel tubs which were full of coal back onto the track after derailments, and walk down roadways carrying the large drills used for making the holes for shot firing, which must have weighed more than a hundredweight each. They seemed to be able to work hard and steadily all day long without showing the signs of fatigue which he was certainly feeling as a sixteen-year-old. He could see though that his own strength was growing and he expected that as the years passed he would also acquire the sort of strength and endurance that was commonplace amongst the men of the mine.

Underground, the pressures in the strata cause the roof to slowly, yet continually, move down, and the floor to rise and the sides of the tunnels to collapse. This involved resetting props, building new packs from rock to stabilise the walls, and digging out the floors of the tunnels and then re-laying the narrow-gauge rails, which went out to the districts where the coal was being mined. John progressed and started to work with these gangs and at nineteen he could see that he was pretty close to moving onto a face.

In many ways, this promotion was controlled by the manpower available. In the case of injury or a death he could be expected to move up; otherwise, he would have to wait until one of the regulars became too physically dilapidated to deal with that most demanding of jobs underground. This required the ability to shovel up to twenty tons per shift into the waiting steel tubs. Generally, men were moved from the faces in their forties as by then they had effectively become too worn out to continue there.

John was always aware of the potential dangers and more than usually alert to the possibilities of injury in difficult situations, and he was very good at avoiding them. Although no one down a mine can avoid the bad luck of a sudden roof fall or the consequences of a major explosion, he minimised his exposure to risk in the most effective manner that was open to him. He kept his arms and legs out of the way of the various continuous cable systems that were used to draw some of the tubs down main roadways. He took care to avoid rollers and the various drive shafts he encountered elsewhere. If shot firing was being carried out, he always retired to the safest distance possible and with a preference for sitting behind a tub or roof support to avoid any fragments that may be propelled back down the roadway due to the explosion. Some colliers were much more cavalier in their attitudes to safety, but for Mckinley the measures he adopted where just common sense.

John noticed that 'the Fates' slowly picked off the careless ones down the mine. He overheard conversations in which so and so was described as unlucky when he had lost an arm or suffered a crushed chest or broken pelvis. He thought that luck had very little to do with it in many of those cases.

In some ways, John had started in mining at the worst possible time. Conditions had improved slowly during the century due to the introduction of improved safety measures. New machinery introduced to increase production also helped with some of the more dangerous tasks, such as the manual undercutting of the coal at the face prior to shot-firing. However, the world economy had once again turned against coal.

During the Great War, every ton was needed urgently to feed the huge needs of the armament industry and the railways and the huge British Merchant Marine and Royal Navy Fleets. However, diesel engines were slowly being introduced on newer ships and on trains, and after the stock market crash of 1929 industrial demand also slackened.

At Bullcroft, the 1920s had been profitable and employment at the pit had peaked at over three thousand. However, the worldwide depression started to bite after that and recruitment ceased, apart from pit lads. The situation throughout Britain varied, with the old pits, which worked narrow seams that were often less than two feet high, struggling to survive. These were situated mainly in the North East and Scotland and many would have closed if the market had been allowed to work in an unfettered way.

However, the Mines Act of 1930 established a quota system with his pit allowed to produce only 700,000 tons a year. Despite this, the Bullcroft Colliery Company remained profitable, though short time working began to bite into the incomes of the colliers with ever increasing severity as the decade progressed. The pit was operating at about sixty percent of the capacity in 1931, which meant that the men were working, on average, a three-day week.

All in the village had suffered severely during the 1926 strike, which went on for over seven months. In the thirties, the lack of demand for both coal and labour snuffed out any prospect of industrial action. Thus, John and his fellows knuckled down to their situation and made the best of it. The company was a leader in industrial relations in many respects and in 1934 hard hats were introduced; prior to this, most miners wore a cloth cap underground. This headgear provided scant protection from roof falls as even a minor fall was sufficient to cause a skull fracture.

This sort of injury to the brain could be fatal due to swelling unless a trepanning operation was carried out in order to relieve the pressure. Each collier at the pit was given the option of renting a helmet or buying one from the company at half price. A further innovation was the free provision of a pint of milk at the end of a shift as it was thought that this might help with the dust. Milk was also very cheap and provided the sort of nutrients that miners badly needed and often did not ordinarily get.

One of the jobs Burkinshaw had given young John, was to drop off the air samples that the undermanager had taken during his shift underground, at the small colliery laboratory. The lab was staffed by the colliery chemist and an apprentice chemist called Ben Dimon. Ben was about John's age and they knew each other from the village. They had attended the same junior schools and had been taught by the same teacher in successive years. Young Dimon was very bright and had gone on to the Grammar School in Doncaster. Their teacher, who had tutored and evaluated the two for their scholarship exams at the junior school, knew that Mckinley was the brighter of the two and was in fact exceptional.

Dimon had shown aptitude in chemistry and after matriculating and obtaining his school certificate had obtained employment at the colliery. Matriculation was a precursor to the General Certificate in Education that later on awarded separate O-levels. It required all round ability shown by passes in five subjects, which included English language, mathematics, and a foreign language. It was possible to pass nine subjects, however failure to pass in any of the mandatory ones meant that although you received a school certificate you did not matriculate—matriculation of course being essential for entry into university.

John had been given a leather satchel containing glass bottles sealed with rubber bungs, each one having writing on it. The undermanager had used these to sample the air quality at certain points in the roadways underground, sucking the air into the bottles using a rubber aspirator, especially at the entrance to and exit from the coalface. These particular bottles had the legends, '10 yards in-bye,' and '10 yards out-bye,' respectively, written on them. These codes on the bottles indicated airflow into, and away from, the coalface.

Ben was slightly surprised to see John entering the small building, but as he was the only one around he invited young Mckinley in and offered to explain how the samples of mine air were analysed, knowing very well that his guest would understand him. He took the bottle labelled in-bye and held it over an open mercury bath from which a small glass tube protruded. He inverted the bottle and deftly removed the bung and placed it on the end of the glass in such a manner that the mercury made a seal with the outside air. He explained that fresh air contains about 0.03% carbon dioxide and 20.93% oxygen, with the rest being mainly nitrogen. He went on to say that underground the coal gives off methane, and both it and the percentage of carbon dioxide increases as you move along a face.

151

The samples of air which enter the face were, usually, little different from fresh air, but on travelling through it quite a big pick up of methane occurred. He told John that on this particular face the out-bye sample usually shows about 1.0% of methane and 0.4% carbon dioxide. Ben explained that some types of coal contain little or no methane, but in Yorkshire the coal is classed as being bituminous, and this type contains a lot of gas. It is also excellent house coal and very good coking coal.

He sat down and using a mercury reservoir connected to a rubber tube, drew gas down the glass tube from the upturned bottle into an apparatus which he said was called a 'Haldane' after its notable inventor. He moved gas from the bottle into another glass tube that had a very narrow neck marked out in fine black graduations. He then turned a tap when satisfied that the correct quantity had been taken in. John was fascinated by the way the bottle that was held upright by the rigid glass tube floated in the mercury bath. Ben manipulated various taps and pumped the mercury reservoir up and down moving the sample back and forth several times through a liquid, and then made a measurement.

He said: 'The first job is to absorb the carbon dioxide in a potash solution; we measure the reduction in volume that gives us the quantity of the gas which was present initially.' After that he turned on a platinum filament that glowed white hot and then pumped several times up and down so that the gas flowed in and out of the glowing chamber. He then turned the filament off and manipulated more glass taps and did the same pumping operation and the gas bubbled through the thick grey potash solution once again.

Ben said: 'The hot platinum gets rid of the methane by combustion, but as burning methane produces carbon dioxide and water vapour, we have to get rid of it again before we measure the reduction in volume of the methane; also, we have to make a correction for the oxygen used up. The next step is to absorb the oxygen in another liquid, we then calculate the inert gasses by difference. The final step is to take the bottle to another apparatus and measure the amount of carbon monoxide.'

It was all very strange to John, but he followed what was happening and thanked Ben profusely. On subsequent visits to the lab he asked questions and filled in gaps in his knowledge, especially in respect to the dangers posed by the various gasses underground.

The elder chemist called Bill Staunton told him that the Germans in particular seemed to have an especial aptitude for chemistry and they had first carried out accurate gas analyses in the previous century. He looked over his half-moon glasses and said in a semi-serious manner, 'Your dad might have noticed that during the last war.' John took the point at once, realising he was referring to the first use of chlorine gas by the detested Boche.

On subsequent visits, the young Mckinley learned all he could. He was genuinely interested and well aware that in the dangerous environment below ground the information he was obtaining might have survival value. He was told about the dangers of methane, or firedamp as the miners called it, which formed an explosive mixture with air once its concentration reached about six percent. Many of the old hands could recite almost as a litany the names of the pits at which major disasters had occurred due to explosions. Barnsley Oaks, 361 killed. Number 3 Pit Hulton, in Lancashire, 344 killed. Senghenydd, in South Wales, 439 killed. In addition to the major national disasters, all miners remembered the smaller more local incidents such as the 88 men killed at Cadeby in 1912 just before the war, and of the very recent explosion in 1931 at Bentley Pit just three miles down the road, at which 45 men had died.

He went on to learn that it was not just methane explosions which were deadly, but that coal dust explosions had been as bad. He also found that there were other hazards such as inundation by water, which had taken 90 men at Heaton Colliery in Northumberland, or by quicksand, which had killed 26 at Gwendreath in Glamorgan, although these two disasters had taken place in the previous century and it was assumed that modern methods of mining had eliminated the possibility of this occurring. John grimly noted, much later in life, that an inundation had killed several men at the brand new Selby Coalfield in the 1970s.

Their union delegate took every opportunity he possibly could to explain that the deaths due to the main disasters were just the tip of the iceberg and that many authorities did not count an incident as a disaster if the death toll was under twenty-five. He went on to say most pits do not have a major disaster but that does not stop 'em killing one, two, or three men every year. By the end of its relatively short working life, Bullcroft had claimed 88 lives. Brodsworth, a bigger pit that had a somewhat longer life, running from 1906 to 1984, claimed 140. Neither had experienced any sort of major incident.

In his visits to the lab, John learned about blackdamp, to give it its old name, or carbon dioxide, as the scientist knew it, and about after-damp which was the mixture of gases left after an explosion. Although oxygen would be used up in an explosion and the gasses remaining could result in asphyxiation, far more deadly than that combination was the carbon monoxide which could also be produced.

Ben explained to John that concentrations of as low as 500 parts per million were sufficient to kill someone, and consequently the mine air from the various working districts was monitored daily for that gas by the lab. He said that it was produced by the underground 'heatings' which occasionally affected the mine. Burkinshaw told John later that the coal that had to be left in the wastes caused the problem. These were the areas left behind as the face advanced. Here some of the props were removed and the wastes were left to collapse slowly as the weight of the overburden of half a mile of rock exerted its inexorable pressure. He said, 'You can't stop rogue airflows through it no matter how well you pack the roadways, and parts of it heat up and catch fire because of "spontaneous combustion." Some pits are more liable to it than others, and unfortunately those in this part of Doncaster are prone to it.'

Mckinley learned to watch out for the signs of a heating starting. Sometimes you could smell them due to subtle changes in the odour of the air flowing down the return roadways. On some occasions the sides of the roadways would become warmer than normal due to the fire. He learned that the most valuable sign of a heating was an increase in carbon monoxide levels in the samples that were taken for analysis.

The colliery chemists were almost invariably the first to know that a problem was starting and could draw it to the attention of the mine management for action. This usually consisted of digging the heating out and dousing the area with water. If this was not possible, sealing the sides of roadways with a compound called Hard-Stop, which was similar to Plaster of Paris, could be effective by reducing the airflow to the fire. It was subsequently explained to John that in the very worse scenarios you would have to seal off both the intake and return roadways. This resulted in not only the loss of the face but could mean that the whole district of potential coal reserves became sterilised. In the very worst cases, he said, 'you can lose the whole bloody pit.'

John did not worry unduly about a disaster at the mine; he knew it was a well-run colliery and he had confidence in Burkinshaw and in the Deputies and Over-men who controlled the way it was worked. He also knew that the employers at Bullcroft Main Collieries Ltd were amongst the better gaffers. Some would sacrifice anything, including the lives and bodies of their workers, if it meant extracting a little more profit from a pit. Despite his confidence, he always kept in mind the fact that working underground was dangerous. You could never give the mine an inch; it would take an arm or break a back or kill if not watched constantly.

John knew that the unwary or stupid were most likely to be claimed by the monster, but he minimised risks for himself in the best way that he could. He would always check roof conditions before starting work rather than assume that everything was all right. He would take the trouble to sit next to a pit prop while he was having his snap. He saw to his own safety by taking a large number of small measures that soon became second nature to him. He was well aware that only a fool took it for granted that everything was fine. Everything was not fine! The mine was not a kindly place; it took no hostages.

Time passed and Mckinley's genetic gifts in respect of strength and hard work transformed him into a powerful youth and he was thus asked to come into the mine on the Saturday and work with Ewan Williams and a couple of other blokes on an urgent job. Though one of the periodic heatings had erupted at the pit it wasn't initially considered serious as it was in an old district and all the salvageable equipment had just a few weeks previously been taken from the face.

Stoppings were being built at the ends of the two roadways that had serviced the face. The one at the out-bye end had been completed and a full brick construction had augmented the seal that had been constructed beyond that wall of rock, sand bags and broken equipment. Work had then been transferred to the in-bye end but there was no particular urgency. In normal circumstances, due to airflow directions, gas build up in-bye was not a problem. Parts of a temporary stopping had been constructed of rock debris and damaged tubs but you could just see over it into the tunnel at the other side. Many of the props in the roadway had been removed and the roof was already coming down beyond the half-completed seal and soon the gap would close naturally due to compression of the strata.

However, Burkinshaw had an instinct about heatings and explosions and he was getting an itchy feeling on his scalp. That instinct was telling him that something was not quite right and he could not quite put his finger on what it was. Perhaps it was the sounds from the worked-out face or the smells; he just did not know what it was but there was some-thing strange happening and he was uneasy. Because of his instincts about the situation, he now wanted the work finished as quickly as possible.

Loads of bricks had been delivered from the colliery com-pany's own brickworks and had been stacked near the seal with bags of ballast and sand and cement ready for use. He asked the workers he had assembled to start to throw rub-ble into the narrow gap which remained and then finish it off with sandbags. 'Pack 'em as tight as you can,' he said. 'You've got a full shift and more if you need it, but I wanted the brick-ies to be able to start on Monday.' He departed saying: 'I'll be back in two or three hours to see how you are going on.' Though he would say nothing to the men, he wanted to check the other seal and take air samples to be absolutely sure there was no leakage there.

There was a manhole built into the side of the roadway near the start of the seal. This was an upright construction about the size of a telephone box and had been intended for men to step into if loaded tubs were passing. The colliers had put their snap tins and Dudleys on the low bench at the back of the hole and then set about their tasks. It was clear from the start that there was only room for two to shovel the rub-ble into it.

The other two in the team were the Thompson brothers. Both were handy lads in their early twenties and both keen amateur boxers. Williams suggested that they work and work about, with two shovelling for a spell and the others filling sand bags in the main roadway. The actual seal was being built about twenty yards down the old tunnel. This was deliberate policy, as the stump end of the tunnel would provide a useful storage area for rails, props and other equipment, which could be needed urgently as the mine workings advanced.

The Thompsons started the task and John and Taffy started to fill sandbags and move bricks up the tunnel, stacking them in the centre of the roadway in a place that would be in easy reach of the brickies. After a while, Taffy and John moved up to take over the heavier of the two tasks. Williams knew that the Thompsons would not ask to be spelled, but he knew that alternating the periods of light and then heavier work would see the job done quicker. He had also noticed Burkinshaw's unease. It was unstated, but Ewan was far from stupid and could easily read the undermanager's concern.

The four paused and took long drinks from their water supplies. Williams said: 'We have moved most of the bricks down but there's a tub full of cement bags about thirty or forty yards down the roadway. You should be able to push the tub up here; if you can't you will have to carry 'em up one by one. There's about twenty of 'em.'

They went to put the Dudleys back in the manhole. John leant in, put his down, and then turned to come out of the small gap.

At that second, a sound caused Williams, who was standing just behind Mckinley, to look towards the stopping. He could still see just above the rubble and became aware of a sheet of orange flame moving rapidly towards them. He jumped towards the manhole, pushing John in front of him and covering the younger man with his powerful body as best as he was able.

They both heard a roaring sound. The roaring of demons released from an inferno deep in the bowels of the earth. The flame roared down the old roadway and the temporary stopping absorbed most of its force and intensity. However, a huge sheet of flame shot out over the top of the incomplete working, dislodging some of the material at the top. John could feel the searing momentary intensity of the blast as the flames shot past them. Almost as suddenly, the flame surge extinguished and a powerful draught of air moved past them, being drawn back into the old workings to fill the deficiency left by gas used up in the combustion process.

John felt sick, dazed, and had difficulty breathing for a few moments; Williams stood up and said, 'Are you alright?' John nodded. The Welshman took a step back. 'I'm not,' he said. John could hear the sound of the two Thompsons running towards them. Just as they arrived at the manhole, Williams slumped down on both knees. John stood, groggily, and reaching out towards the older man, realising that the whole of his back above the belt appeared to be a charred and smouldering mass. Alan Thompson reached for one of the Dudleys and dowsed the charred area. Williams moaned and then fainted with the pain.

John shook his head to clear it and looked down the roadway; he could see the dim glow of a fire in the far distance. As he could feel air flowing past his face down the tunnel he rapidly reasoned that an explosion must have occurred somewhere in the old district and that they had just caught the tail end of it. He knew that the fire in the distance would consume any residual methane and that a further explosion was unlikely, but it could possibly occur if there were still large pockets of the gas that had not been used in the first explosion.

He began to think more clearly. 'We've got to get Taffy out,' he said. 'There's an emergency stretcher in a canister about two hundred yards down the roadway.' The younger of the Thompsons set off running down the uneven ground to get the apparatus. His next thoughts were to get the casualty away from the immediate area of danger. He said, 'We'll have to try to carry him down to the main roadway and get him around the corner just in case we get another blast.' The two men supported the slumped figure between them, trying to avoid the area of charred flesh on the older man's back. They had just about got him to the safe area when Joe Thompson arrived. John said: 'Get him on his face on the stretcher and let's move him to the pit bottom.' They all worked methodically and efficiently; each knew what was needed and no more words needed to be exchanged.

They headed off, taking turns at the stretcher handles and moving as fast as they could. They had been travelling about twenty minutes when they saw a light. Burkinshaw was moving towards them, rapidly. He said, 'Keep going, lads. I heard the thump of the explosion and I've sent word to the surface to get help and get the rescue team down here. What did you see?'

'Sheet of flame,' said Mckinley. 'It shot out past us, and burned Ewan.'

Three more lamps could be seen approaching, and then a fourth. It was a party from the pit bottom followed by Ron Hopkins, their Deputy, who had just been going off shift. Burkinshaw said, 'You three help these men get Williams out as fast as you can.' Then turning to the Deputy: 'We will have a look at how things are. We'll be out fairly soon; if not, you know where to send the rescue teams.'

The stretcher-bearers set off at almost a trot and the two officials walked back to the seals, testing for gas as they did so. The blast had dislodged some stone dust, which still hung in the air, but the roadway was standing well with no evidence of damage or gas flows out of the waste. The under-manager coolly assessed the situation. At the place where the men had been working, he could see some rubble, which had been blown from the top of the pack, but the structure was intact. He also noted a definite glow which indicated that a fire was raging some way down the tunnel. He was not immediately concerned as he had dealt with 'heatings' in the past.

The two walked down to the completed seal in the return roadway. As they approached, Hopkins held his lamp up looking at the flame: a blue cone above it would indicate fire damp but there was no sign of its presence. 'The seal looks all right,' he said. Then, as they got closer, Burkinshaw said, 'Bloody hell! Can you see that?' The deputy looked but couldn't see anything different. The older man said, 'Look at the seal!' Hopkins looked closely at the edges of the structure. 'Christ!' he said. 'The whole bloody thing's moved.' The two concluded that the explosion must have initiated in the return tunnel fairly close to the seal. The force of it had been sufficient to move the plug of rock and brickwork which was several yards thick about a foot down the tunnel.

Closer inspection revealed some fine cracks in the brickwork and at the edges of the structure. Burkinshaw sniffed the air near them hard. He said, 'I think some gas is getting out here, probably not much though. We'll leave it and get out to organise the teams.' They walked back to the pit bottom.

Hopkins said: 'Do you think it's bad?' The undermanager knew that the Deputy was asking if he thought the pit was in danger.

The older man said, 'No, we were lucky. For some reason the methane built up a lot quicker than I have ever known. However, the seals are nearly complete, and the fire down there should be getting rid of any more build-up of methane and might self-extinguish. We need to finish the stoppings as quick as we can and then the fire will eventually burn out behind them due to lack of oxygen.'

After organising gangs of colliers to start the work and arranging for tools and equipment to be moved to the site, he phoned the pit manager from the small office at the shaft side, explaining what had happened and how he was dealing with it. He said, 'The inspectors will have to be involved. Will you ring them?'

His boss said, 'Aye, leave that to me. I'm giving you full responsibility to deal with things down there. Pay what overtime you like, within reason, and make sure the pit's safe, but tell me: was everything in order?'

Burkinshaw knew that he was asking if there had been any contravention of the safety requirements as laid down in the Mines and Quarries acts. The undermanager reassured him. 'Everything was spot on. We were unlucky, it was just a freak explosion.'

Commons was a crafty old sod, sharp as a razor and a natural politician who was used to dealing with the pressures from the mining company directors and with the periodic visits of his Majesty's Inspectors of Mines. His craft was legendary but he was also very well aware of his duties under the various acts that gave him responsibility for everything that occurred within the colliery's curtilage, both above ground and below it.

An example of his craft, which was whispered about in certain quarters, was the tale of the vagrant who was found dead just inside the boundary fence of the colliery. He had instructed the finders to lift the body over the fence, as he didn't want it found on the premises, and to keep their gobs shut. He said, 'It's nothing to do with us. Moving it a few feet won't make the slightest difference and I like to keep the pit yard tidy! Let the local authorities deal with it.' The pit top foreman did as was instructed and told the two removal men: 'Don't say a word about this, tha might be in trouble if tha does.' He also saw that they got a couple of hours of overtime paid on top of what they had earned.

The foreman couldn't work out why Commons wanted the body moved. It didn't seem to make the slightest difference to him where it was found. What he did not know of course was that a body found inside the colliery's boundaries would involve a Coroner's Court. The manager would have to attend it as the responsible person and the manager just did not want hassle that he could easily avoid by moving a corpse six feet.

Sam Commons knew that in these present circumstances notification of the inspectorate was unavoidable and that he would need to meet them and go through the rather ritualised process of inspection with its subsequent reports and recommendations.

He telephoned the personal number of the local His Majesty's Inspector of Mines. The HMI said, 'I will be there first thing tomorrow morning. Keep everybody out of the pit apart from the rescue teams and those working on the seals.' He went on, 'I am sure that the rescue lads will have a canary? Please make sure that they do and that one is kept on site till the job is complete.' He went on: 'Also, I want air samples taken in both stoppings every four hours and in the roadway either side of the tunnels entrance. Tell the lab that I want them on shifts and that I want a full analysis daily and a methane and carbon monoxide analysis on the other samples taken.'

Mckinley and his workmates got to the pit bottom as fast as they could carrying Williams, who was moaning in pain and shivering. The elder Thompson brother said, 'It's shock.' They covered his lower limbs with coats to try to keep him warm but Taffy could not bear anything to touch his back or shoulders. When they got to the pit bottom, the cage was waiting for them and they went straight up the shaft into daylight and fresh air.

As the wire mesh gates opened, they were met by the black colliery ambulance that was waiting at the side of the shaft, and by young Dr Lawrie. He made a rapid assessment of the injury and said to Williams, 'I am going to give you something for the pain.' He then made an injection of morphine and went on: 'No point trying to dress the burns here. Get him straight to hospital. They will be able to cut the remnants of his shirt off and start treatment.'

The doctor turned to the others and said, 'Was anyone else involved?'

The elder Thompson said, 'John was with him when the flames got him.'

Lawrie said: 'Let me have a look at you. Have you any injuries?'

Mckinley said, 'No, Ewan took all of the blast. He pressed himself into my face and chest, I could feel the heat and it took my breath but the air got sucked back into the stopping and then I could breathe again. I think we must have just got the tail end of it.' He looked down and lifted his hands and said: 'It seems to have scorched the hairs on the back of these.'

The Doctor looked at him and said, 'You have superficial burns there. Get them dressed at the medical centre.' He looked at the young man's eyes and said: 'You don't seem to be too bad but you might have a reaction later and suffer some shock.' He told the medical centre attendant what dressings to use and said, 'I will be round tomorrow afternoon

163

after church, to see how you are.' He turned back to the medical room attendant and said, 'Make sure that he has a large mug of sweet tea; if he doesn't feel well at any time sit him down and keep him warm, and if needs be get him a lift back home.'

He turned to the other men saying, 'Are you all alright?' They told him that they had been nowhere near the blast and were fine. They had all seen injuries before and the occasional body being brought out of the colliery, and were hardened to seeing crushed and maimed flesh.

Burkinshaw came out of the pit at that moment and said: 'I'm getting gangs organised to go back down and finish the seals. If you lads want it you can have a twelve-hour shift; though I wouldn't blame you if you had had enough for one day.' The Thompsons agreed at once but said, 'Can we get off and get something to eat first, we're famished. We'll be back in a couple of hours.' Their gaffer replied, 'Of course, come back when tha's ready.'

News that something major had happened got round the village like wild fire. If it had been a normal working day scores would have converged on the pithead in search of news. Fortunately, most men were at home and the relatives of the few who had been working were rapidly reassured.

At that moment an old car pulled into the pit yard, and out of it climbed a local reporter who worked for one of the Doncaster papers. He walked across and said, 'Somebody phoned the paper. I understand men have been killed.'

The undermanager very calmly deflected the question, saying 'No one has been killed; it's the usual gossip and exaggeration.'

The reporter persisted: 'But there's been an incident, a serious incident.'

The official said, 'There are always incidents at pits. We seem to have one or two fatalities every year in common with all the other pits round here. You don't seem to be bothered usually. Anyway, as I said, nobody has been killed; we're just doing some work to seal off an old district. If you want any more information, you'll have to talk to the manager or Mr Humble the managing director.'

He was just turning away when the local Catholic priest arrived. The man was about forty, and sparely built. He was very white faced and approached Burkinshaw and said: 'I have been told that there has been an explosion and that it's a major disaster underground. If so I would like to go underground to be with the men.' A group of the workers at Bullcroft were Catholics and these were the immediate concern of the priest. He was reassured that there had been only a minor explosion but no one was dead and teams were working to make sure everything was safe.

Burkinshaw said, 'Don't worry, it's not another Bentley! None of your flock was involved. One man was injured but he is Welsh and a Chapel man, I understand.'

The old miner had little time for religion. His experience of life led him to believe that life was short, grim and unforgiving and that what little happiness was available was to be enjoyed in the here and now. He had little expectation of an afterlife and thought that heaven sounded a dull place, in which he would not particularly want to spend his eternity. However, he noted the relief that flooded across the priest's face and saw that some colour was returning to it. He said, 'We're all glad that we're not bringing bodies out of the pit, but its good of you to offer to go down.'

The priest looked at the floor and said, 'I would have had to go down; our place is with the men when they are in extremis. Yet I must confess I am glad that I was not tested on this occasion.' The undermanager looked at him questioningly but remained silent. The priest looked him straight in the eye and said: 'I have always dreaded hearing about a major disaster. If one occurred I know what I must do, but the fact is I am badly claustrophobic!'

The undermanager looked at the man with new respect and said: 'Fine Father; hopefully we will never have a disaster

165

which needs your services at this pit.' He then turned away to continue the urgent business of organising the shift.

The undermanager walked towards the offices and saw one of the deputies talking to a group of colliers. He strode over to them and explained the situation, saying: 'The Thompsons know the workings; work with them and start to fill the top that's blown out with rubble and mix some concrete and throw that in with it, and then tamp it in with pick handles. The brickies will follow you down shortly and they will build a full brick seal. I want that filled with concrete and rock as they build it. When they finish that one, move to the other stopping and do the same; it's been dislodged a bit and we want to be absolutely sure that it holds.'

He took the deputy to one side and said, 'Make sure you watch the air flows at all times! If there's any sign that gas is coming back out of the district get the men off the job straight away. Test for gas every few minutes and make sure you have a canary in both stoppings.' There were some things that the men just did not need to know, and which would probably have been misinterpreted by them if they had been told.

The old gaffer had had experience of a bad heating at Markham Main. This was one of the other collieries that made up the Doncaster Collieries Association, which was a sales organisation set up to maximise profits by the owners of Bullcroft, Hickleton, Brodsworth, Yorkshire Main and Markham Main Collieries. The fire had started in the shaft pillar, which was the large area of coal left under the shafts and headgears in order to ensure the stability of the strata above those structures by preventing subsidence; due to its location the area could not be sealed off. All the men had been withdrawn from the pit and the heating was being dug out and the hot area quenched by hoses which had been run into the area by mine rescue teams wearing breathing apparatus.

Although it was not generally known, the pit had nearly been lost due to the incident—the major difficulty had been the levels of carbon monoxide that had built up. Some of the gas was always present in return airways but this was usually just in concentrations of a few parts per million. In a bad heating this could rise up towards a hundred parts per million and in really bad ones to over a hundred. In the Markham fire, for some reason, unprecedented levels of up to two thousand parts per million of the monoxide were being generated.

Though the fire was extinguished after a few days, one thing in particular had burned itself into the undermanager's brain. One of the rescue team had been walking out after his shift and his nose clip had become loose due to sweat, and had dropped to the floor. The brigades-man had picked it up and put it back on without thinking about it. After a few minutes, he had dropped down unconscious. His comrades had gone through the standard procedure and removed his re-breather set and put him on a spare one and brought him out of the pit on a stretcher; luckily, the man was coming round as they exited the cage. Afterwards he said, 'I couldn't have taken more than a couple of breaths of the contaminated air.'

Burkinshaw had grimly realised that it had almost been enough to kill the man. This was what caused his insistence on canaries being taken underground. He knew that by some accident of evolution, canaries and birds generally were more prone to the effects of the deadly monoxide poisoning. Thus, they would show signs of distress and drop off their perches before the gas affected the workers. On one occasion, where the rescue teams had been putting on a display at the annual sporting festival which was run by the miner's welfare, one prim young lady had said how cruel, sacrificing canaries in this way. Burkinshaw had dryly asked her if she would prefer miners to be sacrificed instead!

Seeing the embarrassment and confusion this had produced, he realised that the young lady had spoken without thinking, a not uncommon state of affairs in his experience. He had thus been kind to her and explained that if a canary did drop, the men would withdraw and the canary's Perspex cage would be sealed and flushed with oxygen from a small

cylinder that accompanied it. He said, 'It is rare for the monoxide to get to a level where it affects even a canary, and if
it does they usually recover. They are far too valuable to be
lost: they are specially trained for the job!' Though he could
see that young lady had taken him seriously about the special training, he and the two deputies with him maintained
straight faces until she had walked off.

Underground, the operation went like clockwork. The
men worked solidly, changing shifts every twelve hours. The
undermanager commented afterwards that: 'Those must be
two of the solidest stoppings ever constructed.' After visiting
the pit on the Sunday the HMI inspected the area and had a
look at the analyses produced by the colliery chemists. These
showed nothing abnormal and the inspector gave his permission for resumption of production on the Tuesday morning.
He made the proviso that a daily air sample must be taken at
the fronts of both stoppings for a few weeks to monitor the
atmosphere there.

John was emerging from the medical room at the pit as
Cud got there. 'Thank God you are alright,' his stepdad said.
They walked back towards home. Cud was well aware what
shock could do to a man because of his war experiences. He
said, 'We'll get you home and get something warm inside you
and get your feet up.'

John said, 'Bugger that. I'm calling in at the club for a
drink; have you got any money?' The older man rummaged
in his pockets and pulled out a florin and some coppers. John
said, 'Will you go home and tell mam I'm alright? I'll see you
later.'

On passing the Working Men's club, they separated and
Cud went on home. Despite the tea at the medical room, John
had a hell of a thirst. He ordered a pint, downed it quickly,
and then ordered another which went down almost as fast.
Someone came into the bar and loudly began to tell a half-
baked version of the story to a group sat playing cribbage.
'They say that Taffy Williams and young Mckinley got badly

hurt or killed.' John looked over saying nothing and ordered a third pint. One of the cribbage men said to the gossip: 'If tha looks over there, tha'll see his ghost stood at the bar having a pint.'

The purveyor of woe reddened and sheepishly approached the solitary drinker. 'Can you tell us what happened,' he said. John looked straight in front of him and said, 'No,' very pointedly. The doom-monger beat a hasty retreat and left Mckinley to his drinking. John said, 'Get me a whiskey, a double, and another pint.' He was unused to whisky but wanted to feel the dulling effects of alcohol as fast as possible. He downed the whiskey and took a hard swig of the pint. At that moment, he started to feel a little strange. He put down the beer and walked to the back of the pub where the long urinals of the Gents were situated. He passed next to one of the two washbasins and then, as the full realisation of what had happened caught up with him, he turned and was violently sick into one of the basins.

John arrived home white-faced and was fussed about by his mother. He was asked if he wanted anything to eat but said: 'Not yet. I'll try something in a bit.' He sat in front of the kitchen fire, occupying the old wooden chair which Cud normally sat in to have his pipe. Margaret had often said to him, 'I don't know how you can sit there; you must be scorching.'

Cud, however, remembered freezing nights in Flanders during the Great War, and which of the two situations he preferred. He liked to soak up the heat, luxuriating in it almost as though in a hot bath.

John sat reflecting, his quick mind analysing what had happened. First, he needed to know how Taffy was going on. He knew that gossip was unreliable and that it would have to come from one of the management or a medic. He determined to visit the pit the next day to find out. He then had a good hard think about himself and the pit. He knew that for some an incident like the one that he had just experienced could finish them for work underground. He felt though that he would be all right and as he rationalised the events he was

169

sure that it had just been a freakish accident. He was also well aware that if he and the Welshman had been standing the other way around it would have been him being carried out of the pit passing out in agony.

After a while, the smell of the stew that had been cooking and his long spell without food, and the effects of hard work and a recently emptied stomach, kicked in, and he asked for some food. Margaret served him a large plate of stew in which floated several of her delicious dumplings. 'There's plenty more,' she said. The pan had been intended for the whole family but she had realised the situation and sent the kids off to the fish-shop to get their suppers. John finished the plate and was joined by Cud at the meal. Margaret said, 'You might as well finish it off,' and shared the remainder between them.

John said, 'Have you eaten?'

'Oh yes,' she lied, wiping the last of the gravy from the pan with a piece of bread and popping it in her mouth. She would have some bread and cheese later, she thought.

There was a knock at the door and Cud answered it. Burkinshaw was standing there and was promptly asked into the house. He said, 'I've just dropped in to make sure you're alright. That is,' he said, 'as alright as anybody can be who's just gone through that.'

John said, 'I'm OK, but what about Ewan?'

'I was coming to that,' was the reply. 'I knew you would ask. You know what hospitals are like, they don't tell you anything. They say he is very poorly. I had a word with Lawrie after he had seen him and he wasn't optimistic. He said that from what he could see the burns were very severe, but he couldn't make a prediction on outcomes and that the burns man at the infirmary would be best placed to tell us. He will contact him later in the week and then update me.'

John sat, mulling the information over in his mind. He wondered if it was worth trying to ring the hospital. He said, 'Has anyone tried to contact his family? He has a sister I believe, still living in Wales.'

The undermanager replied, 'Yes, the colliery clerk has looked through our personnel records and we have notified the police and they will take a message to the address we have. It's in some unpronounceable place up in the mining valleys north of Cardiff. If it's a mining family, they will be used to dealing with accidents at the pits. Anyway, we will find out soon enough.' He went on, 'Very well, John, I won't waste your time and intrude any longer. I have things to do, but keep this in mind: don't hurry back to the pit. Have a few days to your-self if you need them and come back to work when you are ready.'

Mckinley looked up at him and said, 'I'll be back there when the pit starts. When does tha think that will be?'

Burkinshaw said, 'With this type of incident tha can never quite tell. The HMI will have to be satisfied that it's safe to work, but it could be as early as Monday or Tuesday and I look forward to seeing you there.' He turned to Margaret. 'Sorry for disturbing your evening, missus. Make sure he gets a good night's sleep and has a lie-in tomorrow.' He nodded to Cud and then left, leaving John ruminating and looking at the fire. John had already thought everything through and knew he had to be back underground as soon as possible to test his nerve.

11

Mckinley and the Siblings

The kitchen at number thirty-nine was very small; it had a red tiled floor with a small pegged rug in front of the fire. It contained an old deal table, covered with oilcloth. This was a cheap, pre-plastic, waterproof surfacing that served as a tablecloth. The table could seat four people comfortably but it was pushed up against the wall with just three chairs round it. A fourth stood in the hall under the coat hangers next to the front door and could be brought in when it was needed. The arrangement was made to give Margaret as much working space as possible in the kitchen. This facilitated washing, especially when clothes needed to be dried round the fire during the many rainy or cold days.

The washing arrangements were very basic; in the corner was a copper that was built into the kitchen next to a large stone sink, which had ends supported by bare brickwork. The arrangement was designed so that a flue ran into the side of the chimney from a small coal grate, which stood under the copper. On washdays, the fire was lit and clothes were boiled with soap flakes. They were then put into a zinc-plated tub, and whirled to and fro manually with a tumbly-peg. Any ingrained dirt in the collars was then attacked using a corrugated rubbing board and a bar of soap. Rinsing the clothes after washing was done in the large tub, again with the assistance of the tumbly-peg. Sometimes the washed items were finished with a final rinse in the large stone sink and then wrung out by hand.

The men did not get involved in the washing; that was women's work. However, on occasion they were cajoled to join in the hand wringing if an item needed to be dried rapidly. The strength in the miner's forearms proved remarkably effective in squeezing the last few drops of water from the smaller pieces of clothing. The larger items were rolled through a mangle, consisting of a cast iron frame and a pair of large rubber rollers that were turned by a weighty handle mounted at the side. This apparatus stood in the bathroom next to the tin bath. When the copper was not in use it was covered with a round wooden lid.

A gas pipe ran down from the roof to a gas tap, which was connected to a flexible hose. This in turn was linked to a single gas ring that was used for cooking or for boiling a kettle when the coal fire was not lit. The fire worked an oven that was set into a black cast iron range at its side. Dinners were cooked using a combination of a gas ring and the oven with extra pans being boiled using the hearth of the coal fire. This fire was kept in, winter and summer, due to its use for cooking. Judging the process could be tricky and once or twice a year the kitchen would be filled with the horrible smell of burning potatoes.

The men ate alone whenever they arrived back from the pit. It was expected that the meal would be ready and served immediately they returned; the men were always ravenous from their exertions at the mine that involved a seven and a half hour working shift. This time did not include the journeys down and up the mine in the cage, and the walks down the roadways, which often extended more than two miles out from the pit bottom to the work place. The walk from home to the pit and back also needed to be added to the working day. On workdays, Cud and John usually set off at twenty past five and arrived back home before three.

Margaret and the other four children usually ate separately during the week but the whole family sat round the big table in the living room for Sunday dinner. It was big in the sense that the seven members of the family could all just about squeeze round it. The two older men sat at the ends with Margaret and the eldest daughter one side and the three smaller children crammed along the other side.

On Saturdays, a three-quarter shift was worked and the men got out of the pit at one pm. This was fish and chip day and this luxury was purchased from the chippy at the end of the road. The meal was always carefully timed, with one of the kids sent out with a small cloth bag and the money and told to wait until they could see the men walking down the lane towards them. They were instructed to go in and join the queue and then to get home as fast as their legs would carry them after they had been served.

The order was always the same, fish and chips twice and fish patty and chips five times. The two men each had fish and chips and the others the patties which were cheaper than a fish and consisted of a small portion of fish in between two large slices of potato; the whole thing was fried in batter. Lots of bread and margarine and brown sauce and salt and vinegar were always available at home. The men usually had a pickled onion with their servings and large pint pots of tea were also consumed. John always found it a particularly satisfying meal for a reason which he could never quite explain.

After the meal, the men would wash and Cud would sit in the kitchen enjoying a pipe of the foul 'black twist' tobacco he was fond of. He had a pipe rack mounted in the living room and over the years had amassed half a dozen pipes of various types. He had won one at a fun fair and got another during a day outing to Cleethorpes. The others had been birthday or Christmas presents, but from among them all, he always turned to a battered old briar pipe with a much-chewed stem. He spent much time cleaning the thing with a penknife, which had a blade at one end and a long spike at the other. This was used to poke out the mouthpiece and rid it of the accumulation of tar and ash that could interfere with the draw on the pipe if it was not removed.

A standing joke, which he relished, was used each time a curious child saw Cud cleaning the pipe and then asked what the spike on the penknife was for. They were invariably told that it was for getting pebbles out of horses' hooves. They would often innocently regurgitate the information for the benefit of others, much to the amusement of Errington senior.

In his mid-teens, Mckinley would have a nap after work, lying on the old horsehair sofa in the living room. In the colder parts of the year a coal fire was always lit there in the afternoon and he would nap till about five and then get off out to see his two special pals Arthur Howarth and Quiller Jones. The three would roam the village and the country paths round it looking for something of interest.

This could be as simple as just watching the harvesting in the summer evenings when the horses and threshing machines were out utilising the long days and working as late as possible in order to get the harvest in. Sometimes there would be a cricket match on one of the local grounds and they would sit with a bottle of pop and a packet of crisps or nuts and raisins watching the play. The matches always ended with the teams entering the wooden pavilion and sharing a plate of sandwiches and scones. Tea was available but some of the men would take pint bottles of John Smith's Tadcaster bitter, or a similar beverage, which was consumed after their sporting exertions. A group of the younger men would have the food and then depart immediately and call in one of the local clubs or pubs and exchange tales of the week's events or talk about the match whilst enjoying several pints.

Saturday nights were the time when most of the village went down to the club or pub. A singer or comic sometimes appeared at the larger Working Men's clubs and on this night they were filled to overflowing with thirsty miners. The club committee kept beer as cheap as possible and it was always a half-pence cheaper per pint than that sold by the various public houses that were dotted through the mining townships. It was said that when the mining industry went into terminal decline later in the century, no one shed more tears than the brewers, who for decades had made fortunes quenching the thirst produced by the hard work and heat and humidity of work underground.

Margaret did not like clubs, but when money allowed she liked to be taken to the snug in the Bullcroft Hotel and sit with friends and drink three half pint bottles of Milk Stout during the period between seven and nine. Cud was not a big drinker and found the arrangement boring. He would buy a milk stout and a bottle of Guinness for himself and dutifully spend a half hour in the pub with his wife while he enjoyed a pipe. He would then go to the bar, get two more bottles of the milder stout for Margaret, and then leave the small animated group. He would excuse himself under the pretext of having to pay his number in the weekly sweepstake, which was held at the Club next door. He would have a couple of bottles there and spend an hour or so chatting to various workmates or cronies in the bar.

He was always sure to get back to the Moon by nine. By then Margaret would be getting to the end of her third glass. She would want to be escorted back home well before ten and certainly before closing time of ten-thirty. She knew very well that there would be rowdy behaviour and that occasionally a fight would break out with some of the young bloods in the village deciding to have a go under the influence of drink.

The police were rarely involved when this occurred and the matter was settled with fists only. Use of the boot would produce rapid intervention from those around. Head butters and boot merchants were considered a form of low-life and were banned from the club or pub if those forms of attack occurred on the premises. Weapons such as knives were never used; they were considered cowardly. At one New Year, a drunken fool picked a bottle up and tried to use it but he went down under a hail of blows from all sides before it made contact with the intended victim. Mining was a man's world but mining communities had rigid rules based on their own code of honour, and woe-betide those who tried to go outside it.

In some families, both the wife and husband drank heavily and left young children at home for long periods while they did so. Occasionally a disaster would occur due to a fire breaking out or the kids playing with a gas tap or engaging in some other dangerous unauthorised activity. In these cases, the parents would always be ostracised by their neighbours. There were no social services to speak of, though in exceptionally bad circumstances, and they had to be really bad, children would be taken into care. In Cud and Maggie's case, when the children had been younger, she did not go out on Saturday nights. It was only when her eldest had reached twelve years of age and thus could be left at home in charge that she felt that she could indulge in her small weekly pleasure at the pub.

John fulfilled the duty at first, but when he started work it was felt that it was no longer fair to ask him. Thus, when he started to earn, the duty passed to Lily, his half-sister, who was two years younger. John had undertaken the burden dutifully and had made Saturday evenings entertaining for his brother and three sisters with card games, Snakes and Ladders or Ludo, and by reading to them from the weekly comic cuts. Lily did not like the burden that was placed on her and spent the Saturday evenings entertaining herself, listening to dance music on the wireless or reading her mother's 'Red Letter' or library book.

The Red Letter contained romantic stories and was printed as cheaply as possible on coarse paper with ink colours restricted to red or black. The library books she chose were invariably light and romantic. She would sit in the living room with them reading, and divorcing herself from reality, with the younger three told not to bother her and to find something to do.

John could not work out how the five of them could be so different. Admittedly, the other four were only his half brothers and sisters but they were so different it was almost as though they all had different parents. Lily was bright and always in the top half dozen at school. She, like John, had passed the scholarship exam, which entitled her to a grammar school place, and like him, she did not take it up but left after three years at the secondary modern school.

In character, she was more or less totally self-centred—her whole universe revolved about herself. Vapid and shallow and with a tendency to hypochondria and hysteria, she focused on snippets of information about society activities which were reported in the papers and in the occasional woman's magazine or radio or film journal which came her way. She knew lots about film and radio stars, especially the female ones, and read avidly those stories of how they had come from nowhere after being 'discovered' in mundane occupations by some famous producer.

She was attractive enough but no great beauty, and had a habit of leaping in front of any camera which was being used at weddings or at any other function. It was almost as though she thought that the photographic record of herself, looking as film starlet-like as she possibly could, would in some way be transmitted through the aether in the direction of the studio chiefs, who would instantly recognise star material and whisk her away into a life of glamour and high romance.

She was not stupid, but seemed not to connect the fact that the various stars, who she modelled her life on, were not only strikingly good-looking but also highly talented and usually very intelligent. She knew that very ordinary girls like Gracie Fields could make it to stardom and the glamorous life style, and she constantly fantasised that it could happen to her.

Her maternal grandmother did not help matters. Margaret senior had been educated at a private school in North Wales. She had learned to read French and could speak Welsh fluently. This was something that was unfashionable at that time and yet her father had insisted on it due to his family history. There were still a few faded studio posed photos of her in an old family album showing her in the dresses typical of a middle class Victorian young woman, and a few of her as a well-dressed and well fed child.

Lily's fanciful aspirations were not helped by Margaret senior's tales of life amongst the well to do of fifty years previously—the stories of difficulties with servants and riding in carriages and what were considered correct manners. She had also been told that one of the family ancestors four or five generations previously had been from the minor aristocracy of France. He had apparently fled to England during the revolution of 1793. This fact more than any other sealed Lily's ruination and condemned her to the unreal and snobbish world in which she existed.

Three of Lily's favourite books were Dickens' *A Tale of Two Cities* and Baroness Orczy's *The Scarlet Pimpernel* and its sequel *The Elusive Pimpernel*. Visiting the world portrayed in those novels, she could easily see herself being transported away into a world of splendour by some dashing nobleman; after all, she had an affinity by blood.

The second sister Peggy was different again. She had an excellent contralto voice and if she had been given the chance would have liked to be a singer. As it was, she was pretty much a plain Jane, very matter of fact in attitude, and very down to earth about her prospects in life. She had managed to get a job at a local sweet factory on leaving school. Her priorities were husband, husband and husband. Because of her looks, she was undiscriminating in her choice and finally settled for a miner called Arnie Metcalfe.

Arnie was a rough character who early in life had determined that he would live it in order to maximise his personal priorities, which were smoking Park Drive cigarettes, boozing and cricket. He was prepared to tolerate family life, but as far as he was concerned it was up to the wife and kids to grab what they could from what he provided. This tended to be limited by his reluctance to work anymore than the minimum shifts necessary to pay the basic bills and furnish his personal needs.

John's younger brother had been named after his dad and as there could not be two Cuthberts in the family he was known as Bert, and this was used by everyone apart from his teachers. At school, he got the full benefit of the appellation bestowed upon him at his christening and he hated it. He grew into as good-natured a man as can possibly be accommodated within the human frame. Generous to a fault and always eager to help others, though he did not like to be patronised and put upon. He had inherited or learned his dad's capacity for the dry and sarcastic put down, usually delivered with a smile to anyone who dared to travel down those unrewarding avenues.

Youngest of all in the family was Alice, who was the polar opposite of her eldest sister Lily in temperament. Within her welled a deep concern for her fellow human beings. She was strong willed and defiant as a child and went on to become, via the RAF nursing service, one of the old-school nursing sisters, taking no nonsense from either doctors or patients. Seemingly hard as nails on the outside, she had a heart of gold on the inside, and this coupled with great personal generosity.

Her self-willed conclusions about life first emerged when she was eight. She came down from her bedroom and after a piece of toast for breakfast announced that she had decided that she would no longer attend school. She did not like it as she could not see any point in it; she said she was going to get a job at the pit with her brothers instead. Margaret said, 'You are going to school! Get ready now!' The response was a wall of defiance. Maggie had a fiery temper but did not often lose it. On this occasion she did, and in a fine fury grabbed Cud's pit belt and chased the young lady out of the house and almost to the school gates, screaming after her: 'Don't you dare defy me!' After that, Alice re-evaluated the situation and decided that she would go to school after all, but under protest.

In 1937 Burkinshaw did the family another favour by taking on young Bert at the pit. There were still some employment opportunities, but due to the general depression, you were considered one of the luckier ones if you could manage to get a job. The production quotas meant that most men were getting only three day's work a week at best. It was well known that coal from Brodsworth and Bullcroft was some of the best in Yorkshire and attempts were made to improve it further by a process known as washing.

The ignorant, on hearing this term, understood it to mean cleaning the 'dirty' coal in some way before it was sold. However, the process was a highly technical method of separating high-grade coal from that which was contaminated with mudstone or other minerals. Very pure coal is light and has a specific gravity of about one point four. Rock minerals have gravities of well over two.

When the undifferentiated mix of minerals came out of the mine it was first passed through a combination of conveyers and vibrating grids called screens. Old men, lads, and women would take lumps with obvious large amounts of rock contamination off the conveyers, and this would be discarded onto the pit tip. The remainder was dropped into a thin slurry made up so it had a specific gravity of one point six. This resulted in the low mineral content material floating and the higher mineral content stuff sinking. The 'sinkings' were also discarded and then, after sorting the coal by mechanical sieving into various useful sizes with names such as singles, doubles and cobbles, the high-grade coal was sold.

Mckinley had chatted to Ben about the coal, as one of the labs functions was to analyse samples of coal for ash content. Ben had told him that they had four thousand tons of the best quality house coal stockpiled in the pit yard. He said, 'It's been washed down so that the ash content is only four percent and we still can't sell it.'

Bert was very pleased with his job; he was working at the pit like his dad and older brother. He was being paid nineteen shillings and sixpence per week. He gave his grateful mother seventeen shillings and with a full two and sixpence a week to spend on himself, he thought himself one of the most privileged boys in the village. He also knew that in a year or two, when he stopped growing, he would get some new clothes, maybe even a suit as Sunday best. This would really mark his transition from the childhood days of ragged jerseys and hand-me-downs to the full world of adulthood.

Lily had left school in 1932. She had tried to get a job as an usherette at the local cinema but was regarded by the manager as too young. She felt that wearing a nice uniform and working in the cinema environment would bring her close in some way to the sort of dream world to which she aspired. However, the best she could do was to obtain work as a part time waitress at the large cafe in Doncaster, which was situated near to the main railway station and the Grand Theatre. The hours tended to be unsocial with attendance always required on Friday and Saturday afternoons and evenings, as these were major days out and also market days in the town. The wages were poor but at least she did get some small tips, which she saved to spend on makeup and on clothes.

Her dissatisfaction with her lot grew and she spent much time looking through the situations vacant pages of the News Chronicle. Most of the jobs advertised were for men, with a whole section devoted to the various schools and colleges offering training for young men in wireless telegraphy. For a fee of fifteen pounds inclusive, the young man could gain the Post Master General's Certificate (second Class) in that essential art. Large numbers of posts existed for keen young men who were prepared to join the huge British Merchant Marine as Wireless Officers. The skill required above all others was a high speed in sending and receiving Morse code. Although radio messaging was available by then, wireless telegraphy remained predominant as the major means of sending and receiving information at sea until long after the Second World War, due to its clarity and reliability. It also had the advantage of being able to be transmitted over the huge distances between continents and lent itself to encryption. This was done not only for military purposes; many industrial and commercial interests would also use coded messages to protect commercially sensitive information.

The men's columns offered every variety of employment from Assistant Porters to Vacuum Tube Pumpers (Neon). Some types of work for women, such as Shorthand Typists, were totally beyond her reach due to the lack of opportunity to develop the skills needed to do the jobs, and their locations, which tended to be in the large southern cities and in the capital. Situations for girls around Doncaster seemed to be restricted to work in hotels or for sewing machinists or as domestic servants. A small number of very unappealing jobs were available in factories or hospitals. The last thing in the world that Lily wanted to be was a Bakelite Polisher or Ward Maid in a Cancer Hospital. This was that strange pre-plastic era of the 1930s. Bakelite, which was always dark brown in colour, was the only plastic then in common use; nylons, polythene, polyesters and the like were still awaiting discovery in the years to come.

Week by week she scanned the columns until she came upon an advert for duties as a maid in a large household in central Manchester. It was made clear that no heavy domestic work was involved and that a charwoman and a cook and scullery maid and a chauffeur cum handy-man were employed. Lily applied and it transpired that the job was just what she wanted. The house was a large Victorian property near the centre of the city. The cook and chauffer were about forty years of age, married, but they had been unable to have children. All the servants apart from the char woman lived in and were accommodated on the top floor in rather spacious bedrooms with fireplaces. Lily shared her room with Sally, the scullery maid.

The cook was responsible for the purchase and preparation of food for all meals and her husband maintained the car and drove occasionally if its owners, the Naysmiths, were to attend some social function. Most of the time Naysmith drove the splendid Bentley Motor car himself. By profession, he was a mechanical engineer, and by virtue of his talent he enjoyed a substantial income because of the various patents he held and from his very lucrative engineering consultancy. His wife was called Norah and she told people that she felt that he had difficulty keeping his hands off the steering wheel and would probably prefer not to be driven by staff at all if he could help it. It was something that the men appeared to understand and to sympathise with, while the women just could not grasp her husband's strange urges in respect of this matter.

Lily's job was to help with making the beds, do some light dusting, to serve at table, to clear the dishes and to circulate with drinks before dinner at the weekly dinner parties that were held on most Saturdays at the residence. Her employer was wealthy and could easily have afforded more staff. Yet those which the Naysmiths had were more than adequate because during most of the week there were only the two of them in residence at the house besides the servants and thus the effort of preparing and delivering meals was not onerous.

Naysmith generally preferred a light lunch following a morning preparing drawings or doing calculations in his office. Mrs Naysmith usually shopped in central Manchester or visited various friends while he worked. They sometimes lunched together and then, in the afternoons, he liked to work in his engineering workshop, which was built into two of the substantial cellars in the house. He had designed racking systems, a lift, and had various devices such as drills, milling machines and a small metalworking lathe installed. The walls were covered with hangers in which hung many types of tools and gauges, the whole place possessing a tidiness characteristic of its proud owner's meticulous and mathematical mind.

The two sometimes visited the theatres in Manchester in the evenings, usually about once a week, and had season tickets to the Grand Theatre, which was visited each year by the renowned D'Oyly Carte Opera Company, who put on a season of Gilbert and Sullivan.

Thursdays was always a Bridge evening, sometimes at the Naysmiths and sometimes at the houses of their friends. The Bridge party usually involved four couples who were fed from a cold collation of hams, chicken, game pie, cheeses and the like. Lily helped to lay it out and set out the drinks from the cabinet. After that, the party helped themselves, usually finishing with cigars and port, or with cocktails and cigarettes for the ladies.

Naysmith was an inveterate experimenter even in this department, persuading the girls to try this new cocktail or that one, which he had heard about on his last visit to London or Birmingham. Mrs Naysmith studiously avoided these concoctions as they could be quite potent, and always restricted herself to a small sherry.

The domestic work of the household was considered by the staff to be far from onerous, and they thought how lucky they were to be employed by the couple. The older servants all knew horror stories about 'Maids of All Work' being kept at it for ridiculously long hours. 'She did everything from the cooking to the cleaning. She even brought the coal up from the cellar to keep the fires burning,' said the cook, 'and they were so mean with her. She was in a freezing garret. In winter, she used to sleep in an old overcoat and socks. They even begrudged her the food she ate and that was the cheapest they could get.' There was much nodding and tut-tutting at the disgraceful treatment and much satisfaction expressed at their own situation.

Once a year their employers departed Manchester to spend a month on Scotland's beautiful west coast, near Tarbet. The inventor had acquired a medium sized property there, high in the hills, overlooking the sea. It was in a beautiful spot and was looked after through the year by a gardener who in addition to tending the shrubs maintained a kitchen garden and greenhouse, which were planted in order to be productive during the visit.

The gardener maintained the house when necessary with painting and the occasional repair. The house had six main bedrooms and two loft bedrooms for the servants. This enabled the Naysmiths to invite friends to stay with them while they holidayed. A girl was employed during the summer break and bicycled up from the village each day to clean and do washing and ironing. The chauffer saw to the fires in the house and the whole enterprise worked swimmingly well.

The female servants were dispatched by train the day before the inventor and his wife left by car. The master and mistress travelled up with the chauffeur in the Bentley with the suitcases and trunks containing clothing and all sorts of tinned cakes and preserves and wine. The gardener was instructed to take the shutters down from the windows in the summer and open the windows and light the fires in order to get the place aired in the week before the party arrived.

The two also spent a week before Christmas in Central London at the Dorchester Hotel. Naysmith, ever the practical analyst, thought the place over expensive but put up with it because it facilitated his wife's need to shop and visit relatives and the need to give the staff their annual week's holiday with pay. The two were very comfortable in the very wealthy and dynamic City of Manchester, but in the absence of staff a week in a good hotel was a very acceptable sacrifice, which they felt they could endure.

He usually visited various museums during the day, concentrating on those that had some link to engineering. Occasionally, there was an exhibition of some new type of machinery that he also liked to visit and run his vastly experienced eye over. There were also trips to some of the latest shows or reviews or plays, such as those being written by that frightfully witty new young playwright called Noel Pierce Coward. They both agreed that his comedy *Hay Fever* and the romance *Private Lives* were particularly good.

During the Christmas break, Lily returned home to the grey mining village in which she had grown up. Previously she had thought it was normal but now she knew it was depressingly drab. Her eyes had been opened to another world and she liked that world far more than her own. She was full of stories about who had done what, the parties in the house, and even of the theatre. The Naysmiths generously allowed the staff the use of their theatre season ticket on days when they did not need it. The cook and chauffer usually did not bother to avail themselves of that privilege but Lily saw many of the lighter plays such as 'The Ghost Train,' and grew to be very fond of the works of Gilbert and Sullivan.

Mckinley often heard her empty-headed chatter to her mother and sisters on her occasional returns to 39 Briar Road, and had tersely made the occasional remark designed to bring her back down to earth. After a description of one of the sumptuous 'Bridge' buffets he once said, 'You would think they would welcome sausage and mash or toad in the hole for a change.' This was to no avail—the remark just seemed not to register in that fantasy-filled brain. Lily gaily sailed on, living vicariously in that exotic world to which she was both necessary and peripheral. She just did not appear to have the ability to analyse, contrast environments, and realistically appraise her own situation. On her visits home, which she regarded as 'her holidays', she was always singularly unwilling to join in the household chores; the young lady was permanently on send and never on receive. John thought that his half-sister was heading for a big and disillusioned fall and when it occurred he would have little sympathy.

When the accident that had almost cost him his life occurred, his brothers and sisters greeted the news in different ways. Lily was away in Manchester at the time but Bert was downcast and seemed very thoughtful when he heard about it. The next day he scraped his pennies together and came back from the Off Licence with a pint bottle of beer for his older brother. His actions, which were far louder than words, spoke volumes about how he felt about his John.

Peggy was very matter-of-fact about the accident, and said that at least you didn't get brought home in the pit ambulance. She had witnessed this awful sight twice, with the ambulance turning into a street and attracting frantic women who followed it down the street, all of them in dread of which house it would stop at. The body inside would be carried out on a stretcher covered by a blanket and the widow would be assisted by her neighbours in dressing it and laying it out in a coffin in the parlour in preparation for burial. The dread with which the ambulance was received into a street was prompted not only by the personal loss but also by fear of the dire economic circumstances for the widow and family that would result from that loss.

Alice just hung around John's neck and was reluctant to leave him. She had a treasured cloth doll and asked him if he would like to loan it so that he could sleep with it, she could do no more. Lily, at John's insistence, was not informed of the incident. She found out, though, on her Christmas weekend visit. Mckinley thought that the hysterical reaction, in which somehow Lily placed herself at the centre of the drama, was more or less what he expected.

Ewan Williams died ten days after the explosion, the severity of the burns was more than a human frame had the capacity to repair. He had been drifting in and out of consciousness at the hospital on morphine with his sister by his side. John, Burkinshaw and the Thompson brothers had visited him but none of them had been able to stay long due to the distressing nature of the man's condition.

The funeral was arranged for the following Saturday afternoon. Miss Williams had contacted the local Baptist Chapel and asked if the preacher from her own small chapel in Wales could hold the service. The request was readily acceded to. It would have been rejected out of hand by most other established churches in the area, due to difficulties with the fees due to the incumbent. The local Pastor humbly asked if he could be permitted to assist.

Thus, a small man with a shock of wild and longer than usual hair arrived to conduct the service. Several of Williams' cousins had made the trip up to Doncaster by train; they were accommodated overnight in various houses in the village. Miss Williams was a schoolmistress; she was older than her brother and had never married. Her chapel and the small light of hope it shone into the grey wet misery and hardship of life in the valleys was the mainstay of her existence. The Burkinshaws had very generously offered to put her up and she had accepted with profound gratitude.

The small building was filled to overflowing, with many standing outside near its entrance. Most of those who had worked with the Welshman at Bullcroft colliery attended. John was at the funeral escorting his maternal grandmother. She had insisted on this as she had visited Miss Williams at the Burkinshaw's house and the two had talked animatedly for several hours in that mother tongue which John's grandmother had not heard or used since her youth.

John had never heard a service like it. The flowing oratory of the old preacher with his shining eyes and rather wild appearance was obviously heartfelt and sincere. John had attended as few church services as he could possibly manage and thus was not an expert in such matters, but he had sufficient experience to realise how poorly the pious and pallid stuff he had heard in C of E establishments had compared with this magnificence.

Although what he heard there was not likely to convert him or dissuade him from what became a lifelong agnosticism, it gave him a profound insight into why others were drawn into it and why they were held so firmly by the beliefs which this type of preaching inspired.

He remembered in particular the hymns, which were sung with a strength and feeling that were totally alien to his Anglican experiences. This was probably helped by the Williams family and by the many others of Welsh extraction who had attended the service. He also remembered the Bible reading, which was delivered in precise and poetic Welsh by Miss Williams. His grandmother went through it with him later using her own small leather bound copy of the New Testament, which was printed in her native tongue.

Most of all he remembered the power of the preacher who had ended the proceedings by saying to the congregation: 'To use a line taken from Exodus: "a stranger in a strange land," let me finish here by deferring to that land and quote to you some lines from your great national bard, which I am sure you will feel are appropriate on this occasion for our dear brother, Euan.' The visiting preacher on this occasion had used the correct form of the name, a fact mostly lost on those not originating from that wild and beautiful principality.

He then launched into the dirge for Fidele, in the manner which seems to come as second nature to the Welsh, a race who are fortunate to be gifted by the gods in the skills of oratory and in using their own lyrical language, a language which is richly endowed with a natural poetry in its native rhythms. On this occasion, though, he used the English language, but with a passion and force in its delivery that John had never heard the like of:

Fear no more the heat of the sun
  Nor the furious winter's rages
Thou thy worldly task hast done
  Home art gone and ta'en thy wages.
Golden lads and girls all must
As chimney-sweepers, come to dust.

Fear no more the frown o' the great
  Thou art past the tyrant's stroke:
Care no more to clothe and eat;
  To thee the reed is as the oak:
The sceptre, learning physic must
All follow this and come to dust.

Fear no more the lightning flash
  Nor the all-dread thunder-stone;
Fear not slander, censure rash;
  Though has finished joy and moan
All lovers young, all lovers must
Consign to thee and come to dust.

No exorciser harm thee!
  Nor no witchcraft charm thee!
Ghost unlaid forbear thee!
  Nothing ill come near thee!
Quiet consummation have:
And renowned be thy grave!

After it, there were muted murmurs of amen, but for the most part the congregation stood in hushed silence at the beauty of those wonderful words.

12

Mckinley and the Grammar School Boy

Life continued to drag its impoverished way through the barren thirties in the North of England. John progressed at the mine, until at nineteen he was 'fortunate' to become a face worker. Fortunate, because in normal times the physical effort demanded by the work on six days a week ensured that most men became physically worn out after about 25 years on the face. The two and three day working which was all that was needed in order to achieve Bullcroft's government-ordained quota of coal had meant that some of the older miners had been able to continue on the faces longer than normal. In addition, they were reluctant to leave the face to work in less well paid jobs such as packers, stone dusters, or on the haulage systems which got the coal and waste out of the pit and which moved men and materials into it.

However, the fates intervened in the form of dissatisfaction, which had eaten into the minds of a group of men who had come to work at the pit in the twenties from Derbyshire.

They were a clannish lot and still had copies of the weekly *Derbyshire Times* delivered to them via the local newsagents. Two of the younger ones saw an advert for skilled mine workers in Australia and took the chance to take the offer up. They wrote back a few months later and a small group of brothers and cousins and their families subsequently followed them there, thus leaving vacancies in the face teams. Because of this, John found himself working on a coalface alongside his stepfather.

By this time, Lily was no longer a cost to the family and John and Cud each brought in about two pounds ten shillings a week. This tended to be a little more in winter when there was a greater demand for coal and less in summer when households were burning much less of it. Peggy had started work and the family were just managing. They were all well aware that in some mining areas men had been laid off for months or even years due to the lack of demand for a particular colliery's coal, and had to subsist on the miserable and means-tested dole in order to survive. John thought that this was grim. After the twenty-six weeks of national insurance stamps were used—these might bring a family thirty or forty shillings a week depending on the number of children—the family then had twenty-six weeks on transitional benefit at a lower rate, before being thrown to the mercies of the local Public Assistance Committee. The rates for a man and wife dropped progressively from twenty-six shillings to twenty-four and then to twenty-three for those out of work more than a year.

The means-test was hated, because the man from 'the dole' would arrive and poke round the house and in the larder looking for any evidence of extravagance or of clandestine employment. On one occasion a half pound of butter which had been given to a housewife by her sister and placed in an earthenware pot to keep it cool had resulted in accusations from the fat and bowler wearing successor to Mr Bumble the Beadle. He did much muttering about the unemployed being expected to use margarine rather than butter and told the couple that they would be likely to find themselves before the Assistance Board to explain themselves if he made such luxurious finds in the future.

John had many empty days to fill and had developed a habit of taking a bus into Doncaster after dinner on a Saturday afternoon. He would wander down to the central library and later round the fish and fruit markets as the stallholders started to pack up and frequently came upon stalls that were getting rid of fish, meat, fruit or vegetables cheap. He was under a standing instruction from his mother to buy any he thought were suitable but to be careful that they were not going rotten. He avoided the fish as it would have had to be cooked on the day it was bought, but he frequently arrived home in the evening carrying a bag of oranges or apples or even chestnuts when they were in season. The fruit was never in prime condition and could often be bruised or damaged, but as he was paying less than a third of the price which would be charged by the village greengrocer, he thought that cutting damaged areas out of an apple or orange was a reasonable forfeit for obtaining fruit which the family otherwise would not have had.

On one afternoon he ran into a youth he had not seen since Junior School, called Geoffrey Fisher. He had been in John's class and was reasonably bright but not exceptional, usually finishing eighth or ninth in the various class tests in which Mckinley invariably came first. Geoff was the son of the local tobacconist who had the shop at the top of the lane. It was near two schools and the pit gates. It was opposite a cinema and near the bus stop. By virtue of geography, it had the potential to be a gold mine. It was transformed into one by his mother who had a wonderful smile, which made all who entered the shop feel very welcome.

The shop sold cigarettes, pipe tobacco, snuff and many types of sweets. These were arrayed in large glass jars along the back of the shop so that they could tempt those entering. There were many varieties of boiled sweets such as acid drops and pear drops, aniseed balls and gob stoppers, orange and lemon slices and the like, with softer ones such as wine gums, or Pontefract cakes for those who didn't have the teeth to tackle the harder ones, or the desire to make the sweet last as long as possible by sucking it until it became a small remnant which could then be crunched between the back teeth and swallowed.

Some of the older and sharper miners' wives and widows

were of the cynical opinion that 'her smile is worth a fortune,' and so it was. Whether it was produced by a naturally joyous disposition or an instinctive grasp of sales psychology in an era before such a science existed, no-one knew! Some thought that they did know, but some people never have a good word for anyone, especially when they can see that they are getting a very good living out of others who are struggling.

John had not exactly been friends with Fisher but on one occasion had intervened when a couple of the school bullies had him cornered near the outdoor block, which housed the school lavatories. John stepped between them, with that very determined and unwavering look which he adopted when his mind was firmly made up to use his fists and was inviting them to try it on with him. Very sensibly, both declined the offer and after that young Geoffrey was never picked on again. The young man always felt a debt of gratitude to Mckinley and would thus always acknowledge him long after their paths had diverged.

The head at John's Junior School was always proud of getting about half a dozen of his pupils through the annual exam that would qualify some of his top year for grammar school places. Most of them did not take their place up, but the head thought that the achievement of the necessary standard said something about his school and the ability of his staff and himself. He would scan the results when they were published, noting how his school compared to the others in the locality. There always followed casual mentions of the results to governors and councillors or any others who he thought could usefully receive the knowledge that his school was doing well.

The head was selective in his comparisons, always avoiding mentioning the results from the schools that served the middle-class areas in the posh ends of the town for the very good reason that these areas provided the bulk of those who actually passed and, in most cases, then went on to attend the grammar school.

Mrs Fisher had seen her son's school reports and had

arranged to see the Headmaster in order to ascertain the young man's chances of passing the exam. She was told that he was borderline and that he may pass but she was not to become optimistic about the possibility. The lady in question was ferociously keen that her son should go to the grammar school and thus arranged for special tutoring for her son. This made a considerable difference to him and much to his surprise and to that of his teachers he was one of that year's successful candidates.

Mrs Fisher was acutely aware of the importance of station, and she remembered very well the rigid class distinctions of her youth; of being made to feel inferior by young ladies whose fathers were in the professions because her father, as a grocer, was 'in trade'. She was determined to move onwards and upwards and constantly pushed Geoffrey senior to achieve. Although the shop brought them in a very good living, she had persuaded him to create a partnership with three of the adjacent shopkeepers, to set up a small wholesale business. This was also doing well and her husband eventually bought out his initial partners and had now started to accumulate a small portfolio of investments.

Geoffrey senior had recently joined the golf club and invitations were being issued to attend lunches at the Danum Hotel and to go to an occasional race meeting. Although his only interest in football extended to the possibility of winning the football pools, one of his contacts had taken him to a Doncaster Rovers match at which he had sat in the seats reserved for the directors. The finer points of the match largely passed him by and his mind kept wandering to the pools and the possibility of the Rovers achieving a draw. He always marked them in for a draw and noted that on the previous weekend Littlewoods Pools had paid out the huge sum of 1,480 pounds and 15 shillings for all those achieving the first dividend.

During his social rounds, his political opinions had been sounded out and he had been introduced into the local Conservative Club and put up for membership.

His wife was aware that the next step for her family would be to have Geoff junior enter one of the recognisably middle class occupations or even try for university. She thought that the latter would be somewhat beyond his reach, but some sort of junior managerial role at one of the railway companies or at a local gas works would do. She would be very happy to settle for a son as a bank clerk and the considerable status that that occupation carried in those days.

It was on a damp and cold Saturday afternoon in Doncaster that John bumped into young Fisher. The latter, having obtained the new shoes he had come into the town for, suggested that they get out of the drizzle and have a pint at one of the many pubs in the market place. John had nothing but time on his hands and was prompted by curiosity to agree to the proposal. The young man chose a pub called The Black Bull. It looked all right from the outside but when they entered the bar they were greeted with the sight of several heavily made up and mature ladies. They seemed to hover in the bar area, almost all of them smoking cigarettes and from time to time leaving, mostly with older men.

John realised at once what was happening but young Fisher was somewhat confused by the nature of the transactions taking place. His confusion increased when he became aware that one of the matrons was very obviously looking him up and down whilst placing the cigarette in her mouth in the most insidiously erotic manner imaginable. At the same time seeming to give signals of a very sexual nature with it. Mckinley pulled Geoff to the other end of the room, they got a seat at a small table, and John laughed and told him if he ignored them, the women would ignore him.

The blazing coal fire in one corner and the crush of bodies in the place made the room nice and warm. Geoff bought them a pint each and John said, 'How's it going? It's been a fair time since I last saw you.'

Geoff replied: 'Oh, its fine really,' and then looked at John saying: 'The women near the door were looking at me when I came in. It was as though I was some sort of tasty serving at a luncheon – it made me feel quite strange.'

John thought about explaining the situation to him but said, 'Don't worry about them, they probably want to get you to buy them a port and lemon or something.' Although he had very limited experience in the area, he had heard that one or two pubs in the marketplace were well known haunts for prostitutes and he now realised that this must be one of them. He had been watching one in action: she was using the cigarette as a prop with a sort of sleazy disinterested look, with lowered lids and pursed and full lips, in order to try to provoke some interest from the very green young Geoffrey. Mckinley, who was dressed in a shabby jacket and cloth cap, had deserved no attention whatsoever, but Fisher who looked quite well-to-do in his smart blazer and grey flannel slacks was obviously thought to be worth a try.

He wondered what would have been the result if Geoff had bitten and taken the bait and had been drawn into conversation with the woman, who must have been in her late thirties. He noted that now they were seated she had turned her attention to a sallow faced individual who had just entered the pub.

The two men exchanged updates, John giving as brief an account of mining as he could. Geoffrey told him that after grammar school he had obtained a job in the accounts section of the Railway Plant Works, which was situated next to the Station and was a major manufacturer of locomotives and rolling stock.

John asked, 'How did you find it at school?'

Geoff replied, 'Well, it was alright, I suppose. I wasn't in the top class but I managed to matriculate and that gave me the chance of a good job.'

'Did you like it there though?' said his inquisitor. 'What sort of things did you do?'

At this point, John noticed that the lady smoker was leaving the premises accompanied by the sallow faced individual. He seemed to be perspiring and was trembling slightly and had a look which was a cross between agitation and excitement, which seemed very, very, strange.

Doncaster Grammar School was an all boys institution, ancient in origins, dating back to 1350. It was very proud of its traditions, which included sending a small group each year up to Oxford or Cambridge Universities. The school served the County Borough of Doncaster and took some pupils from the West Riding areas surrounding it. The young Mr Fisher had started there but at the end of the first term he had transferred to the nearby Mexborough Grammar School, as by then his parents had been able to afford a very nice house in the private close which was quite near to the grammar school in that township.

'At both of them,' Geoff said, 'the main sport was rugby, which I had never played. It was always soccer at junior school, as you know. I did manage to represent the school at cross-country running in the matches we had with the other schools.' By the others, he meant the small group consisting of Thorne, Hemsworth, Normanton and Pontefract Grammar Schools, which then collectively served the needs of that part of the West Riding of Yorkshire to the south of Leeds and to the East of Sheffield. He went on: 'It had a fairly low status compared to Rugby and Cricket. I was accepted, sort of, but I didn't like the snobbery.'

'What do you mean?' said John.

'Difficult to say, exactly,' Geoff replied. 'But there were always undercurrents and snide remarks which indicated to me that the teachers had far more time for the sons of local doctors, solicitors, bank managers, farmers, or owners of the larger businesses than they had for the sons of shopkeepers.

'They seemed to equate us with market traders, but at least we were above the handful of kids that got there from working class backgrounds.' It was made very clear to them by some teachers that they were there on sufferance, and they had to put up with the occasional belittling remark, especially if they drifted into the local dialect or did not pronounce their aitches. That group were left with a distinct if unstated impression that they were not welcome at the school. 'Not all the teachers were like it, but there was enough of that sort of small-minded snobbery in some of 'em to make those kids feel uncomfortable in the place.'

Mckinley expressed surprise that people intelligent enough to have university degrees would behave like that.

Geoff said, 'If you scratched the surface they were riddled with snobbery.'

'What do you mean?' said John.

The young man expanded: 'Well, we had a teacher, a strange bloke; he taught biology but was very religious and uncomfortable about any reference to sex. One year he was our form teacher, and in the form periods he was supposed to hold little discussions intended to improve our minds and to engender respect for our rulers. We had topics such as "What is the function and purpose of the Monarchy?" and "Does the law of England fairly serve its entire people?" Things came up that I had never thought about, such as the fact that in republics, such as America or France, all the people are called "citizens". He pointed out that we were all "subjects" of His Majesty, and then asked if any one minded being a subject rather than a citizen. No one did, but of course we had never thought about it.

'Anyway, one day we got onto the topic: "What are the professions?" He asked us which occupations could be classed as professions. Doctors and lawyers came up first, and he agreed that they could be classed as such. Then one kid said what about engineers? However, he lost him in a maze of rubbish about what do you mean by engineers. Somebody else said scientists, but he was not having that and pointed out that most scientists had a technical education and did not have degrees and just did work in labs. The church came up but that fell into the category of a calling or vocation. He was scornful when somebody suggested nursing. We could see where he was going and most of us avoided it, but his smarmy little teacher's pet finally managed to get in with, "Teaching, of course, sir." He preened himself and said, "Yes, we can include that because teachers, from ourselves up to university professors, all have degrees."

'Barry Hickman jumped in and said, "But most teachers don't have degrees, they just have a two-year teacher training certificate." The form teacher replied, "Yes, but we are talking about two different things: at the Grammar and Public Schools we teach at a professional level. At the other schools, it tends just to be the basic three Rs." His parting shot was, "There are just *three* professions: Medicine, the Law, and Teaching."'

Geoff said, 'How snobby can you get! At the school, the Head had a car, as did the ex-Major who took sports, but he or his wife had inherited some money and they didn't have kids. There were one or two others who had old bangers but most of 'em couldn't afford to run cars and certainly not expensive cars like my father's; but he was only a shopkeeper!'

John shook his head at the stupidity of the mindset which produced such delusions.

However, as life went on, John realised that such distinctions were only important to the small-minded. Differences in status, which were so miniscule that they hardly existed, were obviously very important in making some people feel better about themselves. An old collier, who had made the very unusual move of deciding to buy his own house, gave a glorious example of this attitude to himself. His motivation was the memory of one of the very bitter strikes that had seen his parents thrown out from a house, which was owned by the colliery company he worked for. He reasoned that if he bought one he could never be evicted from it. All the other owners or tenants on that street worked for the railway company.

He wryly explained to young John that he had always been a contractor underground, doing some of the more dangerous work involved in driving new tunnels. He had been part of a small gang who were paid on the yardage driven. They always earned a fair bit more than face-men and always had a greater risk of death and injury. He said that the thing that got him was although he usually earned at least three times as much as any of the railway workers on his row, none of their wives would speak to his wife.

'Why was that?' asked John.

'It was class distinction,' he said. 'They were the wives of railway men and she was only the wife of a miner.'

At that point, Mckinley noted that the tart was leaving the pub once more, with another punter on her arm. This one had the dress, bulk and ruddy-faced look of a farmer.

Geoff went on: 'Now I've got into industry I realise that there are dozens of graduate level professions; anything from accountants, chemists, to civil engineers, and dozens of other sorts, and most of 'em are paid a fair bit more than the teachers were at the Grammar School.'

John knew very well what he meant about working class pupils being penalised or pulled up, because outside the classroom the mass of the populace would use the dialect contractions peculiar to South Yorks. With 'have not' becoming han't, wouldn't becoming wun't, 'does not' becoming dun't, and 'could not' producing some very strange looks amongst the peoples of the South when their delicate ears were exposed to the expression which derived from the contraction of those two words.

Geoff carried on with his tale: 'There was one youth in our class that I really felt sorry for. When we started there, our form teacher went round us having us say who we were and what our fathers did. Most said Doctor, Works Manager, Lawyer or something similar, but this one kid said his dad was killed in the war but his grandfather was a company director, and the teacher sympathised. They were all OK. I said that my dad ran a couple of businesses and she nodded at that. A couple more kid's dads ran shops and they just got through with a nod, but I felt that her lips were starting to curl into the sort of supercilious look you get when some people talk to someone in trade.

'The last one was called Trevor Briggs, and when it came

to what his father's occupation was he said, 'My dad drives a crane at the power station!' She looked at him and said, "Really, so *what are you doing here!*" Trev looked really crestfallen. After that she rode him every chance she got.

'He bit his lip and took it for six months, saying nothing. Then one morning she made another belittling remark about his background after she had collected the dinner money. Trevor stood up and said, "If you say anything else about my parents I'm going to belt you one." The woman stupidly launched into a tirade about lower class guttersnipes and their parents who had ideas above their station, and little Trevor hit her in the guts as hard as he could. He must have caught her just right cos she hung onto the side of her desk for several minutes trying to get her breath.

'After that, she sent one of the kids to fetch the deputy head and Trev was dragged off.

'The head gave him a stiff caning and expelled him from the school on the spot. I heard that he ended up at Doncaster's toughest secondary school in Mexborough and when he was there, he always came top in every subject but he was always kept in the lower class. They were going to show him what you got if you dared hit a teacher. After that, I heard he was knocking round with the wrong crowd. I think he will end up inside.'

John mused about the situation, shaking his head in disbelief. At this point he noticed the woman smoker re-enter the premises. The sallow faced individual was nowhere to be seen. She exchanged some coarse pleasantries with one of her compatriots. John heard fragments of it and could hear them cackling at the joke as they moved towards the bar. She produced a ten-shilling note and got both of them a gin and lime and then lit another cigarette and started to glance round at the various punters in the pub for her next victim. He was not long in coming. John noted to himself the subtleties of the situation as he quietly observed the way that the oldest profession in the world was operating in Donny.

He turned back to Geoff who went on: 'Another thing about it was they all wore gowns and mortar boards like Will Hay in that film. One boy made the comparison and he was given a double detention; I thought the teacher was going to roast him alive. Every one of them spoke with a posh accent—they all sounded like Ronald Coleman to me. It sounded so strange, and in at least three cases they made slight slips. I am sure that those teachers had taken elocution lessons. I'll bet their backgrounds were no better than yours or mine but they acted like they were part of the upper classes.'

'Do you think it was worthwhile going there?' John asked.

Geoffrey said, 'I've just described the things that took the edge off the experience for me personally. It was nice to have the chance to go there; it has been sort of therapeutic to get it all off my chest. I've never told anybody else. Lots of my seniors at work went to the Grammar; they wouldn't appreciate any criticism of it, and my parents certainly would not want to know, especially my mother!

'But, yes, I will always be grateful for that education. I don't think I could have had a better one if I had gone to public school. It's just that I never quite felt comfortable inside my own skin while I was there. I was always guarded about my background and although my dad had started to make quite a lot of money by then, I felt that I never quite fitted in. Anyway, at the end of it all, although I could have stayed into the sixth, the chance of a job came up and I took it. I'm looking after my dad's books now and working part time for an accountancy qualification.'

John explained about the short-time working at the pit and Geoff said, 'Yes, it's even affecting our place. Fortunately, salaried staff don't have any reduction. If you are on salary it means you get so much per annum and they can't change that and don't seem to want to.'

At this point John noticed the tart leaving the premises again. This time the punter was a bespectacled individual with thinning hair. The man looked to be about fifty and was following the lady smoker meekly as though being led off to some dark fate over which he had no control.

Shortly after that, John and Geoff left the Bull to go their separate ways. As they parted, Geoff looked at him and said, 'Do make sure you keep in touch and have a drink with me a bit more often in future.' Then, with much sincerity, somewhat mixed with anger and sadness, he said: 'It's a pity you didn't have the chance to go there; you would have excelled.'

13

Mckinley and the Wonderful Thirties

The long agony of the Depression years wandered on in the North like some half-starved troll ravening through an arctic bleakness in search of food and warmth. In 1936 the Jarrow Hunger Marchers had come and gone but to little avail. The Government had changed in the previous year with the Tory, Baldwin, taking over from the former Labour leader, Ramsey Macdonald, in yet another National Government; but this was merely an exchange of seats around the top table. Policies seemed unchanged and the government remained immobile, going nowhere and stuck in that Sargasso Sea comprised of lack of imagination, pacifism, timidity, and a desire to maintain a balanced budget. What ideas there were tended to pull the great ship of state in opposing directions! Thus, it stayed firmly where it was, stuck in that turgid swamp of inactivity, which in those days comprised government thinking.

The Doncaster pits were lucky. With their thick seams of high quality coal, they kept working but at reduced capacity. In some areas they shut down completely or had lay-offs for weeks or months. One of John's abiding memories was of seeing undernourished and listless men queuing outside the dole office with looks of hopelessness on their pinched faces.

For many in the South and the Midlands, things were relatively good, with the great brunt of unemployment falling on the old industries such as mining, steel making and ship building, which were concentrated in the North of England,

Wales and the South of Scotland. Things seemed to be getting worse on the international scene, with Japan engaged in conquests in China and Mussolini doing the same in Abyssinia. Elsewhere, a strange looking and intense little character had come to power in Germany, and in America Roosevelt was elected for a second presidential term in 1936. His electioneering promised a 'Second New Deal', which was a huge raft of initiatives underpinned by government expenditure, designed to bring unemployment down. These had some effect, yet despite them, unemployment in the USA stayed above ten percent during the whole of the 1930s.

In 1936, Mckinley read in the Friday December 11th edition of the *News Chronicle* the headline: EDWARD VIII ABDICATES—To Broadcast as a Private Citizen Tonight!

The paper had cost him a single penny, which in those days comprised one two hundred and fortieth part of a pound. John was as surprised as anyone was. It became obvious from the pages of the paper that the crisis had been brewing for months, but the first news of it had only just broken as far as the public in Britain were concerned.

John noted, with some cynicism, the reverential tones in which both the departing and incoming monarch and his family were described. His mind as usual absorbed interesting facts. He had known that the former king had been given seven Christian names. Names which young debutants and many other sorts of young women would recite rapidly, almost as a litany, whenever he was mentioned. They usually followed the glazed-eyed recitation with a comment such as 'I always do that. I don't know why!' He found that the names, which were Edward, Albert, Christian, George, Andrew, Patrick and David, had been awarded in respect of his grandfather and great grandfather, his religion and the four patron saints of the four countries he was to rule. By a fortunate coincidence, Edward's father had the same name as the English patron saint and thus was included in the list.

He also read, with fascination, of the origins of the Prince of Wales motto, which he had known was *Ich Dein* and was supposedly German for 'I Serve'. Popular legend said that the motto had first been used by the Black Prince. He had adopted it after the battle of Crecy in honour of John, the blind King of Bohemia, who had fought there and been killed at that great English victory. The legend, however, had no factual basis. He learned that according to Welsh tradition Edward Longshanks, acting with that cunning which had characterised all of his lineage, had promised those chieftains of the principality, whom he had previously battered into submission, that he would present to them 'a Prince untarnished in honour who spoke no word of the hated English tongue.' He subsequently produced his newly born son to them with the words *Eich Dyn*, which translates as 'Your Man' in Welsh.

At the pit during a snap break, John was asked what he thought about the abdication. John said, 'Simple then, isn't it? He had the choice between a bit of skirt or being King. He put his personal interests first and not the needs of the nation! He had been offered compromises, but he wouldn't take them. He is a spoiled brat used to having his own way and determined to get it at any price.'

Some present looked at their feet and some murmured agreement; the one or two natural loyalists kept quiet. He was gratified to find that after a while his view became almost the orthodox view at the mine, and though he was neither pro- nor anti-Monarchy, he realised that what had happened had made him think less of the institution and of the former king.

Mckinley had by then met two or three petulant individuals who seemed to think that everything around them should be ordered to serve their personal needs. He thought that Edward was one of those. After that though, he always kept his own council or passed such matters off as a joke. Even when asked if he thought we should declare war after the German aggressions in 1938 and 1939, he said, 'Yes, as long as it's against France. I want to be on the winning side.' He thought war was coming though, and thought that he would prefer to be as far away from it as possible when it did break out again.

At work, he easily absorbed the new lessons of the coalface. In his father's youth the pits had been worked mainly by the pillar and stall method. This meant leaving pillars of coal as roof supports and extracting only the coal between the pillars. This wasteful process became redundant when almost all of the valuable mineral began to be extracted by digging two tunnels in parallel, about two hundred yards apart. The section of coal between the tunnels comprised the coalface, which was advanced day by day by a three-shift method of working. The first involved the manual undercutting of the coal, with colliers crawling under the un-supported coal face using picks and shovels to extract the coal at its underside. This was usually done in the afternoons. Secondly, the face was drilled at various points and charges inserted and the holes stemmed. The charges were then detonated electrically to break up the coal, which would collapse down towards the undercut and outwards into the clear area behind the face.

In the third or day shift, between 6 am to 2 pm, colliers went onto the face and the Deputy used his stick to measure off the coal into the portions, which comprised each man's 'stint'. These usually amounted to about ten tons. Occasionally, if absenteeism was high, colliers would be asked to share an extra stint or even to do a double and shovel twenty tons. As payment was made on the basis of number of stints, most were keen to do the extra work. The colliers shovelled the coal into the tubs that were then hauled away by the pony lads. As the face advanced, the colliers would set props under the newly exposed roof, and move the rail tracks, which carried the low tubs forward by a few feet, in order to keep up with the face advance.

John was told how lucky he was as the past dangers of the job were explained. They now had a machine which would do the dangerous undercutting. This was a band saw with very tough teeth that sliced easily into the base of the coalface to a depth of about six feet. This eliminated many of the deaths or injuries, which had previously occurred due to falls or collapses of the coalface while men were working to excavate the narrow gap underneath it. They now also had compressed carbon dioxide blasting charges, which eliminated flame and considerably reduced the dangers of a methane or coal dust ignition.

To top it all, since 1934, they all had hard hats as well. A downside to the advances was that the men who were working the electrical under-cutters were having to work in dust so thick that it was hard to see more than two or three feet in front of them. Local doctors, later on, started to notice an increase in the lung diseases of pneumoconiosis and silicosis. In these diseases, the dust causes scarring of the lung tissue and the disease is progressive, once it has been initiated, and cannot be reversed. Over a period of years, the man inflicted gets shorter and shorter of breath until he ends up housebound and needing an oxygen cylinder to breathe.

John noticed that ponies seemed to be used less and less and that engine driven wire ropes were now being used to pull the tubs, and conveyors were increasingly coming into service. All this was intended not to make the job easier but to increase productivity and reduce costs. The machines and ropes introduced new dangers. He knew of one haulage man who had lost an arm after he had reached inwards while the conveyor was running to try to free one of the rollers.

In the course of his travels round the mine, John would still see his old pony from time to time. John always made sure that he had a treat in his pocket to give to it if he came across that patient and affectionate beast. He was always attuned to Pete's moods. He had noticed that it seemed to shy away from a new lad called Keith Piddock, who was now driving it. The youth was rough with the animal and cursed it for being awkward.

John noted the behaviour and then, after seeing some heavy weals across his old friend's back, he quietly followed the youth and pony down a heading and found him there, laying into it with a thin iron bar. John leapt forward, snatched the bar out of his hand, and then brought it down on Piddock's back and shoulders, causing him to cower down and cover his head with his arms. Mckinley then lifted him up bodily by his throat and explained that if he ever saw a mark on Pete again; even if the marks had been caused by some accident, he would give him the biggest thrashing anybody had ever had in his life. As he departed, he said, 'I'll be round at the stables myself to look him over at the end of the shift.' He watched as the youth slunk off muttering to himself. In the days following, John kept an eye out for Pete and asked Quiller and Arthur to look out for him as well.

As it turned out, the youth was not only vicious but stupid as well. Burkinshaw had heard him shooting his mouth off about what he was going to do to the pony and what he and his brothers would do to John Mckinley. The undermanager moved him off the ponies and on to one of the worst jobs in the mine, shovelling out coal and spoil which had fallen off one of the conveyors at one of the junctions. The location was lonely, dank and dark, and because of the ventilation flows at that point, cold. The youth was miserable due to the task he had been given, but even more miserable due to the remarks from the other pony lads. One would ask if he was enjoying his 'promotion', and another would reply 'neighhh'. Then they would all walk off laughing, leaving the solitary shoveller alone in the darkness.

John heard about the threats and sought out the youth's older brother who worked on the afters' shift. He had learned by then that the best way to deal with threats was to confront them directly, and he asked the man for a word outside after seeing him at the club. The man was taken aback at the request, but John looked at him with his usual brooding directness and explained the situation. If the brother had turned nasty, John was confident that he could deal with it. He had done some boxing with the Thompson brothers and they had wanted him to get seriously involved with the sport, thinking him an excellent prospect for the club, but after learning the fundamentals of the gentle art he had drifted away to other things.

The brother, as is not unusual in these situations, was completely ignorant of what had happened, and said, 'Look, John, sometimes you get a wrong 'un in a family and he's ours. I don't know how he turned out like that, he just did.' He went on, 'If I'd found out what he'd been at wi't pony, I'd 'ave brayed 'im meself.'

John made certain that everything was all right between them saying, 'You know what it's like down the pit; we all need to stick together.' Keith's elder brother knew exactly what he meant; in the case of emergencies, petty score settling was the last thing that was needed.

In those impoverished days, leisure time was a problem for Mckinley due to lack of money. He liked a drink but he was not prepared to get into situations where his mates were buying and he could not stand his corner when his turn came. His visits to Donny often included a visit to the Black Bull, not that he intended to use any of the girls there. Nevertheless, the place was warm and he could get a pint and sit next to the fire nursing his drink for a long time.

He had been at the cinema in Doncaster during the evening a few weeks earlier and had been making his way back through Town to get the last bus. He had cut through the market place to get a bag of chips for his supper. He was walking down one of the back alleys near the Bull enjoying his snack, and had just finished when he heard raised voices. He came round a bend in the alley and could see a man and woman arguing. She was being pushed back into a doorway and was cursing and trying to get free. Both were oblivious to John's presence. Suddenly the bloke pulled out a cutthroat razor and held in next to her cheek, saying: 'If you don't do what you are told you know what you will get.' The woman went very silent and was obviously very afraid.

John stepped forward and grabbed the spiv's wrist. The

man was quite thick set but in his late forties and past his best in terms of strength, and also obviously a smoker which meant he would rapidly get out of breath if a fight started. John held the razor so that it could not be used. The spiv came across with the other fist and tried to clip him on the jaw. Mckinley blocked the punch, then kicked the man hard at the side of the kneecap, and followed it with a couple of hard punches to the face. One of them caught the spiv full on the nose and he staggered back, dropping the razor and reaching for a handkerchief to staunch the flow of blood.

John picked the razor up and stepped towards the woman's assailant who then decided he had better leg it before he ended up being cut. He disappeared, running with a marked limp and holding the handkerchief to his face and cursing as he went. John turned to the woman and asked if she was all right. She said, 'Yes, thanks, dearie, just a bit shaken up.' He then realised, now that he could get a closer look at her, that it was the middle-aged tart that he had seen in the Bull on that afternoon that he had run into Geoff.

She said, 'Don't I know you from somewhere?'

John said, 'Yes, I saw you in the Bull a few weeks ago. It was a Saturday, and I was in with a friend.'

A flicker of recognition crept over her face. 'Yes,' she said. 'I remember. Your friend looked as though he needed leading astray.' She smiled at her own joke and went on: 'If you ever get in there again come over and we'll have a chat.'

After making certain that she was all right to get home on her own, he left her, wondering if what he had just seen was one of the routine hazards of her profession or if there was more to it.

The year drifted on towards 1937. The Christmas was bleak, with festive cheer in very short supply due to the lack of money. The face workers were only paid if there was a productive shift, but mining conditions are not standard and unchanging as they are in a factory or railway works or in a school. The face had advanced and run into an area where the shale overhead was less stable than usual and thus the shot firing operations had caused numerous stoppages and coal getting shifts had diminished due to roof falls. Two weeks into December, both John and Cud came home with wages of only a few shillings each for the previous week. Margaret said, 'I've paid into the Co-op Christmas club and we should be alright for food.' However, John was thinking about not having the price of a pint and the Christmas and New Year's Eves were approaching.

In the mining villages, these were times of very special celebration for the men at their clubs; the feeling of goodwill which ran through the places had to be experienced personally to be appreciated. These evenings had something magical about them. The radio programs were always more joyous and more entertaining for those few days. Also, perhaps it was the bits of tinsel and holly that the bar staff put up, or that people always seemed to be more cheerful than usual, with an almost forced determination to enjoy that brief respite from the drabness of everyday existence that permeated the rest of the year. Cud always made a point of putting a sprig of mistletoe up in the entrance hall at number 39, as this would legitimise any kisses that were bestowed on those entering the house, especially on New Year's Eve.

John's one bright spot was Mona. They were developing into a committed couple and despite all the apparent difficulties she was determined to make an honest man of him. He had despondently explained the hopelessness of his prospects but she was cheerfully undeterred, saying, 'For someone like you, something will happen.' She knew that her young man was unusually talented and was sure that he would find some way of exploiting his inherent gifts. She did not know how this would happen, but to John she seemed to have a burning faith in him and an optimism that chances would arise and his promise would be fulfilled. He hoped she was right, but deep within felt an awful pessimism about his own prospects and of those around him.

*

On the Saturday before Christmas, Peggy came in from Doncaster just as Cud was urging silence on everyone so that he could go through the ritual of marking his penny Pools. He did 'Vernons' rather than 'Littlewoods' as he thought that, although the dividends were lower, there was more chance of winning on his particular choice of pool. The event always followed the same pattern, with excitement at the start as the results started to come into the room over the crackling and uncooperative wireless set. The excitement would mount on those rare occasions when Cud had selected matches at which a draw had occurred. He did not seem to notice that his success rate seemed to follow the pattern set by the football matches, which could throw up anywhere between about six and twenty such results.

On one occasion, he actually managed the seven draws that gave him the twenty-two points, which, normally, would have given a fair dividend. He was almost incoherent with excitement, holding the paper up in triumph, shouting seven draws, seven draws! However, that week had resulted in an exceptional number of drawn matches and it was announced later that Vernons would only be paying out on eight draws, and even here, the pay-out was in the eighty pounds range rather than the thousand or so that the pool usually made. Cud briefly thought about packing it in but when the collection agent came round on the next Tuesday he once more parted with his precious sixpence; after all, next week he might win!

Peggy had gone upstairs during the pool marking but came downstairs later, saying: 'There's been a bad accident on the A1. Somebody has been killed, I think.' She had no further details but on Sunday, the bombshell dropped. Quiller and Arthur came down for John to take him out for a drink before Sunday dinner. He was not keen as he was skint and did not like to sponge on his pals, but the two jollied him into it. They had just settled at a table in the bar when one of the pit's first-aiders came in, talking to the driver who acted as part-time chauffeur for the pit manager and also as the ambulance driver.

They were talking about the accident the day before, and the first-aider said, 'We got a phone call because we were only a mile away. It happened on the A1 just before the turnoff down to the village and the ambulance from the hospital was out. There was nothing happening and Burkinshaw gave us the nod but told us not to hang about.'

The St John's Ambulance Brigade man said, 'How do you think it happened; was it ice?'

The driver said: 'No, I think it was his tyres—they were just about bald and we have had nearly a month's dry weather; that always seems to make the road more slippery with oil and rubber from the tyres after a shower. I've always noticed that it's at its worst when it's like that. It's worse than ice because you are driving at normal speed and all of a sudden you are skidding and you aren't expecting it. We had a heavy shower about an hour before the crash.'

'What about the injuries?' said the first-aider, with professional interest.

The witness replied, 'Well, he had cuts to his face and some chest injuries caused by him slamming into the steering wheel; I think he had some broken ribs. The woman didn't have a mark on her, but she was dead; the crash snapped her neck.'

'Was it a married couple?' his companion asked.

'No, it was that Osbourne bloke that lives up the top end of the village; you know the one with the barber's shop in town, and his daughter.'

John went white with shock. He took a deep breath, turned to the ambulance driver, and said: 'Are you saying that Mona Osbourne has been killed?'

The driver nodded. 'That's her name. Young woman, attractive, what a bloody pity!'

John returned to the table, downed his pint, and muttered to his pals: 'I've got to go; I've got to see about something.'

Both were taken aback at John's very unusual behaviour, but accepted that if he said he needed to do something that it would certainly be the case. He would not be hurrying off away from his beer unless the matter was urgent.

John walked out of the club and then up the lane in the blackest despair, hoping against hope that it had been someone else. He had to check, to make certain. As he neared the Osbourne residence he could see the lights on but, unusually for the daytime, the curtains were closed. He saw a woman come out of the house next door but one and asked about the accident. The woman he questioned gave him a stern look and said, 'Why do you want to know?' John told her that he knew Mona well and was going to be seeing her later in the week. The woman said: 'Hmmmm, yes, it's true! Him and that bloody car of his! Mona's in the hospital morgue and he's in one of the wards with his ribs strapped up and a broken arm and collar bone. His sister has just come over and drawn the curtains and is sorting things out.'

After that, John walked down the lane and up the bridle path towards the church. He was walking aimlessly with no sense of where he was going or of time. He walked in abject misery for a couple of hours, thinking things over. At about two-thirty he realised that he was near the end of Briar Road and thus hurried down it towards home.

His mother said, 'Where have you been? We had our dinner about an hour ago. Has something happened? I was starting to get worried.'

John muttered, 'Oh, something important came up!'

His mother said: 'I thought those two had kept you drinking till throwing out time.' However, she could tell that her son had not been drinking and went on. 'Well, I covered your dinner with gravy and put it in the oven between two plates to keep it warm; it might be a bit dried up at the edges.' She retrieved the meal and set it down before her son who started to eat it but with little enthusiasm and in silence.

After he finished he got up and said, 'I've got to go out.'

His mother looked concerned and said, 'You're not in any trouble, are you?'

He looked up and gave her one of his brooding looks and said: 'No, I'll be back later.'

He left the house, walking off into the dismal and fading afternoon light of that drear, drab and lifeless December day.

14

Mckinley and Choices

There is a tide in the affairs of men,
Which taken at the flood, leads onto fortune
Omitted, all the voyage of their life
Is bound in shallows and in miseries.

Mona's funeral was held a week later. John attended but stood at the back of the church not wishing anyone to know of that passionate relationship he had briefly shared with his first love. Mona's father was helped in. From his grey face Mckinley could tell that he was in considerable physical pain and undoubtedly wracked by the mental anguish of losing his only child. The vicar did an adequate job but John promised himself that the bit about sending a pure and unspoiled maiden back to her maker, although incorrect, would remain a secret which only he and his beloved would ever know about.

A month after the burial, on a bright yet freezing January day, he visited the grave with snowdrop shoots he had dug up in the wood and set them all around the grave.

He stood meditating for a short while, fond thoughts, memories and regrets running through his mind. Lines of poetry seemed to emerge from nowhere for a moment and then sink again in the tidal swell of his grief: '*sweets for the sweet*'—'*Lay her i' the earth; and from her fair and unpolluted flesh may violets spring*'. He mused: 'It will be snowdrops in your case, my darling girl.'

He turned and left the graveyard, not looking back, his mind now focused on other things. He was not a sentimentalist, he would not brood; what had happened had happened. It was just as it was with Williams; those gods or demons of chaos, who seemed to control the universe, had swooped unexpectedly once more, and had snatched away someone who was so very vibrant and full of life away from him. He never returned to the grave, but as the years went by he heard people talk of one place in particular in the churchyard, where a carpet of winter white came each year to beautify the place where a young woman lay.

In the following weeks, he thought things through. At work, he was lucky if he got two shifts a week and most of the time hardly had the price of a pint. His young brother had just started work and only his youngest sister now remained at home as the only non-contributor to the family finances. He had no other ties, so now he thought was the time to move off and away from the pit. If he did not do it now, he realised that he probably never would, but he was perplexed in respect of which direction to jump. He had thought of various alternatives, like a move to Australia, but that sounded hot and harsh and snake infested and had little to offer but sheep farming or other forms of agriculture. However, there did seem to be some mining that seemed to be out in the wilderness hundreds of miles from anywhere. He thought that the last thing he wanted was to be stuck in some mining camp where the only things to do on a Saturday night was boozing and then brawling in frustration due to the lack of female company.

He thought about the Navy, but was put off more than anything by the chats he had with the woman he had saved from the razor. He had gone into the Bull one afternoon and was standing at the bar when the woman moved over and said to the barman, 'This one's on me.' John started to protest but she fixed him with a firm look and said, 'I owe you!' He got the drink, she took him over to a quiet table round a concealed corner at the bar end, and the two started to chat.

The woman had been christened Agnes but she hated it. 'Aggie,' she said, and grimaced. 'No, I use my second name, which is May, but I tell 'em it's Mae, like in Mae West. The punters like it, they think it sounds tarty.' She introduced him to some of the other girls, saying, 'He's a friend, he's not after anything, and so don't get any ideas.' John found that after that they seemed relaxed around him and quite friendly. Over a period of several months, her life history unfolded and she explained to the relatively green young man how 'the game' operated in Doncaster.

The man who had been threatening her, it turned out, had been the member of a razor gang that had moved into the town in order to make money out of illicit gambling, prostitution or anything else they could get into. A particularly acute police superintendent had been on to the crew almost as soon as they arrived and had immediately involved the C.I.D. The spiv threatening Mae had wanted her to work for him but she had always been an 'independent' and did not like the idea of being pimped and made to be constantly 'on the batter'.

She liked to please herself and have time off if she felt like it, and to keep all of the money that she earned. As it worked out, after a particularly bad razor attack in the middle of the town, the police had swooped and arrested the whole of the gang. The upshot was several years with hard labour for the leaders and two or three years for the small fry. Mae didn't think that they or any more like them would be back in Donny for a long time.

She explained how she had started on the game: 'My old man was a drunk. I left to live with a sister and her husband, but he had a hard time keeping his hands off me. I had a good figure and was pretty. I tried several jobs but the boredom of doing wiring in the electrical factory was unbelievable. The money doing waitressing was poor and blokes used to try it on. One of the other girls at the place was doing a bit of part-time punting on the quiet; she explained to me how to do it. At first, it was difficult and the first time I had it I was scared to death, but after a bit we rented a place over a shop and I went full-time as a pro. My friend got married soon after, but I've been at it ever since. I'm thirty-seven now, so it must be nineteen years since I started.'

She went on to explain that there were different levels of prostitution in the town and that at the bottom were a group of girls who frequented the Woolpack on the other side of the market square.

'I'd heard it was rough,' said John.

'It is,' she replied. 'You don't want your dick anywhere near any of those slags, but if you want a dose they are the ones to get it with!' She went on: "They are a mix of the thick ones, the mental, and the ugly, who can't get any better than the dregs. They service the labourers, the lorry drivers that stop off here, and the odd weirdo that likes the rough tarts and similar sorts.

'There are one or two high class girls who get into the posh hotels or work from flats in the nice bit of Donny near the racecourse. They deal with professionals and visiting businessmen. When I was younger they used to pull me and one or two others in if there was a race party or some sort of group visiting. Sometimes it was at a flat but more often than not they would book a private room and we'd have a meal and drinks and they would take us off to their bedrooms at the hotel.'

'I thought that the hotels weren't keen on that sort of thing,' said John.

'Don't you believe it,' she replied. 'If you tipped the right people you could have had an orgy in the main ball room if you wanted to.'

He remembered her discourses on the Army and Navy; she had a lot more time for soldiers than sailors and told him: 'The squaddies are mostly fit and youngish; they get some beer down 'em and then want to shoot their load up some girl. It's usually pretty fast and they are mostly OK. The Navy lot tend to be older and I avoid 'em. I've found that if ever something nasty gets spread among the girls it's from some bloody sailor who's picked it up in Singapore or Port Said or Malta.' She mused a while and John wondered if it was due to a bad experience of her own. She went on: 'Sometimes it's a long-distance lorry driver that's stopped overnight in Donny on his way from Hull or Liverpool. If you ever want a dose, pick a girl up near the docks in one of the big ports; it's almost guaranteed.'

Over the following weeks, Mckinley was thoroughly educated about the dynamics of prostitution in Doncaster. Mae pointed out one girl who seemed very unpleasant and was constantly abusive to several of her clients. She had false teeth and a small mouth, which seemed permanently twisted into a vicious snarl. Mae said, 'She's really got her hooks into one bloke in particular; he's the sort that likes it. The smaller she makes him feel the hotter he gets for her.

'She puts him on display, sitting on that long seat near the window, and sends him for drinks using her foul mouth. He loves it. He has a good job and spends absolutely every penny he can spare on her.

'Another pair are mother and daughter, who work from time to time as an expensive twosome.' She pointed out another of the regulars in the Bull, who was a big, buxom and attractive blonde. She seemed none too bright but seemed to be one of the most popular of the girls in the pub and was constantly in and out of the place with various clients. Mae commented: 'That dopy bugger! She actually likes cock. She won't last long.'

She explained to John that very few of the girls actually enjoyed sex with the punters or got any satisfaction from it. Mae said, 'It's all part of the game; you find out what buttons to push to get 'em in and out as fast as you can. If they like slutty you do slutty. If they like chatting you chat. You want 'em gone fast but interested enough to come back for more, when they have the money of course. They orgasm and you certainly don't, although you fake it as though they are really getting you hot. Even now,' she said, 'it never ceases to amaze me what arouses some people.' He recalled his excursions into Krafft-Ebing and was perhaps less surprised than Mae thought, but this was the first time that he had run into actual evidence of fetish interests and he found it all profoundly interesting.

Mae's own clients presented a fair variety of punters, with some of them interested in quite strange activities; she would feed John tit bits but would never identify the actual male involved. 'After all, one of 'em might be a relative of yours or the local vicar,' she said, with a wicked laugh. He thought it was very unlikely, but as Mae said, 'You never know!' One thing that did take him aback was the fact that some of her clients did not want intercourse; he thought that the act would be an almost automatic requirement of the transaction.

In his own mind, he was not exactly sure what counted as a fetish. He had read of men who could be reduced to jelly just by looking at a feminine foot in high heels, and of those who liked to be bound, spanked, or caned. He also grew to appreciate that a wide variety of female forms were sought out. Some always wanted a very slim girl. Others liked the rounded and feminine types with the wide hips and ample breasts like Mae's, and others liked very young girls. Some always went for those built like amazons and others would only ever consider the very petite ones. He knew that many, including himself, liked high heels, stockings, and suspenders, but was that the norm?

The prostitute's clients seemed to be driven by urges deep inside them over which they had no control. One of the aspects of this, which John found fascinating, was, 'what had put these desires there in the first place?' They seemed so very firmly locked deep within the minds of the various punters that Mckinley realised he was looking at some of the fundamental drives that propel people through life. He also realised that he was receiving an education from Mae that went way beyond anything he could ever learn at a university. He was learning about the true nature of sexual relationships and of how sex and sexuality could be used to motivate and control people. What the older woman was giving him was priceless.

As the cruel winter merged into a drear spring, John realised that he had had enough. His thoughts focused more and more on joining the army. He had information about how it had worked from Cud, but realised that the life of a soldier in peacetime is very different to that in wartime. Fortunately, information about it came to him from an unexpected source.

He had explained his predicament to Mae who took him to see the landlord of a pub called the Wellington Arms. It was up in the industrial area set in between the town centre and the A1. The place was small yet busy due to its nearness to a local brass foundry that, surprisingly, was still working on two shifts. She told him that they did a mix of work, some for the military, some for industry, and some for the building trade, and as a result had managed to keep going almost full-time.

The landlord was an ex-sergeant-major who had served his time and got out with his full pension and taken on a pub. He had the ideal qualifications for it as far as the brewery was concerned. He could deal with drunks and he had a wife and daughter who would comprise his staff. Unfortunately, soon after taking the place on, his wife had died of complications after an appendix operation at the local infirmary. However, that was ten years previously. His daughter had now married and moved on into her own pub. Though a fair bit older than Mae, he had made it clear to her that if she was ever interested in changing occupations he would be very pleased to enter into a matrimonial arrangement. Though Mae had told him it would be impossible, as word would get around that he had married a prostitute and it would ruin his reputation, he still seemed keen and was obviously very fond of her.

She took John up to his hostelry on one of the free nights she gave herself, when lack of money meant that although there were still many who would like to enjoy the exotic pleasures that she offered, few could afford to pay for them. The landlord was called Bill, and by some 'Uncle Bill'. He was a large man with a clipped military moustache. Powerfully built but going somewhat to seed, John thought. It was a Wednesday night, which was always the slackest in the town. The weekends were all right, as pay packets had arrived, and Tuesday's market day always boosted trade, but by Wednesday, everyone was skint. The two arrived on the premises and Mae made the introductions. The landlord bought her a large gin and lime and John a pint. He smiled and said, 'Don't worry, lad, you're not paying. Mae tells me that you helped her out of a very nasty situation; that took guts.' He then engaged in conversation with Mckinley and proceeded to give his shrewd and extensive appraisal of army life.

Bill enlisted at sixteen and had seen service in the Boer War and in India and during the Great War. He explained to John how matters had changed in the army, and how during the Boer War about six thousand troops had been killed by the enemy and about three times as many by disease and infections. The Great War had seen vast improvements with about equal numbers killed by disease and enemy action. He said, 'That's your first lesson. If you are posted abroad, you will get lots of medical advice; follow it scrupulously. If they tell you to bathe you do it, if they tell you to sterilise your razor do it. If they tell you to put pink powder on your balls four times a day do that. A lot of the lads I knew who caught something did so because they failed to follow the basic common sense advice they were given.'

He smiled and said, 'You must have been told: "never volunteer!" Well, that is generally good advice, but sometimes it might just suit you to volunteer; the alternative might be worse. Try to be one jump ahead. Listen to the jungle drums, ignore the gossip, but you might find there are useful contacts, say in the telegraph office, who know about postings and the like. Try to find out. There might be loose talk in the officer's mess, a steward or bandsman might hear something. Another good thing to remember is, never try too hard; don't be sloppy—that will get you in bother—but don't try to be among the best or you will find that if you are thought very smart you might get picked out for special escort duty or extra parades if they want to impress some bigwig.'

He continued: 'I take it you can handle yourself with bullies. You've got a pair of broad shoulders and I don't think you will have any bother. If it happens, always remember: never back down. All bullies are cowards inside. There are certain types to watch out for and not to trust. Look out for the thin faced ones with a wolfish look, as if something is eating 'em deep inside. Shakespeare knew what he was talking about when he said: "*Yond' Cassius has a lean and hungry look; he thinks too much such men are dangerous.*" And look out for the fat sly ones with slitty eyes. They are the connivers, the manipulators, the types that will always make a bullet for someone else to fire because they know better than to fire it themselves. 'If they want to complain, they get somebody else to stand up, make the complaint, and then get the manure that always falls on somebody who rocks the boat. You see, the army just cannot have it! Forget about all notions of fair play if you get into a bad situation. Just grit your teeth and put up with it, it will pass. The officers might tell you that they will listen, but that's just for show, just so they can tell the generals later: "I put it to the men and there was no dissent," or something similar. Never complain in the mess or on parade. You might be able to have a quiet word with an officer or NCO if you think something bad is happening or likely to happen.

'Even there, you have to be careful and pick an intelligent one. Lots aren't. They do it by numbers, bark orders, and expect to be obeyed without thinking about the situation they are in and the situation they are putting the men in. Sometimes, the powers that be are so stupid that they provoke a mutiny as they did in 1919, but that was among conscripts who wanted discharge and didn't like hanging about after it was all finished. I very much doubt that you would now get a mutiny in the regular army.'

They paused and had a drink and Bill said to Mae, 'I know you find all this very boring, dear, but the lad needs to hear it.'

Mae, who was looking a couple of the burly foundry workers up and down, replied, 'Not at all, you keep on.'

The old soldier continued: 'If a war starts you can guarantee they will get it wrong. The Boers ran rings round us until the officers started to get ruthless. Those buggers had a nasty habit of blowing our troop or supply trains up or ambushing them. The officers stopped that by putting a wagonload of Boer prisoners in front of each engine. The Boers thought it wasn't cricket, somehow, but they got much less keen on using dynamite after that.

'When the last lot started, we were sent to France with the British Expeditionary Force; we were beautifully equipped—equipped for war in the veldt that is. We only had about one bloody machine gun per battalion, and we were being drawn into trench warfare with next to no mortars or hand grenades or howitzers, and not even damned trenching tools. When it all finished I accidently saw some civil service reports that were marked confidential. The army started the war with only eighty bloody motor vehicles! Eighty! In the whole bloody army! We were not prepared for mechanised warfare in any way. The Germans had six thousand graduate mechanical engineers at the start of the war but because of the way our universities gave priority to theology, classics and arts subjects, we had the magnificent total of just three hundred. It would have made us weep if we'd known about it.

'It was all horses then, with a cavalry mentality that was about fifty years out of date. We didn't have field telephones or wireless at first, so all messages were carried by officers on horseback. They could have drafted Wellington in as our Commander-in-Chief and he would have fitted in just fine.

'I saw other stuff about future preparedness for war. They pointed out that our chemical industry was way behind the

Germans and we couldn't manufacture enough explosives at the start of the war to fill our needs. We were even surreptitiously shipping loads of khaki dye in from Germany after the war had started so that we could dye our bloody uniforms.

'Our commander-in-chief was a general called French; he was sixty-two and he should have been retired. He was cavalry through and through, and thought we were going to fight the bloody war on horseback. We ended up at Mons with two divisions and we beat off six German divisions with rapid rifle fire. We were so good at it that the Huns thought it was machine guns. We had sixteen-hundred casualties, a number that was thought to be horrendous at that time. Anyway, after that it was all confusion, advance, retreat, no proper coordination with the bloody Frogs, no coordination at all, as far as I could see. The French were retreating so we had to. We stopped the Germans at Le Cateau. After that, we marched two hundred miles in thirteen days in full kit. Sometimes we only got four hours sleep a night. The situation must have been critical and French wanted to take us out of the line to refit.

'We started to advance and the Huns stopped us at the Aisne. I think they found out by accident that entrenched men with machine guns could easily stop infantry or cavalry attacks. We saw what they were doing and copied them. That started trench warfare. That got into its stride in November at Ypres. We fought the Germans to a standstill but I found out later that by then, more than half of us who had come into France in the summer were casualties by the end of Wipers. What a bloody mess. After that it got nastier and nastier; it was just hard slog all the way.

'On the second day of the Somme, I got a shrapnel fragment straight through this muscle, here; the Doc called it the latissimus. Nasty, it bled an awful lot and hurt like hell but turned out not to be serious. That took me out of the line and back to Blighty for a fair bit because the wound would not heal. That probably saved my life, 'cos the Somme went on for five months and we ended up with four-hundred-thousand British casualties and sixty-thousand of them on the first day and twenty-thousand of 'em killed.' John looked at him in amazement. 'Yes, four-hundred-thousand, I said,' was the response. 'After that slaughter, the volunteers dried up and they had to bring conscription in.

'Anyway, it went on until 1918. By then the Americans started to arrive in numbers, the Germans were exhausted and near starving, and it ended. We lost almost a million men, the French more than that and the Germans more than both of us put together. What a bloody waste! By the end, though, our lot had started to get it right. We ran into attack, we didn't walk in anymore assuming the shelling had done for 'em. We had tanks and our aircraft were beating theirs and we had more of 'em.

'Nevertheless, what a waste, what a mess! Confusion was the order of the day, confusion and crass assumptions about the Germans. The guts of the ordinary Tommy saved it in the early days. We had huge numbers of cavalry in reserve all through it with hundreds of thousands of horses. I found out later that we had used more shipping in bringing forage across for them than were lost to all their submarines during the whole war. They thought that if the infantry could break through, the cavalry would ride through the gap and then cut 'em down in open country. They waited and waited but a real opportunity never came.'

He went on animatedly: 'I've read a lot about weapons and battles, after all as a Regimental Sergeant-Major it was my game; I was expected to know! As good an example of the thinking as I can give is about the cavalry sword or sabre. It went through hundreds of years of development and by the Napoleonic war it was so good that the French lancers complained about having to face our troops armed with it.

'You would have thought that a lancer would have the advantage, wouldn't you? The fact was that they used to pick tall men for our cavalry and a sabre held with arm outstretched was about six inches longer than a lance. Just occasionally, somebody in the bloody army has a bright idea, but it might just have been a lucky accident. Anyway, by 1910 the cavalry sword was thought to be just about as perfect as it could get. The only trouble was that by then the machine gun had rendered the cavalry obsolete. Though from what I hear, even that hasn't fully sunk in yet, judging by the number of cavalry regiments still about.

'Of course, if you'd been in it as a miner you would have been in one of the tunnelling regiments. Both sides were at it, with the idea of getting a very large explosive mine under the enemy trenches and then detonating it just before an attack. Amazingly, we had some good successes doing it. But don't you believe the bullshit about our marvellous tunnelling units. There was counter tunnelling and some nasty knife and bayonet fights underground and explosions with lots of men's bodies never recovered. Another thing one of our miners told me was they did their digging by candle light. When they broke into the German tunnels they found out that they had electric lighting and better digging equipment. See what I mean about our lack of engineering officers?'

Mckinley was fascinated. Bill paused and got some more drinks sent across to the party and then went on with his lecture. 'Another thing, the army in peacetime is a totally different kettle of fish, especially if you can get posted somewhere nice and warm and healthy; big parts of India are like that but there are disease-ridden hellholes like Quetta that you need to avoid.' He expanded, 'Not much happens and the big enemy is boredom; the officers are wrapped up in the fine social life which the army offers them and they leave the routine pretty much to the NCOs. If you fancy it, remember in peacetime promotion is slow because it's dead men's shoes. People aren't being killed and there's not much opportunity. I went up to RSM fast because everybody round me was dying of something nasty or getting killed. I would hate to be a lance corporal now in the Indian Army waiting for five or ten years before I got the second stripe.

'However, I tried it, and as things are round here now I wouldn't blame you if you gave it a go. Just take my advice, try to out-think the system. Never argue with an officer or NCO! Just give it, yes sir, no sir, three bags full sir. Try not to draw attention to yourself. Don't be too smart or eager, but don't be sloppy or a member of the awkward squad. The army likes to make the occasional example of someone who steps out of line. They feel it might help to keep the others in line! Never forget there are always people in the military who are cunning and who want to build a reputation at somebody else's expense. This at its worst could mean shooting down some natives like that idiot Dyer at Amritsar, or having one of your own men shot to demonstrate to the high ups what a fine disciplinarian you are.'

'What do you mean?' said John.

Bill replied, 'Well, I might be being cynical here but the worst examples I can put forward were the French. If things went wrong on the Western front in an attack or something, as they frequently did, they had the nasty habit of choosing some men from the offending regiment, by lot, to face the firing squad. The men chosen might have been performing bravely but they were still shot. You see how it works! This gave the politicians the impression that the generals had a firm grip on things and were determined to maintain discipline at all costs. No wonder the French troops were on the point of mutiny at some points in the bloody war.

'Mind you, some of ours weren't past that sort of thing. I can remember one bloke, a sergeant, who had run out of ammunition. The Germans were attacking and very near, so he jammed his rifle across the trench to bar their way and shouted, "The Huns are upon us," and told everybody to run. He was court-martialled and shot for throwing his weapon away.'

'You're joking!' said Mckinley.

'No,' said the ex-RSM. 'He faced the firing squad for it. I've no doubt it helped the careerist officer who pushed it through to get a bit higher up the greasy promotional pole.'

'Any particular reason?' asked their inquisitor.

John said, 'It's got a good reputation and I've a friend who was in and he told me all about it, the good bits and the bad.'

'Who might that be?' said their potential recruiter.

John told him about Bill. The sergeant looked straight at him and said, "Bill Turnbull up at the Wellington Arms, will he vouch for you?'

John replied, 'Well, you'll have to ask him, but I'm pretty sure that he will.'

He could see that the recruiting sergeant had instantly mellowed and become more relaxed and even enthusiastic. 'Good outfit, the West Yorks,' he said. 'The Prince of Wales Own. Calvert's Entire, that's their nickname. "Difficulties do not Deter", "Nec aspera terrent", that's the regimental motto, and they're proud of it. Impressive battle honours too: Namur, Waterloo, Sevastopol, the Somme, of course, and lots of others too, including Corunna.

'You know the poem?' he said, looking up. John had seen it but Arthur and Quiller looked blank. He went on: "It's a port on the north coast of Spain. Napoleon's armies drove our lads back there in 1809 before Wellington got properly stuck into 'em, and they disembarked safely due to a famous rear-guard action, but the CO, Sir John Moore, was killed. Look it up: it's in the *Oxford Book of English Verse*. I'm not much on poetry but I think its bloody good.' He launched into the famous second and then the closing stanza:

We buried him darkly, at dead of night,
The sods with our bayonets turning,
By the struggling moonbeams misty light,
And the lantern dimly burning.

Slowly and sadly we laid him down
From the field of his fame fresh and gory;
We carved not a line, and we raised not a stone,
But we left him alone in his glory.

'That's poetry!' the older man said. He laughed and went on: 'I could bore you on military history for hours.' He took some forms from a drawer. 'Signing up is easy. You get the King's shilling of course, and then you are in. How long do you fancy you can sign up for? Nine years or for the full job lot of more than twenty?' The three stuck to the agreed plan and enlisted for the minimum. He told them: 'You need to wait until you are ordered to report for initial training. They take about thirty at a time—that's called a troop. I want to be right about it with you lads, expect the training to be hard but once you're through it and sent to your unit, things get a lot easier. I'll give you all a chit and you can see the local board later this week for your medicals. You all look pretty fit but you need to pass it to get in the Army.

'Alright then?' he said questioningly, looking at the three. 'Let's get the forms filled in and start you down the route to becoming soldiers.' He pulled out a bottle of ink and three old pens, each of which consisted of a nib mounted on six inches of slim dowel. He winked and said, 'This is the first test, whether you can read and write! Don't worry if you can't, we can always send you to the Pioneers.' He laughed heartily at what John realised must be some sort of internal army joke at the expense of the Pioneer Corps.

The three were used to the scratchy old pens, which were the sort that had been use in schools for decades; the iron nib replacing the much older quill which was much softer and thus needed frequent sharpening. They wrote in silence, their concentration on what they were doing, and then handed the forms across the desk. The NCO padded them with blotting paper and said, 'That's good, you've passed the second test.'

Quiller fell for it and said, 'What's that?'

'No crossings out or mistakes that I can see,' was the response. 'And no blots. I hate blots, they're sloppy. I hate sloppiness.' He chuckled!

He looked over John's form last, taking a little longer over it than he had done over the others. He gave him an odd sort of look and said, 'That's a very nice hand you have there, son. Are you sure you work at the pit? Some of the officers don't have handwriting as neat as that.'

It was John's turn to smile. He said, 'Well it's nice to know I'm good at something.'

The sergeant twisted his mouth into a thoughtful sort of expression; it entered his mind that he had seen two good recruits and another with potential, real potential.

Potential was something that the officers asked him about from time to time. Which lance-jack had the potential to do the duties needed for that extra stripe? Which trooper had potential to play rugby or join the regimental boxing team? Who had the potential to be circumspect and make a good steward? There seemed to be many different kinds of potential and the old hand had learned to be very cautious in his recommendations. Even if he was prepared to put a name forward, he had always slipped in the odd caveat just in case it didn't work out. The last thing he wanted was it bouncing back in his direction if he had backed a loser.

The NCO said, 'Everything clear then? As far as I am concerned, you're in the army now. Please don't get into trouble in between leaving here and when you report to barracks, it ruins my filing system. And finally, if you have any questions, feel free to ask.'

The three declined his offer, thanked him, and walked out into the street. The Sun was just coming out and the neglected Donny street had started to look almost cheerful. Mckinley wondered if it was a good omen.

They made their way down the slight incline in the direction of the market place.

'I feel like a drink,' said Arthur.

'You got any money?' said Quiller.

'Two bob,' Arthur replied, 'but that includes my bus fare.'

John said, 'We'll have one back home, it's cheaper, and I'm keeping it to one because I have a few things to see to; I suppose you have as well.'

'Like what?' said Quiller.

'Like telling your parents that you've signed up,' said Mckinley. 'How do you think they will take it?'

'I never thought about that,' said Arthur.

'Well you better think about in now!' came the amused retort.

The three had a pint when they got back to the Skellow Grange Working Men's Club; they sat in a corner and talked things over. John allayed their fears, saying: 'Millions have done it and by all accounts it's not a bad life if you knuckle down to it, and let's face it, what are we looking at if we stay here? Years of short time working underground in shitty conditions and scratching our arses for the price of a pint. After training we can be sent anywhere; we will see the world. And there's another good thing about it just now,' he went on. The two looked at him and John looked back as though he was talking to a couple of pudding heads: 'We aren't at war! Soldiers get shot at if there's a war on, didn't you realise that? You should have joined the Navy!' The two laughed and soon afterwards the recruitment party broke up and each went his separate way.

It was 1937 and Chamberlain had just succeeded Baldwin as Prime Minister. Hitler had reoccupied the Rhineland with German troops the year before but this was of little concern to Britain's leaders. The general view was that it was a reoccupation of the Reich's own back yard. John could see little prospect of war looming in the years ahead but things were afoot of which most of the populace had little knowledge. Government policies had resulted in huge expenditure on the Air Force and on the Navy, whilst the Army had remained as a poor relation. In many ways, Mckinley and friends had been lucky to get in to the West Yorks, as by the mid-thirties the Army had been reduced in size to a little over two-hundred-thousand men. It was organised on the basis of home defence and the security of the Empire.

What John did know about were his own circumstances:

the short time working, the dirt, the grime, the dangers, and the lack of money. He walked down Briar Road looking at the unkempt privet hedges and occasional patch of snapdragons that brightened some gardens, down at the grit in the gutters and the occasional fag end and used match. The cast steel drain covers had an almost surreal appearance as grim entrances to the subterranean world of the local drains and sewers.

Half way down the road was the change from wooden fences to the low red brick walls, which marked the transition from council houses to those owned by the colliery company. Rents were always a little lower in the 'pit houses'. Cud was paying five shillings and fourpence a week for theirs, but those a little further along the road grumbled because they had to fork out more than six shillings. Some gardens were neat but many were largely untended, with the grass growing in clumps and the occasional dock or thistle enhancing the general untidiness of the plot.

One garden stood out, with pansies, geraniums and similar flowers growing within neat borders that surrounded a well-kept lawn. The occupiers of the house were both retired and had no children, and the small plot of colour at the front of their house was their pride and joy. The council's policy, and to a much lesser extent that of the Colliery company, was that the front gardens should be kept tidy. The policy was almost never enforced, unless junk such as a discarded bathtub or similar rubbish started to accumulate.

The neat little garden was often held out as an example by wives to husbands who were too weary from pit work to do much about theirs. For most, about the best that could be done was the occasional rose bush or lilac tree with the grass hacked back into the semblance of order three or four times a year with a sickle or scythe. The pair with the neat little garden had invested in a small rotary hand mower and it was thought by the neighbours that they must have had money to throw away because they owned such an advanced machine.

243

John arrived at the arched passageway, known as 'The Jennel,' which marked the entrance to the back door of number 39. The small house was one of the middle two in a small terrace block of four. Cud kept the garden pretty neat but the one next door had been untended ever since the tenant had done his back in at the pit and gone on 'light' work on the surface. The slate roofs gleamed with the wet of a recent shower and yellow sulphurous smoke curled up from the chimneys of all houses in the block. He turned left, walking past the brick coal shed, and entered the house by the kitchen door.

Margaret was in the middle of the unending cycle of washing. She turned and asked, 'Do you want a cup of tea and something to eat?'

John said, 'I'll get a drink of water.' He ran the tap for a while to get the water cold and then filled a glass and sat at the small kitchen table. 'Is Cud around?' he enquired.

'No,' replied Margaret. 'He's gone down to Luke's place to help him put a pane of glass in, the kids have managed to break one with a cricket ball. Is it anything important?'

'It might be,' he replied. She turned away from the steaming copper and faced him with a quizzical look on her face.

John would have preferred his stepfather to be present, feeling that somehow it would be easier to deliver his news if he was there. His mouth twisted into a grimace that indicated he was in difficulties with the matter.

Margaret said, 'Well, now you've started you can't leave it hanging in the air.'

John looked at his feet and then straight at her and said: 'Me and Quiller and Arthur have had it about up to here with the pit, with no money week after week. We've joined the army!'

Margaret went an unbelievably deathly white and then rushed from the kitchen and upstairs. He followed her out into the passage and looked up. He could hear her scrabbling for something in the bedroom. She returned down the stairs and screamed at him, 'These are your father's. You'll end up like your dad.' Then, reaching the bottom stair, she threw the blood-stained identity discs at him that had been sent back to her with her dead husband's possessions.

John's hand tightened in a furious reflex about the glass of water he had been carrying, and he felt it break under the pressure of his powerful grip. Margaret swept past him into the kitchen and sat in the chair next to the fire with her head in her hands, weeping uncontrollably. John put the remains of the glass in the bucket, which was kept under the sink for ashes, and looked at his hand. There were a couple of small cuts but no serious damage. He ran water over the cuts to clean them and then wrapped a rag round his hand. He turned to Margaret and said, 'Sorry mam, but I've had enough, being here with no money and no prospects is nearly as bad as being dead. We're off in the army, we'll look after each other, and it's not the same as at Gallipoli!'

Margaret looked up and stopped crying. 'I hope so,' she said. 'I couldn't bear it if you were killed. You're all I've got left to remind me of your dad, your real dad.'

'Don't worry,' he reassured her. 'I'm a big lad now. I can look after myself. Think about it! Nothing's happening in the Army, no wars or anything. I'll be safer there than down the pit! Bloody hell mother, it's not so long ago that I was almost killed there.' She looked up in acknowledgement of the truth of what he had said. She knew that Cud had experienced a couple of narrow escapes due to falls of ground at the face and thus, slowly putting things in perspective, she started to come round from the initial shock of being told the dreadful news.

He said, 'Are you sure that you are all right? I have to go out and see people.' She nodded and even managed a weary smile; John smiled back and then left after putting his best jacket on. His best jacket was a brown garment that he had spotted on a second-hand stall in Doncaster market. He had examined it and could find no sign of damage or wear and saw that it was made of thick and durable tweed. He said to the stallholder: 'It looks almost new.' The woman, who had a Woodbine in the corner of her mouth, said, 'Yes dear, it's made up in Scotland. You can see on the label, its Harris Tweed and it almost never wears out.' He tried it on and it fitted perfectly. She was asking for twelve shillings and six pence but had accepted ten, which was all he had on him.

His first port of call was the pit. He was sure that he would find Burkinshaw still there in his office near the medical centre. He walked in and asked George the office lad if the undermanager was in. George said yes. John asked if he was on his own, and the young clerk affirmed that he was. The door was slightly ajar and a voice from within called out: 'Is that young Mckinley? Come in!' John entered the office and found his old gaffer sat in an ancient high backed leather swivel chair with his feet on the desk. He was smoking his pipe and had obviously just finished his day's reports. 'What can I do for thee?' said the older man, beckoning him in.

John looked straight at him and told him that he was joining the Army, saying, 'You set me on at the pit, Mr Burkinshaw, and I wanted to tell you straight away. I didn't want it to seem that I was throwing it in your face, but with the short time working, I have had enough. The trouble is, I just can't see things picking up either. I can't go on for year after year like this. Me, Quiller Jones and Arthur Howarth are off together.'

The older man pointed towards a battered chair with his pipe stem. He said, 'Sit down, lad. Does tha want a cuppa? I've just had a pot brought in.' Mckinley thought, why not, and nodded. Burkinshaw shouted through the door: 'George get thissen in here!'

The young clerk poked his head round the door and said, 'Yes sir.'

'Get another mug and pour the tea, one for my visitor and one for me,' was the rather brisk order to his underling. The clerk scurried about doing his master's bidding, wondering what was going on. He surmised it must be something important. Maybe Mckinley was being given some special job or even being considered for training as a deputy or something similar, he thought.

'Ok, tha can go now,' said his superior. 'Close the door on your way out. Nosy bugger that one. He'd be ideal working for the assistance board. He'd love prying into people's pantries and cupboards.' The old man sat back and said: 'You're not the first, there's been a steady drift out of the pit for about seven or eight years now. Some abroad, some down to London, some in the forces, mainly the younger men without ties like thessen. If I was in your shoes I'd do exactly the same. Not the forces though, I'd try Canada or America if I was a young man.' He passed the tea to John and took a long swig at his own. 'I wouldn't say this to everybody, but if things do pick up and tha wants to come back, there'll always be a job at this pit for thee. I've only got a few years left but I'll put the word in with the right people so you're set on wi' no bother.'

Burkinshaw asked which regiment he was joining and then about Cud and his mother and family, and went on to grumble about the government. 'It's all their bloody fault,' he said. 'They're up the owners' backsides, bloody Tories! They're all in the same clubs down in London and from the same schools.' He laughed and said, 'I shouldn't say that as a manager, but I've got to the stage now where I'm getting too old to care.' The conversation ended with the tea, and John left thinking about his next port of call.

That journey was the most painful of all. He made his way slowly up through the village to the lonely looking house where he knew Mona's father still lived. The man had slowly recovered physically, but John knew from conversations with others that he could not forgive himself for the accident in which his only daughter had died. He thus went through life never smiling, and stooped as though a great millstone of guilt was fastened round his neck. As John walked towards the house the precious hours he had spent with his first love welled up into his mind. He recalled their chats about poetry, literature, what was happening in the world and what would lie in their futures. He also knew that he had to put the matter to rest; he could not afford to dwell morosely on the what-might-have-beens of life, he had to move on and live in the immediate world which surrounded him. But he did need a memento of his darling Mona.

Mckinley, with leaden steps, approached the portal of which he had such joyous memories, almost having to force himself through the gate and up to the entrance to the place, which Mona had first invited him to enter on that summer's day of vanished dreams. He stood for a while listening but could hear nothing, no wireless or any sort of movement. He stared at the small brass knocker and then, taking it firmly in his hand, knocked loudly five times on the solid oak door and then waited. It seemed that an age passed and he was just on the point of knocking again when he heard a sound from deep within the house. After a while, he heard slow footsteps and then a key turning. The door opened and a pale unsmiling face looked down at him and said, 'Yes!'

John said, 'I wonder if I could have a word, sir? It's about Mona, I was one of her friends.'

The pale face hovered over the step for a short while looking at him, searching for some memory of recognition, and then with a sad sort of look said, 'Please come in.' John followed him in. He was taller than the older man and could see that he seemed to be a little lop sided and was walking with a limp. He led the young man into the familiar parlour and sat down and picked up a glass that looked as though it was half-full of whisky. 'I'm having a drink, would you like one?' said the older man.

John declined, and being very careful to be correct and very formal in his mode of address said, 'Let me come straight to the point, sir. I was a close friend of Mona's. I've known her for quite a few years and we had quite a few interests in common: books, music, and the like. We used to chat when we ran into each other in the country lanes round here or at the library.

'There are some things I would like to say: she used to tell me how fond she was of you; she said you were very close. She used to tell me that there's nobody like her dad, she was very proud of you.' He looked at the man in the dim light and could tell that he was battling with the pain of inner emotions, with tears welling up and filling his eyes. He went on: 'I thought I should say it, sir, because I think Mona would like you to be in no doubt of what she felt about you.' He paused a while, till Mona's father gained control of himself and could be spoken to once more and actually take on board what was being said to him.

After a short while, John said, 'Would it be possible to have a photo of Mona? I know it's a big thing to ask but I am leaving the district and would like a memento of her. If you have a photo she will always be young in it and it will give me great pleasure to look at it now and again and remember how she was.'

He would have liked to fill his carefully constructed sentences with all the superlatives that could describe a young woman filled with the strong instincts of her sex, with the wildness and poetic beauty of that free spirit which he had lost forever. He was deliberately mundane and matter of fact. He went on: 'I was at the funeral; you were in a pretty bad way after the crash so you probably didn't notice. I didn't go to the tea at the church hall after it, although everyone in the church was invited. I always feel that those things are for family and close friends.'

His companion in the room had seemed to grow older and more stooped. He got up, rummaged in a drawer, and then went over to a studio taken photo of Mona that was placed, icon like, in the centre of the sideboard. He lifted it up and turned to John, saying: 'I don't have many photos and none which I would give away. I'm afraid I never had much opportunity to take them; I was too busy working. However, I do have the negative to this one, and some others taken at the studio. I will let you have a loan of it and you can have it developed.'

249

He took out three small, fragile looking, thin glass plates and put them in an envelope and handed it across. 'It's important not to get fingerprints on 'em,' he said. 'There's a good chap down Crossfield Lane who does photography as a hobby, it's the one on the corner, number twenty-three I think. His name is Reg Beaumont. If you say I sent you, I'm sure he will do you copies for a few bob. But, whatever you do, make sure you get the negatives back to me.'

The man seemed to have livened up and became much more animated, asking John about himself. The younger man was deliberately vague, but did say that he was leaving the area to join the Army. Mona's dad became sad again, perhaps thinking of friends or relatives he had lost in the Great War. He suddenly said, 'The Church has been on to me about Mona's gravestone. The grave has settled now and it's getting a bit overdue. I've been trying to think of a suitable sentiment, but whatever I come up with seems mawkish, or much too cold, or silly, like "rest in peace" or "in fond remembrance". Have you got any idea about what she might have liked?'

John thought hard and said: 'There was a poem of Byron's which she was particularly fond of; you might like to use the opening or some of the other lines, they might be appropriate.'

'How does it go?' said his sad companion.

John, using his remarkable gifts for memory, delivered the verses perfectly in a measured tone, which captured the metre exactly:

We'll go no more a roving
So late into the night,
Though the heart be still as loving,
And the moon be still as bright.

For the sword outwears its sheath,
And the soul wears out the breast,
And the heart must pause to breathe,
And Love itself have rest.

Though the night was made for loving
And the day returns too soon,
Yet we'll go no more a roving
By the light of the moon.

'What about, "Love itself here rests"? The line is changed a bit but the metre is preserved; I am sure she would like it.

The older man's eyes grew bright and he reached in the sideboard for pen and paper. 'I'll write that down.' He then said, 'Thank you very much young man, you really did know her well, didn't you? I know that her favourite poets were Byron, Shelley and Keats.'

John smiled and felt that the atmosphere of gloom and misery in the room had lifted somewhat. He said, 'She used to call the last two Sheets and Kelly, and then lift her eyes to the heavens and say may Calliope forgive me!' The older man looked blank, and John said, 'She's the muse of poetic inspiration; Mona knew a lot about poetry.'

John then made his excuses and left clutching the precious photographic negatives. He called in at the photographers on his way home and arranged for two prints to be made from each negative. One of them a large portrait size and the other one just of his Mona's face which would fit nicely into his wallet.

Some years later, he learned that the words he had suggested to the grieving father had been carved into the imposing headstone that was erected in the ancient graveyard where his lost love waited out eternity, sleeping there through the seasons under the shade of the old Mulberry tree.

16

Mckinley meets the Army

If you're cast for fatigue by a sergeant unkind,
Don't grouse like a woman nor crack on nor blind;
Be handy and civil, and then you will find
That its beer for the young British soldier.
Beer, beer, beer for the soldier...

Rudyard Kipling

The British Army in 1937 was a strange beast—starved of funds, badly equipped and with the minimum number of troops thought sufficient to serve the needs of home defence and that of the Empire. It had been obvious to 'the thinkers' in the Army from the twenties onwards that the next war would be a largely mobile and armoured affair, but thinkers such as Liddell-Hart, Fuller and Hobart were few and far between and usually junior in rank to the old buffers who held sway. Though tactics and deployments had been worked out by gifted individuals, the dead hand of the old guard at High Command determined priorities. This, combined with the bean-counting attitude of the Civil Service and the inability of the elderly men of politics to grasp the new realities as Germany raced to rearm, saw only 375 armoured vehicles in British Army service in the year Mckinley joined the West Yorks.

The High Command were so out of touch that in some circles the continuing value of the cavalry horse was still being discussed. The Civil Service had generously allowed a new tank to be built nicknamed 'the Matilda' after a cartoon character called 'Matilda the Duck'. This was due to its spindly suspension and an appearance of waddling progress. It was to be built, but amazingly the prime requirement was not speed nor armour or even firepower, it was the clerical stipulation that production costs should not exceed a maximum of £12000.

The Matilda was envisaged as an infantry support tank with a maximum speed of eight miles an hour and a machine gun as armament. The building down to a price rather than up to a specification had lumbered the army with an eleven-ton vehicle with only 65mm of armour. The whole concept indicated that its initiators were thinking in terms of static First World War tactics rather than those which would be required for the highly mobile conflict of the next war.

As hostilities approached, government mechanisms creaked into action with new designs of tanks being commissioned, but by the time they arrived it was almost too late. The Civil Service, in that crass way in which only it is capable of operating, had vastly overestimated the likely number of civilian casualties due to bombing and had prioritised really important things like the ordering of six million shrouds so that the expected corpses should be decently disposed of.

Mckinley and Co had all passed the Army medical and were categorised as A1. This signified that the three were in excellent physical condition, and were considered suitable for service anywhere in the Empire. The appellation has since lost its specific meaning and passed into everyday language for something considered to be first rate. All of them had been sent travel warrants and were ordered to report to the West York's main barracks in York. They were to arrive on the first Tuesday after Easter Week to begin their basic training.

On the Monday night prior to departure they arranged to

have a last few drinks in their old haunts in Doncaster and to finish off in Skellow for a last one at the club. The three were in that devil-may-care mood which sometimes grips young men who have severed their everyday ties and put their futures in the hands of fate. There were jokes on the bus about Donny being a dump that they would be glad to see the back off, and whether the Sergeant Major would be kissing them good night by the end of the week. In John's opinion Arthur was far too ugly to qualify but Quiller just might manage one. The mood that gripped the three, had a sort of sad gaiety. They all knew that this particular evening marked a major change in the lives of three young men who had seen little of the world outside the pit and its immediate surrounds.

They got into the town at about seven, and John insisted that they call at The Nelson first. This was a little out of their way but sold an excellent pint of Bass and he wanted to remember how good it tasted before embarking for alien parts and having to endure inferior ale or, even worse, that awful muck which was served in the South of England.

The place was quite empty; the three sat looking at the wonderful deep colour of the Bass and savouring it as it slowly went down. The barmaid was a blowsy, big-breasted girl with light blond hair and about thirty years of age. She sat at the end of the bar reading a paper and taking long and languid drags on a Park Drive. From time to time, she looked their way. Mckinley observed this without her being aware that she was being scrutinised. He couldn't quite work out whether she was showing sexual interest or was just bored.

Eventually, with two of the glasses drained and Arthur just finishing his, the girl came across to collect the empties. As she bent forward over the table she gave John a smouldering look which could mean only one thing. He asked her if she always worked Mondays. She warmed to the interest and said, 'I'm in most nights, but Wednesday's me night off.'

John replied, 'The boys and me have something on tonight but I might be back to see you one night when I'm on my own.'

'I bet you say that to all the girls,' she said with a rather dirty and inviting laugh, and then busied herself wiping the table, looking pleased at the interest he had shown. She gave John a last look, half-challenging, half-inviting, and John winked at her and rose to shepherd his two mates on to the next pub.

John led them towards The Danum, a name derived from that of the fort and small township that the Romans had established at this crossing point of the river Don. People of a certain mentality liked frequenting the place because it sounded posh and the management did its best to make sure that it appeared so, adding to the exclusiveness of the place by selling the most expensive beer in the town.

As they approached the entrance, Quiller said, 'We're not going in here are we, it's for the nobs?'

John said, 'That's exactly why we're going in. I've never had a drink here and I want to see what the place is like.'

He led them in through the posh portal of what the management considered 'the best hotel in Doncaster'. They could see a large lounge and a sign in the corridor which pointed and exclaimed 'Residents only!' Mckinley was tempted to try it purely for devilment. He walked a few paces down the corridor until he could see inside. The seating was of a plush velvety kind that he had not seen before but there was no barman, just a bell with a polished wooden sign inscribed with the words 'ring for service.' He thus turned and led his two comrades the other way, into the lounge.

A frosty face barmaid greeted them with the words: 'Don't you want the bar? The public bar's round the back!'

'No,' said Mckinley. 'We want beer; we can't afford the bar! This is a public hotel, isn't it?' This somewhat confused the defender of that bastion of the middle classes. From the lack of any smart cut and the somewhat ordinary appearance of the clothes of the three, she had taken them for miners or labourers of some kind. However, John's quick-witted reply had left her guessing. She revised her opinion and wondered if the three might be connected to one of the racehorse owners who were in the town for one of the periodic bloodstock sales. They certainly were not owners, but if they were connected to racing she would deign to serve them.

The woman was about forty and straight up and down with no figure to speak off. She wore a high-buttoned blouse and had a markedly prim appearance. She pulled the three pints quite sloppily, overfilling each glass. John thought that the woman probably needed glasses but for some reason did not or would not wear them. He was careful to give her the exact change for the beer, which cost almost half as much again as that in his Working Men's club. He took the pints and directed his companions over to a corner table so that the three could sit with backs to the wall and observe the comings and goings in the lounge.

It was a quiet night and the young men chatted about what they could expect in the coming weeks. John tutored the two in what sort of things they might expect and said, 'Above all, we stick together! It's like in *The Three Musketeers*: "All for one and one for all!"' He went on: 'It will be tough, I expect, but it is tough working down a pit and if explosions happen I've already got some experience.' His two companions laughed and were sure that everything would be fine. John reminded them: 'Look at the fix we are in: no money, no prospects, just years of the same till we kick our clogs. Some of the old timers have told me that it can be comfortable after the first few weeks. We just keep our noses clean, don't answer back and do what we're told; even you two can do that can't you!' They all smiled and sat back to enjoy their pints.

Customers in the bar were few. One old timer, who looked like a clerk, was drinking a glass of stout at the bar and reading a paper. Occasionally he made comment to the barmaid about some matter of national importance but she was pretty much ignoring him. Mckinley became aware that her gaze constantly turned in their direction and particularly at him. He ignored her at first but then caught her directly in his gaze as she was looking and acknowledged the look with something resembling a half smile and half scowl, with just a very slight nod of the head. The woman looked away immediately and turned to a brisk wiping down of the counter. He could see that she was now studiously avoiding looking at him. After a while, he said to his two companions: 'It's not bad beer in here. Expensive though. We'll just have another half and then go down to the Bull. There might be someone there I want to see.'

He got up, presented himself at the bar, and said to its guardian, 'Another three halves of your excellent beer if you please.' She reached for the glasses and started to fiddle with the pump and then fill the glasses. John turned on the roguish charm and said: 'I hope you don't mind me asking, but my two mates were trying to guess your age. They think you must be about thirty-two-ish but I told 'em with your looks and trim figure you would be younger.'

'Oh!' she said, smiling, 'as a matter of fact I am thirty-seven, but a lady never discusses her age.'

'Well,' said John, 'I would never have guessed it. What's your name by the way?'

'Oh, it's Jane,' she said. 'Plain Jane.'

'Far from plain,' said a roguish voice, which Mckinley recognised as his own. 'And I would have put you closer to twenty-seven.'

By now, Jane was almost simpering with pleasure. John guessed that the sort of flattery he was pouring out came her way pretty rarely. He took her hand and placed the money in it, making sure that their two hands lingered in contact a little longer than usual, and then took the glasses, saying, 'I must look you up the next time I'm in this part of town.' She smiled in anticipation, not quite knowing what to say.

The charmer returned with the drinks and engaged his friends in studious conversation. He could see that Jane was now showing decided interest with frequent smiling looks in their direction. However, he continued in animated conversation with his two friends and seemed not to notice. They drank quickly and then rose and as they walked past the bar, John said, 'I'll be seeing you, Jane; I hope you'll remember me.' She blushed and stuttered a reply in the affirmative as the three smiling pitmen left her posh premises.

As they walked down the lane, Arthur said, 'What was all that about? Tha didn't fancy her, did tha?'

Mckinley replied, 'No, a bit too old.'

Quiller joined in, saying: 'A lot too old if you ask me, but I could hear you buttering her up. You're Donny's version of Errol Flynn when you feel like it.'

John roughed his mate's hair up, pushing him off the kerb and said to both, 'There's one thing about it.'

'What's that?' they asked in unison.

'If we ever get in there again she won't be asking us if we want the public bar, she'll be breaking her neck to serve us.' They walked on and a look of understanding came over their faces at his ruse. They might have reacted angrily to the invitation to use the public bar or even have accepted it if she had become stroppy, but neither could or would have turned the situation round to their advantage in the way that John had.

They got to the Bull, and as John expected, Mae was there with a couple of the girls who were talking to a balding character of about fifty. He wore a rather loud suit with a silver watch chain hung just over a waist-coated paunch, which descended down to a pair of well-creased twill trousers ending in a pair of comfortable looking brogues. The man was very obviously sweating, although the bar was far from warm. Why do they always do that, John thought, having seen numerous punters who seemed to be in a similar condition prior to leaving the Bull with various varieties of interesting females?

The two women seemed an odd combination, one about forty and with a severe look, and one in her early twenties who also looked a bit nasty. They left with the commercial traveller, as Mckinley later discovered he was. Mae turned and greeted John very warmly as he introduced his two mates. She told them, 'John's a very good friend of mine, my knight in shining armour.' He explained to them later how he had got to know the older woman. He asked her what she wanted to drink and insisted on paying for her gin and lime rather than allowing her to stick to her usual insistence that she would buy the drinks.

The four settled down to enjoy their beverages and he then told her that it was a sort of farewell, as they would be starting in the Army the next day. Mae looked sad and said, 'Oh well, you're young, you'll see a bit of the world.' Then, looking urgently straight at him, 'But make sure you don't get killed!'

John laughed and patted her on the knee and replied: 'We're big boys now, Mae, and we're going to look after each other and I'll make sure that whenever I'm on leave I'll be down to see you to make sure that you are alright.'

She smiled and lit a cigarette.

Arthur said, 'Where's the lav?' Mae pointed to a door at the back.

Quiller said, 'I need one as well,' and they both got up and walked through the bar in order to use the very basic urinal at the rear of the premises.

John indicated the door with his head and said, 'What was all that about?'

His companion replied, 'Oh, mother and daughter team! They are expensive and occasionally give "unusual" services together. They don't get in here very much, not their sort of clientele.'

'What do you mean by "unusual"?' said her curious young friend.

'Well, put it like this,' said Mae. 'They will be at it for hours and he will be a lot poorer and very sore in certain parts of his anatomy when they have finished. And another thing, he won't be able to wait to get back for more of the same; when they're like that they're like drug addicts.' John looked quizzically at her but she said, 'You don't want a blow by blow description, do you? If you really want to find out, save up the ten or twenty quid that they charge and I'll get you an introduction.' He was not that curious and thought that an investment of more than a month's pay was unlikely to reap the sort of dividends in satisfaction which he would enjoy from paying for their services. He thought of his earlier readings of Krafft-Ebing and knew that further details would be forthcoming on the future occasions when he saw Mae.

His companions returned and he stood up. They all reached down as though given a signal, which was indeed the case, and finished their drinks. He said to Mae: 'We've got to go, other people to see, but I'll be back and that's a promise.'

Mae shook hands with Quiller and Arthur and turned to John and put her hands on his shoulders and with a poignant look told him to make sure he stayed safe and to come back soon. She then kissed him slowly on the lips, which was something she never did. The kiss spoke volumes, of longing, of sadness, of desire and fond farewells, and as he turned to go, he could see tears welling in Mae's very sad and attractive eyes.

Their next stop was the Club. They had fortuitously hopped on a bus just as it was about to leave town. John reckoned that even with the slow rate at which the vehicle trundled through the various villages on the way back to Skellow, they should be in the club for about nine; plenty of time for a last couple of pints and some goodbyes if anyone was interested. Half an hour later they walked through the rather dingy portico at the back of the club. The main door was kept shut through the early part of the week, and those thirsty colliers who had the price of a drink congregated in the bar at the rear. It was always smoke filled, with groups sat around usually playing dominoes or cribbage. In one corner, a couple of dartboards were being punctured with more enthusiasm than accuracy by a group of listless looking youths.

At that time and for many years after it, notices could be seen in working men's clubs which prohibited card games but which did permit dominoes or similar, with the stern injunction that they were only to be engaged in for 'small monetary stakes'.

261

Cud came over as soon as they entered and the three were rapidly surrounded by about eighteen or twenty others, comprising various relatives and workmates. Three pints were immediately placed in their hands and it swept round the bar that the three were leaving to join the army in the morning. Yorkshire miners are by nature a dry, taciturn, and hard race, but there were looks of approval from some of the old sweats. It was made clear to the three that they would not be paying for beer tonight. Quiller said, 'Bloody hell, if I'd known that I would have been in here at half-six.'

A heaped tray of cheese and onion sandwiches appeared from behind the bar and the three were urged to get stuck in, which they did with enthusiasm. The rest of the group then helped themselves and the tray was refilled with fresh bread covered in pork dripping and then passed round the bar. It turned out that Cud and a couple of the others had paid the steward for the grub which was the standard fare on the occasional games nights which the club took turns to host, along with the others in the locality. The mining community weren't much good at expressing emotions or given to oratory but the three left the place with the warm glow of knowing that they carried with them the very best wishes of all of the men of that small and insular community which they were leaving.

John arose next morning, got washed, and then checked the small suitcase which he had carefully packed at the weekend. He was surprisingly clear-headed and could smell bacon as he entered the kitchen. Margaret had prepared a breakfast of bacon, eggs and sausages, which was a rare treat indeed and marked his mother's determination to send her son off in the best way possible, knowing that she could never do it in words. He sat down to eat the meal with enthusiasm, with lots of brown sauce and bread and marge and tea.

Cud and young Bert had made farewells earlier and gone off to the pit to get in one of the few shifts which were now available and which were too valuable to lose. Peggy had also gone off to work, but Alice, his youngest sister, kept hanging about near him. When he finished the meal, he swept her up onto his knee and said, 'Well then, Gypsy,' which was his nickname for her. 'You will look after your mam while I'm gone.'

She did not speak but climbed from his knee and went into the parlour. She returned immediately, placed a small packet of chocolate biscuits in his hands, and said, 'I got you these 'cos you might get hungry.'

He said, 'Well, thank you darling. Cadburys! My favourites. I'll eat 'em on the train.'

Alice scurried off, rather pleased with herself, and then returned clutching her beloved rag doll. She said, 'You can take Molly as well if you like, in case you get lonely.'

John had to pause and choke back emotion and took a long swallow from the mug of tea. He then said, 'No! I've told Molly that she's got to stay here and look after you.' Alice looked rather pleased at that but at least she had made the offer of her most treasured possession.

After the breakfast, John bustled about, grabbed his jacket, and checked the small amount of money that he had and his travel warrant, and then made his last farewells to his mother. She was on the point of tears and hugged him to her very hard. He said, 'Don't worry, mam, this will be an adventure and I'll soon be back on leave.'

He then set off for the bus station to meet his two compatriots. He had arranged it so that they would have plenty of time in case of transport breakdowns or delays and thus the three got an early train into York and then made for Strensall Barracks, which was then the home base of their regiment.

They asked directions and were told that the Barracks could be reached by bus or a longish walk through the city. They had plenty of time before the two-o'clock stipulated for reporting and thus decided to walk. John had told them it would be useful as they might be there for months, and they needed to get a feel for the place. The three had never been to York before and thought that the city had a cleaner and quieter air than Doncaster. Its buildings seemed older and classier in some way, and the river Ouse, which ran through its centre, was a more substantial and picturesque river than the variable and dirty river Don of their hometown. John mentally ticked off the street names and places that they had been given, noting the likely looking boozers as they made their way to their destination.

Eventually they arrived at the gates and reported at the guardhouse as instructed. The corporal there said, 'You'll be part of the new troop. You're a bit early. I'll get you over to the drill hall and you can meet some of the others.' He then said, 'Follow me,' and marched smartly across the large parade ground with his charges in tow.

They entered the drill hall, which was a very large school-hall-like structure with black painted iron rods across the lower part of the ceiling. These formed structural reinforcements to the hall, which had been built about a century earlier. Crossed flags were mounted prominently in one corner. One was the Union Jack and the other was some sort of regimental banner with a list of names embroidered decoratively on it in a long descending sequence. Round the walls were numerous photographs of groups of men. The front rows were seated with an officer in the centre and with various NCOs either side of him; the remainder appeared to be fresh faced troopers.

John noted that the officer and most of the NCO's wore moustaches. These were not the generous and flowing growths of an earlier generation; all now had the small, neat, clipped and disciplined appearance of what he came to appreciate was a military moustache, army style. The Navy favoured full beards if facial hair was to be worn at all, and the strange new breed in that pubescent service known as the Royal Air Force had started to affect that eccentric facial accoutrement known as the handlebar moustache.

In a later lecture on poison gas and how to combat it, one dry old senior instructor had explained that military moustaches had become much smaller or had disappeared during the Great War due to the fact that the seal between the face and gas mask tended to be broken by a large growth of hair, and that death was often the result. He said: '"The Fly boys" don't seem to think that they will ever have to breath mustard gas up there in their wonderful machines, and even if they do it won't affect 'em as they seem to think they can walk on bloody water.' Mckinley formed the distinct impression that the Army's opinion of the most junior of the armed services was a very low one at that time.

Six antique wooden benches were set out in front of a small low stage. Everything was highly polished or seemed to smell of polish. The other distinct odour was one of excessive neatness and order; the place was so neat and orderly that the meticulous scent of it seemed to permeate the air. The benches were set out in perfect symmetry with exactly equidistant spacing. Their ends seemed to be lined up to the nearest sixteenth of an inch as far as he could tell. The same precision in spacing appeared to apply to the various photographs arranged around the walls and to the eager ranks displayed within them.

The Corporal left them saying that tea and biscuits would be arriving at half past one but they would have to amuse themselves for the next forty minutes or so. He turned and marched smartly out of the hall and back across the parade ground. Two other young men were in the hall and the three wandered to the corner in which they were stood. John said, 'I suppose you're here for the same reason as us. This is Arthur and the other one's Quiller. I'm, John, John Mckinley.'

The two youths introduced themselves as George and Walter. 'We're called Geordie and Walt,' they said in an accent which indicated they were from somewhere near Newcastle. 'We decided to join up together; we come from Middlesbrough.'

'Any particular reason?' asked John. They replied that they had worked in a brick works but were fed up of the constant layoffs and short time working.

'Pretty much the same as us,' said Quiller.

'We worked in the pits,' joined in Arthur.

At that moment the door opened again and eight or nine others were ushered into the room, by a private this time. The two groups eyed each other up for a few seconds until John said, 'We're all in the same boat; we might as well get to know who's who.' A round of introductions started with Mckinley carefully noting names, faces and attitudes. He was a firm believer in the expression that the first impression is often the best one.

A third group entered the hall and the escorting the private said: 'I wish you new recruits would all arrive together, it would save me an awful lot of marching about.'

The group had now swelled to more than twenty. Three or four were smoking nervously, and one was enjoying a pipe. The corporal arrived with another party of five men and then looked around. He barked out, 'Who gave you lot permission to smoke!' The faces of the smokers fell. The corporal smiled and said, 'Don't worry about it, but remember this: after the coming session you will only smoke if given permission to do so, or in designated recreational areas. You may look around you and notice that there is nowhere in this hall to deposit your cigarette ends; you might now like to work out where you will deposit them when you have finished. You certainly will not deposit them on this highly-polished floor.' This caused a look of consternation on the faces of the smokers. He went on: 'There is a sand bucket in the corridor through that door,' pointing to a side door, which led out into a glass covered walkway which led to the next building. There was a look of relief from the slaves of nicotine, but after that John noted that they hurriedly finished their smokes and went outside to get rid of the fag ends.

Two more men entered the room followed by the corporal who shouted: 'Silence!' The room fell still. He went on: 'Tea and biscuits will be served directly; you are now all here apart from one. Eat up smartly and visit the lavatory if you need to; the sergeant will be in to talk to you at fourteen hundred hours. That is two o' the clock to civvies, but you are soldiers now. In the army, we use a twenty-four-hour clock. If an attack is starting at six o'clock, we need to be very clear if we mean six am or six pm. It saves an awful lot of red faces if we call 'em 0600 hrs and 1800 hrs. You will be getting out of your comfy little bunks at 0600 hrs, and lights out will be at 2100 hrs. If you need assistance, it will be given by a cheery little army bugler who will play all sorts of nice tunes to help those of you who can't tell the time.'

He turned and marched smartly out of the room. A couple of minutes later a tea trolley was wheeled in with about three dozen mugs on it and a large urn, two jugs of milk and two tins containing sugar. Another followed it on which were placed two large trays; plain biscuits were heaped on one and slabs of brown cake on the other. One of the two Catering Corps' privates shouted, 'To get the tea, turn the spigot at the bottom! Help yourselves.' He then turned and left.

Mckinley had strategically positioned Arthur and Quiller near the door through which he was pretty sure the refreshments would enter. They were thus the first to serve themselves with tea, and each then grabbed a large chunk of the cake and a couple of biscuits. John said, 'Parkin; not bad,' and the three ate and drank heartily as the others queued to get their mugs filled.

At two pm, or 1400 hrs, the door swung open and in marched the corporal, a sergeant, and the Regimental Sergeant Major. The two junior NCOs were smart but the RSM stood as though he had a vertical steel rod inserted in his spine. He turned to the corporal and said, 'Get the men in order, Corporal Bell.' The corporal screamed: 'Silence!' and followed it with: 'Now arrange yourselves as smartly as possible in these benches, filling them from the front.' The group started to amble towards the seats. The corporal screamed, 'Do it now, not next week!' His shout caused a considerable acceleration amongst the group moving to be seated. Mckinley thought that there might be an awful lot of screaming during the coming weeks.

The RSM turned to the group and said in a quiet voice, 'In a short while I will turn you over to Sergeant Enderby to begin the process of turning you into the sort of soldier we want in the West Yorks. This is a very fine regiment, with a proud history, as you will see from the battle honours inscribed on the regimental colours. It is one of the very best regiments in the British army, if not *the* best. It is also one of the oldest. It was formed in 1685 and after that saw its first action in Flanders in 1693 under King William III. You will train together and I am sure become one of the very best of those troops which make up the regiment's B company. Train hard gentlemen, and try hard; if you do so we will try our very best for you.' He nodded to the sergeant: 'Take over, Sergeant Enderby,' he said, and marched out with a precision and smartness which struck Mckinley as being so near to perfection that it was almost as if the RSM was some sort of very finely tuned mechanical mechanism.

The sergeant said: 'We can't expect you to be smart at this stage but you will start your drilling tomorrow. You will be taught how to march. You will be taught how to salute. You will be taught how to address an NCO and how to address a Commissioned Officer. You will be taught how to wash, how to shave, and how to present yourselves smartly and to the standard which the army requires. You will be taught about army regulations and discipline. The RSM told you that if you try hard for us we will try hard for you. What he didn't tell you of course was what would happen if you did not try hard. All I can say, gentlemen, is if I were you I wouldn't want to find out.'

A murmur rippled through the ranks. The corporal screamed 'Silence!' Mckinley noted that he seemed to be very good at doing that.

The sergeant then said, 'Thank you, corporal.' He turned to the group and said, 'From now on I will be addressing you as troopers; you will never hear me use the term gentlemen again. From now on, keep silent until you are invited to speak.

I do not like muttering in the ranks. I usually find something very unpleasant to do to those who engage in this very ill-disciplined practice. The Army cannot have ill-discipline! The army will not have ill-discipline at any price! Get that simple fact very firmly in your minds.'

John was starting to get the picture. Cud and others had told him all about how the army worked, and had explained many of the pitfalls. On one occasion, Cud had told him: 'It's like this, one day the army might want you to run at a trench in which there are people who are firing a machine gun at you and throwing grenades in your direction. Your natural instincts would make you very reluctant to do that because you might think you might be killed.

'The army instils discipline at every turn, and from the moment you get in, so that if ordered to do something which your instincts tell you is not a very good idea, you will still obey the order. In a few cases the instincts overcome the training and leave someone cowering at the bottom of a dugout.'

'What happens then?' said Mckinley.

'Oh, the military police shoot them,' Cud replied. 'The choice was: will be killed, or might be killed or wounded; most men saw the sense of it and went over the top.'

The sergeant explained about meal times and gave a brief explanation about training. He said, 'Before I turn you over to Corporal Bell to get kitted out, I will take any "sensible" questions, but before you ask let me speak about leave. You will stay on camp until we think you are smart enough to be seen off it in uniform. I always feel that explaining that simple fact to new recruits tends to make 'em try very hard to become very smart as soon as they can. When you pass out, and by that I mean that you will have completed your basic training in a satisfactory manner, you will get a weekend's leave. For the first few weeks, you will find your entertainment inside these walls. We have a film on Saturday evenings and there is a library. Magazines, cigarettes and beer are to be had at the NAAFI. Their canteen holds a snooker table and you can play ping-pong.

'For those keen on sport, Wednesday and Saturday afternoons are given over to sport. We have regimental rugby and football teams, and a boxing team. We have access to a swimming pool and you will learn to swim. You can train with barbells and Indian clubs in the gymnasium and one of the sergeants is trying to get an amateur wrestling team started. Now, if you have any questions put your hand up and state your name.' One hand went up. 'Name,' said the sergeant.

'Albert,' said the unfortunate questioner.

'Your surname,' screamed the NCO. 'I'm your sergeant not your bleeding maiden aunt.'

'Smurthwaite,' said the eager recruit. 'Well,' he said, 'I was wondering how long it would be before we got to shoot a rifle.'

The sergeant took a deep breath. 'Never,' he said. Smurthwaite looked crestfallen.

'Never?' he repeated.

'Never,' said his tormentor. 'Very dangerous things, rifles, especially the loaded ones. We never shoot a rifle! We shoot the bleeding enemy! You fire a rifle! Is that clear Smurthwaite?'

'Yes,' said the woebegone one.

'Yes what!' screamed the NCO.

'Yes sir,' replied the startled Smurf.

'Yes *Sergeant*,' screamed the red-faced NCO. 'You only use sir when addressing a commissioned officer, is that clear?'

'Yes,' said the harassed Smurf.

'Yes, Sergeant!' screamed the NCO.

'Yes, Sergeant,' said the victim.

Enderby looked to the heavens. 'Gawd give me strength,' he said. 'Any other "sensible" questions?'

Unsurprisingly, there were none.

Mckinley could tell that quite a few in the troop were struggling to repress smiles or chuckles. He kept his face perfectly straight, knowing that the unfortunate Albert had served Enderby's purposes perfectly. If the group had been given instructions on how to address officers and NCOs it would have gone in one ear and out of the other as far as some were concerned, but now all of them would remember, especially the unfortunate Albert.

The next step was to have the troop kitted out. They were marched to the stores where the quartermaster sergeant and his men issued kit bags, boots, belts, gaiters, greatcoats, caps, mess kits, and the 1922 Pattern Service Dress—serge. Serge was a cheap thick woollen material and the uniform was dyed khaki. Service Dress was a five-buttoned jacket with four large pockets; it had been introduced in 1902 to replace the traditional red coat of the British infantry soldier. The design, which was relatively tight fitting, had been adopted more with a regard to looking smart on parade than to functionality. Although the 1937 battledress had just been introduced, this was not yet available for the West Yorks Regiment.

The troop were then marched to the large barrack room which would be their home for the next few months. There were thirty-two beds in the room, each with a metal locker at its side. Enderby said, 'Right, you lot. Lay your kit out on your bed according to the diagram on this sheet of paper. Take your time, do it right, and try to remember it. Every time there is a kit inspection you will be expected to lay your kit out for inspection very neatly, as per the diagram. Don't worry, you will get plenty of practice.' He had brought four troopers with him and they showed the new recruits how to fold and stack the clothes and lay out the mess kit, boots, shoe brushes, etc. 'Right,' he said. 'Check it and make sure nothing is missing.' A few items, inevitably, were missing, and the NCO sent one of the troopers off to the stores with a list to obtain them. Once these additions had been made, he walked down the beds looking at the various attempts and making a mental note of the smarter and not so smart layouts.

He then issued the order for the men to get out of their civvies and into uniform. After the civilian clothes were stowed at the back of the locker, he said, 'I can now report to the officer that you are all fully kitted and ready to commence training. From this point on you will wear your uniform. You will learn to keep your uniform very tidy and presentable. From this moment, you are responsible for all your items of kit. If any go missing, replacements will be provided, but you will pay for them. Look after your kit. Stow it in the lockers as indicated in the diagram.'

Mckinley had been paying attention to what had been said very acutely, and he knew that sloppiness could result in sanctions by the NCOs. If the troopers were sloppy, the officers would have a go at the NCOs, who would then visit their ire on those responsible. He had made a mental note of the required positions of his equipment and in which order they were stacked. He realised that correct folding would take a little work but he would make sure that Arthur and Quiller went through it with him until all were very proficient at the task.

Enderby then said, 'As we have some time to fill, Corporal Bell will now spend it teaching you how to come to attention, how to stand at ease, how to salute and how to march. Your proper training in that will start at 0700hrs on the parade ground tomorrow.'

The corporal then went through the basics for more than half an hour with the men stood at the foot of their beds stamping down to attention and trying to achieve what they thought was a snappy salute and standing at ease. The corporal said, 'When you can do this properly, we will let you loose on an officer. I am sure he will be totally amazed by your efforts.' He had one of the troopers march up and down between the rows and said, 'Look at him; head erect, back straight, left foot swings forward at the same time as the right arm.' After that, he marched them back to the drill hall. The heavy wooden benches had miraculously disappeared and the group were made to march up and down the hall and shown how to do an about-turn.

One trooper had difficulties in that his left arm always wanted to move forward in unison with his left foot and right arm with right foot. He did it several times despite being bawled out by the corporal. Eventually the troop were stood at ease while the unfortunate Albert was marched up and down in front of them until he was sweating profusely, being stopped and started and told to always start on his left foot and at the same time swing his right hand forward. Eventually he started to get it right.

The corporal glared at him and said: 'You'd better think about this one, son, and make sure that you get your various limbs working in order and in army fashion. We can't have twenty-nine of the troop marching left right, left right, and you marching left, left, right, right; the RSM will get very annoyed if you do.' He then stepped very close to Albert's face and said, 'The very last thing in the world that you want to see is the RSM when he's very annoyed. Is that clear trooper?'

'Yes, sir,' said the panicking Albert.

'Yes, *Corporal!*' Bell screamed at him.

Bell said: 'It's about a quarter to six now, so I'm going to march you lot across to the mess hall so that you can sample the wonderful cooking of our head chef. I am sure he will have prepared something very special just for you to celebrate your arrival here. After that, you have a couple of hour's free time and you can visit the mess for a pint or two before lights out. I am assigning trooper Brooks here to accompany you and keep you out of mischief. He will bring you back to your luxurious bedroom before lights out and the sergeant may have some last words. He might even tuck you in and kiss you goodnight and wish you sweet dreams before he leaves you to get your kip.'

The group of fresh recruits were marched across to the mess hall, which was a long building with about twenty tables and benches on either side that sat ten men each. They were the first to arrive and as the food was not quite ready the group were told to get a mug of tea each and then queue for the grub. The trooper leading them said to the catering private, who was getting a large urn of mashed potatoes ready for serving, 'I've brought the new troop across, try not to poison 'em; the sarge will be very upset if you do.' The trooper was told to fluck off! Or something sounding very similar.

After a couple more minutes, the food was ready and the catering private shouted: 'Right!' An unenthusiastic lance corporal had emerged and the two rapidly dished the food out to the waiting men. The meal consisted of corned beef stew with peas, mashed potatoes, and a lump of sultana pudding with custard that the trooper described as 'spotted dick'. Other men came into the hall in dribs and drabs until it was about a third full.

Mckinley said to the trooper, 'I expected more than this.'

Their guide said, 'Yes, something's afoot. Most of the top brass are down in London and everyone that can be spared is off getting their back-leave in. I expect the barracks will be back to normal by the beginning of May.'

The catering corps lance corporal shouted: 'Seconds, anybody?' and the chaperoning trooper said, 'Come on,' and led a wave of the men who had got out of their seats with him to the front of the queue. John was third in the line followed by Arthur and Quiller. All took a further lump of the spotted dick. Although the meal had been filling, John reasoned that the training would be energetic and he knew from his underground experiences that lots of food would be essential. The group gravitated over to the mess building after the meal and the three had a couple of pints whilst sitting to one side and sizing up the rest of the troop.

They were led back to the barrack room at eight-forty-five and the sergeant came in and did a head count. 'Nobody's deserted, then,' he said. 'It can't be all that bad.' His final comments were, 'OK, lights out in a few minutes. If you need to go, go now, and I will be seeing you early tomorrow morning. Very early.'

17

Mckinley Becomes a Soldier of the King

The 'eathen in 'is blindness must end where 'e began,
But the backbone of the Army
Is the Non-commissioned man!

Rudyard Kipling

John slept remarkably well considering the strangeness of his bed and surrounds. He was awoken by a bugle and started to get dressed. After a couple of minutes, Corporal Bell rushed in, shouting, 'Come on; look lively you 'orrible lot!' The troop dressed, grumbling as they did so, and were marched out onto the parade ground. They spent almost an hour being drilled in the basics of marching and in saluting and were then marched back to the barracks for what were described as ablutions. This was for strip washing and shaving at the many washbasins with wall-mounted mirrors in the lavatory block.

A breakfast of porridge followed by boiled eggs with bread and margarine and a large mug of tea was an acceptable start to the day, Mckinley thought. He could hear some more grumbles from some of the other recruits about the food and especially about the time at which they were expected to rise. The trio from the mines just smiled at this, as they were very used to getting out of bed at that time or much earlier. John had started to size up the rest of the troop. He had exchanged words with a couple of lads called Travis and Wild who were from Hull. They had done some work on the trawlers and like many of the families from that city had been brought up as hard as nails. John thought that they were all right and later found that one of them had thumped one of the skippers in a row about money and after that had found it hard to get work. The two were no nonsense types, loyal, and with a distinct sense of right and wrong.

About a dozen of the intake had evidently been unemployed or had been in part-time or short-time work since they had left school. Four of the group were very young and had joined the army as soon as they were able, in search of adventure or perhaps to escape from home. There was, of course, 'the unfortunate Albert,' who had worked on the railways and had tired of the low pay and tedium of the hard physical work involved in maintaining the track. Of the remaining eight, four looked as though they were unused to physical work.

It transpired that two were domestic servants who had been 'let go' due to the falling incomes of their employers. One was a furniture salesman and another had worked in a pawnshop. One recruit created no sort of impression whatsoever but Mckinley's antennae sensed that the remaining three were problem cases and would bear watching. He made a mental note of the names of all of the troopers and started to call all of them by their first names apart from those three, Brenner, Burns and Collins. The BBC, he thought: probably bent, barmy and crooked.

After breakfast, there was another long session of square bashing and saluting practice. After a while the ex-furniture salesman who considered himself a bit of a wag ventured to say that his elbow was getting tired as a result of all of the snapping his arm up and down. Enderby marched him out to the front and explained, in that kindly manner which only sergeants in the service of his Majesty the King are capable of, that saluting was very, very, important. 'Some time very soon I am going to have to let you do one of these near an officer, and when I do you will salute him very smartly, is that clear?'

'Yes, Sergeant,' said 'Sales.'

'Good,' said the sarge. 'Now just show the rest of the troop how smartly you can salute. Show me... now do it again... and once more... Hmmmm,' said the sarge, 'I don't think you've quite got it, do it again... and again. Mmmm, I think you're getting there; just do it again three or four times more so that I am absolutely sure.'

Most of the rest of the troop once again struggled to suppress smirks as Enderby tortured the unfortunate comedian. Later that night in the NAAFI, John overheard Wild saying: 'He better not try that on me.' John waited until they were alone and explained to the troop's hothead that it wasn't personal and it was all part of instilling discipline. 'You can't have someone in the army give an order and then get mocked. It undermines authority. You can see that, can't you?'

Wild was not stupid, he was just hot-tempered and could see it fine now that it had been spelled out to him. John said, 'Just grit your teeth and keep your gob shut if anything like that happens to you. If you do what you are told, smartly, they will never get the chance. If you lose your temper and the sarge loses some teeth, you'll do six months in the Glass House and then get kicked out of the army with a dishonourable discharge and you'll never work again.'

Wild said, 'Oh, I never realised that.' After the talk he, like Arthur and Quiller, and also Travis to a certain extent, would follow Mckinley's lead when difficulties arose. After that, although John could see Wild colouring up in anger from time to time, the ex-trawlerman always managed to bottle it up, especially if John managed to catch his eye, and he eventually passed out as one of the best in the troop.

Halfway through the morning there was a tea break, again with biscuits. John had noted that slightly more than half of the group were smokers and that a top priority with those, and especially after food, was to satisfy their craving for nicotine. This seemed to be the established order of things with smoke breaks being an accepted part of any stoppage. He could also see that Collins especially was heavily into it, lighting up as soon as he got a chance and taking very frequent drags at the cigarette. If he got the chance, he would light a second, when the other troopers seemed quite happy to enjoy a single smoke. Mckinley noted later that during sporting activities or P.T. it was always the smokers who seemed to be the first to get out of breath.

There followed even more square bashing and saluting. John and a few others were now completing actions such as 'About Turn,' by numbers, or 'Quick March,' smartly and almost without having to think about it. The unfortunate Albert and a couple of others were clearly struggling. John thought that in the case of those two it was probably due to lack of physical fitness, but in Albert's case there was something deeper involved.

A lunch followed, with the food served once again being filling yet inexpensive and from a culinary point of view uninspiring. At two o'clock the troop were marched across to the drill hall and stood to attention. The sergeant made it very clear that there would be no talking in the ranks. He told the troop to stand at ease and marched off smartly through the double doors. He returned escorting a young man who wore the single pip of a second lieutenant.

Enderby screamed at the group as he entered the room: 'ATTEN–TION!' The entire group, perhaps catching the note of urgency in their sergeant's voice, complied very smartly, obeying the order, even the unfortunate Albert. Mckinley realised that the young man walking in must be about the same age as himself. He appeared to be a rather serious type, a little less than six feet in height and slim, but with a sort of wiry build and lean look, which told anyone who was bright enough to read the signals that the young man was a sportsman of some kind.

He asked the sergeant to stand the men at ease, which he did, while watching the whole group as though he was some sort of hovering falcon who was about to swoop and gobble

278

up any who did not stand smartly. When the troop was at ease, the young man, whose name was Algernon Tasburgh, began to speak. The totally cut glass accent of the man fell strangely on John's ears. He had heard people on the BBC speak like it, and Dr Whyte, of course, at the prize giving ceremonies back at school.

Sharpe, and virtually everyone else working for the local authority or in any other official capacity whether in mining or within the local authority or elsewhere within the town, spoke with a correct, polite northern accent, which did not dip into the local dialect shortcuts, and with the aitches always pronounced. It was a clear and confident voice. The man might be young thought John but he was clearly used to giving orders and having them obeyed. It was also clear from what is now known as body language that the NCOs held the Lieutenant in considerable respect.

The young man started to speak, welcoming them into the regiment and making clear that he was their troop Commander. There followed advice about the strangeness of it all and his expectations of them. He followed that with some measured and obviously proud words about the regimental history and battle honours. He said, 'It has probably been explained to you that our regimental motto means "difficulties do not deter". This is well illustrated by the fact that the Regiment, up to now, has been awarded six Victoria Crosses. They represent a fine tradition which I expect members of my troop to uphold.' His final words were: 'Listen to your NCOs, all of them are very experienced. If you want to get the very best out of the army, allow them to get the very best out of you!'

He turned to the NCO and said, 'Carry on, sergeant.' The older man snapped to attention, threw the younger man a very smart salute and then turned to the troop and screamed, 'Attention!' The men obliged and the officer strode off smartly and out through the doors of the drill-hall. The sergeant was pleased that the troop had performed reasonably well. He knew that with the indications that he had, even at this early stage, he was confident that in a few weeks his troop would be very smart, very smart indeed, except perhaps for one of them.

Mckinley learned later that the lieutenant was from one of the local landed families, and had recently come into the regiment via Sandhurst and Cambridge. He was the youngest son of five and could thus expect little in the way of an inheritance, and for this reason he had decided on an Army career. The family apparently had long associations with the regiment and the young Tasburgh engendered considerable respect by virtue of this and by being one of the University's athletics' blues.

In the following days the troop settled into the routine of practicing to march smartly and salute. Weapons training was gradually introduced and the young soldiers were shown the Short Magazine Lee Enfield Mark III rifle, otherwise, puzzlingly, known as rifle number one. The sergeant instructor explained that there was a modified version known as rifle number four Mark 1, which had been about since a 1926 redesign. He explained, looking up at the heavens for some sort of divine guidance as he did so, that he expected that the regiment would be getting them any year now.

The sergeant was called Len Housley and he seemed to Mckinley to be just a little on the obsessive side when it came to small arms. He had run into engineers who had similar characteristics in the mining industry. They talked about engineering at work and during leisure. If they had hobbies, they invariably involved engineering. The other NCOs tended to avoid him and one had remarked in an unguarded moment, 'Old Housley, he can spew small arms specifications like other people spew diarrhoea. The only difference is that after a few days they usually stop, but he never does.'

However, John thought that mastery of the basic tools of a soldier's trade was essential, and for that reason he gave what the older man said his very best attention; listening carefully as he described the wonders of the weapon. He learned that the Mark 1 was a compromise between the shorter carbine carried by the cavalry and artillerymen and the longer rifle which had previously been used by the infantry. It thus became the standard weapon used by the whole army. It had a 25 and one fifth inch barrel and used a ten-round magazine filled with .303 cartridges. Housley waxed lyrically about the bolt mechanism which, he said, was of ingenious design. Because of the way the bolt was locked by lugs at its rear, he said this rifle had the fastest bolt action of any rifle in service anywhere in the world. A trained man could fire up to thirty aimed rounds in a minute with it. He went on: 'I suppose you have all heard about the battle of Agincourt:

Once more into the breach dear friends, once more: or close the wall up with our English dead.

'That's Shakespeare, telling us about Henry V, urging his men to one last attack. Very poetic. If it comes to it, you're much more likely to get the RSM screaming some much less poetic words, urgently, in your direction. If it gets really hot, he might even be profane!'

Housley paused and looked around with amusement on his face to see if they were getting his joke. He could see by the glint in Mckinley's and some of the other's eyes that some of them at least had the wit to be appreciative. He went on: 'At that battle, in 1415, which if my arithmetic is correct was more than five hundred years ago, Henry V, with a force of ten thousand men, which included about eight thousand English archers, faced a force of sixty-six thousand French. Some claim that we lost twenty-five rankers and four officers, and the French more than ten thousand. This was due to the devastating rate of fire of our bowmen. Some authorities seem to think that between them they could fire twenty-seven thousand arrows a minute. Think about it! It took nearly five hundred years but we now have a weapon that can fire faster than they did. The big difference is that the army expects you to do a lot more damage with an aimed .303 slug than they could manage with un-aimed arrows fired from the longbow.'

He stripped the rifle down with what seemed to be loving care, explaining each part of the mechanism to them and how it interacted with the others and what to do in the case of blockages and the vital importance of keeping the Mark III clean. He put the rifle back together and stripped it down again but a little faster this time. 'Are you all getting this?' he asked. Some of those present murmured faint affirmations, but Mckinley remained silent, although his eyes had been fixed on every action that Housley had carried out, and he had logged the sequence of moves needed to dismantle and reassemble the beast.

The next part of the exercise involved each man being issued with a weapon for drill and practice purposes. The NCO said, 'Right-ho! I want all of you to attempt the dismantling.' John did this rapidly and easily. The Sergeant circulated, looking down at the various parts and making sure they were arranged in the prescribed order. He said: 'Fine, I want you all to start from the top. Let's see if you can put them back together. When you've finished, put the weapon down and snap to attention.' John was easily first to do so and this earned him a look of intense interest from the instructor.

About half a dozen had not managed the reassembly and the Sergeant patiently circulated, explaining to each what he needed to do. He said: 'Alright, we'll do it a couple more times, but by the end of the week I expect you to be getting it correct; a couple of weeks after that I expect you to be able to do it in your sleep. If you don't, I can always arrange some extra sessions during the evenings. I am sure you would rather be doing that anyway, rather than swilling beer down at the NAAFI.' He usually found that the threat was sufficient incentive to make all recruits pay attention and rapidly become proficient in the vital exercise of taking a rifle apart and putting it together again.

In the weeks following, the troop learned the wonders of the No1, Mark 1 bayonet, the type 36 Mills grenade, the Lewis Gun and the newly arrived Bren Gun Mark 1. The men were allowed to familiarise themselves with all of them, both on and off the firing range. Mckinley paid considerable attention to everything he was told, on the basis that these were the basic tools of his trade. He felt that a firm grasp of all aspects of these weapons could be a lifesaver if a war ever did start again. The only surprise during that stage was during grenade training, in which they were given un-fused grenades to practice with. 'The unfortunate Albert' delivered the surprise.

The troop were told to lob the grenades as far as they could on a range which Housley had arranged to be marked with lines made with football field line whitener at one yard intervals starting at 25 yards. This was an innovation of his own and he was rather proud of it. He knew that a type thirty-six could usually be lobbed between thirty and forty yards. The miners and two Hull lads easily lobbed the grenades, which weighed one pound and eleven ounces, well past the thirty-yard mark. About four of the troop couldn't make that line. However, Albert flung the grenade in a long arc, which easily exceeded forty-five yards. Housley's mouth dropped open after seeing it. He instructed Albert to throw a second grenade to see if the first throw was a fluke; again, it ended yards beyond all the others. He had seen the forty-yard mark exceeded occasionally but he had never seen a grenade flung as far as this trooper had. He made a mental note: Albert (Grenades)! After that, Albert found the other NCOs seemed to give him a little more leeway if he was slow or made his usual errors.

It was explained that the type 36 grenade was primarily a defensive weapon and was usually deployed during attacks by the enemy. Housley said to the troop: 'By the feel of it you may think it's made of steel, but steel is very tough, it doesn't break easily; that's why the mark one bayonet is made of steel! This grenade case is made of cast iron, which you could smash, if you tried, with a sledgehammer. The indentations in the body mean that the grenade shatters along them and throws off dozens of fragments, which are nearly as much danger to the thrower as to the enemy. Thus, if you lob a live grenade it must be from cover. If you ever need to throw one standing, my advice is to hit the deck immediately afterwards, preferably with your helmet facing it. You have between four and seven seconds, with a standard fuse, before the thing detonates. Treat the type thirty-six and all other weapons with a great deal of respect, they are designed to kill people; if you are careless with them they might just kill you!'

Mckinley had much less time for some of the rest of the six weeks basic training, which was designed from the army's point of view to produce troops who would obey orders without too much thought or without any thought at all. It was thought that their effectiveness in action would depend on command structures and not on individuality or on innovatory use of weapons. Thus, the Troop endured the drudgery of Squad drill, Platoon drill and Company and Ceremonial drills. Mckinley saw real value in the field signals, field drills and field craft and other exercises in which they learned to judge distances and how to lay down various patterns of rifle fire. He absorbed these like a sponge.

The Troop were shown training films and subjected to various lectures on regimental history, the history of the British Army, map reading, elementary tactics, and so on. They were shown propaganda films that reinforced the notion of a great and invincible Empire and the racial and weapons inferiority of any potential enemies. The rather pallid and godly Padre who gave a lecture entitled 'Moral Turpitude and its Consequences' provided the only light amusement.

His message was supposed to aid the army in combating the venereal disease, which during the Great War had affected about one man in five. The padre was struggling from the start in his quest to save the group of young and lusty young men from 'the Wages of Sin' by his inability to say the word 'sex' or any other word connected with it. Injunctions to avoid 'women of doubtful reputation' just did not have the same impact as, 'avoid those juicy whores, they may look inviting but you will regret it! They can give you some very nasty diseases!' Many of the padre's other vague and euphemistic references to 'the pleasures of the flesh' and to 'fallen women,' left many of the Troop slightly confused.

A subsequent lecture by the dry old Scottish medical officer, who explained the symptoms and consequences of contracting gonorrhoea and syphilis in a very laconic and matter of fact and yet very graphic manner, had the right effect. This was done with the aid of some revolting photographs of badly affected organs and of victims in the late stages of the diseases, and even with photographs from autopsies. He was very forthright about some of the very painful treatments involved in unblocking inflamed urethras and the like and was gratified when he saw that some of the men were wincing at the prospect.

Unusually, he spoke to the troop on an almost casual, man-to-man basis, rather than on the very stiff, officer to man manner that they were accustomed to, and this went down very well with them. He finished off with the words: 'You will find yourselves in situations where you haven't been near a woman for months, and afterwards on leave in those dubious places which are to be found throughout the Empire, where nubile young ladies will offer you sexual pleasures for a small fee. My advice is just to get drunk and avoid those pox-ridden tarts at all costs! If you must indulge, do wear a French letter; these provide a physical barrier to the infection being passed to you. If you catch anything, it is of course an offence in the army; they regard getting the pox in the same way as damaging yourself with a self-inflicted injury.'

The M.O. had been in the army for more than twenty years and knew that, inevitably, some of them would fall through the safety net he had tried to construct. He also knew very well that this was much more for the benefit of the Army than its young recruits, due to a desire to have them maintained in a fully functioning manner. Even so, he found the sexually transmitted diseases to be unpleasant and had experience of certain cases of them being fatal. Thus, he would prefer to deal with as few of them as possible. Later that evening, Mckinley and a lot of the troop had rather more than their usual three or four pints of beer. After all, they were now nearing the end of their basic training and had been living a monastic life during which all had become very physically fit. After five pints, Arthur said, 'Shall we have another?' John said: 'Yes, we've had advice from one of the best doctors in the army and he told us to get drunk. We'd better obey orders.'

After the basic training finally finished the troop had a small passing out parade, but due to the absence of most of the regiment it was a very low key affair with the salute being taken by a lowly captain, who was the most senior officer available. After that, the group were granted the customary leave and allowed to travel home, with the stipulation that they should travel back home in uniform. The three Doncaster boys did so, as did the others, all with a certain amount of swagger and arrogance due to their newfound smartness and the status of being privates in the West Yorkshire Regiment.

After they got back home, John and the boys did the rounds of the various pubs in Doncaster. In doing so, John discovered that certain women seemed to be looking at the men who were now in uniform with more interest than he had previously experienced. In a couple of pubs he noted that landlords were now unwelcoming and made remarks such as, 'We don't want any trouble here lads, do we?' They seemed uneasy to have the troopers on their premises. It had escaped John's notice previously but it seemed that soldiers had a tendency to indulge in fisticuffs, especially if some loud mouth tried to take a rise out of them or be sarcastic about the uniform. Some pubs, and it tended to be the posher ones such as the Danum, had an unstated policy of discouraging men in uniform from drinking there. The experience brought to his mind another of Kipling's Barrack Room ballads entitled Tommy:

I went into a public 'ouse to get a pint o' beer,
The publican 'e up an' sez, "We serve no red-coats here."
The girls be'ind the bar they laughed an' giggled fit to die,
I outs into the street again and to myself sez I:

O it's Tommy this, an' Tommy that, an "Tommy go away";
But it's "Thank you, Mister Atkins," when the band begins
to play...

...For it's Tommy this, an' Tommy that, an' "Chuck 'im out,
the brute!"
But it's "Saviour of 'is country," when the guns begin to
shoot...

Although the era that the poet had been writing about was the nineteenth century, or at its turn, the experience left John under no illusions as to what he could expect whilst in uniform, at least in peacetime!

He and the boys made a point of calling in at the Black Bull to see Mae and reassure her that he was all right. Mckinley noted a change in her attitude, which had turned from that of a grateful and worldly-wise friend to one of almost maternal concern.

They went on to the Wellington Arms to fulfil the promise to Uncle Bill. The old RSM evinced considerable pride at their presence in the pub, and that in turn made them stand a little more erect and try to insist that they would pay. Bill would have none of it. 'While you're here, boys, the drinks are on me.' He made light of the matter, saying: 'You boys are on a private's pay. I've got my army pension and a good living out of these thirsty foundry men on top.'

He went on: 'And when you're on leave make sure you come here and see me. I know a bit about human nature and you three might not want to come 'cos you're not paying. Make sure you do, though. You can tell me what's happening in the army and that will be royal payment for me, surrounded as I am by big, daft, thirsty labourers!' His voice had been raised deliberately in making the comment so that the half dozen foundry men in the pub could hear him. They returned the comment with good-natured banter, advising him to sod off down to Chelsea and join 'the Pensioners' and similar. Here was a group who could not care less about soldiers and possible punch ups; they were a rough crowd and would probably have welcomed a fight as light entertainment.

Mckinley tried to stay away from home as much as possible during his leave; he knew that he would have to face an overly concerned and anxious mother there, which he did not want. At the club, Cud made him go through the main points of his training, most of the time nodding but occasionally chipping in with a bit of advice about cleaning kit or drills. He was particularly interested in the new Bren gun. He had experience of the older Lewis light machine gun during the Great War and knew very well that it had a large range of possible malfunctions and stoppages.

He said to John, 'How do you find it?' John replied that it was lighter and easier to carry than the Lewis gun and that his sergeant had been sent on the first course run for army instructors and had seemed very impressed. 'He seems to think it is a lot more reliable than the Lewis and is impressed by how accurate it is and how easy it can be stripped and assembled.' He laughed and said, 'Even Albert can do it.'

'Who's that?' asked Cud.

'Oh! Albert Smurthwaite, he's the squad's thickest recruit. If he wasn't so good at throwing grenades, they might have had him out during training.'

Cud mused: 'It's a lot like being down the pit in the army! I found that it was the ones that were not too sharp who seemed to be the ones that always got picked off by snipers or who were too slow getting their mask on in a gas attack. I wouldn't get too pally with the bloke; in action he might be a liability.'

Mckinley laughed the remark off but he knew there was a deadly seriousness underlying his stepfather's concern.

*

The leave passed all too quickly, and soon the troop reassembled at the barracks. The place was much fuller than when they had first arrived and something was obviously afoot. The officers were unusually active and the NCOs were scurrying about like blue-arsed flies. The rumour in the NAAFI bar that night was that the Colonel was expected back from London in about a fortnight and something big was likely to happen. 'The troop' were now fully-fledged private soldiers of the king and although treated as green new-boys by some, generally those from the other squads treated them on the basis of how they performed during working hours and socially. The embargo on leaving camp was now lifted and information was forthcoming about the best pubs in the area and of those best avoided. Mckinley noted that Brenner seemed particularly interested in where the local whores could be located, but most of the rest seemed to be interested in drinking or finding out where local dances were so they could meet a nicer class of girl.

At one such dance Albert had words with John about girls, bemoaning the fact that he could never get them to dance or if he did they rapidly showed lack of interest in him soon after. He said, 'I just don't know what's wrong. If you walk up to them you have 'em giggling and friendly in no time but I seem to get tongue-tied and they walk off.'

John tried to explain the subtle art of 'the chat up,' to his comrade in arms but knew that he was probably wasting his time. He said, 'This is the important thing, Albert: you have to talk to them, it doesn't have to be deep, it doesn't even have to make sense, you can say virtually anything, just be lively and show that you like 'em.'

He, Quiller and Arthur relaxed with a drink and watched as Albert, now fully instructed in the sweet-talking arts, tried to make headway. Eventually, he persuaded a large and plain lass from one of the sweet factories in York to take to the floor for a waltz. After it ended, Albert stood there and they could tell that he was straining in an effort to find some appropriate endearment. After what seemed an age, during which the girl seemed to be on the point of drifting off, Albert stuttered and said the first and only thing that came into his head: 'Tha dun't sweat much for a big lass!' The girl glared at him and went back to her friend at the other side of the room.

The three spluttered into helpless laughter. Later on, the woebegone Albert said to Mckinley, 'But you said I could say virtually anything!'

John smiled and said, 'I will sort out some lines for you Albert. 'A good one is, that's a nice dress, it really suits you! Do you think you can remember it? After that, ask her where she's from and if she has a boyfriend. Don't talk about yourself unless she asks you.'

Life back at the Barracks settled into routine. Mckinley realised that the Army liked routine and did not like people or events that disturbed it. Thus, as a troop they were now assigned regimental duties according to the normal rotation, with the pressure of intensive squad drill lifted from their shoulders. Just enough was done to keep the men smart. Much more P.T. or physical training was now introduced and two afternoons a week were devoted to sport. John, Quiller and Arthur were heavier and more muscular than most due to their experiences shovelling twenty tons of coal on hot and cramped coalfaces. They would have fitted into the rugby team, but it was Rugby Union and they had all played some amateur Rugby League, which was hugely frowned on by most of the officers as an inferior game played by 'paid' professionals, and were technically barred from playing by the Union code which then disqualified anyone from joining its ranks if they had played League. All of them could have made passable backs in the soccer teams but John persuaded his pals to choose boxing, on the basis that, 'it might be useful in our game.'

The choice was fortunate in that the senior PTI in charge of the noble art had been a noted amateur wrestler in his youth and was keen to impart his skills to those who were interested. They had all observed the junior PTI was a lance corporal of about forty who had been involved in more than three hundred boxing contests. He had been a mainstay of the army team, which always put on a good showing during the Inter-services and regional and national Amateur Boxing Association matches. John could see a sort of blankness in the man's stare, and slowness in grasping the point of a question. This was combined with short temperedness if he was pressured. This all led John to think that he had possibly endured more punches than were good for him. The man was certainly not 'Punchy', which was the slang term for the punch drunkenness which was sometimes seen in those boxers who had become brain damaged by too many blows to the head; but his example was disconcerting to those contemplating participation in 'the noble art'.

Thus, after some basic boxing training during which Mckinley was careful to disguise those skills he had picked up back in the village boxing club with the Thompson brothers, John and his two pals gravitated towards wrestling. Sergeant Budd, their instructor, was Cornish by extraction and had done some Cornish wrestling as a youth before moving over to free-style, or catch-as-catch-can as it was more generally known.

Budd was another of the army's surprises. Like Housley who seemed to know everything about small arms, the PTI sergeant was very competent in gymnastics and could instruct superbly in boxing, football, rugby and hockey, but his real love was wrestling. He had managed to secure a rather spacious attic space above the stores and had installed a makeshift wrestling mat made of canvas stretched tight over wood shavings. The construction was unorthodox but very effective at enabling the men to take a fall without damaging themselves. He had managed to gather about a dozen acolytes together and had hopes that one particularly promising lad would do well in the regional championships.

The basic methods of breaking falls by absorbing the force

291

by making sure that the arms or legs reached the canvas first were imparted to the newcomers, and then the major throws or takedowns were taught. As Budd explained: 'In England there are several forms of wrestling. It's particularly strong in Cumbria and Lancashire and in Cornwall. The styles are all a little different and in Cornwall stiff canvas jackets are worn, 'a little like what these Ju-Jitsu wallahs wear in Japan,' he explained. 'The jacket gives you more purchase when you get hold and you have more chance of throwing your opponent in that style than in the others because of it.

'Internationally there are two styles, the Graeco-Roman where you can only take hold above the waist. That's very ancient and is the style used in the Olympics. In the free-style, which I teach, you can throw with waist and shoulder or arm holds and you can take 'em down by catching any part of the legs or tripping with the legs. If you were really good you could try for the next Olympic team,' he said laughingly.

'Where's that then, sarge?' asked Arthur.

'The one in 1940 is scheduled for Tokyo,' was the reply. 'It will be interesting to find how the Japs go on against the East European and Persian and Indian wrestlers.'

'Are they any good?' asked one of the others with a note of surprise in his voice.

'Some of the best in the world,' came the reply. 'It's one of their national sports, they've got thousands of clubs. In England it's just a few dozen.'

Budd was extremely knowledgeable about his favourite sport and was always pushing to find a champion, but John and the boys enjoyed it for its own sake and were interested in absorbing the useful skills without pushing themselves to the sort of extremes needed to become competition winners. They found that even with their mining backgrounds they all became more muscular around their arms and shoulders and all went up a waist size in trousers. The Cornishman laughed when he heard them talking about it, saying, 'Don't worry about it, boys. All wrestlers build up a thick muscular mid-section, that's where most of the strain is felt when you are trying to throw or hold somebody down. A lot of the wrestler's strength is in the trunk. You'll have to trade that in against losing your chances of ever becoming male models or ballroom dancers.'

The two Hull men had chosen boxing as their sport and lots of the training was done in common. Rope work for fleetness of foot and endurance, and work with dumbbells and Indian clubs for upper body strength. The five drank together as a group and were thought to be the hard men of the platoon. No one was going to mess with them if they had any sense. All five agreed that one real bonus of their afternoon pursuits was that they stayed warm and dry whilst the rugger, hockey and soccer players often came in after their exertions drenched and covered in mud.

For various reasons, the Colonel was delayed and did not arrive back at the Regimental HQ until late July. The initial bustling about by NCOs had slackened but now it redoubled and tended to be fiercely loud when commands were given to the men, especially if officers were anywhere near. Housley became rather obsessive about kit inspections and made absolutely sure that everything was in order as far as his troop were concerned. As Bell explained: 'The CO's a stickler for it; although he's not very likely to carry out a kit inspection, if he does and he's not happy with it there will be hell to pay. Housley will be in the bad books 'an he'll take it out on me, 'an I'll bloody well take it out on you lot. So just be sure everything's right.' On the quiet he had a word with John and asked him to keep an eye on Albert and help him if he needed it; and with a very obvious wink suggesting it might help him when he filled out the duty rosters. John, of course, agreed.

The Colonel had words with the officers on the afternoon after he returned and arranged for a full regimental parade two days afterwards, during which he was to impart his important news to the men. He may have been under the illusion that all would be kept under wraps but it leaked out, of course. Mckinley heard Housley talking to Bell and he was sure that he heard the words: 'It sounds like bloody India!' At the subsequent parade, the adjutant, who read out the orders, confirmed all this. The regiment was to be kitted out, inoculated, given lectures, have a generous period of home leave, and would then depart for Southampton by train in the first week of September. Some heavy kit would precede them and depart from the Hull docks. Embarkation from the port was somewhat dependent on tides and weather, but they should be on their way by the middle of the month.

John had never seen the Colonel before and it came as a considerable surprise to him that at the parade the CO and two escorting officers were mounted on three very splendid looking horses. Apart from issuing a couple of brief orders, their leader seemed very aloof. He was sharp featured and rather small but sat with considerable ease on his mount and seemed to be part of it when the two of them eventually moved off after taking the salute at the march past. John noticed that Housley and some of the other NCOs were sweating under his godlike gaze. This gave him an insight into the considerable power and authority which could be exerted by senior officers, and he made a careful mental note of it.

When the opportunity arose a few days later, he asked Bell about 'the Colonel' and was told, 'Oh, very well connected, Colonel Grimston, he's the second cousin of a Scottish earl. I think the family name is Sinclair. He came to us from the cavalry; his three main interests in life outside his family are the regiment, horses, and shooting grouse.' When John said he was a bit surprised to see the officers mounted in an infantry regiment, Bell smiled and said, 'You always get that, even in the armoured corps; the top men sit on horses while the tanks and armoured cars whizz by. It's historical, many of the top people in the army are related to each other or connected in some way and a lot of 'em come from the cavalry regiments. It hasn't really changed since Waterloo—troops on foot and officers mounted; that's the way it is.'

John asked him how the posting would affect married officers and if the colonel's wife would be travelling out to the great sub-continent with the other wives. 'Oh yes,' said Bell, 'but if the Regiment has a long posting in India—and we can probably expect at least three years; the last time I went it was four years—then after the first year, she will be back here for four or five months every year when it gets hot and nasty. She's a fair bit younger than him, their boys are at school in England, and that's part of her excuse for coming back. When she does leave, it doesn't help the Colonel's temper one bit and it's a good idea to keep out of his way. The adjutant tries to keep him busy with regimental matters, tiger shoots or other shoots, and they get up to headquarters a lot, but he can be a bugger when she's away, so be warned.'

It was early days but all the scraps of information that John absorbed were being put together in his keen mind to form a model of the dynamics by which the regiment and the army itself worked. He realised that none of the new troopers were married, or if they were they were keeping very quiet about it. Many of the older officers and NCOs had wives and married quarters were available. However, Mckinley learned that arrangements varied, with some intending to follow their husbands and others not, largely depending on family circumstances.

The prescribed program of preparation was put into effect with the MO being scrupulously careful to see that all the men received their inoculations and advice on how to deal with bites, fungal infections and all the other joys of a hot climate. The pallid Padre gave a talk with slides entitled 'The many tribes and religions of India.' In it, he managed to make it clear how superior Christianity was to all other beliefs. He emphasised the nobility of the European nations and especially that of the English in imposing their cultural norms on the many races under the sway of the British Empire.

The Padre illustrated his belief in his creed and the high purpose of his country with quotes from Rudyard Kipling. He presented them almost as scientific analyses of the Imperial condition in which the British found themselves, and as such, unarguably accurate. Both of the poems had been written many years earlier, the first stanza was chosen for its religious content and was from a poem called 'Recessional':

If, drunk with sight of power, we loose
Wild tongues that have not Thee in awe,
Such boastings as the Gentiles use,
Or lesser breeds without the law—
Lord God of Hosts, be with us yet,
Lest we forget, lest we forget!

The second was from a poem called 'The White Man's Burden'. It presented the British Imperial Presence as an act of noble duty and sacrifice rather than as being necessary for the maintenance of the commercial interests within that large Empire which Britain had almost accidentally acquired. The British presence in the sub-continent brought in very rich material rewards and presented considerable career opportunities for those who, perhaps from lack of background or connections, would have been unable to access them in a small and insular island. The stanzas chosen went:

Take up the white man's burden—
Send forth the best ye breed—
Go bind your sons to exile
To serve your captives' need;
To wait in heavy harness,
On fluttered folk and wild—
Your new-caught, sullen peoples,
Half-devil and half child.

Though John admired Kipling's use of metre and his skills in versification, he also realised that the poem was a product of its time and pretty much prior to the advent of socialism or of trade union power. He realised that his own working class were just one-step up from the sullen peoples of the poem and wondered what Karl Marx would have had to say about it. Later in the mess, one half-drunk old trooper let loose the gem: 'Bloody white man's burden; when he read the bloody title I thought he was going to talk about bloody marriage!'

18

Mckinley and Port Said

After the pre-embarkation leave, during which John had spent as much time with his family as possible, he spent hours devouring various tomes and encyclopaedia articles about India and 'the Raj'. He was amazed, first by its size and secondly by the huge diversity of its races and religions. He and most of those others at that time on the very small island on which they lived, had had almost no exposure to the world's other belief systems. It seemed to him that India was at the confluence of all of them. Islam had penetrated well into the northern states while Hinduism held the major sway in the centre and south. Buddhism was still a considerable force in Ceylon and in other enclaves in southern India, and in the adjacent states of Nepal, Tibet, Burma and Siam.

The sub-continent was home to many other minority sects such as the Sikhs and Jains. It had become the home of the last adherents of Zoroastrianism, who were now known as Parsees. John's eyes were opened by the huge variety and complexity of the various beliefs, which were now starting to be presented to him. Christianity, which he had not been impressed with for years due to the way that many of its purveyors had behaved to him and friends and family members, seemed to be increasingly narrow in outlook as a result of his readings. It also seemed that Christianity had not taken much of a hold there until the British had arrived. He had found little evidence of a Jewish presence but he was sure that somewhere or other in the many bustling commercial centres, those enterprising peoples were certain to be found.

He checked on the likely route the regiment would follow. This would almost certainly be via the Suez Canal. He had been taught geography during the 1920s by the 'deadly Capes and Bays' method in which pupils were made to memorise every inlet and promontory around large sections of the coastline of Britain and many other, mainly British Empire, countries. He could remember that India was about two thirds of the way to Australia and that it was huge. He remembered his Geography teacher had pointed out that it was about twenty-five times the size of England and about one third of the size of the United States.

His researches unearthed the facts that London to Bombay, by sea, was six-thousand two-hundred and sixty miles and that there were four possible ports of call on the way to that city. To Gibraltar was thirteen-hundred and thirteen miles, Gib to Malta another nine-hundred and ninety-one, Malta to Port Said nine-hundred and thirty-six and Suez to Aden thirteen-hundred and ten, with the last leg, Aden to Bombay being sixteen-hundred and fifty.

He was told by the old sweats that it would probably be Southampton to Malta or Port Said, and then on to the coaling station in Aden before the final balmy cruise through the Arabian Sea to Bombay. The likely travelling speed would be at about two hundred nautical miles per day at best, with additional days to get through the Suez Canal. They were looking at a journey of about a month if you included the stops. The old sweat said: 'You're lucky to be travelling at this time of year. In midsummer it's just about unbearable on a ship through Suez and the Red Sea, especially on a troop ship!'

A small advance party had embarked for India with most of the necessary equipment, the officer's personal trunks, and the mess silver, in the middle of September. The bulk of the regiment gathered and departed for Southampton about a fortnight later. Kit and men were checked and double-checked, and they embarked on a fine October morning on the 18000 ton Shaw, Savill and Albion Co. liner, the *SS Ceramica*. The ship was heavily segregated, with men and NCOs on the lower decks and the officers on the light and airy top deck with access to the outside at virtually any time they wished. The men and NCO's had restricted access to the large rear-deck where parades and services were held.

The Colonel left the running of things pretty much to the NCOs and the junior troop commanders with the injunction that the men were to be kept busy. Tasburgh joined his regiment just before embarkation due to a pressing need to attend the wedding of one of his cousins who had been snapped up by a guard's officer, whom she had met during her year as a debutant. The cousin held the triple attraction of being very pretty, a good horsewoman and an heiress. In discussions about the nuptials, Tasburgh senior, looking very seriously at young Algy as he said it, stated that the first two were a bonus but the prime consideration was her financial expectations.

The standing of the bride's family was taken for granted, as it was rare to marry outside the accepted circle of the landed gentry. There were a few reluctantly admitted additions from the newly wealthy classes, but it was usually felt that they did not have the backgrounds that would enable them to act correctly in all social situations and to deal properly with servants. After all, these people, unlike the families they were marrying into, did not have the breeding and had not had generations of experience in these matters. However, the considerable quantities of money, which they brought, or would bring, into the older families usually lubricated the transactions to a sufficient degree to permit these 'mixed marriages'.

Tasburgh arrived in Southampton in a chauffeur driven limousine accompanied by a very tall and strikingly good-looking young woman; they strode, arm in arm, to the foot of the gantry by which the officers had boarded. She declared loudly, 'I told you we would be in plenty of time, darling. I'll make my farewells here. I positively must dash as mommy would like the Bentley back as soon as possible.' The Colonel and adjutant were having coffee on the upper deck and observing comings and goings whilst dealing with reports of various junior officers and NCOs.

Grimston leant forward and reddening slightly he said in a somewhat prickly voice, 'Isn't that young Tasburgh? Rather late isn't he!'

The adjutant, who was the son of a solicitor and also a consummate politician, rapidly replied: 'Yes, sir, and isn't that the Duke's youngest daughter seeing him off?'

Grimston looked again and said, 'Yes, I believe it is. We must keep an eye on that young officer. I feel he has considerable potential within the regiment. What do you think, Sherbroke?' The adjutant, of course, couldn't agree more with the older man's assessment.

Algy made his way into the ship, found Enderby, and inquired if everything was all right with the men and if all were present and correct; he was assured that the full troop of thirty had arrived and been berthed within the vessel and that no problems had arisen. He then made his way to the upper decks, found his batman and enquired about his kit and personal effects. He was told that everything had been checked and unpacked as needed and all the small comforts needed for the voyage were to hand. After that, he made his way up to find the Colonel to report his presence and to apologise for arriving at the vessel so late. Grimston would have no apologies, saying: 'My dear boy, these things happen, we can all be late. I was young once myself. I understand entirely.' This wasn't entirely accurate as he had never been late for anything in his life, including his birth which had been two weeks premature.

Down in the bowels of the vessel the men had been berthed on tiered bunks at four to a cabin. These were small and normally held only one or two of those second or third class passengers which had formerly been carried by the ship. Meals were to be taken in three rotations with the men got into and out of the dining area as rapidly as possible. The liner had been on contract to the army since 1935 and the owners had been glad of it due to the reduced demand that had come about during the depression years. It had steamed all over the Empire's sea-lanes delivering troops and returning them to England after tours of duty had been completed.

All naval and sea faring matters were dealt with by the civilian officers and crew, who reported to the ship's captain. The catering staff and foodstuffs were also supplied by the company and delivered by its crew, who had the advantage of long experience of catering afloat. Mckinley didn't notice much difference from normal army fare apart from the fish dishes, which were served much more frequently than in barracks, and he found that they had much more fresh fruit provided than previously.

The officers dined in a separate mess and were attended by their own batmen and Catering Corps personnel. The diet of the officers was vastly superior to that of the enlisted men and it was augmented by a plentiful supply of fruit preserves and a very well stocked bar. The Colonel had explained: 'We are in rather cramped conditions and thus dinner will consist of only four courses, followed by coffee. Brandy, other beverages and cigars will of course be available after that.' Because of the regiments enforced change in location and cramped quartering, Grimston was quite clearly prepared to rough it, but only to a certain extent!

The Colonel made it clear to the junior officers that he wanted things to run like clockwork and that the secret of this was routine, which would consist of ablutions and then breakfast, and after that cleaning of kit and kit inspections followed by calisthenics in the mornings. After the large afternoon meal, which most of the men referred to as dinner for some reason, the early afternoon would be free. The men could read, see the padre, write letters home or occupy themselves in some other useful manner. The MO would be available from ten until midday. Outside those hours, the sick bay attendants would deal with minor complaints unless a medical emergency presented itself. After the evening meal, films would be shown, weather permitting, on the large rear-deck on Wednesdays and Saturdays and the mess would be open for two hours only for alcoholic beverages following the meal. Lights out would be at ten pm.

The crew told Mckinley that the stretch from Southampton to the Straits of Gibraltar was one of the smoothest they could remember; a brief stop was made at 'the Rock' for coal. The ship then made excellent time until about half way to the first intended major stopping point, which was Malta. Then, a huge gale broke out and the ship slugged on through it. After a wireless message about storm damage affecting port facilities in Valetta and due to the emergency berthing and delayed departures of several other vessels, the captain of the *SS Ceramica* told the Colonel that it would now be necessary to berth at the secondary destination available to them, which would be Port Said.

It was John's first experience of the sea and he came to realise that its vastness was a highly unpredictable entity of hugely variable moods. He asked one of the ships engineers about the rather worrying metallic groaning sound that he could hear in the ship, but was told: 'Don't worry, that's normal. Think of the ship as a long steel beam being lifted by the huge waves. Like all beams it will flex, but it's designed to do that and those sounds are always there in high seas.' Mckinley hoped he was right. After forty-eight hours in the force ten gale, during which a substantial proportion of those on board spent much time being seasick or at least feeling very, very queasy, he concluded that his decision to choose the Army rather than the Navy had been the correct one.

Grimston wasn't too pleased about the interference of the elements with his precisely planned itinerary but there was little he could do about it. He would have preferred the men to have been allowed shore leave in Valletta where there was little chance of anyone going missing. Port Said was of a much more international character than Valletta due to the location of the city at the entrance to the Suez Canal. It was about twice the size of the Maltese port and its bars and brothels had an unsavoury if not notorious character. The Colonel did toy with the idea of restricting the men to the ship but was enough of a realist to grasp that after almost two weeks at sea, some steam would need to be blown off.

He let the authorities know that there would be several hundred thirsty young men let loose within the port on the following day and personally reminded the NCOs that he considered them responsible for the behaviour of the men within their own troops. He set a curfew of 11pm for return and had warnings issued to the men regarding their behaviour. The warning was augmented by a matter-of-fact refresher talk from the MO regarding those possible unpleasant diseases that may be contracted during liaisons of a sexual nature and the ready availability of those diseases within the city.

The ship crawled gratefully into the port at the tail end of the huge storm during a late evening on what looked like being a glorious October day. The ship's captain informed the Colonel that they would need forty-eight hours at least to load various necessary supplies, repair minor storm damage, and do essential cleaning of some of the toilet areas in the lower decks. Grimston thus resigned himself to letting the men loose into the area of mysterious small streets and alleyways, which started just outside the entrance to the docks.

After breakfast, the men thus drifted into the Souk in large groups and found various establishments keen to sell them cold beer, and other delights. Others visited the bazaar and looked over the amazing and exotic range of wares for sale. Most items seemed to be hand crafted and were different to anything most of them had ever previously seen. One trooper gormlessly commented, 'It's nothing like Woolworths, is it!' John had talked about what he could expect when abroad with some of the old hands and had been given much advice about the various native denizens he might encounter, most of it of a very dismissive or disparaging nature. Nothing prepared him for the vigour and enterprise of the young kids, however, some of whom couldn't have been more than seven or eight, in trying to sell him everything from small crude carvings of the Sphinx to their big sister. He was familiar with the listlessness and poor health of many of the youngsters of his own locality, and so the brown and healthy appearance of these young entrepreneurs came as a surprise to one inculcated with notions of the inherent superiority of the English.

It was obvious that there was a wide variety of intentions amongst those disembarking. Most were just going to go with the flow and drift along with the rest of the lads and have a drink and a laugh whilst looking round. For most, it resembled a day trip to Blackpool, with many new and exotic excitements on offer. The major difference was the warmth and incredible blue sky. A minority set out from the start to get totally rat-arsed, some did so broodingly, staring into their drinks, and some stupidly because they had a taste for it, which had been denied or restricted for weeks. A few toured the bazaars and haggled, and yet still paid far too much for small gifts for mothers or wives or sweethearts at home. Fights broke out and a couple of drunks were returned to the ship under escort to face the Colonel's displeasure.

A few headed straight for the brothels, but most, after a rather brief and unsatisfactory unloading of pent up desires, returned and caught up with the drinkers. John, Art, and Quill, as the troop now called them, stuck together, and after a few drinks wandered round the bazaar, frequently shooing off small groups of begging urchins that they encountered. John had seen Brenner earlier with a peculiarly intense and strangely white-faced expression, heading off down an alley. When the trio reached the end of it, he had disappeared but John could see several women of various ages stood in doorways or sat on small balconies overlooking the thoroughfare. He could also see some older men sat smoking outside a small cafe and a couple of nasty looking characters hovering near the girls. 'Well, we know what he's after then,' Art said.

The afternoon and evening merged into one and the sky changed from light to dark over the course of just a few minutes. Most of the men then started to drift back towards the ship, the groups becoming larger as they neared the docks. One mild mannered and slightly built trooper had been got thoroughly drunk by his pals because it was his birthday. He then decided he wanted to fight the biggest member of a naval shore patrol, who towered about a foot above him and was about twice the drunken man's weight. After several attempts to persuade him to be on his way, the huge sailor, who carried a large baton, handed the stick to a companion whilst the reckless attacker lunged towards him once again. As the wildly flailing man approached, he undid the chinstrap of the steel helmet that was standard equipment for patrolmen, took hold of the front of the brim and swung it down in a rapid arc on to the head of the birthday boy. The very dazed and limp soldier was then handed over to his compatriots with the instruction to get him straight back to the ship, or else. No-one was sure what the 'or else' entailed, but it sounded sufficiently unpleasant to impel them rapidly in the direction of their berths.

The three had walked back slowly, retracing their steps, and had almost reached the entrance to the alley up which they had seen Brenner disappear a couple of hours previously. A group of about six other troopers had just passed the entrance when a couple of the unpleasant characters seen previously came charging out of the alley brandishing knives and shouting.

John looked round for a likely weapon and got ready to fight, and the six troopers turned and looked back; but after scrutinising them briefly and then turning to look up the street past the returning trio, the two cutthroats went back up the alley. The narrow passageway seemed to be in quite a hubbub, with several women gathered around one particular door just beyond the small cafe.

'I wonder what all that was about?' said Quill.

'Probably not paid her,' responded Art.

John remained silent. He was uneasy, sensing that something far more serious had happened. After about another hundred yards walk, during which several small groups of soldiers had coalesced defensively into one, they were passed by a large shore patrol hurrying towards the end of the alley. A couple of minutes later, an alert looking army captain and two military policemen wearing pistols, strode purposively after them.

By ten, most of John's troop had gathered in a largish hostelry within sight of the ship and were exchanging yarns and having a last couple of beers. One young trooper was telling his mates about a dive they had found where exotic dancers were performing. His description was vivid. Most of the audience sat in raised areas around a stage that was at about waist height to the twenty troopers or so who were leaning on its edge, drinking and leering at the girls and making rather un-gentlemanly suggestions, all of which were greeted with uproarious merriment.

Eventually, an older and very acrobatic dancer emerged. One of the old hands muttered to the rest: 'This is the one I told you about.' They watched as the woman, who must have been in her early thirties, did handstands and then arched her torso and touched her feet to the floor in front of her. She did the splits and similar moves and slowly disrobed to the beat of a small drum and some sort of stringed instrument.

After each veil was discarded she said in broken English, 'You want see more, boys? I want money.' The troopers and others threw pennies onto the stage, which a fat little man wearing a fez scurried about collecting. Eventually, she said, 'You want see titty?' A loud and raucous chorus of affirmation arose from the crowd and more coins showered onto the platform. After the collection, she removed the sequined bra covering her breasts and a large cheer went up.

She looked lewdly at the crowd of lusty squaddies. 'Want even more, boys?' she said. A cheer went up and the fat little man bent down towards the audience and shouted, 'Half-crown,' and placed a small object on the floor and pointed to it. This mystified most of those there but the old hand, who was wise in the ancient customs of the place, reached forward and placed a half crown in the small device so that it stood perpendicular to the floor. The dancer now stepped forward and slowly did the splits over it, lowering herself until the coin vanished between the lips of her vagina. She then rose to the delighted cheers of the soldiers, lifting the coin as she did so. She turned away and then flipped the coin to the be-fezzed coin collector.

She now looked at the audience even more lewdly and said, 'You want to see again! I want plenty money.' The coins hitting the stage now included some small silver ones in addition to the normal shower of copper and brass. The little man pointed to the holder. This time several eager hands vied to place the required coin in place. The dancer repeated the trick again, and several times more until no more coins were donated. After a last collection, she bowed off and a young belly dancer took her place on the small stage. After that, the troopers started to drift away for some reason.

After the young soldier finished telling the tale, a couple of the older men opined that what they had participated in was 'disgusting', but most of the others seemed to want to know exactly where the joint was and seemed to be highly approving of the consummate artistry of the acrobatic dancer. After a last drink, John and the rest started to drift back to the ship. When they reached it, in addition to the crewman who was guarding the entrance to the gantry, three military policemen scrutinised faces as the men filed aboard. Quill muttered as they walked along the deck, 'What was all that about?' John did not have any idea what had happened and did not reply, but he was sure that if one of the regiment was involved he knew who it was.

On the next day, the Provost Marshal of the Port Said garrison marched onto the *SS Ceramica* with several of his men.

He had made an appointment to see Grimston after breakfast, and the two spent about half an hour with the adjutant. After the meeting, Grimston emerged looking seriously displeased. After a conference with the senior officers, the men were told that they had an hour and then there would be a full kit inspection followed by full parade and inspection on the dockside after lunch. Most of the troops were still feeling dull or half hungover from the effects of last night's beer and set about their tasks with the usual mixture of grumbling and the minimum effort that was needed to comply with the order. However, by two-thirty, all were stood to attention while Major Porter, who was the second most senior officer after the Colonel, made the inspection, accompanied by the Provost Marshal and one of his men.

John realised that they were being scrutinised as well as being inspected, and had a fair idea who was being sought. The Provost Marshal told the Colonel that the description he had been given probably fitted about a quarter of the regiment and thus there was little possibility of identifying the man, but he felt that pressure needed to be applied. He advised that there should be no further shore leave. Grimston, who was experienced in dealing with problems presented by the occasional 'bad apple' in the barrel, knew that sailing away as rapidly as possible was the best option. Thus, he arranged with the ship's Captain to expedite repairs and loading and sail on as soon as was convenient. The men were dismissed and told to meet their officers on-board in their respective troops. They were told that an unsavoury incident had taken place ashore, the ship would be sailing on to its next destination after tea, and that no one was to leave the ship under any circumstances

Nothing was revealed about the nature of the 'unsavoury incident' and the ship left the port that night, sailed onwards through the Suez Canal, and then down the long stretch comprising the Red Sea. Mckinley thought that the cloudless evenings, the balmy air, and the low and beautiful sunsets seen across the calm waters were magical. He had never known anything like the warmth he was experiencing. This increased day by day as they sailed down from latitude thirty to about latitude twelve, which marked their exit from the Red Sea into the Gulf of Aden. The officers, of course, enjoyed iced cocktails in the evenings served under pleasant awnings erected on the spacious after deck. The men had to make do with beer, sacks, bales, and wooden benches on the overcrowded foredeck.

The ship put into the coaling station at Aden for twenty hours to replenish stocks and make up the shortfall resulting from the rapid departure from Port Said. It arrived at about two a.m. and the men were woken at six by the sound of the grab discharging its first load of steam coal into the hold. John explained to one of the inquisitive squaddies that coal came in different varieties and the longer it was in the ground the less tar content it had in it. The very best coal in terms of energy content was anthracite and the next best was steam coal, which burned hotter and was much less tarry and smoky than the bituminous coals which were used to produce house coal or which were consigned to coke works. He said that's where your coal gas, coal tar, and coke for steel making is made. He explained that older coals tended to be worked in Wales in deeper and thinner seams of maybe only a couple of feet in height, and that at his home pit of Bullcroft they mined very good quality bituminous coal in thick seams of up to seven feet.

'Two feet!' said the aghast soldier. 'How do they manage that?'

John replied with a wry chuckle, 'The Welsh miners are very short.'

19

Mckinley and Mother India

The key of India is London.

Disraeli

In India's sunny clime, where I used to spend my time
A serving of his majesty the King.
Of all them heathen crew the finest that I knew
Were brown eyed maids who taught me how to sin.

A trooper's modified version of Gunga Din

Mckinley first ran into Hugo Brody-Bollers on the *SS Ceramica*. He had come aboard in Aden, pleading urgent business back in India and had been found a berth. This was not strictly in accordance with regulations, but on the basis that the tea trading company he worked for supplied the Army and that his father was a Baronet, his request was granted.

Bollers was viewed by some in England as a rather odd character; after studying oriental languages at Oxford he had secured a job which meant he could travel through India, Burma and Siam. He had now been out in that area for about eight years. He had used his leave periods to visit Japan and French Indo-China. His passion was not tea but the languages and culture of the Far East. Though he was very efficient in his occupation, the major part of his energies were directed towards increasing his knowledge of that vast area which was then very conveniently under the sway of the British Raj and its European neighbours.

Bollers was a broad-shouldered shambling blond, careless of his personal appearance, but he had obtained a double first and a rugby blue at University. He was the third son in line of succession to the Baronetcy. He had two sisters, one of whom was rather dull, very horsey and a mainstay of her county set in Nottinghamshire. The younger sister was much more like Hugo. She had also obtained a first, this time in modern history at Girton. She had also decided that she was a socialist and had gone off to work for one of the left leaning departments at London University.

Bollers and his younger sister were regarded as being 'different' because they did not quite fit in with the normal patterns and expectations of upper class life. This was undoubtedly due in part to the piercing intelligence which both possessed. His two elder brothers were both in the Guards, the middle one as a career soldier, the eldest one as a stopgap and for social contacts until he was required to take over the family estate and farms from his father, who was the ninth baronet in the family line.

On the *Ceramica*, Bollers tried to avoid the officers if at all possible as he found their conversation dull. He was uninterested in army matters generally as well as in horses, cricket, drinking and marital prospects. He had found himself a quiet spot on a part of the deck near to that used by the enlisted men. He had purloined a deck chair and spent long periods reclining in the shade and reading the *Bhagavad Gita* in the sacred classical Sanskrit of the original. He shared the spot with Mckinley, who had been using the same shaded area since Suez. It was surrounded by bales containing equipment or provisions of some sort and thus quite private. After observing John writing down all the answers to a newspaper quiz, he made the remark: 'Very few troopers would have known that.' This was followed by an immediate apology: 'Sorry, old chap, thinking aloud. But really, they wouldn't!' The question in the paper was, 'Wedge shaped characters used by the Assyrians?' John had written Cuneiform, which was the correct answer.

After a few words, Bollers realised he was talking to a trooper of somewhat unusual quality. After that, he laid aside the *Gita* and rather took the younger man under his wing, feeling that he was under something of an obligation to do so due to his initial rather patronising remark. Mckinley was keen to know about India and fill in some of the gaps in his knowledge with information from someone who had first-hand experience. Bollers, who shared some of his cleverer sister's socialist notions, insisted that they should be on first name terms and was very keen to oblige.

He said, 'Right from the start you should realise that India is a hugely complex and diverse society both in its peoples and religions, and that most of the British there are remark-ably stupid regarding them; they don't even understand the distinction between the Hindu classes and castes. Hindus, of course, make up the bulk of the sub-continent's population. The British in India seem to work in a sort of bubble in which British practices and lifestyles are preserved. Another very important thing is that you should make your own mind up and above all else avoid stereotyping; take them as you find them, please be very open minded.' Throughout the discussion, Mckinley further impressed Bollers by asking a series of tersely framed and very perceptive questions, which made it abundantly clear that he had absorbed every word that had been imparted to him.

Hugo gave a brief explanation of the four Hindu classes and explained that these were much more rigid than in England. The Brahmans, or top caste, study, teach and perform religious ceremonies. The Kshatriya is the nobleman and warrior class. The Vaisya are the merchant and artisan and farming class. The lowest class are the Sudra and these are menials and labourers. Below all these classes lie 'the untouchables'.

'There is no intermarriage between classes. One important lesson is that the class structure is not built on power, conquest, or wealth as in Europe. You are born into your caste and willingly accept it and its rights and responsibilities. It is almost as if the members of the four belong to separate species. The four classes work like the parts of a great machine, but each independent of each other.' He went on to say that there were probably thousands of sub-castes depending on trades, tribal affinities and social standards and the like. He said: 'You will probably have heard of "the untouchables." These are the people who carry out occupations such as scavenging, butchering, brewing and tanning, which are considered impure.'

Mckinley asked what Hugo meant by social standards. Bollers smiled and said, 'Certain practices such as re-marriage of widows or eating meat would tend to lower the standing of a caste, and others related to Brahman practices can raise it. It is a little different from the way English social standards arise, isn't it? Those tend to be determined by birth, school and the position in society of your parents.' Over the next few days, Bollers drew a comprehensive sketch of India for the young soldier and recommended some useful sources from which more could be obtained. He said, 'I would not discount Kipling, read *Kim* and *Plain Tales from the Hills* and the poetry. His view is a little over romanticised but he certainly had a feeling for the place. He was born in Bombay, had a native nurse, and could speak Hindi before he could speak English. He was a keen observer and his satires and criticisms of some of the less admirable aspects of colonialism are well worth looking at.'

He raised his copy of the *Bhagavad Gita* and said: 'Something like this is well worth reading as well. Reading in the original Sanskrit might be difficult for you but there is an excellent and poetic English translation by Sir Edwin Arnold.

It contains some profound stuff; it is interesting to compare it to the advice given in Christian scriptures. There, everything is cut and dried with the message presented as though it is factual and cannot be challenged in any way. You must have had it pounded into you at school or in church: obey the law, believe in Christ and follow his teachings unquestioningly and eventually you will be rewarded by salvation and resurrection of the body.' He opened the book and said: 'I am by no means a Hindu, but consider these lines for example. I find them more subtle and thought provoking than the stories in the Christian scriptures:

'Now I would hear, O gracious Kesava!
Of life which seems, and the soul beyond, which sees,
And what it is we know—or think to know.'

He explained, 'Kesava is one of the many Hindu names for the god Vishnu.'

The remaining few days of the ocean voyage passed rapidly but not without incident. For Mckinley some of the sights were wondrous. The slow-moving Dhows with their full-bellied sails reminded him of Shakespeare's immortal lines in *A Midsummer Night's Dream*:

The fairyland buys not the child of me
His mother was a votaress of my order
And in the spiced Indian air by night
Full often has she gossiped by my side,
And sat with me on Neptune's yellow sands
Marking the embarked traders on the flood,
When we have laughed to see the sails conceive
And grow big-bellied with the wanton wind;
Which she with pretty and with swimming gait
Following—her womb then rich with my young squire—
Would imitate and sail upon the land—

He marvelled at the strangely attired crews and the occasional sight of a porpoise or dolphin slicing gracefully through the water, and at all the other varied sights, sounds, and magical atmosphere of a great ocean near to the equator. A sour note presented itself with the disappearance of Trooper Mills. His absence was noticed the day after the vessel had set sail from Aden. Mills was a quiet type of bloke who kept himself to himself and the others had hardly noticed his presence during training. Checks and searches were made and everyone was told to keep an eye out for their comrade. A further day passed with no evidence of him at meals or anywhere else.

At Aden, mail caught up with the regiment and was transferred from one of the steamers that had left England a couple of days after the *Ceramica*. The Adjutant ascertained that Mills had been one of the troopers who received a letter. No trace of it could be found and enquiries were made by radiotelegraph back to his hometown. It eventually transpired that the young lady whom Mills had been seeing had written saying that it was all over between them. No body was ever recovered; it was charitably assumed that Mills must have fallen overboard rather than jumped. B troop, by virtue of the loss, was now reduced to twenty-nine men.

The *Ceramica* finally put into Bombay and the regiment began to disembark. Mckinley saw Brody-Bollers on the quayside; he was in deep conversation with a small dark-skinned man and looked concerned. John surmised he was receiving bad news but did not want to distract him from what was obviously important business. He filed past with Art and Quill but just as he drew level with Bollers he heard a creak from above and looked up. One of the ropes round a load being moved from the ship by the crane had snapped. In a split second, he realised that it was starting to topple and would probably land on Bollers and his companion. He took a running dive and knocked Bollers forwards and his companion to the side. The load just missed all three but split open on landing and a large crate toppled over onto the dark-skinned man's leg. Bollers lay, momentarily in shock, and Mckinley and several other troopers leapt to the side of the crate and lifted it away. It was evident to Mckinley, who was familiar with broken limbs because of his experiences underground, that the leg was broken.

He told the small man to lie still and sent Art off at a run to get the MO or anyone with medical expertise. The MO quickly arrived and took charge, ordering a stretcher and splints, which he rapidly applied. 'Don't worry, old chap,' he said. 'I think it's a simple fracture, you should be up and about in no time.' The dark-skinned man murmured thanks through lips that were grimacing with pain.

Bollers approached John. He was white faced but had fully grasped the significance of what had happened. 'I owe you a debt of gratitude, old boy,' he said. 'I rather think that you just saved my life. It's a pity about Ram, he's one of my buying agents, very able feller; he'll be out of action for a few weeks or even months.' He went across to reassure his employee and then turned back to John: 'He was telling me that a steamer with several dozen tons of our tea on board has gone down in a damned Typhoon. Most of the crew were saved but it's a valuable cargo lost and the insurance never makes up for it.'

The two shook hands and Bollers said, 'I hope to see you again soon; please look after yourself.' Tasburgh had heard the noise as the cargo fell and been made fully aware of the incident. He approached the two. 'Well done, Mckinley,' he said. 'Very fast thinking.' He turned to Bollers: 'Is there anything we can do for you? I have a staff car and can drop you off in the city or at the infirmary.'

Hugo said, 'I appreciate the offer, old boy, but actually I have a car and driver just beyond the pier area. I have some urgent matters to see to and then must see that Ram is properly looked after until he recovers; perhaps we can have a drink in the mess sometime?'

Tasburgh said, 'I look forward to it,' and then excused himself to supervise his troops departure from the docks.

The regiment were to be loaded onto ancient open army lorries and transported to their new accommodation; new in the sense that it was new to them—the actual buildings had been constructed in the 1890s with raised bases to avoid flooding and rot. The buildings were roomy compared to the home barracks in York, and well ventilated. Thus, the regiment settled in and rapidly adapted to its new life in those balmy climes.

In many ways, the next two years were an unreal time, which seemed to drift by slowly in a permanent summer. The regiment had exchanged the heavy, woollen, 1922 pattern service dress for the lightweight cotton khaki drill and the unloved three-quarter length shorts, known as 'Bombay Bloomers'. The Wolsey pattern cork 'solar topee' was also issued, and although it was intended to provide some relief from intense sunlight, Mckinley thought that the effect of the shorts and topee was rather comical and wondered if knee length shorts and a lightweight forage cap wouldn't have been better.

The Army had long experience in India. Talks were given and leaflets issued about the various diseases and infections that would be encountered. The MO had explained the problems: 'The heat seldom gets below the high seventies and can move into the mid-nineties. The climate is dry from mid-October through winter, but then humidity starts to build up to mid-May and then the rains start, and although we do not get the sort of Monsoon deluge experienced in the north west of India, through July you can expect at least twenty inches of rain a month. This might seem a lot by British standards but around Darjeeling it could be over a hundred inches a month. That is about two years' worth of Manchester rainfall. The natives are used to it and we cope with it. Those that are able to, go up-country for the rainy season. India is tremendously variable in respect of climate. Delhi, for example, only gets about twenty-five inches of rain a year, the climate there is very tolerable and that is why the Viceroy lives there and why so many government and army department offices are located there.'

In terms of army duties, the routine was undemanding. A certain amount of sport, P.T. and drill was expected. The drills intensified if a major ceremonial parade approached. There was a small amount of weapons training and use of firing ranges, but as the army was starved of funds and because bullets cost money, as few of them as possible where used. Apart from that and occasional lectures or compulsory medical parades to check for the clap, the trooper's life was easy.

The officers busied themselves with mess dinners and the social life, which consisted of long garden parties at which various marriageable daughters of administrators, clergy, plantation and factory owners, and so on, were displayed to the younger officers, in the hope that they would be removed from the parental home to a state of marital bliss. Gymkhanas and polo matches were popular and so was cricket, all with the inevitable and extended social component firmly welded into the structure of these events. From what Mckinley could make of them, they seemed almost Edwardian in character, with fragrant women, wearing long gloves and dresses and always carrying parasols, floating in between the tables, gossiping and surreptitiously eying up the young officers who relaxed, drank cocktails and smoked cigars, and acted like young lords.

He was also aware that although some of the females behaved in what seemed to be a very heavily mannered way, which amongst the sillier ones could seem quite ridiculous, a very effective intelligence network was operating amongst them. The officers were classified according to family and monetary status with breeding and antecedents rather than wealth being the major consideration. Some of the shrewder mothers reversed the ranking of these marriage parameters in their own minds, realising that in the final analysis a few tens of thousands in the funds had the prospect of being far more use to them than being related by marriage to a penniless young 'honourable'. This mindset, however, was relatively rare and the snobbery of position and class still held rigid sway over the vast majority.

As regards the rest, the officers left the management of the troopers largely to the NCOs. The troops were to be kept smart, occupied, and discipline was to be maintained. Drunkenness, insubordination, and slackness were to be stamped on. Liaison with native girls was frowned on, mainly due to the difficulty that a pregnancy would cause the regiment. It was realised that use of whores would occur. Although the officers did not wish to talk about it, they were realistic enough to know that it was inevitable.

Once again the stern injunction was given that French Letters were worn and any form of V.D. avoided at all costs. Failure to do so was a chargeable offence, as it constituted a self-inflicted injury that would be certain to be detected as the more painful symptoms of the diseases started to present themselves. John thought that only the meticulous and rigidly clockwork thinking within the British Army could have equated getting the pox as a result of a hurried drunken encounter as being the equivalent of shooting oneself in the foot to avoid going 'over the top'.

One other factor, which made the time around Bombay seem unreal, was the huge abundance of very cheap native labour. Although agriculture and the jute and cotton mills and other industries employed very many, the population of the district was huge with the city itself having more than a million inhabitants. Due to this, there were always more hands available than work to occupy them. Thus, smartly attired Indian servants were to be found all over the domestic quarters. The officers and their families lived like landed gentry because of it.

The NCOs and families lived well, with wives unburdened of most domestic chores, and in barracks, kit was always kept spotless. Even at the level of the private soldier, the boredom of keeping his kit presentable was relieved by the simple expedient of collecting a penny every week from each of the troopers. The resulting half crown was pressed into the eager hands of a raggedly attired native who seemed to want to run errands, bull boots up to an incredible shine, or blanco belts or webbing to a standard rarely seen in England, all day long and, moreover, to do it very cheerfully.

The B troop servant looked to be in his early forties. He was about five feet four and so sparely built that John wondered where he got his energy. He could have been little more than eight stone but seemed to work continuously without the slightest complaint and often in a temperature and humidity that left the troopers laid out in a state of torpor, sweating on their bunks until the afternoon heat had subsided. He wore a shabby loincloth and little else.

The man's name was Chota Pahar. However, with that exquisite wit which is only found amongst rankers in the British Army, the troopers had christened him Gandhi due to his undoubted resemblance to that sage. Gandhi was treated with good-humoured bluster by most of the troop with much use of injunctions to *Juhldi, Juhldi,* which was the native word for hurry. This was often connected to threats to kick his arse if he didn't; the threats of course were never carried out and although Chota was a native and thus naturally inferior to the British, most of the men had a sneaking respect for the man due to his sunny nature and seemingly inexhaustible capacity for work.

The one exception to the general attitude was found in Brenner who, whenever he wanted Chota to do something, delivered his order with a vehement unpleasantness which most of the rest of the troop did not like. On one occasion, the small servant was bumped into accidentally by one of the troopers and spilt a glass of beer that Brenner had sent him for. The liquid spilt over the end of his bunk and a few drops spattered his boots.

Brenner reacted with an unreasoning fury that was totally out of proportion to the incident, which was clearly not the

Indian's fault. Grabbing a thick leather belt, he made for the servant, screaming: 'You fucking clumsy wog,' and with the clear intention of laying into him with the buckle end of the belt. John jumped up from his bunk and caught Brenner's wrist just as he was about to bring the buckle down on the shoulders of the cringing and frightened native. Brenner had above average strength but this was nowhere near the raw animal power of Mckinley.

John looked him in the eyes and said in a very quiet and deadly voice, 'I wouldn't, if I was you.'

Brenner had two choices: he could take a crack at Mckinley or back down. The grip round his wrist was so tight and powerful that it felt as though his bones might fracture. He snarled, 'OK,' and Mckinley relaxed his grip. Brenner turned away with a nasty curl to his lips, snarled, 'You fucking clumsy twat,' and walked out of the room.

John turned back to the visibly upset Chota. The man had previously put up with bantering and good-humoured threats but had never been anywhere near to being assaulted. He said, 'We can't have that sort of behaviour, can we, Mr Pahar? As compensation, I am going to award you sixpence from the regimental funds.' He took the small silver coin from among several in his pocket and placed it in the man's hand.

'Oh thank you, thank you, Sahib,' said the now beaming barracks' servant. He had been given more than a day's wage, but most of all Trooper John Sahib had called him Mr Pahar.

Thus, the easy life drifted on through 1938. The troopers experienced their first rainy season and broke out the oilskins and galoshes. Grimston had hoped to move the whole regiment for exercises during the rains into the hilly semi-desert of the north but financial constraints had defeated him. John rarely saw the colonel as his wife had departed for England and summer with the children. After receiving news that the exercises were cancelled, the colonel found it necessary to go off with the adjutant for urgent consultations in Delhi, and he was expected to be away during June, July and August. The rains curtailed most of the regiment's soldiering and time was devoted to eating, drinking, and cursing at and coping with the wet. John marvelled at the verdant growth that sprang forth during the rains. He was far less impressed with the huge burgeoning of the flying, crawling and slithering life that accompanied it.

On another level, some of the things which Hugo Brody-Bollers had said to him were starting to make sense. His mentor was of the opinion that the British time in India was ending: 'Rich pickings for a few years yet, maybe', he said. 'Who knows?' He had explained that in past years, cotton had flooded from India to Lancashire and then made its way back as yarn, cloth and garments, but this was ending. The Indians were setting up cotton mills and getting cheaper cotton goods from Japan. With the loss of markets, India was thus becoming a liability. The political mood had also changed since the massacre at Amritsar in 1919 when the now infamous General Dyer had ordered his troops to machine gun an unarmed crowd; 379 had been killed during that madness. The Civil Service was horrified and Dyer had been recalled to England. On his return, he had faced an inquiry but not a court martial. The incident had inflamed Indian nationalism and given great impetus to the movement lead by Gandhi.

'Why did he do it?' asked Mckinley.

'Moot point, old boy', said Bollers. 'On the one hand there had been lots of unrest and Dyer thought that the crowd needed a lesson, a bit like Napoleon with the Paris mob after the revolution, "a whiff of grapeshot" sort of thing!' John looked nonplussed. Hugo said, 'The quote comes from Carlyle's *History of the French Revolution*. Apparently, the French mob had become a bit uppity and Napoleon cured it with a few rounds of grapeshot. The big difference between the two of course was that they were rioting and the Indians were demonstrating peacefully.

'I am cynical about it, personally. I would like to think that

Dyer was a raving lunatic, but he was not, although he did not appear to be too bright when he appeared before the enquiry. The other obvious explanation is the one frequently observed through recent history, where a military type has sought to gain a reputation and thus promotion by military action against the natives, preferably natives who are vastly inferior in terms of armaments, of course. Sometimes they come unstuck, like Chelmsford did at Isandlwana in 1879, but the massacre there was more due to his incompetence as a military commander than promotional aspirations.

'Anyway, who really knows? All I can do is venture an opinion. The upshot of it all, of course, was that he gave the ghastly Gandhi his chance and he has been fomenting unrest ever since. When I say ghastly, of course, that is from a British commercial point of view. The Indians think he is a saint and he is highly regarded by some of the Liberal elements back home. What does seem clear is that with the Government of India Act of 1935 the British are slowly relinquishing power and appear to be enjoying their last years in control. India is certain to become a Dominion pretty soon in my opinion.'

He went on: 'Our government has tried to deal with Gandhi by spells of imprisonment alternated with invites to London to sit at the high table for pow-wow. They perhaps hoped to impress him with all the flummery, pomp, and grandeur in London but he was totally underwhelmed by it all. After seeing Parliament and the Horse Guards parading and all the rest, he was asked what he thought about Western Civilisation and he replied that he thought it would be a good idea! The King was very uneasy because he would not conform and wear a frock coat and top hat and bow and scrape in the royal presence like everyone else; he had never seen anything like it. Churchill was furious at his "disrespectful" informality. After all, fancy going to meet his Imperial Majesty wearing a shabby blanket and a ragged loin-cloth!'

The rains passed and the easy life resumed. John had found the small Indian wrestling club that Sergeant Budd had told him about. The man in charge was about fifty and of large build and had been a regional champion. A white man in the club was unusual but not unknown; there was no deference to him because of his race. It rapidly became apparent to John that those there were accorded status according to their ability on the mat and not according to race or creed.

The place was financed by a small mat fee from those attending and the sale of drinks and snacks prepared by the head wrestler's wife. There was a large class of juniors on Sunday mornings, with those who could afford it paying a few annas as the fee for their instruction. At the club, John found that he was stronger than all the others, but was nowhere near as lithe and flexible. The head wrestler watched him shrewdly and recommended an exercise routine with lots of vigorous stretching and some Indian club work to improve his deficiencies.

John worked at it assiduously, and found after a few months that he was much looser, and had become even more powerful than previously due to some hard wrestling bouts with his compatriots. Back in camp during the callisthenics sessions, he showed a new flexibility that surprised the instructors and caused them to think that he should be invited to join their ranks. The approach and suggestion that he would soon make corporal if accepted was rebuffed diplomatically, on the grounds that he did not wish to be separated from the two pals he had joined up with: 'We made a pact when we joined and I don't intend being the one to break it.'

Lt Tasburgh, although running the troop at arm's length through his NCOs, was shrewdly aware of each of his men's capabilities. He was also privy to the letters they sent home, as he had to censor them in case any vital military details such as dispositions or dysentery outbreaks reached unwelcome eyes back home. He could see that this young soldier wrote in a highly articulate manner and in a very well-formed copperplate style, which he felt was beyond certain of the officers he knew. He was also well aware of his ability to react rapidly in nasty situations, as had been demonstrated by his actions when the load had fallen on the quayside. Thus, he initiated an approach regarding promotion, but was told by the NCOs: 'He's just not interested, sir. He wants to stay with the lads, he says. They are all from the same mining village and have some sort of agreement to stick together.'

20

Mckinley and the War

The news from home filtered slowly back into India, seeming almost as though it was from another world. There was talk of alliances and growing distrust of Hitler as he started to acquire his first territories. This caused some excitement in military circles, as it appeared that finally the Army would have some money spent on it, with its home strength being increased to thirty-two divisions. This, of course, could mean promotional opportunities instead of the morale-sapping, dead-men's shoes advancements which had existed for many years. In March, Hitler seized Czechoslovakia and, finally seeing the danger, France and Britain entered into a treaty with Poland in a vain attempt to deter the Führer from further expansion. Rearmament got underway sluggishly and the Army slowly began to spend money on the sorts of arms that would be needed to fight a European war.

Little changed in the sub-continent; exercises and arms training were permitted to be stepped up a little as long as they did not interfere too much with the full social lives of the officers and ruling classes. In the ranks, it was the usual mix of drills, sport, boozing and occasional visits to the low-life dives in the city. At the end of the rainy season the news broke that Hitler had invaded Poland, and then news came over the wireless that on 3rd September, Britain had declared war on Germany.

Things had changed since the First World War. In 1914,

war was declared by Britain on behalf of the home country and the whole of the British Empire. By 1939, the Dominions of Australia, New Zealand, Canada and South Africa were free to decide for themselves if they entered the war. The Governments of Australia and New Zealand followed the Mother Country's example and declared war at once, without consulting their parliaments. The Canadians waited for their parliament to decide and declared war on 10th September.

South Africa had a strong Boer element in its ruling white population and a prime minister of Dutch descent who favoured neutrality. However, its parliament eventually voted by 80 votes to 67 to go to war. By this time, the Indians had gained powers at provincial government level and were slowly being nudged towards Dominion status. The Viceroy, Lord Linlithgow, declared war on Germany in a foolishly peremptory manner without consulting any of India's political leaders. Mckinley became aware that this caused huge anger and resentment amongst the nationalists, which the British government attempted to ameliorate later by promising that India would be granted full Dominion status after the war had been won.

At home, the conflict plodded through its early months with little actually happening. News trickled out to the regiment and other units after being given a suitable gloss to keep up morale. The first major adverse event was the sinking of *HMS Royal Oak* in Scapa Flow on 14th October with the loss of 786 lives. The event was put down to a mixture of bad luck and the underhand and dastardly cunning of the German U-boat commander responsible for the sinking. In the middle of December, news was received that three plucky, smaller ships had attacked the pocket battle ship the *Admiral Graf Spee*, which was subsequently scuttled off Montevideo. This seemed to even things out somehow and was a big boost to morale.

In France, the British Expeditionary Force was slowly built up to a strength of ten divisions. By May 1941, the Germans had 134 divisions on the western front, the French had 94 with everyone waiting for something to happen. In April, Hitler unleashed his forces and seized Denmark and Norway. In May, a full-scale invasion of France was undertaken and with amazing rapidity achieved complete success and the humiliating surrender of the old enemy. By early June, Dunkirk was over, with most of the British Expeditionary Force (BEF) saved but most of their equipment lost. It was now 'backs to the wall' time with Britain on its own in Europe. The defeat brought new urgency to bear, even in India. The West Yorks and other units were moved across to the eastern side of the sub-continent and took up new quarters in Calcutta. It seemed to the authorities that any threat to India would come from the east, in the form of Germany's fairly recently acquired ally, Japan.

Mckinley was not impressed by the new city and he tried to avoid it if possible. He did not like the inevitable cluster of 'wogs' which seemed to attach itself to any white man in the town. They cheerily shouted for 'Buck-shees' and he knew some troopers would throw a few annas or farthings amongst them and be amused as they scrabbled in the dust for the coins. He felt somehow that this was degrading and knew that the best way to get rid of them was not to encourage them in any way. 'The mob' usually made their way to the centre of the city on the Saturday nights to what were loosely described as nightclubs.

Some members of the troop picked up girls and indulged in that drunken and perfunctory sex that afflicts young men filled with testosterone. Others got drunk and worked out their frustrated urges in fisticuffs. Brenner went in to town on the lorry that carried the rest but always disappeared as soon as he got into Calcutta, going off towards the area of seedy brothels that most troopers avoided. John had some idea of what he was about and back at camp had noticed him furtively visiting some disused wooden storage buildings. One day he quietly followed him and had a look around after Brenner had left. He found a haversack stuffed at the back of a cupboard and inside it was a small, nasty looking, whip made of knotted strands of rawhide, and some short lengths of rope. The haversack always accompanied Brenner on his sojourns into the town.

On the Saturday evenings, Mckinley usually went into Calcutta with the rest but came back early after a few pints. He was far from being a sentimentalist but felt sorry for the bar girls, most of whom were Anglo-Indian. They seemed desperate to click with one of the lads and perhaps fantasised about marriage to some innocent young man and being romanced back to Blighty as a soldier's bride. They usually tried to claim that they were English. One evening he heard one saying that she had been born in Livery-pool which was ten minutes from Blacky-pool; the remark caused raucous laughter among the lads but the girl had no idea what caused it.

John was very aware that important things were happening, most of which went over the heads of his comrades in arms. He saw through the gloss put on the various British reverses by the papers. He learned that several Indian divisions had been transferred to bolster defences in the Middle East. Although the NCOs had been instructed to remain tight-lipped about anything they heard, army gossip and information from new arrivals made it clear that by September 1940 the losses in France had largely been made up. The Royal Navy was guarding the Channel approaches and a million of the newly formed Home Guard backed sixteen fully equipped army divisions on the south coast. John thought that the prospect of a German land invasion was now unlikely. He realised that the danger to his own family would come from air raids and from starvation due to U-boat attacks. Because of their relatively isolated location in Yorkshire, the danger from the former did not worry him unduly. 'In Skellow, there's more chance of getting killed at the pit than by the Luftwaffe,' he told Art and Quill.

Heavily glossed news came through of various setbacks, while huge coverage was given to minor victories and then to major ones, especially to the Battle of Britain. The RAFs eventual victory over the Luftwaffe and the superiority of the Spitfire over the Messerschmitt was to his mind portrayed in almost comic book fashion. Mckinley realised that the defenders must have a fuel advantage as they operated over home territory. He also knew from an RAF contact that the German plane was about as fast as the Spitfire and almost as manoeuvrable, and what is more had fifty-five seconds of fire power from cannons as opposed to the Spit's inferior fifteen seconds of fire from machine guns.

Nevertheless, he was as delighted as the rest that finally the Top Brass seemed to be getting something right. In November of 1940, news arrived that half of the Italian fleet had been put out of action at Taranto by a squadron of ancient torpedo planes. There also seemed to have been success in the desert against the Italians. In May 1941, news came through of the sinking of the *Bismarck*, with much justifiable prominence given to it in the media. The sinking of *HMS Hood* during the early part of the same engagement was portrayed as a tragic accident and a great source of sadness, but it was also played down considerably.

After his failure to defeat the RAF, Hitler loosed the Blitz on British towns and cities. Many buildings were destroyed but mercifully the civilian casualties were nowhere near the hundreds of thousands or millions that had been predicted by the tidy minds of the Civil Service. In India, the West Yorks increased its program of lectures. More small arms training was arranged and a good deal of physical training. Some small-scale exercises were carried out but the social life of the officers continued as usual and the rankers still spent most nights drinking in the mess. In June 1941, news came through that Hitler had invaded Russia and the pressure of the Blitz had slackened due to the transfer of much of the Luftwaffe to the east for the Russian campaign.

In December, in the week before Christmas, John was making his way towards the regimental HQ. He had just reached the bottom of the set of imposing steps that led up to the main entrance when a group of officers approached and John snapped out a very smart salute. A captain at the rear stepped forward and said, 'Mckinley, my dear chap. Delighted to see you again.' The Adjutant glared at the captain due to his casual overfamiliarity with a trooper, but the officer was having none of it; he turned to the rest and said: 'That young private saved me from being killed or seriously injured when we landed in Calcutta. Very fast thinking, just the kind of trooper we need at the present time.' He murmured quietly to John, 'We must have words later old boy, but I am rather tied up at present. Do excuse me.' John snapped out another salute and the party walked up into the HQ building.

A couple of days later Bell told him that he was required in the main buildings by a Captain Brody-Bollers. He said, pointedly, 'I hope there's not a problem.'

John said, 'Don't worry, Corp, it's probably about his sister!' The cryptic remark left Bell totally nonplussed and even more concerned than before.

He eventually found the office he had been directed to at the rear of the HQ. It was a rather untidy place and a corporal who had a cigarette dangling from a corner of his mouth (he always had a cigarette dangling from the corner of his mouth, as John later discovered) said, 'Oh, you're Mckinley. Go straight into the Major's office.'

John said, 'Don't you mean captain?'

The corporal said, 'He was until half an hour ago; his promotion has just come through. Someone up there really likes him, or perhaps they are impressed with what he is doing.'

Bollers was sat in a cane chair reading what looked like some sort of Chinese script. He looked up at Mckinley. His shirt was open at the neck and he wore a yellow silk cravat. 'Sit down, old boy,' he said warmly. 'You must be wondering what all this nonsense is about. All of this is totally confidential of course, and you are not to breathe a word about it to anyone. As you know, I have spent many years in the Far East as a tea trader. But one of the chaps at my club asked me before I left on my jaunts eastwards if I wouldn't mind keeping my eyes and ears open regarding any sort of military equipment, troop dispositions, transport and the like, should I come across it; a sort of unofficial, unpaid, agent, if you like.

'I passed the info back from time to time and tried to tell the dimwits in the foreign office that something big was happening and not to underestimate the jolly old Japs. It appears that they weren't actually all dimwits and when the eggs started to break I was invited to a very interesting chat with a very senior intelligence type.' The corporal brought tea in and poured three mugs full of the refreshing liquid. 'This is Kirkwood,' Bollers said. 'Lives on tea and cigarettes. He was one of my buyers in China. He speaks excellent Chinese and can read Mandarin and has fair Japanese, which improves daily. Scruffy bugger, but do not let that fool you. Very keen mind.

'To get to the point, after Dunkirk and due to some very real concerns about the Japanese, rapid moves were made to strengthen the intelligence section in the far eastern command. Strings were pulled and I moved from having been one of the most lackadaisical members of the officer cadets at my public school to being a full-blown captain in the proper army, and now very rapidly a major. Actually, that is probably because I have managed to pick up some very useful stuff and feed it back to HQ in Delhi.

'The regulars do not like it one little bit, but it has been explained to the upper levels, in the most gentlemanly manner possible, that I report straight to high command and do not fall under their authority in any way. After the Pearl Harbour disaster they have also been instructed to give me their fullest cooperation, and I understand that the word fullest was very strongly emphasised to them. London thinks that the American setback will neutralise the Yanks in the Pacific for up to two years and that we might have to hold the fort here very much on our own. In the longer run, of course, with the Russians and the Americans now in the party, we will undoubtedly win the war; it is just a question of doing it in the most effective manner possible and with the fewest casualties.

'We have been monitoring radio messages and other intercepts and trying to get a handle on their codes. There is a huge volume of traffic. We have some native clerks transcribing the stuff from recordings. We have scoured half of India to find them, but in a population of hundreds of millions it is surprising what turns up. We have an Anglo-Indian girl who worked as a nanny for one of the diplomats who was posted to our embassy in Japan. She could speak English and four of the Indian native languages when she went. The memsahibs showed no interest whatsoever but the nanny was bored out of her very active mind and rapidly learned Tokyo Japanese from the lower orders employed by the embassy. She even picked up a working knowledge of some of the dialects.

'I'm trying to put it all together. I spend most of my time reading transcripts and picking out those that have high volume code words or look important for other reasons, and send 'em back to HQ for decryption. What I badly need, old boy, is someone who is intelligent, reliable and above all quick-witted. I want you to act as a messenger and driver for me and to report to me directly. It would also be useful to know what the ordinary chaps are thinking about the present state of affairs. I can feed that in with some useful suggestions, perhaps, about training and moral. I'll have you paid as a corporal during the secondment. I do not know how long it will last but I suspect when they do realise what is happening they will move us to the centre of things, probably to Delhi. At that point, old boy, I'm afraid you will probably have to return to your regiment, but I think by then you might have picked up some useful insights into the way the jolly old Japs operate.'

Although Bollers had considered that it might be useful, he did not have an overriding need for John's services. However, he had been given carte blanche in respect of acquiring necessary personnel. Thus, by having John assigned to the intelligence section, he thought that in some small way he could repay his debt to the younger man by removing him for a while from the boredom of regimental routine. As a result, Mckinley found himself transferred to special duties in the small and very informal intelligence section.

He moved his kit across to the quarters assigned to that unit and had the unusual luxury, for a while, of his own small room. The big bonus as far as he was concerned was exemption from parades and especially the hated Sunday morning church parades. He had sought out Art and Quill in the mess just after his assignment and told them that he was on temporary duties elsewhere and would be back eventually but he did not know when. He advised them to keep their noses clean, keep their heads down, and to avoid promotion at all costs.

A group of military policemen were assigned to guard the entrance to the corridor that led to the section. They operated unobtrusively, sitting inside the doors next to a phone. Only authorized personnel were to be admitted. All others needed to be cleared first via the phone. Bollers told them that this included officers, and they were to allow no one to try to pull rank to get past them.

'What do we do if they try it, sir?' asked the sergeant Red Cap in charge.

'Well, you shoot them,' said Hugo.

'But what if it's the adjutant?' said the sergeant.

'Oh, him especially,' came the laconic reply.

The sergeant told his men that they would not shoot officers who tried to enter the inner sanctum. Nevertheless, they would tell them that they had received very specific orders from the highest level to let no one pass without authority and that it was a matter of high security and they would have to arrest them if they attempted to get past the guard.

'Do we really do that, sarge?' said one of his squad.

'Oh yes,' said the sarge. 'We do it very apologetically and nicely and take them back to the Colonel and hand them over for a bollocking.'

'We don't shoot them, then?' said one disappointed voice.

'No,' said their chief. 'Loud bangs give me a terrible head-ache and I don't like the sight of all that blood. We don't shoot anyone unless I give the order, is that clear?'

'Yes, sarge,' said the disappointed voice.

The sergeant had been in India for nine years and was very wise in the ways in which officers and rankers operated. He knew that the occasional officer had been despatched by troopers after trying to bully or bluster his way past guard posts. About four years previously he had been involved in an investigation after two hard-bitten older troopers had shot an officer in the small hours after he had suddenly appeared and had approached them without warning.

The man in question was thin faced and seemed con-stantly agitated. The troopers had nicknamed him 'Twitchy'. It had seemed that Twitchy had wanted to gain a reputation as a disciplinarian. He was a full lieutenant but promotion was painfully slow. He longed to be a captain and it appeared that he was determined to get there based on a reputation gained at the expense of those who served under him. He was noted for handing out unnecessary punishments for minor infringe-ments and was pretty much detested by all of his men.

After the rains had ceased he had adopted the practice of occasionally prowling around at night and suddenly appear-ing at sentry posts in the hope of taking the men off guard, in order to be able to gain brownie points with his superiors by jumping on those slackers for some minor infringement. On one occasion, he appeared and was not challenged as both troopers recognised him. He tore into them because they had not meticulously adhered to regulations. Though both pro-tested that they could see it was him and not some sort of interloper, it was to no avail. Both were subsequently con-fined to barracks for seven days for failing to issue the proper challenges.

The two old sweats had both sworn on oath that a stran-ger had appeared at about two am and had been challenged in the appropriate way, but had not responded—just marched towards them with something in his hand. A second challenge 'halt or I fire' had been issued to no effect and the troopers had thus felt compelled to fire to protect the base and themselves. They made no mistake, two shots rang out simultaneously, and unfortunately Twitchy lay dead, shot through the chest and head, the swagger stick he had been carrying still grasped rigidly in his fist.

The redcaps had told the CO that the troopers had followed standing orders correctly and that it was a pity the officer had placed himself in the unfortunate position that had caused his demise. They also ventured the opinion that it was clear that there were no grounds for disciplinary action against the men. The CO had thought that the officer was somewhat odd and had not liked his obvious promotion chasing. He also did not like the notion of an officer being shot. But the army was about rules and procedures and the two privates had followed them exactly and could not be faulted. The only route which was open to him, to express his displeasure, was to have the men marched in and explain that he was very unhappy about the affair and that he would be watching every move they made in the future. The two were very apologetic and saluted smartly and then left the august presence of their CO.

In informed quarters, it was believed that Twitchy had jumped out and the two had just shot him. Thereafter, both men were very careful. They sat together in the mess and took good care not to drink to any extent and become careless about what they might say. They had about eighteen months left to serve and then they were out of the army and back to Blighty, time served and on a full private's pension.

21

Mckinley and Intelligence

Various things stood out for Mckinley during the months he was with the intelligence unit. He was particularly impressed with the very clear picture that Bollers had of what was happening. Almost everyone else he spoke to was either in the dark and fearful, or jingoistic and overoptimistic. Though reverses had occurred, the worst of them being the surrender of over a hundred thousand British and Commonwealth troops in Singapore, Hugo remained sanguine and very sure of eventual Allied success. He explained that lessons would be learned by analysing the reasons for the failures and that the Japanese would face greater and greater difficulties as their supply lines became stretched and as they came under increasing attack from the Americans. This would drain their manpower and resources, he said.

He had explained that Singapore had fallen due to a mixture of incompetence by Arthur Percival and Gordon Bennet, who had been appointed as the British and Australian commanders in Singapore, and to a series of crass assumptions about what the Japanese were capable of by the higher levels within the army and the government. The orthodox view was that the Japanese would be unable to advance through the 'impenetrable' Malaysian Jungle, and certainly not with tanks. It had been discovered with considerable chagrin that this was something that they could do rapidly and apparently with little difficulty.

Bollers told John that Percival had not strung the large quantities of barbed wire with which he had been supplied in front of the defences, despite repeated requests by the Brigadier commanding the Royal Engineers that he should do so. When finally pressed into giving an explanation, he said that he believed to do so would be bad for the morale of troops and civilians.

'Bloody good job that Haig didn't think that way on the Somme, eh!' said Hugo. 'Well, at least he surrendered with his troops; by all accounts, he seemed to have almost lost his grasp of reality when he was surrendering to Yamashita. He seemed fixated on having 1500 troops left under his command in order to police Singapore while the Japanese took over. He really did not have the slightest grasp of Japanese psychology or their military code of Bushido. Finally, Yamashita got fed up of the wittering from Percival, banged the table, glared at him, and said, "Will you surrender!" At that point, Percival lamely said, "Yes." Gordon Bennet, the Australian CO, apparently paid a fishing boat skipper to get him out of it and he is back in Australia and in very bad odour, by all accounts.

'Since then we have been fighting a retreating action and learning about the Japanese warrior the hard way. The units down there are not properly equipped or trained for jungle warfare and air cover is patchy. However, as the Japanese advance, things will swing in our favour. We will start to get the right sort of commanders and equipment and men. The Chinese are moving down under Stilwell to protect the Burma-China road, which delivers supplies to the Chinese from the railhead in Lashio. The likelihood is that they will be overrun and forced to retreat, but at least it takes pressure off our chaps.'

He went on: 'War has a strange habit of sifting out the ept from the inept.' He shot a look at Kirkwood after noting his eyes moving skywards in disapproval. 'No such word as ept, is there, old boy?' he said to the crossword devouring Corporal.

'No,' sneered the linguist from the corner of his mouth not

holding his cigarette. 'Inept is from the Latin word *in-eptus, in* meaning not and *aptus* meaning apt!'

'Ah! Thought so,' said Bollers. 'Very clever, Kirkwood,' he said to John in a conspiratorial sort of way. 'Very precise with words. He has a low opinion of the officer class in general and a tendency to be insubordinate. If he worked for anyone else, he would have had a career as a spud-peeling private. He thinks that the notion of Military Intelligence is a contradiction in terms, don't you Kirkwood?' The sergeant just looked back at him in a supercilious way and carried on with what he was doing. 'Rhetorical question, eh? No reply required. Quite right,' said Bollers.

The final and invaluable lesson that John learned from Brody-Bollers was about the Japanese. For years, all aspects of Japanese culture and language had fascinated the Major. He said, 'I found a copy of Lord Redesdale's *Tales of Old Japan* in the library at home when I was a child. Baron Algernon Bertram Freeman–Mitford Redesdale, there's a name for you. It was fascinating stuff, tales like the forty-seven Ronin and of Samurai feuds, folk tales and descriptions of low life around Yokohama. I suppose that triggered it all off. The main thing to remember about the Japanese and Japan is never to believe any of the crass tosh you see in the papers or newsreels about them. It seems to be put together by bumptious, old school imperialists who really don't have a clue about it.'

Bollers went on: 'Extremely interesting culture the Japanese! They and the British are both island races and there are similarities, but the geography is different. Japan has many active volcanoes and is subject to severe earthquakes. Its main landmasses stretch approximately between latitudes 30 to 45 while Britain is located between latitudes 50 to 60. Both are in the northern hemisphere. That fact took some time to get into my head, because it was well beyond India and well towards Australia; as a kid, I always pictured it as being in the South. The northern bits can have cold winters with temperatures down to minus 20 up in the mountains. The southern islands have temperate winters and hot dry summers. It has a land area about half as big again as Britain but much more of it is not suitable for agriculture due to the mountains and volcanoes. About sixty of those are still active, by the way. The area seems to be geologically active for some reason and the islands have many earthquakes, some of 'em very severe.

'The Japanese are an Asiatic race, technically mongoloid, but they are not the original inhabitants of the islands. The original peoples are called the Ainu. Only a few thousands of them remain now, on the northern island of Hokkaido. Racially, these peoples seem to be Caucasoid and not dissimilar to the southern Mediterranean types. They have wavy hair as opposed to the straight hair seen in the Asians and their skin colour is light brown. They are also unusually hairy. There are remains of Ainu hill forts in Hokkaido, probably constructed as they attempted to defend their last island stronghold from the ancestors of the present Japanese. The situation there must have been similar to the displacement of the Celts by the Angles, Saxons and Jutes. They, of course, were pushed off into the mountains and moors in the West of Britain as the Germanic tribes moved in.

'The other similarity between our island races is the warfare between the different clans and tribes. This went on for centuries, as with us. A major difference was the length of our feudal periods. Ours was relatively short due to the rise of the mercantile class in the fourteenth century and the proximity of European countries and the trading relationships that developed between them. Their feudal period was much longer and was much more rigid. In their case, they only had one real continental neighbour, the Chinese, and neither of them were much interested in trade or cultural exchanges.

'That system ceased less than a hundred years ago. The feudal discipline, instilled during those long centuries, still appertains, and is one of the reasons for the present success of the Japanese army. They are tough, very fit and used to privation. The soldiers obey even to the extent of falling on a

344

grenade if ordered to. They do not grumble like the British Tommies, who have been used to democratic freedoms for decades. Their obedience, actually, can be a weakness—they are used to obeying and not to thinking. The Japanese soldier is much more like a feudal vassal than our men, with the privates and NCOs owing complete allegiance to the officers and the officers owing complete allegiance to their commanders who owe complete allegiance to the Emperor, who incidentally is regarded as a god.'

He went on: 'The Japanese managed to stop two Mongol invasions in the thirteenth century and this in turn enabled them to maintain centuries of isolation. If we compare them to Britain, our history went broadly: peace under the Romans, then invasions by small tribes who gradually became bigger until they were all united under a single king in the tenth century. From that time on, with one or two wobbles, England has been a single country under a single monarch with a gradual transfer of power from the monarch and barons to the people.

'Compare that to Japan, old boy. Perhaps because of the geography and thousands of small islands, the rulership has oscillated between periods of unification and thus stability, and periods of fragmentation where the barons took control with resulting anarchy due to the incessant clan warfare. The periods of stability were usually brought about when one clan gained dominance and a Shogunate was established. Shogun translates literally as 'first in war' by the way. We would call him a military dictator. They ran a military government whilst allowing the Imperial court to continue its activities connected with high culture but with little political power or money; because of that their royalty was held in tremendous respect but had little real influence.

'At about the period from when we were ruled by Alfred the Great to Richard II, power was gradually lost in Japan by the Emperor to the provincial barons. The country lapsed into civil disorder, and then civil war broke out between two clans of Imperial descent, the Taira and Minamoto. In 1185,

Yorimoto Minamoto was victorious and became Shogun. Although rulership subsequently passed to the Hojo clan, they kept a lid on things and governed effectively until about 1280. With their decline and fall came the most anarchic period ever known in Japan, with constant clan warfare and resulting bad government and lawlessness until 1615. That was the date when Tokugawa Ieyasu overcame the last resistance and became undisputed Shogun of all Japan. The last Shogunate kept things stable until nominal Imperial power was restored in 1868 under the Meiji Emperor.

'I hope I'm not boring you, old boy,' said Bollers, 'but I find all this absolutely riveting and actually it is the root of our present difficulties. If we understand what drives the Japanese military psychology it will make our task of defeating them easier. If you have any questions, just fire away.'

'I've heard of the Samurai, they were more or less the equivalent of our feudal knights, but what is a Ronin?'

'Ah!' said Hugo. 'They were a sort of vagrant Samurai class who had lost their positions and were no longer attached to a major household. They sort of drifted around like flotsam looking for work as mercenaries or bodyguards and the like. The word actually translates as "wave-man".

'The group of statesmen who took power in the Emperor's name realised that Japan must be opened up to western technology, especially military technology. We can date their drive to industrialise from that date. By 1904-5, they were sufficiently advanced in warship and armaments development to defeat the Russians in the Russo-Japanese war. The progress from almost medieval weaponry to modern armaments in less than forty years should have rung alarm bells with someone. In fact, it did with one or two of the brighter individuals in the civil service and army, but at higher levels no one was listening. Almost another forty years have passed and their military equipment has been improved at a faster rate than in any other nation. Finally, now that our ships and planes are being destroyed by theirs, the threat is starting to sink in.'

346

John absorbed all of it. He realised that they were up against a powerful enemy yet was also sure that Hugo was right about what would happen. It was just about getting all the cogs in the British war machine working together. He could see that the Japanese supply lines were getting longer as theirs shortened. The British were being pushed back, but like a spring being compressed, it was just a matter of time before it sprang back very viciously.

The one important thing, which no one seemed to know, not even Bollers, was how far the Japanese could advance before they ran out of steam, although he became much more cheerful when General Slim took charge in Burma. Hugo said, 'He is exactly the right sort of soldier for the job!' Despite this, during May, the British evacuated Mandalay and retreated over the Irrawaddy, and the oilfields at Yenangyaung were blown up. Japanese successes in the east against Chinese armies enabled them to move to Lashio and thus cut the Burma Road. The only option available to the British now was a fighting retreat to India, regrouping and then going back eventually in strength with superior armour and air cover.

By the end of May, the retreat had been completed. Re-supply in India wasn't being helped by Rommel's advance in the desert and the need to divert men and supplies there. Despite all of this, his leader seemed to grow more and more cheerful. In February, the remnant of a large German army had surrendered at Stalingrad. He said to his staff: 'Now they are for it; it seems the Russian Bear has woken up at last and is starting to get annoyed.'

In early June, he was whooping with joy when he heard that the U.S. Navy had destroyed four Japanese carriers and three hundred aircraft at the battle of Midway. 'Turning point, old boy,' he said to Mckinley. 'Critical turning point! Without their carriers they will have to pull their horns in in the Pacific.' With the coming of the monsoon the Japanese advance stopped.

Bollers was also cheered by the increasingly good

intelligence he was getting; his own network was getting better and better and photo reconnaissance aircraft had arrived at long last. In addition, two thousand hill tribesmen from the Assam—Burma border had been formed into a unit called V force under British officers. The original intention had been to enter into guerrilla operations, but as things were working out they were providing invaluable information on Japanese troop movements.

About a month later, Mckinley entered the intelligence office and his CO was in deep conversation with a young and very tough looking captain who had commando badges on his uniform. The commando looked up and said to John: 'I noticed from your record that you are from a small place called Skellow in the West Riding of Yorkshire. I was recently involved in an action in Burma with someone called Plunkett-Green, also from Skellow in the West Riding; did you know him at all?'

John volunteered the information that he did know the man slightly and had heard that after conscription PG junior had joined the medical corps.

Hugo looked at the commando and said, 'You were there, old man. Can you tell the story?'

The commando said: 'During the retreat, things had been pretty desperate from time to time with, for example, bridges being blown up with troops stranded on the wrong side of the rivers. They then had the choice of trying to swim for it or captivity. A constant source of concern was for the injured as cases had been reported of the sick and injured having their throats cut or being bayoneted.

'We were defending a position about a hundred miles north of Mandalay and trying to get everyone evacuated from a field hospital. We had managed it apart from about a dozen of the most serious cases. Japanese infiltration became so strong that we were forced to retreat and leave them, we had no choice. The Medical Officer and a medical orderly called Cedric Plunkett-Green offered to stay behind with the wounded. These were on stretchers under awnings in a large clearing where Red Cross symbols were displayed prominently. I was last to leave and was on the side of a hill with my driver just above the camp looking down with my binoculars. I was not happy about the situation but was hopeful that the Japs would respect the white flag and the surrender of a doctor.

'The advance party of Japanese arrived—three soldiers, an NCO, and an officer. He was carrying a sword and obviously in charge. The MO came out from amongst the casualties and advanced with a white flag in one hand and his other hand in the air. The Jap in charge said something and three of the soldiers went over to the awning. He said something to them all and the NCO stuck a bayonet straight into the guts of the MO and the others started to bayonet the stretcher cases.

'Plunkett-Green must have been in the medical tent because as the bayonets went in I heard a loud scream and he ran out of the tent with a revolver. He shot the one who had bayoneted the MO. The three privates came rushing out from under the awning and Plunket-Green shot two of 'em, but the third managed to get a shot off and he fell to his knees. Even then, he managed to get the revolver up and shot the officer between the eyes, before falling back, obviously severely wounded. Some more Japs burst into the clearing and several of 'em stuck bayonets into Green.

'Another officer arrived, stopped them, and then must have asked what had happened. About half of the stretcher cases had been killed but Green's intervention brought things to a halt. Shortly after that a lorry arrived and the survivors were loaded onto it. The officer gave out some sharp orders. The bodies of our people were piled up, petrol poured on 'em and they were all set alight, apart from Plunkett-Green. For some reason they buried him and they seemed quite respectful of the body.

'It was late afternoon by then and I could see 'em posting guards and starting to get a meal ready from the rations they had taken from the medical tent. I was hopping mad and if I had had any sort of detachment with me or a Vickers, I would have sprayed the lot of 'em. I just had my Webley, of course, so at that point I thought that discretion would be the better part of valour and I sloped off. I was determined to do two things: the first was to report the atrocity; the second was to recommend that medical orderly for a decoration. It was one of the bravest things I have ever seen. He rushed out, obviously with no thought for his own safety, in order to avenge the doctor's death and to protect those badly injured patients. When you take into account that the fellow was not combat trained but just a medic, his actions were even more praise-worthy.

'I was asking the Major why he thought they burned everyone except him.'

Hugo said, 'You can never tell but I think it's a fair bet that they buried him because he was a warrior who fell in action; they would respect that.'

The actuality, of course, was only known to Plunkett-Green, and as he now lay amongst the glorious dead, no one would ever find out. However, the facts were that Cedric was absolutely besotted by the MO. He had observed the approach of the Japanese with apprehension and then looked on in horror as his lover had been murdered. He had screamed loudly when he witnessed the dastardly act and had grabbed a service revolver which lay on the top of an equipment trunk and ran out firing the gun blindly in the direction of the killer and then at the soldiers as they came towards him. The third soldier had put a fatal shot into him, but as he dropped to his knees, his arm came up by reflex and he fired the last random shot that fortuitously took the Jap officer between the eyes.

'I've written it up,' said the commando captain, 'and put in a recommendation for a decoration. He might even get the VC.'

It later transpired that the actual criteria for awards were fairly arbitrary, but Cedric ended up with a posthumous Military Medal. Back in the family home, although his wife was devastated, PG Senior read the citation repeatedly. 'Despite those early disappointments, I always knew the boy had it in him,' he told himself. 'When the call came, he answered it. I knew he would do it.' After that, he always thought of and spoke of his son in the warmest terms. Those fond consolations stayed with him until the day of his death.

The lull in fighting in Burma enabled intensive training of the units in India and facilitated a build-up of equipment. The Japanese reverse at Midway meant that a seaborne invasion of Ceylon or southern India was now unlikely and troops were released from Wavell's southern army for the defence of the north. Bollers thought that things had started to look positively promising. Mckinley always kept close to him, driving the staff car when needed and hand delivering important messages. Wherever they went, another car followed them containing four heavily armed Military Policemen.

It was late August, 1942. The monsoon was unrelenting at that time of year and John trudged to the office wearing an oilskin and wellingtons. He got to the unit slightly later than normal, hung his oilskin on the porch, and changed the wellies for boots. As he walked in, he could feel an atmosphere. Kirkwood and the others scurried round with eyes downcast, looking almost guilty. The corporal had now become a sergeant and was minus the cigarette, which was usually a permanent fixture in the corner of his mouth. Brody-Bollers was sat at his untidy, paper covered desk. He looked ashen. He glanced up at Mckinley almost in a trance; it was as though he was not there.

'Can I get you a cup of tea, sir?' John said, realising that something was seriously wrong.

'Tea, tea,' mused Bollers. 'The ubiquitous panacea for all the nations' ills.' Then, seeming to snap out of it, he said: 'By all means, old boy, let's have some tea. Thank you for the thought.'

Mckinley brought the tea and started to pour it. 'Will you

join me, old boy?' said Bollers, with his usual and unfailing courtesy. 'I've had some rather bad news.' He pushed a telegram across the desk and said, 'Please read it. It's from my younger sister. She's given up socialism for the duration and now works in Whitehall at the Ministry of Defence, very close to the centre of things. Runs into the PM virtually every other week.'

The telegram went:

DEAREST HUGO. WITH GREATEST SADNESS. I
MUST TELL YOU THAT HECTOR AND ALEX ARE
DEAD. ALEX AT DIEPPE. HECTOR IN AN AIR RAID IN
LONDON. WILL WRITE IMMEDIATELY. ROWENA IS
TAKING IT VERY BADLY. FATHER IS TOO ILL TO BE
TOLD. ROSALIND.

The two men were Brody-Bollers two older brothers. An airmail letter arrived about a week later giving the details. Hector had been seeing a female ATS officer to safety after hearing the air raid siren while they were out in London. Unfortunately, he had very urgent business back at the Guards barracks and had decided to risk a return. He was caught by a bomb blast, having just about made it back, whilst sprinting for the entrance to a shelter. Alexander had died gallantly, trying to move his men to safety on the Dieppe beaches. He had been recommended for the Military Cross, but this was little consolation for the loss of a dearly loved eldest brother.

A week after that, a further telegram arrived:

DEAREST HUGO. WITH GREATEST SADNESS.
FATHER DIED LAST NIGHT ASKING FOR HIS
BOYS. MERCIFULLY, STILL NOT KNOWING ABOUT
ALEX AND HECTOR. WILL WRITE IMMEDIATELY.
ROSALIND.

After receiving the news, Bollers had lost much of his light-heartedness. Up to then the war had seemed almost a game, or that was the impression he gave of it. He was now immersing himself ferociously in intelligence details. When the second telegram arrived, he read it, and remarked grimly to Kirkwood and Mckinley. 'Well chaps, as Byron once remarked, "It never rains, but it pours".' He then picked up his signals and carried on reading, seemingly oblivious of all around him.

It was from about this time that the colours in John's universe seemed to change. When he had arrived there, the vivid colours of India had replaced the soft, virginal greens of England. Burning reds and gold had usurped pale insignificant mists at dawn. The tenuous and hesitant whites of home were drowned out by a brilliance which almost dazzled. The huge blossoms, raging with the passion of violent colour, had overpowered his memories of the delicate English blooms. He had been almost overwhelmed by the richness of it all, by the intoxicating, exhilarating madness of the riot of the various hues.

However, his perceptions had changed and the magical colours of India ceased to have an impact. John's world now seemed to be coloured khaki, or buff, or asphalt grey, or insipid green like the peeling paint in the office, or monotonous dark green like the filing cabinets. Something seemed to have sucked all the vitality from that brilliant world, and only the colours of war now seemed to register with him.

About a month passed by. A letter arrived by army courier from the families' solicitors. It was addressed to Sir Hugo Brody-Bollers Bt. Hugo had inherited his father's title and the estates and farms which went with it, along with half ownership in a small armaments factory. After all taxes had been deducted his sisters had received about £20,000 each. Mr Whimshurst, the solicitor, pointed out that further monies would be forthcoming from the estates of his brothers. Both had owned town houses in London and various gilts, equities and debentures, and neither of the men had any known heirs.

Hugo took no pleasure in any of it. His tea trading activities had resulted in considerable personal wealth. He had never expected to inherit anything substantial from his father and thus had made his own arrangements. He would have traded the lot for a single further day with his brothers but that was no longer possible. He now turned his considerable intellect, single-mindedly, to the task. The day after the receipt of the letters, Kirkwood heard his chief musing aloud at his desk: 'Sir Hugo Bloody Brody-Bollers Bart, bollocks, bollocks, bollocks.' The language analyst idly wondered if he should start to address his boss as 'Sir, Sir,' but wisely thought, on reflection, perhaps not!

The pace of intelligence activities and everything else seemed to pick up from that point. Although everything was very hush-hush, it was clear that some sort of major operation was being planned against the Japanese. Morale, generally, was improving; although it was accepted that it would be a hard slog, the high-ups could now see light at the end of the dark tunnel of war, which had almost swallowed Britain, and were now sure of eventual victory.

Early in September, John drove Hugo into the commercial part of Calcutta. It was a monthly meeting where his chief met several of his agents for a briefing in the offices in one of the small steamship companies with which he had enjoyed pre-war links. Even with the interruption of war, the area was still bustling with activity. In addition to representatives of the many races of India, many others filled the streets and alleyways. There was always a sprinkling of whites, Chinese, Malays, Burmese, blacks, half-castes, and even a few Arabs could be seen. Slow moving dhows were still frequent visitors to the port, however they tended to hug the coast and be a lot more careful these days. Although it was felt that any Japanese aircraft or subs this far across the Bay of Bengal would not bother to waste ammunition on these relatively small trading craft, they took as few chances as possible.

John stopped the staff car, and Bollers leaped out and hurried inside the dilapidated building. The meeting usually lasted about an hour. The four MPs got out of their vehicle and stood around chatting and smoking. Mckinley sat in the car waiting. He did not like the look of some of the shifty characters in the area and he wanted to be ready for a quick getaway if there was any sort of native demonstration brewing. After the appointed hour, two of his chief's agents appeared and walked off in different directions. Hugo then emerged deep in conversation with a third as he walked towards the car.

The MPs moved towards their conveyance and were starting to climb into their seats, laughing and chatting as they did so. Someone emerged from a shop doorway on the opposite side of the street. John's eye was attracted by his rapid movement towards the car. The man approached and as he got to the middle of the road, Mckinley could see a gun in his hand. Almost without thinking John grabbed the service revolver which his boss had left on the dashboard before going into the meeting, knocked the safety catch off, swung it up, and fired, just a fraction of a second before the assailant could get his shot off.

Though the weapons seemed to have been discharged simultaneously, John's bullet hit the would-be assassin in his shoulder just in time to knock him back and spoil his aim. Because of this, the attacker fired high and his bullet passed about six inches over Hugo's head. The assailant, though obviously in pain, stepped forward and raised his pistol again. Mckinley loosed two more shots into the man's trunk and he fell back unconscious or dead. Hugo had ducked after the first shot and his agent had dived under the car for cover. The MPs came rushing towards the staff car, fumbling with their lanyards and covers to their holsters, drawing their weapons as the man fell to the ground. Bollers pointed and shouted: 'Bring him! Make sure he is disarmed! Try to stop the bleeding! Bring that pistol to me!' He leapt into the car and an MP passed the attackers weapon through the window. Bollers said, 'Put your foot down, old boy.' Mckinley needed no second telling, he was already revving the engine as Hugo took the seat beside him. They set off at high speed with the MPs just behind.

They had engaged the siren on their vehicle and at the third junction along the road were joined by another escort who had just happened to be out on patrol in the area. This vehicle was a jeep with two MPs in it—one had a submachine gun and looked ready to use it. The base was about a half-hour drive away. The MPs had used the car's radio and within five minutes four truckloads of military police and heavily armed troopers were heading in their direction. The two convoys passed about ten minutes from the base and one of the trucks swung round and started to follow Mckinley whilst the others raced towards the commercial district.

Bollers had remained quiet and in deep thought for about ten minutes. He finally broke his silence and said, 'Slow down, old boy. I think we are out of danger now.' Mckinley slowed to a brisk 40 mph. Hugo said: 'I must thank you profoundly once more, old chap. You have now saved my life on two separate occasions. That really was extremely quick thinking; most people would have just frozen. I did not think that the Japanese counter intelligence was so good or had penetrated so far.'

'You think it's the Japanese, sir, and not some sort of nationalist?' John asked.

Bollers said, 'I took a quick look at the attacker and would say he was probably Burmese. However, there is no mistaking this,' he said, pointing to the failed assassin's weapon. 'It's a type 94 Shiki Kenju automatic pistol. The Japanese army started to get these in the late thirties. They are almost unknown outside of Japanese hands so it must have come down those channels. If he survives those three bullets you put in him, we might be able to extract some information from the blighter. You blasted him with my Webley 38 which packs quite a punch and is very reliable compared to the Shiki Kenju, which, actually, is a bloody awful pistol.'

At the intelligence unit, the guards seemed to double overnight. The guard at the camp gate also strengthened. The communications channels seemed to be red hot and within days a captain of Military Police arrived with a detachment of twenty men. The man was sharp eyed and keen, his men were handpicked and he did not miss a trick. The assassination attempt had been explained to him and the serious consequences that would have arisen if it had been successful. His CO had told him that now they were aware of the threat, further attempts would be unlikely to be successful. The captain explained to his men: 'We got this assignment from General Wavell himself and Wavell is one of the most gentlemanly officers I have ever met. But I did get the distinct impression whilst I was being briefed that should the slightest thing happen to our charge, our next assignment would be guard duty on the Russian front.'

About a week after the attack, a dispatch was received promoting Bollers to Lieutenant-Colonel. The adjutant did not like the promotion one bit, suspecting it was due to family connections. He also thought it was far too premature. Thus, he informally sought reasons for it from his CO. Grimston himself was only partially in the picture as everything was top secret. However, he managed to convey that the work Bollers was doing was invaluable and that as a Colonel he could expedite matters in intelligence and with other channels. In addition, various senior officers such as Group Captains, Majors, etc., would be reporting directly to him. He obviously couldn't be inferior in rank to them.

The adjutant bristled a bit but just had to swallow it. Grimston also said, 'Don't worry, old boy. We are likely to be in action pretty soon and in my experience promotions always flow from that.' The adjutant knew exactly what he meant, realising that gaps occurred in the officer ranks due to premature death in the field from shellfire, mines or bullets. Those fortunate enough to survive could be expected to fill the gaps in the senior ranks. The trick was, of course, to make sure that you were one of the survivors.

The flurry of activity had rather taken Bollers mind off

his personal situation. Further letters arrived from the family solicitor and from Rosalind telling him that their father and two brothers had been buried in the churchyard on the family estate after a joint ceremony for all three. The place had been crammed to the rafters, with a couple of hundred others standing with bare heads outside the church in the English drizzle during the service. The solicitor informed him that his elder brother had left fifty thousand and his younger brother thirty-five, both amounts after death duty. Hugo wrote back instructing that the monies were to be divided equally between his two sisters.

At the unit, all the staff were extremely busy apart from Mckinley, who had been kicking his heels for almost a fortnight as no driving or courier duties had been required. Eventually, Lieutenant-Colonel Brody-Bollers sent for him and said, 'Two things, old boy. The first is that the surgeons managed to save the blighter who took the pot shot at me. He is Burmese and belongs to Aung San's bunch of renegades who are trying to establish a Burmese government independent of colonial rule. We have managed to turn the bugger and he has been very useful. He was not going to cooperate at first but I got Kirkwood to take him off in handcuffs to witness a hanging. Very gruesome by all accounts, and after that he seemed quite keen to help us out.

'We have been able to round up several agents who are working for the Japanese as a result of the information he has provided. They also are being presented with the choice of either coming on board and working as double agents or being hanged as spies. It's marvellous how the prospect of a long drop on the end of a short rope concentrates the mind. We think all of them will come over and join us in our noble task of bamboozling the jolly old Japs with lots of misinformation.

'The second thing I have to tell you is that I am being ordered to the centre of things in Delhi. This unit is considered to be too exposed here; most of the staff will join a large intelligence analysis unit, apart from Kirkwood who will come with me. I can pull strings and have you assigned to that unit, but our regular contact will be lost I am afraid. I also know your views on becoming an NCO, so no point in pursuing that, is there?' he said, looking straight at Mckinley. 'I thought I would seek your views first.'

John paused a few moments, churning things over in his mind. Finally, he said, 'Thank you very much for the offer, sir, but if it's all the same to you I will return to the regiment. It's been very enjoyable, very interesting, even exciting from time to time, but I have a couple of pals in my troop who I need to look after if we are going into action.'

Bollers looked at him. The look was affectionate and quizzical at the same time. 'I thought that would be your reaction, old boy. Lots would jump at the prospect of a cushy number, but not you, eh? Very well, I want you to get through this in one piece, so let me give you a personal and highly confidential briefing; you are to tell no one, they will find out soon enough anyway.

'You have seen the usual propaganda nonsense on the newsreels of course; however, and this is the real picture, it is growing increasingly clear that the enemy is being stretched. He is suffering reverses in Russia and will soon feel the full Allied weight in North Africa. In the Pacific, the Americans and Australians are having successes. Things must be bad because in September Tojo resigned as the Japanese foreign minister.

'Our air strength is growing in India and that of the Japanese seems to be static. In addition, we are getting some of the very latest fighters that will finally outmatch their Zeros. We are also getting some Beaufighters—wonderful! They have four cannon and six machine guns at the front. Their large hydromantic twin props make 'em so quiet, they are on top of the enemy before they know it. The Japanese hate 'em; they are already calling the plane "Whispering Death"—very poetic and very apt.

'In respect of army activities, and do keep this absolutely

hush-hush old boy, two offensive actions are under consideration. One is a major attack down the Arakan, the other will be action by a Long Range Penetration Group under a chap called Wingate. Bit of an oddball, but he has a proven record in guerrilla operations. It will be a volunteer force and may be the better of the two operations to take part in.'

He went on: 'You have obviously picked up bits of Japanese and an insight into how they think, but let me flesh it out for you a little. We have talked previously about the very long feudal period in Japan. During those years, the warrior class or Samurai adhered to a ferocious military code known as Bushido. This demands total loyalty to one's superiors and ultimately to the Emperor. The Japanese will not retreat and will fight to the death if ordered to. They will not surrender and in fact despise prisoners for their weakness for having surrendered. Any prisoners taken can be expected to be starved and beaten. If they strike back, they are executed. The Japs pay lip-service to the Geneva Convention. The message here, old boy, is: do not be taken prisoner by the blighters.

'It is a little difficult to get the differences in our cultures over to a Western mind. Here the traditions grew out of knightly combat, where warfare was often seen in chivalric terms as the supreme form of sport. It wasn't uncommon for the victorious knights to feast the vanquished lords after the battle. Prisoners were generally treated honourably.'

John said: 'I know what you mean, sir. One of the new recruits from my home village told the tale of a captive German officer from a POW camp near the village being taken out riding by a British officer. They were riding down a bridle path and the British officer made the mistake of ordering some of the local youths to get out of their way. He didn't like their response, apparently.'

'Oh? What was it?' said Bollers, smiling.

'Well, they tell me it was a bit 'fuck-offee' in tone,' replied Mckinley with a grin.

Bollers roared with laughter and said, 'Well, that should

have conveyed something to him about the strength of feeling about the Nazis.'

'They weren't going to step aside for a German under any circumstances, sir,' he said. 'They have brothers and cousins out there fighting them. The officer told them that when they were in uniform he would make sure that they were taught some manners. That really annoyed them. They all worked in mining, which is a reserved occupation of course, so they knew he couldn't touch them. The officer tried to ride through them so they tore up grass sods and pelted him until he turned round. But the fact he was out riding with a brother officer, though an enemy one, illustrates the point you are trying to make, doesn't it sir?'

'Yes, all too readily,' said Bollers, smiling. 'If that had happened in Japan until very recently, they would have been slaughtered by any Samurai subjected to such an insult, and the authorities would have considered such a response perfectly acceptable. So don't forget, your enemy will not give any quarter: make sure you don't give any.

'I understand that there are all sorts of fairy stories around about the Japanese soldier being some sort of superman, but that is far from the truth. I have seen the casualty lists and during our retreat the casualties in both armies were approximately the same. I also know that their forces are badly affected by malaria and they have difficulties in getting the quinine and other treatments, and food supplies generally, into this theatre of war; their top priorities are against the Americans and Aussies. We, on the other hand, are now building in strength and getting the upper hand in terms of men and armaments. We are also starting to destroy their supply convoys very effectively.'

Bollers paused and went to a large cupboard. 'I understand other myths circulate, such as those about weapons such as this—the Samurai sword.' He placed the sword, which he had taken from the shelves, in front of Mckinley. 'There are various sorts of Japanese sword but the main one is called the

Katana. They are now being mass produced in millions from pressed steel for the officers and NCOs. They are just ordinary swords, no better or worse than, for example, an army sabre.

'Some of the older Katanas produced by the great Japanese smiths are works of art and are beautifully made to a very high standard. The one before you is one of those. They have very tough blades and are exquisitely sharp. It was said that they were tested on the corpses of convicts and that a single blow could cut through three of them. That may or may not be true, but you are very unlikely to come across one of these. In any event, anyone waving one at you can pretty easily be dispatched with a bullet or bayonet before they get to you, as they are a relatively short sword.'

He looked across at Mckinley: 'You are getting the picture, old boy. The odds are swinging inexorably in our favour, we will clearly win the war, but it will not be without cost. Just make sure that at the last roll call you are on the credit side of life's ledger and not one of the debits.'

The two shook hands and the private left the office. A couple of days later he was back with the mob. Bollers had already departed for Delhi and his new command.

22

Mckinley and the Chindits

Most of the blokes were glad to see John back, especially Arthur and Quiller. There was some ribbing and even good-humoured sarcasm from Corporal Bell. 'So good of you to join us again,' he said. 'We've kept your bed nice and aired for you. I hope it's comfortable enough for you after your feather bed at HQ?' John thought that his bunk might have been reassigned to a replacement, but he was told that one of the new mob had managed to kill himself whilst riding a motor bike at high speed, apparently into one of the many sacred cows that wander around the area.

'We're down to twenty-eight in the troop,' said Art. 'We may or may not get reinforcements before we go into action. Tasburgh is not concerned; he says its quality that counts and the Colonel thinks highly of his unit. That probably means when it starts we'll be placed right in the thick of it.'

'Any news about what is afoot?' Mckinley asked.

'No,' said Quill. 'It's all rumour, as usual, but something big is brewing. You can tell that by the way people are scurrying round.'

It seemed likely that action would start in the dry season that began in November. At one parade a request was made for volunteers for a behind enemy lines operation. Most of the troop adhered firmly to the old army adage of never volunteer. John had rapid words with Arthur and Quiller and told them that it was the one to go for. They asked about it but John just winked and tapped the side of his nose and said, 'Intelligence'. The two realised that he must know something and with their usual trust agreed to follow his lead. They presented themselves to Tasburgh later that day and said that they were keen to join the behind the lines operation. The troop commander was highly impressed, especially as no-one else had come forward.

It was now mid-October. News had just come through of a major victory in the desert at a place called El Alamein. The three musketeers were told to report for training with the Long Range Penetration Group and the remainder of the regiment continued to prepare for the coming action around the home base. The offensive was delayed by heavy rains but it eventually kicked off on 8th December.

The initial results of that main Arakan expedition seemed to be good and the Chindits subsequently set off on 8th February with the intention of creating mayhem behind Japanese lines. The unit had been named after the 'Chinthe', which is a mythical beast, half eagle and half lion, found carved on many Burmese temples. The unit consisted of about three thousand men, with a Ghurkha battalion and a British battalion, and specialist groups including a rifle unit to which the three Skellow men were assigned.

The columns would advance with initial supplies carried on mules, and after that they would be supplied by air. To ensure that high-grade radio communications could be maintained, each column included an RAF officer and four radio operators who would service and use the Mark 1082/83 wireless, which was normally used in aircraft. The set weighed 200 pounds but was considered vital and was carried by a large artillery mule.

The Chindits advanced in two columns, the Ghurkhas to the South were pushed in to provide a diversionary force with the bulk of Wingate's troops about fifty miles to the north. Both columns advanced with much heaving, pulling, and cursing at the fractious mules. Muddy banks were traversed

364

and numerous streams were crossed in which the usual leeches were encountered. The remedy for them was to touch their tails with a lighted cigarette. Those small dark suckers let go their grip from the blood rich flesh immediately and fell to the ground. It had been explained to all the troops never to try to pull leeches off as it would remove the body but leave the head attached and this could develop into a sore that would become infected.

The unit's objectives were to blow up railway lines and harass and attack the Japanese. As far as they could tell everything was going well. Bridges and railway lines were blown and gorges filled with tons or rock via the judicious use of high explosives. Eventually, there were some sharp rifle and machine gun exchanges in defensive actions as Japanese troops were moved into the area in numbers in an attempt to counter the disruption.

Mckinley had no overall strategic picture of the operation and no idea how the other columns were doing. However, casualties seemed light and aircraft were landing and managing to evacuate the wounded. However, the Japanese pressure increased and on 24th March the General ordered all columns to make their way back to Assam. The columns broke into small parties and retreated in good order. Eight hundred or so did not return and were listed as dead, captured, or missing; despite these losses, the expedition was considered a great success.

The three musketeers returned to base in early May having marched about eight hundred miles. They had all been beefy thirteen stoners when they set off. On return, they were down to less than eleven stone. None of them had contracted malaria or any of the other serious jungle diseases, and back at base they all spent several days gorging food and drinking a lot of beer.

When they re-joined the troop, to John's disappointment he found out that Tasburgh had been promoted and replaced as troop commander by someone called Ponsonby. The man was a full lieutenant in his late thirties. He was an extremely unimpressive physical specimen with short, spindly legs; he was flabby without being heavy. The man seemed to have no sort of chin; the flesh beneath his mouth descended in a continuous curve until it met his neck. He appeared to John to be one of the most unfit officers he had ever seen. His previous post had been in charge of some sort of clerical unit and he had clearly been in the Indian Army for the social life and not for combat. Mckinley, as usual, kept his opinions to himself, but he was very disappointed in their new leader.

Training resumed after the Chindit operation and during it all the troop got fitter due to their exertions, but Ponsonby avoided walking if possible. He drove everywhere in his old pre-war Morris. When he did have to march with the men it was obvious to all that he sweated profusely as he did so. Wild remarked, 'I suppose the flabby twat will expect to be driving into action in the jungle when it all kicks off again.' John looked around, thinking Enderby was probably in earshot, but Wild did not care and Enderby, who actually was in earshot, privately agreed. He had remarked to Corporal Bell in very confidential tones that: 'They must have been scraping the bottom of the barrel when they found that one for us.'

The ever level-headed John said quietly to Wild, 'I wouldn't go shouting those sort of things around if I was you. Don't forget, if jankers and other crap duty gets handed out, Ponsonby will be the one pushing it your way.' Wild grunted in a sort of unimpressed manner in response. Mckinley thought it would not take much to push Wild into some sort of serious insubordination if Ponsonby leaned on him but there was not much he could do about it. Eventually, a Jeep arrived for the troop and Ponsonby started to be driven around in it. Enderby opined to Bell, 'Well at least it makes him look more military.'

One final event confirmed everyone in the troop's low opinion of their new commander. One Sunday several of them were playing about at an open-air swimming pool. It was a time for relaxation and letting off steam. Some of the more athletic blokes were making loud splashing entries into the water, some were doing handstands on the diving board and attempting acrobatic dives into the water.

The pool was overlooked by the veranda of the officer's club that was up a sloped banking about thirty yards away. Although the pool was mainly obscured from sight by shrubbery, after a while Ponsonby appeared wearing a solar topee; he was sweating heavily with the effort of carrying himself and his swagger stick down the slope to the poolside. When he got there he said very loudly: 'Stop all this shouting and messing about, you are disturbing the ladies!' The men looked at him with thinly disguised dislike. 'Who is in charge here?' he said. No-one responded as they were all privates and some of them were now glaring at the little man, especially Wild. 'Oh well,' he said. 'Don't make it necessary for me to come down here and tell you again.' With that he turned triumphantly on his heel and made his way back up the hill having exerted his authority for the benefit of 'the ladies', most of whom had been largely oblivious to the high jinks going on down in the pool area in any case.

Wild just managed to contain himself but broke out into an abusive tirade as the little fellow disappeared.

Art said to John, 'What was all that about?'

John said, 'Obvious, he just wants to throw his weight about and show off his authority in front of the women. He is doing it because he can; he's protected by the two pips on what pass for his shoulders. I'm sure they all must have the same opinion of the bloke that we do. If he tried it out of uniform, he would probably find himself very deficient in teeth. Just ignore him.'

Soon after that, news started to filter back about the Arakan expedition. The initial successes had been reversed as a result of very determined Japanese counter-attacks and most of the surviving troops eventually returned to their starting point in Chittagong. The 14th Indian division had lost about two and a half thousand men with many more suffering from malaria and other diseases. The reverse caused morale to slump because the action had resulted in so many casualties with no territorial gains. On the other hand, the action carried out by the Chindits had just the opposite effect and their success was skilfully used in propaganda newsreels.

The Americans were so impressed that they formed a similar unit under Colonel F.D. Merrill. Merrill had been 'Vinegar Joe', Stilwell's chief of staff, and was an experienced Orientalist and linguist. Morale also improved due to successes in other theatres of the war. The Russians were making great advances. By May 1943, the Axis forces had been defeated in North Africa, and Italy was by then tottering on the brink of defeat.

In the intelligence unit, Bollers, though heartened by the overall picture, was growing increasingly concerned about Japanese troop and aircraft reinforcements arriving in Burma. He gauged that they had moved about six or seven divisions in and were obviously planning something big. However, General Slim had things underway also, and a second offensive in the Arakan was to take place as well as a second Chindit operation.

John had expected to re-join the Chindits but as bad luck would have it part of the West Yorks, including B troop, were out on the left of the 7th Indian division when the Japanese initiated their flanking attack by moving up the Eastern bank of the Mayu river in early February. Again, Mckinley had no overall picture, and all he could do was to try to get himself and Quiller and Arthur through it. The Troop had set up defensive positions supported by artillery defending a track in a steep sided gorge surrounded by dense jungle growth on either side.

Ponsonby had found urgent need to return to headquarters from the defences in his jeep, leaving Enderby in charge. A Brigadier at HQ had found even more need to send him back immediately with instructions to hold the line with his troop as long as possible, while a solid defensive position was constructed in what became known as the admin box.

The orders were to delay the Japanese advance as long

as they could and then to fall back and join the rest of the defenders. It was made clear to the fearful lieutenant that every hour that the Japanese could be delayed would be vital and that he was not to leave his post.

Back on the front line, it became obvious that he did not have a clue. Enderby suggested that he should set up a camouflaged command position in a dugout slightly to the rear of the others, which could be manned by the officer and wireless operator, and that he would deploy the troops. Ponsonby readily agreed but said imperiously, 'Make sure that I am kept fully informed.'

Enderby had collared the radio operator who was called Jerry Green and said: 'Look Jerry, we all know how much use the lieutenant will be, so if I send the message "Code Red!" that means we are being overrun. When you hear it, you call down shell fire on these positions and scarper up the side track as fast as you can. We should have a few minutes before the salvoes start to fall.'

He had strategically positioned the jeep about a couple of hundred yards to the rear, concealed by a bend in the track. His intention was to use it to evacuate the wounded if he got the opportunity, as he did not like the idea of leaving anyone behind to the Japs. He divided the men into three groups, with six on each flank and the rest concentrated in the middle portion of the track, each group with a Bren gun. Four troopers from the central group manned the two mortars, which were aimed some way down the central route. Enderby had chosen a good natural defensive position at the brow of a steep slope in the track. Some trees had been felled and dragged back and covered with some of the very dense vegetation. The troop had been placed in twos, in deep foxholes, which were also thickly camouflaged. Artillery support could be called to fire into pre-arranged coordinates by radio.

Enderby had rations and water distributed with all the ammunition, and this was accompanied by the order to be as still and silent as possible. He told Bell to look after the left flank and he would take the right. He looked at Mckinley and said, 'You look after the centre with the bulk of the men. We don't have a lance corporal, so you're in charge. You lot hear that?' he barked at the others; they were delighted to hear it. He also told everyone that if he shouted 'Code Red' the riflemen were to do rapid fire and empty their magazines and then all were to leg it up the side track. He told the Bren operators that if he shouted 'Code Red', to lay down covering fire until the blokes were a few yards up the track. He told the mortar unit to loose all remaining mortar bombs at short range and then sprint for it with the Bren gunners. The side track passed through a slight depression which would give some cover until they were a couple of hundred yards down it and away from the defended area.

Mckinley told his squad: 'We'll probably get the brunt of it in the centre, but they may try a flanking attack as a diversion.' He gave the two Thompson sub-machine guns to Art and Quill and said to use their rifles but if they got really close to use the Thompsons. His eyes fell on the only weapon they had in excess, several crates of grenades. He distributed these generously amongst his comrades but even so, there were about fifty left.

He looked at Albert and had a brainwave. He said to him, 'Look Albert, get in that dugout and when I shout "Now!" I want you to start throwing those grenades as far down the track as you can. Just one thing though, Albert. Remember to pull the pins out before you lob 'em.'

'Course I will,' said Albert, grinning. 'Do you think I'm daft or summat?' John grinned back and nodded good-naturedly at his long-range grenadier.

The Troop waited for the attack. Midday passed and nothing happened. Two-o'clock came and went, and then three. Still nothing. One trooper said, 'Do you think they are coming, sarge?'

'Oh yes,' was the reply. 'Don't worry, they will be shooting at us pretty soon.'

The afternoon passed and then night fell and the men tried to sleep in the dugouts between watches. Eventually dawn arrived and Enderby moved round the men checking on the forward positions. Finally, he checked with Green. 'Everything OK?' he said. 'Radio working alright?'

'Yes Sarge, tip top,' was the reply.

'Have you anything to report, sergeant?' said Ponsonby, with the objectionable officiousness designed to emphasise the difference in their rank and the fact that he thought he was very much in charge.

'No, sir,' he said. 'The situation is static with the troop well prepared to repel an attack.'

'What if they should have tanks?' came the rejoinder.

'Extremely unlikely, sir,' said the sergeant. 'As I understand it, they have come over a difficult range of hills.'

The lieutenant said wistfully, 'I really do feel that I ought to report back to headquarters in person.'

Enderby said, 'Weren't you given very specific orders by the Brigadier to stay here, sir?'

Ponsonby said, 'Yes, but in these circumstances I really feel I should go.'

'I wouldn't advise it, sir,' said Enderby. 'We can report back quite adequately by radio and if you go back the Brigadier will probably have you shot for disobeying a direct order.' Ponsonby coloured up and sat down heavily on his campstool without replying.

The sergeant left without bothering to salute and had been back in position for about ten minutes when Tommy Jackson, who was on the Bren said, softly, 'I think I heard something!'

Enderby said, 'Quiet everyone, and get ready. Pass it on.' After a while he caught sight of movement, and just after that he could see three and then five Japanese privates advancing warily with fixed bayonets up the track, with an NCO about ten yards behind them. They halted when they spotted the felled trees. He thought, 'No fooling them.' The NCO sent one of the men back whilst he looked the position over with binoculars. After a few minutes, about thirty to forty other Japanese arrived. A machine gun was set up facing the felled timber and then the enemy spread out and started to advance slowly, hugging the trees on either side of the approach. The sergeant called quietly across to the mortar crews: 'Try to target that machine gun; it's about a hundred and twenty yards down the track!' The Japanese came on, Enderby said quietly, 'Hold till I give the order.' Tension mounted. They were less than a hundred yards away now, then ninety then eighty then seventy. He knew that the closer they approached the more effective B troop's fire would be in repelling them.

The enemy came on, Mckinley found he was sweating with the tension, but the sergeant knew exactly what he was doing. Finally, just beyond grenade range at about forty yards he yelled 'Fire!' and everything opened up. He estimated that at least a fifteen to twenty of the enemy must have been hit. An order was screamed from the Japanese end and the advancing party hit the deck and their machine gun opened up shortly afterwards, raking the defences. The prone soldiers joined in and a fair hail of bullets swept over the foxholes. Fortunately, the Japanese were firing blindly and no one was hit.

The troop's mortars then opened up and the first salvo landed about ten yards behind the machine gun. The crew adjusted its range and landed two direct hits on the machine gun crew who were frantically trying to dismantle and move it. Enderby shouted: 'You've got it spot on. If anyone else approaches that gun, drop some more on 'em.' He shouted at the troop to pick their targets and fire. Everything opened up and he could see that two or three more of the prone Japanese had been hit. Another order was barked at the Japanese. They rose and dived retreating into the cover of the jungle. 'Rake the sides!' shouted Enderby, and a fusillade of bullets followed the enemy into the greenery.

He shouted cease-fire and told everyone: 'Reload if you haven't done it already.' He then said, 'That's stopped 'em for a while, but they know where we are now and next time they will hit us with everything they've got. Take a breather, boys. Eat or drink if you feel like it. You can smoke now but keep down when you do it.' He crawled across to the radio operator and said to get him the artillery battery. Ponsonby sat sulking on his camp stool. Enderby explained briefly to him and then outlined the situation to the captain of artillery at the other end of the set and said, 'Do you think a salvo dropped just in front of us might deter them, sir? If they think we have strong artillery back up, they may wait until they can bring theirs up.' The captain mulled it over and said. 'All right, I'll launch a double salvo in ten minutes. Tell your troop to keep their heads well down until it's over. We have your coordinates don't we?'

'Yes sir,' said Enderby giving them again.

'One thing more, sergeant,' said the artillery captain. 'I can give support today. However, we will be withdrawing under cover of darkness to the main defensive position.'

Enderby said, 'That's OK, sir. We can delay 'em for a few hours more, maybe a day, but not much more. After that we will be heading the same way as you, those of us that are able to.'

Ponsonby interjected and said: 'I want a full report, sergeant.'

The NCO said, 'Not now, sir, I've got to get back to the troop.' He added: 'Keep your heads down. We are going to have shells whizzing overhead in a few minutes!' He crawled back to the flank and said to Bell, 'Anything happening out there?'

Bell said, 'I can hear something but there's nothing in sight.'

Enderby explained about the imminent shelling and told everyone to keep well down in case a shell fell short. After a short while, the shells whistled overhead and there were a satisfying series of crump, crump—crump, crump sounds, as they landed. He also thought he heard someone scream. He had no insight into the enemy numbers but knew that eventually they would attack relentlessly.

Colonel Oribe was in charge of the advance party of the enemy; in fact, he had two hundred men and had been ordered to advance with all possible speed. There were nineteen dead and seriously wounded after the first advance and twenty-nine dead and seriously wounded because of the shelling. He had sent scouts down a nearby jungle track but they had returned and reported it led in the wrong direction. He considered macheting a route through the jungle for a flanking attack but knew it would take too much time, and time was of the essence in this situation.

He was hampered by lack of artillery and had only one light mortar and three 11 Nen Shiki Kikanju light machine guns. The thirty round cartridge hoppers in each would give just short of four seconds' continuous fire before they were empty. He hoped that these plus the rifle rounds from his attack force would be sufficient to achieve a breach in the defences. His plan was basic and brutal in terms of expenditure of his men, but he would get as close as possible. Open up with the mortar and machine guns and charge the defences throwing grenades. He estimated that the British could not have more than forty defenders and he knew they were inferior to his men in terms of fighting spirit. He also knew that the closer they got the less likely his men were to be shelled.

The infiltration process took until midday, and by then the bulk of his men were dispersed either side of the track, some in shallow slit trenches with others crouched in the green denseness of the jungle. The careless had been sniped at and three more of his men had been wounded.

Enderby shouted: 'Hold your fire, but don't worry boys: in a little while you will be shooting your little socks off.'

It was early afternoon before the Japanese mortar opened up, shifting its angle slightly between bombs in order to saturate as much of the defensive position as possible.

Most of the bombs exploded harmlessly, as the men dipped deep into the foxholes each time they heard one coming over. After about five minutes of mortaring the three Japanese light machine guns opened up. Oribe was using them in turn in order to maintain a continuous fusillade. Each crew had been ordered to expend ten cartridge hoppers, then pick up their rifles and follow the main body of charging troops. After the two minutes or so which was needed to discharge the 900 rounds, the order was given to charge.

It seemed to Mckinley that hundreds of Japanese were coming at him. He gave the order to shoot, and his section opened up with rapid rifle fire and the mortars joined in.

He had almost forgotten Albert but then realised the Japs were uncomfortably close. He screamed at the burly grenadier 'NOW!' Albert spread his huge shoulders and started to lob the grenades straight down the track. Japanese were falling but not fast enough, they were only about thirty yards away now and firing at the camouflaged defences from the hip. John screamed, 'Thompsons!' Art and Quill opened up. The Japanese were just a few feet away when the extra two Bren guns joined in. Enderby had rapidly grasped the situation and moved his Brens to a more central position with most of his men and they were now laying down a deadly hail of fire. Bullets from the Japanese type 99 rifles whizzed around the troopers and some grenades were exploding amid the undergrowth or near the fox holes. About sixty of the Japanese must have fallen before an order was screamed and they broke and ran backwards and dived for cover in the jungle. Though no one was to know it, their problem was the deadly screen of grenade fragments produced by Albert's efforts.

The first group of attackers had got close to them, but the second group had been broken up by the grenades and mortars and then the Brens. The sergeant shouted: 'Shoot at anything that moves.' For the next hour, an occasional shot came from the Japanese in the jungle but importantly the attack had been beaten off.

'What was it they were shouting as they charged?' said Quiller. 'Was it Bonsai?'

'Nearly right,' said John. 'It's Banzai.'

'What the bloody hell are they on about?' said Albert.

'It's a sort of Japanese courage word,' said Mckinley. 'It inspires them. It means "may he live for ten thousand years," he being their emperor of course. Don't forget they are all prepared to die for their emperor, and we are all prepared to let 'em. We will do our best and assist them in meeting their gods wherever possible, won't we?' Most of the troop laughed.

'I think it's bloody daft,' said Albert. 'I might get killed for King and country by accident, but I'm not volunteering.'

John said, 'You keep on with your best efforts to stay alive, Albert, and so will we!' The mood lightened in what they all knew was a desperate situation.

Enderby crawled around, doing the rounds. The foxhole on the far right containing Geordie and Walt had sustained a direct mortar hit; both men were dead. Two more men had superficial wounds from grenade fragments, three others had more serious bullet wounds and one had a very nasty wound in the thigh. He asked John if his section was all right. John checked and found out everyone was unscathed apart from Arthur: 'I've got a mortar fragment in my right hand,' he shouted. 'I can't grip or shoot.'

The sergeant evaluated all the information in a very matter of fact way, the moment was about practicalities and not about sadness for the deceased; that would come later. 'Get the wounded to the rear,' ordered the sergeant. 'Get field dressings on, use morphine if need-be, and move 'em back to the Jeep.' He asked the two with slight wounds if either of them can drive.

The older of the two said: 'I used to drive a dairy wagon in civvy-street.'

'Right,' said Enderby. 'Cram all the wounded in the jeep and then get off up to the nearest medical post. Offload and then make your way back on your own. Be careful, though, in case we have been overrun; we may meet you part way.'

Enderby made his way back to the foxhole containing the radio operator and the officer. 'You OK, Jerry?' he said.

'I'm alright,' came the reply. 'But *he's* not.'

Ponsonby was leaning against the side of the dugout. He was saying, repeatedly, 'My name is Lieutenant Horace Ponsonby. My name is Lieutenant Horace Ponsonby.'

Enderby said, 'He looks OK; do you think its shock?'

'No,' said Jerry. 'Look at the back of his head.' The sergeant looked and saw that a mortar fragment had removed the back of the officer's skull. The brain was exposed and blood was oozing from it.

'How did it happen,' said the sergeant.

'The silly bugger took his tin hat off in the middle of the attack to wipe the sweat off his face. He bent forwards and the back of his head disappeared.'

'My name is Lieutenant Horace Ponsonby,' the Lieutenant murmured.

'Yes,' said the sergeant, but it didn't register with the wounded man. 'He'll be dead in a few minutes,' said Enderby to the radio-man. 'I have a few pressing things to attend to; keep an eye on him, will you?'

He thought about his position. They now had three dead or dying and five others too badly injured to fight. The driver who had gone with them reduced the fighting force by another. He went back to the troop and conferred with Bell and Mckinley. 'We've lost nearly a third of the troop now, do you think we can withstand another attack?'

Bell said, 'Doubtful! The last one was touch and go; if they get in among us we've had it.'

'What do you think, John?' said the sergeant.

'If we had a Vickers machine gun I'd be prepared to try it. It all depends on how many Japs are left. They may be too few for another full-scale attack. It might be an idea for the troop to slope off while we have a chance and just leave a Bren, the mortar lads, and Albert. If you place another Bren at the entrance to the side-track we can leg it when they get close and the Bren can cover as they come through the fox holes into the open on the other side.'

Enderby looked at his watch. It was almost 3.30 pm. He decided that Mckinley's plan was the best one. He said: 'We want two Bren gunners and the mortar lads and Albert to stay for now. I'll stay with one of the Thompsons, and we'll need somebody else for the other.'

John said, quietly, 'I'll stay.'

All the remaining grenades were collected and given to Albert. There were about thirty in all. Enderby said, 'Start to lob 'em as soon as they get nearly in range. We'll be spraying 'em with the Bren and the Thompsons. When you've lobbed the last grenade, leg it for the side track and we will be right behind you.'

Enderby crawled across to Jerry and called the captain of artillery again and said: 'Can you arrange to saturate our position immediately I give the call? Just give us five minutes.' He explained that another attack was imminent and that there was no possibility of holding this one. He said, 'We should be just out of the way and running fast. If you give the buggers a good thumping with shell fire, it could buy us a few more hours before they regroup and start to advance again.' The captain of artillery agreed readily, and said he would follow it with a creeping barrage through the position which should win the retreating troop several minutes more.

The Sergeant said to Jerry, 'Get the radio, keep low, and make for the entry to the side track. When I give you the wire, call the captain to commence firing and then start to hare up the track. We will follow pdq.' He then asked the radio man: 'How's Ponsonby?'

Jerry replied, 'He's stopped breathing, I think he's dead.'

'Right,' said Enderby, registering the fact of death with little or no emotion. He then told Brenner and Ward, who were the two nearest, 'Move him into the foxhole with the dead troopers. Take their dog tags and cover them as best you can.'

He asked the lads on the mortar how many rounds they had left, and was told twenty-seven. He said: 'Right, fire ten at maximum range when the rifle men have finished. Then, I want you both two-hundred yards up the track and when you get there, target our position here. One of you take the mortar shells up there now. I want you to start firing again when the Brens have stopped and you see us sprinting down the track towards you. When you have finished, you can scarper alongside us. Hopefully, with the artillery and you, the Japs will dive for cover long enough for us to get away.'

He then shouted to everyone: 'Right lads, by foxholes from the right, each of you slowly discharge a full clip into the distance, then reload. Then, make for the side track. You can all start moving off when Corporal Bell joins you, and bloody well keep low!' He said to Quiller: 'Can you man the second Bren at the track entrance?'

Trooper Jones said, 'Fine.'

Enderby said to the last defenders: 'Blast away till I say the word and then move straight up the track and run like hell.'

Johnny Oldroyd was the youngest in the troop; he was nineteen and had very keen ears. He shouted to Enderby: 'I think I can hear a truck, maybe two.' After another minute, all could hear the very obvious sound of engines.

'They've stopped well back,' said Bell. 'They don't want to get in range of our field guns. I wonder what's in 'em?'

Four enemy trucks had arrived with food and water, munitions, and sixty reinforcements. Oribe was happy; he knew that his last attack had almost succeeded and he was now sure that the second would do so if he committed all his men plus the reinforcements. A young lieutenant accompanied the new troops and his senior explained that he and his fresh troops would be given the honour of leading the next attack. The lieutenant bowed low and expressed his gratitude for the great honour bestowed on him.

It was now past four.

'Anyway,' said Enderby, 'ignore the trucks. Start firing your clips off and then get away when you've reloaded.'

The plan worked like clockwork. The occasional bullet was returned from the jungle but to no avail. The mortar men started to fire and regular explosions were heard about every ten to twelve seconds for the next couple of minutes.

'Finished sarge,' said the young Oldroyd.

'Ok, get off lads,' said Enderby. He shouted up to Jerry: 'Are you ready?' The radio operator shouted back in the affirmative.

Enderby said to John: 'This is where it gets hairy. As soon as they stand up to charge, fire a full magazine and then run for it. The rise in the track should give us cover and when they get through our defences the second Bren and then the mortars should discourage them.' After the rifle firing, everything went eerily quiet. About ten minutes later, Mckinley could see movement and Oribe's three machine guns opened up.

'OK, Albert,' said Enderby. 'Start with the grenades. They're about fifty yards off but it might slow 'em up.' Albert got through his stock of grenades in record time. Enderby said 'Go!' and Albert needed no second telling. The Japanese machine guns stopped and Enderby shouted at Jerry, 'Artillery NOW!' and the radio operator relayed his vital message to the captain commanding the gunnery unit. In the same breath, Enderby said, 'Fire!'

The Bren and two Thompsons discharged their magazines and Enderby said, 'Move boys!' The Bren gunner hared off, but Enderby loaded a second canister of bullets.

John turned and said, 'What are you doing?'

The sergeant said, 'Bloody well go!' He then spewed his second magazine at the enemy. Mckinley had just started off but heard Enderby grunt. He turned and saw him fall. He could see that the Sergeant had taken a bullet through the chest. His eyes were wide open with the shock of sudden death. Mckinley realised he could do nothing for him and started to sprint. He had managed about twenty strides when bullets started to whistle over his head, and then he heard the Bren at the rear open up.

23

Mckinley and the Jungle

Mckinley continued zigzagging rapidly down the track. The Bren fell silent after discharging two magazines, and about a minute later he heard a salvo of shells flying overhead and dived into the jungle. He rolled over a couple of times and slid about twenty feet down a bank. He crouched low at the bottom of it as the missiles landed. One had dropped a little short and exploded only a few yards behind him. His rifle had gone flying and his ears were ringing from the explosion, but he knew that a creeping barrage would follow soon. He stood and looked to no avail for his weapon, and then adopting a low crouch he moved off following the thin track which led from the base of the bank. His eventual aim was to navigate towards the track and the rest of the troop but for now he needed to put distance between himself and the barrage. He tried to use the sun as a pointer to navigate but it was difficult under the thick green canopy.

Shells started to whiz to the right of him and he moved away from the series of explosions. They occurred regularly and seemed to grow more distant at first, and then started to move back in his direction again. He surmised, correctly, that the captain of artillery had plastered their former position and then dropped shells further down the track towards the Japanese. Then, he moved back from his furthest point of bombardment with another creeping series of projectiles.

John hurried down the track, not sure how close the

approaching shellfire would come. At last the explosions ceased. He thought that the final one could not have been more than fifty yards away, and he hoped that the Japanese unit had been comprehensively plastered and discouraged from any further immediate advance.

Mckinley slogged on, but having no compass his route to what he hoped would be the main track proved tortuously winding and difficult, and he thus navigated with more optimism than accuracy. Eventually he saw a clearing just in front and stepped into it. At exactly that moment, a small Japanese warrior stepped into the same space from the opposite direction. Both exchanged concerned looks but each rapidly realised that the other was unarmed. The Jap stood in John's intended path of escape and he did not intend to give it up. The small soldier seemed to think for a moment and then ran at John and grabbed for his sleeve, intending to try to throw him to the ground using judo.

John struck first, though, clipping his oncoming attacker in the mouth with a teeth rattling jab with his right fist. The Jap took his grip and tried to drop under his larger opponent. Mckinley was far too well versed in the skills of wrestling to be caught, and he stepped over the throwing leg and the two ended up rolling on the ground flailing at each other. Eventually they came to a halt but, importantly, Mckinley was on top.

John grabbed his adversary round the throat and squeezed hard with all the strength which years as a miner had endowed him. The man below writhed and tried to smash his knees up into his opponent's back, but to no avail. He reached up, trying frantically to jab his thumbs into his strangler's eyes. However, John had much longer arms than his opponent and lifted his head back out of the way and squeezed even harder. The man below was making gurgling sounds now and in a last desperate effort grabbed his opponent's wrists in an attempt to ease the unrelenting pressure on his throat. After a short while, he ceased moving. John kept on squeezing hard until he was certain that his opponent was not shamming. John ceased applying the pressure and then sat back looking down at his newly dead adversary. He felt strange; he had never killed anyone with his bare hands and had never expected to do so. It was different to shooting at someone and being shot back at, in some strange way that seemed to be impersonal, fair almost. He realised that it had to be one of the two of them and he was the one who had lived, but the realisation of what he had done left him with a feeling of disgust.

His mind then turned to practicalities; he hurriedly searched through the several pockets of the dead man. In the first he found some documents in Japanese, a leather covered book containing a mix of numbers and symbols, a small map and a photo of a young woman in traditional Japanese dress. In the second he discovered a pound bar of British chocolate—'Taken off one of our lads,' he thought venomously. In a third pocket, wrapped in a piece of oilskin, he discovered a box of matches. In a small inside pocket that he almost missed, most valuably of all, he found a small compass.

Around the bruised neck, he could see a cord; he pulled it from round the dead man's head and a small leather pouch appeared. Inside, he discovered two small gold coins and nine coin-sized pieces of a dark green glassy mineral. He mused to himself for a few seconds and then realised the green objects must be emeralds.

He now had two canteens of water with him, his own and the one that had belonged to the dead man. He stuffed the various objects in his battledress pockets. In addition to his recent haul, he himself contributed a pack of field rations and a Jack knife that was attached to a clip on the back of his belt. In the heat of the encounter, he had forgotten all about it. He removed it from the clip and opened it up. It was not much of a weapon but if he ran into anyone else, he would move in with the knife rather than with his bare hands.

He got up and set off along the track. After a few minutes he could hear shouts in Japanese someway behind him. At least I am going away from them he thought, even if I do not know where I am. He pressed on, hoping to find the main route, but after a couple of hours he realised he must have been moving away from it. He paused to look at the map. Although the features were marked with Japanese ideographs, he recognised the main features on it. From what he had picked up previously, the main Jap force had outflanked the British and where circling back in a southerly direction to try to wipe out the seventh Indian division by attacking from the rear. John thought that if he were picked up by a Jap patrol there would be only one outcome. Thus, he decided to head off in a north-easterly direction in hope of making contact with a British unit.

He cut down a stout young sapling using his knife and carved a point at one end of it. It was a bit basic but he thought it should ward of anything but the very largest of the jungle beasts if they became interested in him. His route was circuitous, but using the compass he kept to his desired path until nightfall. Eventually, he found a couple of large trees and settled down. After eating some of the chocolate he tried to get some rest, leaning against one of the trees with the makeshift spear across his lap.

He slept fitfully, often disturbed by the strange noises of the jungle at night. The noises, which he had often heard before, seemed so much closer and more immediate than anything he had heard previously. On waking, he realised he was ravenous; apart from the chocolate, he had hardly eaten since the previous day. He broke a piece off the dried fruit and biscuits in the field ration and ate it slowly, followed by a long drink of his precious water. He looked at the compass and at the early sun and then set off on his trek. The going was difficult. He kept to the small pathways, which wound sinuously through groves and round cliffs and hills and along the sides of streams.

With some backtracking, he managed to keep up a steady progress, and by midday he thought he must have walked eight or ten miles. He consulted the map but none of the features he had come across seemed to conform to the landscape he had encountered. He rested for ten minutes, ate two squares of the chocolate, and then set off again, walking until it was almost dusk.

The march continued for five days. At the end of them, he had eaten all the field rations and was down to the last few squares of the chocolate. On the third day, he had risked a fire and boiled water in one of the canteens until he had sufficient water to fill both of them. After it had cooled down it had an unusual flat taste, but Mckinley knew that at least it would be sterile. At this juncture, the last thing he needed was a dose of dysentery or something similar. He had heard various aircraft on his trek but on the sixth day he actually saw two of them, which he thought were a Zero pursued by one of the new Spitfire VCs, and the Zero was trailing smoke. A few minutes later, he heard an explosion in the far distance and a couple of minutes later saw the Spitfire again. John checked the flight direction with his compass. It was more northerly than the direction he had set himself, so he adjusted his route to follow that of the aircraft. That evening he boiled more water, ate all but two of his squares of chocolate, and settled down for the night once again.

On the morning of the seventh day, he ate his final supplies and set off once more. He was now starting to feel weaker and suffered from cramps in his stomach due to hunger. He marched on for a further two days, walking in a sort of daze induced by heat and lack of food. On the morning of the tenth day, he emerged onto what looked like a main track. He warily weighed up the risks. Hopefully he had now left the Japanese behind and if he used the main track he would make faster progress and possibly run into a British unit or friendly tribesmen. The track started to swing towards the north east after a couple of miles; Mckinley pondered whether to keep to it in the hope it would swing back towards his preferred direction of travel or whether to take a side track.

Suddenly, he heard an aircraft and then, machine gun and

cannon fire. Almost immediately he heard an engine and realised that some sort of vehicle was speeding in his direction. He rapidly left the track and took cover in the undergrowth. Then, about four hundred yards away, he saw a lorry travelling at top speed towards him. A second later, he saw a Beaufighter in pursuit. The aircraft came in low doing a strafing run with its cannons and machine guns, and the lorry exploded and burst into flame. John heard ammunition going off but after about ten minutes the flammables had all burned off and all that was left was a smouldering wreck.

As he could not hear any sounds from up the track, he decided to risk a quick look. The lorry appeared to be empty apart from the badly charred corpse of its driver. He looked in the cab and on the floor could see a blackened and damaged rifle and next to it, a bayonet. Behind the driver in a metal box he found eleven tins. The labels had burned off but though they were still hot, they seemed intact. John hoped that they contained food. In the road in front of the truck he found a jerry can, and on opening it he found it contained water. He picked the bayonet up, gathered the tins together, and tied them in a piece of canvas which had been ripped from the lorry as it exploded.

He slung his booty over his shoulder and carrying the jerry can made for the side-track. Because of the change of direction of the main track and the possibility of enemy ahead, he had no choice but to make another circuitous detour. He walked for about a mile and then paused; he had to try one of the cans to see if it contained food. His clasp knife had a can opener attachment and John greedily ripped into the top, prizing the can open. He found that it contained peaches, which he devoured greedily at first, but then he deliberately slowed down, knowing what a food overload could do to an empty stomach. He felt his energy flow back and he began to think clearly again. He wondered if news of his situation had reached home yet. He had been missing in action now for ten days.

The tin cans were large; John estimated they must be about a pound each. Just over half the peaches had been consumed and he had no sealable container. He hit on the idea of hammering the top ends of the can together with the base of the bayonet until they folded. He suspended the can by the fold, in his belt for later consumption. He refilled his canteens from the Jerry can and then drank his fill from it and set off once again carrying his precious load.

John made circuitous progress in the direction the planes had seemed to be flying from. He was now seeing two or three of them each day. That night he finished the peaches and then another full tin containing beef stew. After dealing with his hunger pangs he decided to try to consume only two of the cans of food every twenty-four hours. On the second day the first can contained cooked white beans in salt-water—he ate some of the beans and drank a quantity of the water, thinking that he must be getting short of salt because of his exertions and the heat. He split his meals into two, now, one after a couple of hours marching and the second in the evening before he settled down for the night. Now he had the bayonet and his makeshift spear he slept more easily, as he felt confident about dealing with almost anything he might encounter in the jungle.

On the morning of the next day he had to skirt a clearing in which a small Japanese patrol were gathered. He had almost walked into them but had heard someone speak just in time and turned back and then left the path he was on for another which led away from them. Mckinley mused: 'They are further up country than I realised, or I haven't been going in the right direction.' He carried on until well away from the patrol.

On taking his meal, he discovered that the third day's food surprise was some sort of oily fish. He ate it all in one go, knowing that fish had a tendency to go off rapidly in the Burmese heat. The fourth day revealed more peaches and meat stew again, and on the fifth day both tins contained cheese.

It tasted somewhat burnt due to the cooking it had undergone in the truck but John's hunger easily outmatched his mild distaste. On the sixth day, the delicacy was corned beef. He thought that some of the cans must have been captured from his own comrades because as far as he knew the Japanese subsisted mainly on rice. After that final treat, it was back to marching on an empty stomach.

Three days later, he stumbled into a village. It was empty apart from three women and an old man. Mckinley was wary but he approached the elders, pointed to himself, and said slowly: 'British.'

The old man's face cracked into a wide and largely toothless smile: 'Naga,' he said pointing to himself. John smiled with relief. He knew that the Naga tribesmen were loyal allies. The old man shouted and the women went into one of the huts and reappeared after a few minutes with some sort of rice and meat stew and tea. The tea tasted magical, next to a pint of cool beer it was the most welcome beverage John could think of.

John took out the map and tried to converse with the old man but with little success. One of the women stepped forward and pointing to the map said in halting English: 'Japanese here and here! British here!'

'How far?' asked John.

'Four—five days,' said the woman. She pointed at the map. 'Jungle, then river. Walk up side of river, then walk down track through hills.' She then said, 'Bad.' Looking at the map, Mckinley realised the markings must indicate an area of swamp. She continued: 'British, one-day march, other side.' John relaxed for the first time in weeks.

'How did you learn English?' he said.

She replied, 'Missionary come, he teach, he try to tell us that our gods wrong, Christ main man.' Her smile led John to believe that their bringer of good news had not been particularly successful in his endeavours.

The Naga provided him with a shoulder bag and a leather

water holder. They gave him a smallish bag of boiled rice and six fruits, which looked a bit like small pink-skinned oranges. The woman said: 'We have no much food, but two fingers rice each day, one fruit. Five days, six days, you meet friends.' John rested for another hour and after more tea and stew set of in good heart, sure that he would reach safety in a few days.

John staggered out of the jungle into a large British air base nine days later. It transpired he had walked straight past two smaller outposts, having become disoriented in the swamp area. The RAF Regiment sentry who was on duty when the ragged starveling arrived could see straight away that it was a British soldier and did not bother with the formalities.

John said weakly, 'Could you get me to some food? I have not eaten for days and was on half rations before that.'

The sentry called to one of the airmen. 'You! Yes, I mean you! Get this bloke to the MO bloody quick and then to the canteen.'

At the medical centre, the MO gave John some barley sugar and said: 'We mustn't rush it, old man. If you gorge yourself you will just vomit it all back.' The effect of the glucose was amazing—John felt a huge surge of energy. The MO questioned him and said: 'The Japanese attack has been repulsed and they have a lot of casualties. We supplied our troops by air. They held firm at the Admin Box, especially after the Japanese broke through the perimeter into the main dressing station and killed a lot of the doctors, orderlies and the sick. After that, the relieving columns don't seem to be taking any prisoners; not that the Japanese want to surrender of course.'

A nurse arrived with a dish of milky rice pudding. The MO cautioned, 'Eat it slowly. Let your stomach get used to having food inside it again.' He went on: 'The air war also seems to have turned a corner; our older Hurricanes weren't really a match for the Zero's and tended to come off worst in dogfights, but we've just had some Spitfire VCs delivered. They are shooting the Japanese down like Billy-ho. I understand that during the first thirteen days of the battle we shot down sixty-five of theirs for the loss of only three Spits. Bloody marvellous, and apparently not one of those are propaganda figures; the numbers are believed to be totally accurate.'

The doctor continued to chat and John asked if anything had been heard about his troop. The doc said: 'I will make enquiries old man, but it may take a few days. Things have been a bit fraught and men are scattered all over the place.' He continued with his examination, asking if his patient knew what he had weighed at the start of the action, and John told him he was close on thirteen stone. The MO said, 'You are less than nine now and I think you have the symptoms of the beginnings of scurvy. You have been a long time without much vitamin C,' he said. 'What I want you to do is rest and eat a small quantity every two hours or so. How does the milk pudding feel on your stomach?'

John replied, 'OK.'

'No cramps or anything?'

John replied, 'No, I was getting the cramps when my stomach was empty.'

The doctor said: 'Take it easy then and I'll look in later. Is there anything else we can do for you?'

'I haven't had a pint for weeks, Doc, any chance?'

The doctor smiled and thought for a moment and said to the nursing sister, 'See that this patient is given a pint of stout with his last meal this evening.' He turned back to John and said, 'We'll see how you progress. In a few days you may be allowed down to the NAAFI.' He said that he would look in on him later and left with the sister who asked if he thought it was wise to allow alcohol at this stage. The Doctor replied, 'Certainly, Sister. Make sure he has it with some food. The calories in it and the vitamin B will do him a world of good.'

After two days, John felt like a new man and he was starting to eat ravenously. The doctor said, 'We'll keep you in for another couple of days and then we will find you a bed in the out-patients block. You can resume normal meals then, but please do not overstuff. Also you are not to do anything until your weight gets back to at least twelve stone; then you can return to the tender care of the Army with a chitty saying that you are to do only light duties for a month at least.' His patient enquired again if the medic had heard anything about his comrades in arms. The doctor told him that enquiries had been made but he had not yet heard anything. That was not surprising after the battle and the mopping up, which was continuing.

One morning about a week later, the doctor arrived with a sharp faced lieutenant wearing the insignia of the signals regiment. The young officer said: 'I understand you have spent a few weeks wandering round the jungle; I hope you are none too worse for the ordeal?' John answered in the affirmative. The officer went on: 'When you arrived here you had some documentation which was passed straight back to intelligence. I got a message last night from a Colonel Brody-Bollers, instructing me to look in on you immediately and find out if there was anything you needed. I am to report to him, also immediately, after I have seen you.'

John thanked the officer but said he was being well looked after and would be his old self in two or three weeks. The lieutenant went on: 'The second thing was about the documents. They turned out to be pretty important. They were up to date Japanese codebooks and are proving extremely useful.' He produced a map, spread it out, and explained where the hospital was located. 'Could you possibly tell us your approximate location when they were acquired?'

John explained the circumstances under which the books had been obtained and pointed on the map, identifying the gorge where his troop's defences had been, saying: 'It was pretty close to there.'

'Did you notice anything else about the Japanese from whom you took the documents?' asked the lieutenant.

John replied, 'He was unarmed. I went through all his pockets and all I found besides the documents were basics like a compass and some chocolate and a photo of a woman in traditional Japanese costume.'

'What about insignia?' asked his inquisitor.

'That was another odd thing,' said Mckinley. 'He didn't have any!'

'Are you sure about that?' said the officer.

'Oh yes,' said John. 'I was looking for anything of use. A badge with a pin in it could have been handy, but he didn't have any, not even cloth badges.'

'Was he in an army uniform?' said the lieutenant.

'Well, apart from the lack of badges it looked like one.' Although nothing was said, John thought from the knowing look on the lieutenant's face that the Jap must have been an intelligence officer, and with lack of insignia was probably working under cover.

'Can I do anything else for you?' said the young man. 'I really must rush off and report back.'

John said: 'Could you pass my thanks to the Colonel and tell him I really am alright, and I wonder if you could find out what happened to the rest of my troop. When I got separated from them things were pretty hot with several casualties.'

The officer assured him that he would look into it straight away. He then left the ward, walking rapidly and escorted by the doctor. As they walked out towards his car, the lieutenant said: 'If your patient requires anything, the Colonel asks that you provide it and he will foot any expenditure personally, and I do take it that he is alright?'

'Malnutrition is the only problem,' said the Doc. 'He will soon be fine.'

'Thank you, sir,' said the lieutenant, saluting. 'I will be back in touch when I have made further enquiries.'

The lieutenant returned three days later with news of John's comrades in arms. They had made it back to the Admin Box and helped to defend it, and were now resting in Chittagong. 'I am sure you will join them soon,' he said. 'I passed the message to them that you had survived and they were delighted, especially Sergeant Bell.' The young man sent his driver out to the car and he returned with a crate containing a dozen pint bottles of Samuel Smith's Best Bitter. He said, 'These are for you, with best wishes from Colonel Brody-Bollers. I really do not know how he does it! No one seems to have seen this brand of beer out here since 1941. I understand it's a favourite tipple in your home town.' Mckinley grinned in delight and received the gift with considerable appreciation.

Back in the ward, he had thought that he detected a change in attitude, especially in the hard-bitten RAF nursing sister. She was wondering what sort of private merited the personal solicitations of a full Colonel and thought that perhaps it would be wise to accord him the full measure of professional respect which she normally reserved for fellow NCOs. The MO also wondered about it, and covered his back by making it extremely clear to the other medical staff that his patient was in a convalescent state and was not to be bothered or harassed in any way. The invalid thus spent several more days eating heartily and consuming three or four pints of beer each evening.

John chatted to various army personnel and it became clear that although the first attack had been repulsed with thousands of Japanese dead, a second attack had been launched in the general direction of Imphal and the situation was still rather uncertain.

A few more days passed. John was putting on weight rapidly, idling his time away and feeling fine. The doctor had kept an eye on him and eventually said, 'I think at the end of the week you will be fit for release and light duties.'

The following Monday John was discharged and given a seat on an RAF Dakota to an airfield near Chittagong. From there he got a lift to the barracks in the town and found B Troop. All were delighted to see him apart from Brenner and Burns. Mckinley asked if everyone alive after the last attack had made it back, and Quiller said, 'Everyone but Collins.'

'What happened there?' said John.

'Well, you know we were ordered to fire a clip and then scarper up the track and wait for the Corp; well, Brenner, Burns and Collins decided not to wait, so they hurried off and we all followed a bit later with the Corp. They must have been a couple of hundred yards in front of us by then and we heard a couple of shots ring out, and then several more. The Japs had managed to get three or four men up the track and they had ambushed those buggers. Served 'em right. We had waited for Bell and followed when everybody was together.

'Those three had been making haste but Collins had paused to light a fag and the Japs got him right through the gut and lung. The other two dropped and started firing back. When we arrived, we killed the Japs and then Bell ordered Burns and Brenner on ahead. He said, "You wanted to lead off, so you can keep in front now; you will be the first to find anyone else who is waiting for us." They weren't keen but they knew they were in bad odour and so they set off. Collins died there after a couple of minutes; talk about dying for a fag!'

John smiled at the grim humour behind the joke and knew that Burns and Brenner were now total outsiders as far as the troop were concerned, and he was pleased about it.

He enquired about Arthur. Quiller said, 'The injury to his hand means he can't do front line duty. It's not serious but he's going back home for an op on the hand to try to restore some movement and grip. It looks like his active army career is over.' Mckinley was glad to hear it, and knew that now at least one of his close friends would almost certainly make it through the war.

A little later Bell found John, on his own, and said, 'Bloody glad you made it, and bloody well done back there.' Mckinley congratulated him on his extra stripe, but Bell told him that he would be willing to give up all three in exchange for having Enderby back with them.

John said: 'I don't suppose there was any chance of a decoration for his bravery. At the end he seemed to be wanting to face the Japs alone to give us a few more seconds to get away.'

'Oh, I raised it with Major Tasburgh,' said Bell. 'He was sympathetic and told me that he would write to Enderby's family to tell them of his self-sacrifice, and he then explained apologetically that, unless an officer witnesses the action and puts a recommendation in, no medal is awarded.' He went on: 'The bloody adjutant collared me and asked about our former leader; he seemed to want to paint him as some sort of hero leading his troops into action in a difficult situation. I gave him short shrift and told him that he never left the fox hole at the rear and had half his head blown off without firing a shot, and that Enderby had effectively taken command.

'I wondered about being so outspoken, but apparently the Brigadier told the Colonel what he thought of Ponsonby's attempt to retreat to HQ. If you had been around, I would have recommended you to take my place. The blokes would like you as an NCO and you were very cool under fire; you did just the right thing. You certainly have what it takes as far as I am concerned, and Enderby thought so too. As it was, I recommended Travis. The two Hull lads are a bit hot-headed but they have guts and guts is what we need right now. They've made him a lance-jack for now, but he will get full corporal after they've seen how he goes on. The troop are ready for some leave but it looks like that will have to wait until we sort the rest of the Japs out. More and more men and equipment are arriving; it's just a question of getting 'em to the right place so we can do the job.'

John had visited the stores and was now fully re-equipped. The stores corporal, who didn't like replacing every item of kit, asked him if he had any serviceable pieces left. John said: 'Well, there is the clasp knife but that's non-standard. It looks like you will have to let me have the lot.' Late that night he sewed the cache of green stones that he had retrieved from the man he had throttled into the base of his newly issued kitbag.

24

Mckinley and Imphal

A couple of days later Bell came running into the barracks shouting: 'Get your kit together! We are being flown into Imphal.' The troop was ready in less than an hour and on its way with other units to the airfield. B troop and another mob were crammed into Curtiss Commandos for the journey. Mckinley was impressed with the aircraft, which seemed luxurious compared to the Dakotas he was used to, and could carry nearly twice the load of the older planes.

The last man on the plane was a pale-faced and wiry young lieutenant. Bell saluted and the young man said, 'Are you B Troop, Sergeant Bell, I believe?' Bell affirmed that he had found the correct unit. The young man said: 'I've just arrived fresh out of Sandhurst with just some commando training, I am afraid; but you are short of an officer, and thus I have been allocated to you.' Bell went round the Troop, who were told not to salute in the cramped conditions of the aircraft by the young man. He said, 'We'll get all formal when we get off the aircraft, chaps, but now I need to brief you.'

'Oh, by the way, my name is Montague, George Montague.' He opened an envelope and said, 'This is the situation! Apparently, the recent Japanese attack in the Arakan was only part of a larger operation. We have been aware since about the middle of March of large scale troop movements and their intentions are starting to become clear. Their operation is called 'U-Go', and our operation is called We-Stop 'em!' The joke raised a few smiles but Mckinley thought, 'At least he has some wit and a sense of humour and totally lacks the pomposity of the last one.' The lieutenant went on: 'They are advancing over a fairly broad front from the South and East towards Manipur and Assam. Our Divisions have been conducting fierce fighting retreats and are concentrating at Imphal.

'Great efforts are now being made to increase the strength and disposition of our units there. Everything available is being sent to defend the place. We have an abundance of men, and supplies will come in by air. Our job is to hold, until relieved. The Second Division has been ordered across the country to do that but it will take time as they have been undergoing amphibious training on the South Coast of India. However, they are on their way.' He continued rapidly: 'My understanding is that the High Command is supremely confident that Imphal will hold. We have the artillery and aircraft, the Japanese are at the end of a long supply chain, and their aircraft get fewer and fewer each day. The enemy are also moving towards a small hill fort to the north, called Kohima, and it is hoped that the chaps there can also hang on until relieved. They have good defensive positions and will also be supplied by air.' Mckinley read between the lines of what was being said and thought that he was glad to be going to Imphal.

The troop rapidly got to like the easy-going Montague. He, like Tasburgh, was intelligent and had the relaxed confidence that came of money and family connections in England. In addition to a wiry athleticism, he also had an engaging, straightforward boyishness. When asked a question about the senior command he said: 'Totally beyond me, old chap. I expected to be crawling through French woods and ditches sticking knives into Jerry sentries as part of the big show in Europe, which I can tell you is pretty imminent. As it turned out I ended up here, swatting flies in Calcutta before being flown across country to lead you against the yellow peril.' He endeared himself to them by saying: 'I understand you have seen a lot of action and I obviously count on you all to work together as a unit and keep me out of trouble. I am sure that Sergeant Bell will advise me as necessary and prevent me from making too many mistakes.'

At the airstrip, the troop disembarked from the plane. There seemed to be men and equipment spewing out of planes all around the place and there were soldiers and aircrew everywhere. The troop were fed and then rapidly assigned a spot at the defensive perimeter. Mckinley noted with satisfaction that their section of the line was densely populated with soldiers and there seemed to be Bren guns, mortars and Vickers machine guns galore. There were numerous artillery batteries to the rear and, reassuringly, quite a few tanks. The position faced out over open plains. John thought that it was a natural killing ground and wondered what the Japanese tactics would be in trying to breach the defences. The personnel on the ground eventually proved to be so numerous that for a while everyone was put on half rations until the air supply caught up with demand.

Montague had been briefed that the opposing force was the Japanese fifteenth army, which contained over eighty thousand men. About fifteen thousand of these had been thrown against Kohima, which was defended by a single Battalion of the West Kents. Fighting there was apparently very intense but the Second Division was getting close and they were expected to be relieved within a week. He was told, 'At Imphal, if there is a problem it is oversupply; we have more than enough men and equipment to defend against Division strong attacks. They are being repulsed with huge artillery barrages and strafing from our aircraft. The few that do get close are cut down by withering fire from our rifles and machine guns. Mortars and grenades also add to their misery. After we stop them and they move back, we counter-attack with tanks and infantry with the intention of destroying their bunkers and artillery, and they have made no inroads into our defences whatsoever.'

Mckinley made a point of bringing Albert's prowess with grenades to the attention of the new lieutenant and said he can lob 'em nearly twice as far as most men. He got Albert to demonstrate. Montague was mightily impressed and Albert was assigned the task of using grenades during attacks, but generally the Japanese were driven off before his skills were called on.

The only really hot moment was when the troop had been moved into trenches to defend a forward artillery battery. The Japanese came on, charging towards them in considerable numbers, across open ground. The field of fire was excellent. Mckinley could see mortar bombs dropping amid the enemy as they advanced; fire from Brens and Vicker's machine guns joined in but the enemy still came on. At two hundred yards, B Troop's rifles added to the hail of bullets heading towards the enemy. They still came on, led by sword wielding officers and NCOs. At fifty yards Albert started with his grenades, and Stens and Thompson sub-machine guns opened up. The last of the attackers was cut down about twenty yards from where Mckinley shared a slit trench with Quiller. The remainder of them broke and ran, some still falling as the furious fusillade pursued them into the distance.

After that action, during which John could not have been firing for more than two minutes, he had expended five clips of bullets, fifty rounds in all. He asked around the troop and all had done about the same. 'That's about fifteen hundred rounds just from us and we are aiming at targets. Even if just one in ten is effective we must have got one hundred and fifty of the buggers. And what about the machine guns, grenades and mortars as well?'

John couldn't work it out; the attacks were suicidal in his opinion, why were they doing it? In a later conversation with Brody-Bollers he learned that the Japanese had been supremely confident of success. They had expected to overrun defences easily and capture supplies as they advanced. However, the British had learned since Singapore and had become more and more effective in neutralising Japanese tactics. In addition, those in the field had developed a bloody-minded determination to hold their ground and kill as many of the enemy as possible with no thought of surrender. He heard later about the heroics of the West Kents at Kohima; this exemplified the type of determination that the enemy faced and which came as a terrible shock to an army that thought itself invincible.

Though an occasional bullet had come whizzing over their heads, the return fire from the Japanese was miserable in his opinion. After they had been driven back, artillery opened up, pounding the ground at the point where the enemy had disappeared. Four tanks then appeared and moved forward with machine guns blazing, followed by Bren carriers, which also produced withering fire against any concentration of the enemy that they could see. The troop was ordered to fix bayonets and advance, taking no chances. This was after several incidents where an enemy soldier had apparently surrendered and then tried to take some of his captors with him by a grenade attack at close quarters. This order effectively meant shoot or bayonet anything which moved and even some who didn't. B Troop went forward and John noticed that Brenner seemed to take particular relish in finishing off the badly wounded enemy with his bayonet.

Compared to the Troop's jungle encounter the fight at Imphal was a cakewalk. B Troop had regular rotations out of the trenches and regular meals. There was even some bottled beer being flown in. In late April news came through that Kohima had been relieved and the Second Division had turned to the attack around the hill fort and were destroying the remnants of the enemy in the area. By the middle of May, it was becoming clear that the Japanese attacks were weakening and B troop was amongst those withdrawn for recuperation. No deaths had been sustained and morale was high; the only injury was one of the replacements who had managed to get himself shot in the shoulder because of standing up in an over enthusiastic manner to fire at the retreating enemy. Later, John learned that during the whole battle the enemy had suffered over fifty-thousand casualties with over thirty-thousand dead and had lost virtually all their tanks, transport and artillery. Congratulations were passed around all units. General Slim's 14th Army then paused and gathered its strength in preparation to retake Burma.

A couple of days after getting back to barracks, John came down with a high fever and was hospitalised with malaria. The MO was of the opinion that he had been weakened by his earlier experiences and should not have been returned to active duty. 'Malaria is a variable condition,' he said. In Mckinley's case, the first attack was a bad one and he had a high fever, which raged for several days. After treatment with the Quinine substitute, Atabrine, he improved rapidly.

In the hospital, as he recuperated, he ran into the same RAF nursing sister he had met previously. She explained that he would get periodic malarial fevers for the rest of his life; they could be months or even years apart but he would never get rid of the malarial parasite, which would emerge from time to time. She said: 'Keep some Indian tonic water in the house; it contains quinine. When it comes on you, go to bed, drink the tonic water and sweat it out. Most attacks only last a day or two.' John was still in the infirmary when news came through of the D-Day landings.

He had started to like the sister; she had a lively mind and a firm idea of where she wanted to be after the war. Ideally, she would like a couple of kids, but if marriage did not happen she had determined on a nursing career in the services. As he got to know her, they discussed the peculiarities of wartime existence and their likes and dislikes.

John impressed her with his wide range of knowledge and especially of literature and poetry. John said: 'Yes, its strange; before the war I used to read a lot of poetry but since things kicked off against the Japanese it seems to have much less importance.' The sister had gone to grammar school but had left at sixteen after excellent matriculation results, which her headmistress had hoped would encourage her to remain into the sixth and prepare for university. She was having none of that and after enrolling as a nurse at the local infirmary had transferred to the Air Force when it became clear that war was coming. It was also very evident to her that promotion would be much more rapid within the forces' nursing services than outside.

Her name was Jane but she was known to all as Jenny. As the two became closer, she began to loosen up about her desires and aspirations, which had been bottled up since the war started, and tell Mckinley more about herself. On the surface, she looked pretty straight laced, but it became clear after a while that she had a high, but for now temporarily suppressed, sex drive. She said, 'There'll be plenty of time and opportunity for it in peace time!' She did not like alcohol particularly, but she made clear that she was an enthusiastic smoker and that any man in her life would need to be prepared for that.

On the evening before Mckinley's discharge, just after lights out, she made an excuse and invited him into the linen room. The problem was that she was ovulating, and a primeval voice deep inside her seemed to be screaming: 'I want sex'. In the linen store she pulled him urgently towards her. She had removed her knickers before hunting him down in the ward as the most likely candidate to fulfil her, presently predatory, sexual needs. John responded almost as urgently as Jane, who orgasmed rapidly and very violently, struggling hard not to scream due to the intensity of it. Her hips moved hard against his as she experienced orgasm after orgasm, moaning and gasping at the intense pleasure she was experiencing, arching her back as each one took hold of her and ran through every part of her. Her clitoris and nipples were so taut that it felt they might burst as she was overcome by her huge need to be fucked very, very hard. Soon, Mckinley also experienced the excruciating pleasure of orgasm.

After he had finished ejaculating, he stood motionless and she took a deep breath and clung to him for a few seconds,

403

with years of pent up sexual tension, blessedly, released. She then stood back, coolly adjusted her uniform and said, 'We'd better get back to the ward. If we see anybody, you have been helping me to stack the linen.'

Jane walked back to the offices, went into the toilet, and administered a douche containing the mix of contraceptive chemicals she had been told about, in strict confidence of course, by one of the old nursing hands. The older nurse was near the end of her service and had explained: 'In our job sex rears its ugly head surprisingly often. Some girls need it, especially when they are on heat. Some do without it and are miserable or vicious; they are often the religious types. Other girls make do with each other, but I think that is a poor substitute personally; give me a man any time.' She went on: 'Don't have any illusions about romantic love. Sex is a physical need, just like the need to eat and drink, so for god's sake don't feel guilty about it. You are entitled to your share of it, but above all don't get pregnant; there's no need to if you take the right measures.'

After the encounter, John got into his bed and enjoyed the best night's sleep that he had had in years. The next day before she went off shift, the massively satisfied nursing sister said, 'I have got all your details and home address from the file; we keep them there in case we need to write home about a death.' She passed a small card across to him saying, 'Here are mine! If you want to get in contact with me after the war, please write. I hope you do! If I am not at home, my sister will pass the letter on. The house is in Bradford, and Doncaster and Bradford are only about thirty miles apart so you can easily get there by train. Oh, and one other thing,' she said. 'You are the only one since the start of the war; I hope you are flattered.' Jenny gave him a sideways smile, squeezed his hand, and said, 'Make damned sure you live through it and come to me back home.' She turned abruptly and left him, still trembling slightly from the wonderful fulfilment of that very recent and long overdue sex. Jane walked out of the ward lighting a cigarette as she did so. Mckinley did not see her again for two years.

Everyone expected to move back into action with the Division but other events were afoot. Montague returned to the well-rested unit and said, 'Well chaps, as you well know the Army works in mysterious ways, its wonders to perform. It seems that the attack in Europe is going well, but more experienced troops are needed to keep up the momentum. Some schools of thought seem to think that if we do so, it could be all over by Christmas. Thus, some units are being returned home from India while fresher troops take their place in the jungle. We are one of those sections that are being returned. Apparently, we will move into France as part of the Highland Light Infantry division. I shouldn't worry too much, with the boat ride home and re-equipping, and even home leave promised before we re-embark, it will probably be at least two or three months before we see anything like action again.'

Following Montague's surprise news, the journey home seemed to proceed at a very leisurely pace, with movement by train across India back to Bombay, and then several days wait until they could embark. In Bombay, a good deal of beer was consumed by the men as they kicked their heels, waiting idly in barracks for the ship to be readied. Newsreels of the action in France were avidly consumed, as were the various newspaper reports. It was July before the unit set sail in the large former P&O liner Corfu. The convoy made good time; it was explained that the U-boat war had been pretty well won and that any submarines encountered were likely to be working in isolation and would easily be dealt with by the new anti-submarine measures. These had been so effective that they had caused Doenitz to withdraw his submarine fleet from the Atlantic in May 1943. One of the naval ratings who had been involved in that conflict explained to some of the men that at least forty-three submarines had been sunk in that single month and that torpedo attacks were now a rarity due to the very high risks the submarine crews had to take in order to make one. He said, 'We also have air cover all the way home. If we see a U-boat I will be amazed.'

On board the ship, a major from the intelligence corps gave a briefing to all the ships company; his theme: 'The noose is tightening'. He explained that the Russian forces had now entered Poland and were pressing hard on the Germans from the east. The Americans and Australians were advancing in the Pacific towards Japan, and in Burma, he told them, 'As you very well know, gentlemen, things are going splendidly in no small part thanks to your recent efforts in stopping the Japanese. The Americans have just destroyed the last significant elements of the Japanese fleet, have captured the island of Truck, and are starting to attack the Marianas. When they fall, substantial air attacks will be possible by B29s from Tinian and other islands directly against the Japanese mainland. In China, the nationalist army continue to push the enemy out of their homeland.

'The story, gentlemen, is one of successes and advance on all fronts, but let me now turn to what is of interest to yourselves: the attack on western Europe. It should be very plain to you that things are going very well there. A substantial build up has occurred in Normandy and major breakouts towards Paris and the South are inevitable and will occur very soon. As you are very well aware, allied forces are slugging their way up the Italian mainland and with Italy now on our side the conclusion there is also inevitable. Allied forces have been landed in the South of France and are advancing up the Rhone valley. We now have total air superiority in France and at sea. If I was Hitler, and I am very glad I am not, gentlemen, I would be thinking about hanging myself by my swastikas from the top of the Reichstag. Victory is certain. It is now just a question of when. I do hope that we can get you into France in time to be able to join the party.'

He went on: 'At home you will probably find things very different. I understand that some of you have been away since 1938. You will find a huge number of Americans in Britain, especially in the large cities. Theirs is the equipment and manpower which will ensure victory. In France, all armies are under the strategic command of General Eisenhower, and rightly so as our noble cousins have more troops in France than we do. Churchill is also justly proud that throughout the war and up to the D-Day landings we, a small nation of forty-eight million, have had more divisions in the field than our transatlantic allies. However, in the final months of the war we must inevitably accept that we will be the junior party in achieving final victory as the huge manpower of the Americans is brought to bear against the enemy.'

Mckinley thought about what had been said and talked it over with Quiller later. He said, 'I don't doubt anything he said to us; it's what he isn't saying that worries me.'

'Like what?' said Quill.

'Well, the Germans have a first-rate army and as they get pushed back towards their homeland I think they will fight with greater and greater desperation. Imagine what we would have been doing if they had invaded us in 1940,' was the thoughtful reply. 'OK, we are winning, and they are getting hammered by the Russians in the East. We have more aircraft. But I keep adding up the numbers. As far as I can make out we are outnumbering their regulars about five to one but in Germany they have a home guard, and despite the jokes, if it's like ours they will have close on two million men in home defence units, and they will have the advantage of being prepared and of knowing their own back yards. It won't be a cakewalk by any means.'

The sea journey continued, and apart from eating, sleeping, and the occasional lecture there was little else to do but read. There were out of date papers and well-thumbed copies of various magazines such as *Picture Post*, *Reveille*, and *Tit Bits*. However, there was a library with much popular fiction by authors such as H.G. Wells, A.E. Bennet, John Buchan and Hugh Walpole. Amongst the novels, John found a small copy of Palgrave's *Golden Treasury* of English verse and spent many hours reading old favourites and discovering new ones.

A Naval chaplain, who was also making the voyage back, noticed this and struck up a conversation asking John which poets he liked. John replied: 'I like Wordsworth, Byron, Shelley, Keats, Tennyson, Kipling, Hardy and Shakespeare. There are some others but those are the greats as far as I am concerned. I must admit, though, I haven't had a chance to read much poetry in the last five years. I've been a bit busy,' he said, smiling ruefully. 'And poetry doesn't go down well in a barracks or mess unless it's a lewd limerick or bawdy ballad.'

The officer laughed and said, 'I studied Latin and Greek poetry as a classics subsidiary as part of my theology degree at Durham University. If you read Catullus, nothing from a barrack room ballad could embarrass you. If you get a chance though, I would make sure that you read the great Homeric epics, marvellous stuff even in translation. See if you can get hold of a copy of Cowper's translation of the *Odyssey* and the Earl of Derby's *Iliad*. Both are rewritten in English blank verse and thus you get the marvellous adventure stories within the two poems and a sense of Homer's verse.'

He went on: 'Have you had a chance to keep up with any of the latest poetry?' Mckinley replied that apart from the occasional rousing bits of jingoistic verse in some of the papers he had seen, none. The Chaplain said, 'It is being written, and the poems are thought provoking. I think you will find that poetic fashions are changing. This war seems not to have thrown up any of the wonderful poets, like the Great War produced. Perhaps they are around but I have not seen any so far. We may have to wait for the post-war period to evaluate them and I am sure that German and Russian poets and those from other European countries are writing, but they just haven't surfaced in Britain yet. I will look out some of the latest stuff for you. Will you be here tomorrow?'

John replied, 'Unless we get torpedoed, yes sir.'

The next day the chaplain arrived with a folder containing

cuttings from various magazines and papers; there were about ten poems in all. He said, 'You might like to look at these and tell me what you think.' Mckinley read rapidly and after a while the chaplain said, 'What do you think?'

'Most of it is very bleak. I like parts of some poems like Auden's opening of "September 1st, 1939".' John recited the verse, obviously from memory and after just one reading:

I sit in one of the dives
On Fifty-second Street
Uncertain and afraid
As the clever hopes expire
Of a low dishonest decade:

He went on, 'I like the last verse as well but you do get a sense of great despair and of self-absorption, and also a very acute eye for situations.'

The chaplain sat back and looked at Mckinley with new respect. John went on, 'The poem about sniping: "How to Kill," by Keith Douglas, leaves me cold. Oh, its clever, and they snipe us and we snipe them, but it repulses me. It seems cowardly in some strange way. The poem seems very good technically, it's just the subject matter I don't like, but I suppose it is produced by the unpleasant reality of the war we are in. The one I really like is "Naming of Parts" by Henry Reed; that one has a timeless quality which will, I think, ensure that it is remembered for a long time.'

The chaplain dreamily said 'yes' and quoted the second last verse of the poem:

And this you can see is the bolt. The purpose of this
Is to open the breech, as you can see. We slide it
Rapidly backwards and forwards: we call this
Easing the spring. And rapidly backwards and forwards
The early bees are assaulting and fumbling the flowers:
They call it easing the spring.

'I agree with you,' he said. 'I think that poem is very fine; the intertwining of something as mundane as an instruction drill naming rifle parts and the lyrical scenes from the spring garden lifts it far above the ordinary.'

The chaplain turned the conversation and broached the subject of evening services on board the ship, and Mckinley replied coldly with a glint in his eye, 'Not interested, sir!'

The chaplain said, 'Oh well, it will always be there when you are ready to reach for it.' John knew he never would be, but the Chaplain went off thinking that he had discerned something deeply spiritual within this particular private.

25

Mckinley and Port Said Again

In the middle of July, the ship docked in Port Said to refuel and resupply with food and water. All the men were given shore leave on what they were told could be a stay of two to four days. The Port was much busier than Mckinley remembered, with uniforms everywhere in addition to the usual gangs of urchins calling for baksheesh and the older pedlars offering to sell anything and everything that could possibly be sold.

The mob made straight for the fleshpots and spent time getting drunk, whoring, or both. The naive young men who had embarked in 1938 were now hardened and mature men; they had seen privation and hardship and battle. Some of their comrades had been killed and their perspectives had changed, with much more emphasis on the now and the immediate gratifications which could fill the present moment. No sensible talks by army doctors on the perils of the clap, or lectures on inner worthiness from the padres were going to keep most of them away from the hot and willing prostitutes of the town.

John told Quiller that he would rather save it for home and an RAF nursing sister he had met. Quiller just did not like paying for sex and the two therefore avoided the main bars and found themselves having a quiet drink with some older sailors from a destroyer that had berthed at the same time as the Corfu. As they had walked into the town, they saw Brenner in front of them looking quite furtive and heading for the seedier brothel area; John wondered if he was fool enough to be revisiting the scene of his former difficulties.

They had found a reasonably quiet bar and the old salts and the two troopers exchanged yarns about their war experiences and drank steadily, grumbling about the quality of the beer to the barman, who just smiled and got the next round ready. Mckinley never ceased to be amazed at the way fate rolled the dice in respect of service requirements. One of the sailors had spent most of the war doing coastal patrols round Britain. They had occasionally fired at what they thought were passing enemy aircraft but had never been attacked. Another had served in motor torpedo boats in the Irish Sea and had much the same experiences. He said the nastiest incident they had was when a daft new recruit allowed the pressure cooker to explode in the galley. Another, who was drinking harder than all the rest, said he had been on escort duty in the Atlantic during '39 and '40 in destroyers and had been under attack in virtually every convoy he had done; eventually his ship had been torpedoed and they had lost about a third of their crew.

The Admiralty then thoughtfully transferred him to a new berth in the Mediterranean just as the naval action there was getting hot, with the convoys to Malta often losing more than half the ships that had been sent to the island. In the Med his ship had been mined, with the result that several-dozen of the ships company had once more been killed and wounded. He said, 'I was lucky I had been sent up top with mugs of cocoa for the watch. All of a sudden the bow of the ship came flying over the bridge! If I had stayed where I had been ten minutes before that, I would have bought it for sure. The only way that the Captain could prevent the destroyer sinking was to lash it to another and then get moved stern first back to Gibraltar.' During the attacks against Rommel's supply convoys, his previous ship had been bombed and had sunk off the Libyan coast and he had to swim for it. He had just managed to make it to a life raft; he was totally exhausted but had been hauled onto it by a couple of shipmates. He had then been assigned to his present ship, which had been doing Russian convoy escort duty. He explained: 'The winter conditions up in the Arctic are appalling; if a ship goes down it's a death sentence. If you get in the water, even if you get into a boat, you are likely to freeze to death if you aren't picked up pretty quick.

'It's best to be on something like an ammunition ship. I saw one get torpedoed. It was about a mile away from us; it had just got alight, then the thing seemed to explode hundreds of yards into the air and nothing was left, just bits of rubbish on the surface. Everyone on it would have been killed straight off; it's the best way to go up there.' He went on: 'I don't know what I am doing back in the Med but something bad is sure to happen, even with the Eyeties on our side now. We will probably sink in a hurricane or collide with one of our own ships.'

Eventually they all swayed out of the bar, not drunk but certainly replete with a sufficiency of the splendidly cool beer. The sailors had drunk rather more than the two soldiers and the unlucky one of the three was almost staggering as the three made their way back to their berths. John said: 'We'll head back through the red-light district and pick up the boys and get back; we might be able to keep some of the younger ones out of trouble. I wonder what Brenner got up to?'

Brenner had made his way to the extensive brothel area, furtively, trying to avoid people he knew, but on his way there he had not escaped the notice of Mckinley. On the last occasion he had been in the port he had experienced a narrow escape because of indulging his rather special sexual needs, and he knew that he needed to be careful. However, it had been six years or so since that escapade and he looked older, but he took care to choose an out of the way brothel as far away as possible from the one he had previously used. He entered the low door, had a drink at the bar, and then scanned the dingy room searching for any faces which looked familiar. After reassuring himself that there were none, he negotiated a transaction with the madam. 'I want a girl all evening,' he said. 'How much?'

413

The madam was instantly all over him, sensing money; she drew heavily on an aromatic cigarette and told him that they had six girls waiting and asked him to choose. She quoted a price while sizing him up; he looked a rough customer, not really the type who would easily be parted from his wallet after a few drinks, she thought. On a busy night, most girls could expect to have more than a dozen clients, but it was not busy and she gave him a price which was not too exorbitant. He laughed and said, 'That's expensive, but it's OK as long as I don't get disturbed till I have finished.' He said, 'I'll take a few beers up with me.' The Madam shouted and a small, nervous looking, middle-aged man appeared carrying a small pail with half a dozen bottles of beer resting in ice. 'You pay extra for these,' she said. He laughed as he parted with more money for the over-priced drinks.

He had picked a rather plump girl with large rounded buttocks and very full breasts. He thought she looked about twenty-five and more Turkish than Egyptian. He just could not understand why men like the Duke of Windsor went for stick insects; he liked 'em big. What the Hell! They could be Eskimos as long as they served his purpose. They went up to the small room and the waiting bed and Brenner told the girl to undress. He sat drinking a beer, watching her.

She moved to take off her stockings but Brenner said, 'No! Leave those on, I want to look at you.' She looked back at him with big brown cow-like eyes and said, 'You use Johnny?' He laughed and said: 'Of course,' and threw a three pack down on the bed. The girl stripped and he ordered her to turn slowly. She obeyed passively. Brenner enjoyed the sight of the full breasts and rounded belly and the pale flesh hanging over the stocking tops. 'You like to do as you are told, don't you slut!' Brenner snarled the words in a tone of voice that had grown much less pleasant and somehow very urgent. He stood and grasped the woman's breasts, cupping them from behind, fingering the nipples and then squeezing them hard. His hand transferred to the clitoris and he fingered and rubbed it for two or three minutes until he felt the girl starting to lubricate. 'Bend over the bed,' he said, and the prostitute complied willingly.

He said, 'Wait while I put the Johnny on.' The girl waited and relaxed in willing anticipation of his entry. Brenner moved rapidly to his tunic, took out a small brown bottle, and poured some of the liquid it contained onto a large handkerchief. Then he pulled the girl back towards him and pushed the pad over her mouth and nose. She struggled against him for a few seconds but soon had to inhale deeply, and after a few seconds she stopped struggling as the chloroform stupefied her. Brenner had purloined the stuff from the ship's medical centre where it could be found in a number of large brown bottles. He pushed his victim onto her knees on the bed and gagged her with a small rubber gag he had brought with him and then expertly tied each wrist to each ankle with cord so that she was helpless, on her knees with her legs wide apart. She started to recover slightly from the effects of the drug and started to make sounds through the gag.

Brenner cupped her breasts again, squeezed her nipples hard, and said, 'You'd better be quiet, slut, if you know what's good for you.' He reached into his tunic and brought out the small whip which he had always taken great trouble to conceal when in barracks. It was about two feet in length and consisted of several knotted leather thongs which were intertwined at one end to make a handle. Brenner brought the knotted strands of the device down viciously on the woman's inviting and rounded buttocks and said, 'Like I told you, slut, shut up or you'll get more chloroform.'

The prostitute writhed violently, moaning through the gag. Brenner brought the whip down more than a dozen times on the woman's bare buttocks until he could see a series of harsh and blood bright wheals criss-crossing them. By this time, the woman was crying and whimpering with pain. Brenner was now totally aroused at the sight of the well-punished flesh and entered her like an animal, fucking his victim violently until the assault ended for him in a massive orgasm.

After satisfying himself he dressed rapidly and pushed the woman onto her back and used the chloroform again until he could see that she was on the point of passing out. He untied her rapidly, took the gag out of her mouth, and stuffed the cords, the whip and the gag down his battle dress. He gave her a final whiff of the pungent liquid and left her lying in a drugged stupor on the bed. He knew from previous experience that it would be ten to fifteen minutes before she recovered her wits sufficiently to raise the alarm. Brenner left the room furtively, closing the door firmly behind him, and walked down the corridor towards the stairs.

He passed another of the girls and she stared hard at him as he passed, but the well-satisfied, sadistic private was too preoccupied to look back at her.

He walked nonchalantly through the bar and said to the Madam, 'That's enough for me, dearie. I'm off now to have a drink with the lads; thanks a lot.'

The Madam looked up and said, 'You want a drink? We have other girls. You want to relax for a while and try one of them?'

Brenner laughed and said, 'Sufficient to the night is the pleasure thereof,' and then, laughing at his own joke, he stepped out into the night.

What he had not realised was that by an incredible coincidence the girl who had seen him upstairs had been his victim of six years earlier. His leering face was etched indelibly into her memory. She raced down the corridor and pushed open the door from which he had just emerged. She found his victim in a drugged, bleeding and shocked state and realised that rapid action was needed. She raced down the back stairs and alerted three of the brothel's minders to the situation. They were all young men, and they raced upstairs and saw what had happened to the girl, then hared off after Brenner. He had only walked about thirty yards up the alley when they emerged from the door of the seedy den in pursuit of him. For a moment, he thought that the two at the rear were chasing the one in the lead. Then he saw that all three were carrying knives and that he was their quarry.

Brenner sprinted off. On a bend and just out of sight of his pursuers, he turned into another of the narrow byways which ran through the district. He pulled back into a doorway and watched as they ran past the end of the dark passageway. Thinking he had shaken them off he started to walk on, his path lit by light from the occasional oil lamp which shone from the upper rooms that he passed. However, on turning another corner he found himself at a dead end.

Brenner turned to retrace his steps, but so had his pursuers. Their local knowledge had made them realise he could only have gone one way. All of a sudden, three vicious looking Arabs confronted him. He weighed the situation quickly, realising that his only chance was to charge through them and then run for dear life. He lunged at the first, pushing him out of the way and back on his arse and belted the second man very hard in the teeth, knocking him down. The third ducked an incoming blow from Brenner and at the same time stuck his knife deep into the desperate private's side.

Brenner grunted in pain, put his hand over the blood spurting from the gash, and made off. The two other Arabs had regained their feet and now came in for the kill. They caught him up and one slashed at their quarry's face, but Brenner took the blow on his forearm. Hot blood started to run down his arm from the deep gash inflicted by the razor-sharp blade. The other man came rushing in from behind and stuck his knife deep and hard into the wounded soldier's back. Brenner stopped and staggered back and then slowly slid down the wall, giggling as he did so.

His three pursuers stood back, pausing in their attack because of the strangeness of the fallen man's behaviour; he just sat there, coughing blood, seeming to be afflicted by some strange joke. Then, the leader of the three bent down and slowly and deliberately cut deep across the sitting man's throat. The three paused and looked at him as his eyes glazed and he fell silent and slumped down into the red pool of his own fresh blood. Then, grasping their situation as murderers of one of his majesty's soldiers, they ran off, disappearing into the maze of alleyways that were filled with the blackness of the Egyptian night.

Mckinley and Quiller found the rest of the troop in the last bar before the docks. They were all having a last few jarfuls before they left. It was about eleven p.m. and someone mentioned the order to report back before midnight. One lad said: 'I don't give a fuck about that. I'm staying here till I've had enough. What will they do to me if I don't make it back in time, send me off to get shot at by the Krauts?' On the way out to India the young and green recruits had all been fearful of the disciplinary sanctions which would be imposed if they were not back by the stipulated hour, but now no one seemed to care.

At about eleven-fifteen, a Redcap corporal rushed into the bar and asked if anyone had seen Sergeant Bell. One of the lads said that he had been struck down with the shits and had gone back aboard. The man asked if anyone else was in charge. They all looked at Mckinley. The redcap took him to one side and said, 'It looks like the natives have done for one of your mob. We think he is called Brenner. Did anybody see him earlier.'

John said, 'We saw him sloping off on his own towards the red-light district when we came into town, but that was hours ago. That was the last we saw of him. Quiller and me have spent all night yarning and drinking near here with some deck hands from the destroyer docked next to us.'

The sergeant said, 'Anything odd about him?'

Mckinley said, 'Well, when we were here on the way out, about six years ago, there was some funny business. After that, the Redcaps were everywhere and they were stood looking at us all when we got back and boarded the ship. I think he was involved in that somehow; it's just a hunch though, I didn't see anything—it was just the way he behaved.'

418

John continued: 'I don't suppose it was just a robbery gone wrong?'

The sergeant replied, 'We don't think so; he still had his wallet and his watch and his documents on him when we got to him.' The sergeant thanked him for his help and said, 'I may want to talk to you again; you'll be on the SS *Corfu* won't you? How long before you sail?'

"They think it will be at least twenty-four hours and possibly up to three days."

The military policeman then strode into the middle of the bar, shouted for quiet, and then said: 'Sorry lads, there's been some serious trouble; can you all drink up and move back to your ship.'

He didn't wait for any protests but turned on his heel and made for the door and jumped into the car waiting outside.

John said to Quiller, 'We'd best drink up.' He had words with one or two of the others and told them: 'It's serious, anyone late back might find themselves in very hot water. The officers do not like trouble and this is big trouble.' Word got round the group quickly and the mood changed. They all drank up and departed, some in quiet groups and some rowdily, but all were back on board by the required hour.

John sought out Bell when he got on board and told him what had happened. The sergeant looked pale as a result of the bug that had emptied his guts but he told John that he was all right.

He said, 'I've had it worse in India. I had a double dose of them kaolin and opium pills you get in the Bazaar and the runs have finished; I just feel a bit queasy. But thanks for the advance warning; I will cover my back just in case any crap flies my way. I'll get hold of Montague first thing and tell him what you've said. I expect the place will be crawling with military police tomorrow.'

And so it transpired.

The Provost Marshal came aboard after breakfast, formally reported the incident, and then asked to see a Private

Mckinley. John was marched into the cabin that served as an office to find the senior army officer on board, a Brigadier called Sims, the *Corfu's* first officer, the Provost Marshal, Montague, and the Redcap sergeant of the previous evening. The Provost Marshal led off and said, 'Stand at ease please, private. The sergeant here says that you might have been the last of the army personnel to see Brenner before he was killed. Could you go through it for us?'

John went through the evening's happenings again. He had seen Brenner disappear quite early into the rougher part of the brothel area and had not seen him again. He had been drinking all night with another private in the same bar with some older sailors. He gave their first names and ranks. He explained that two were able seamen and one was a galley hand. 'They should be easy to trace,' he said, 'but I doubt they would have noticed anything as they didn't know the man who has been killed and would have no reason to clock him. I only did so because he seemed so furtive; his not wanting to be noticed drew my attention to him.' He went through the incident that had occurred on the troop's previous shore leave and said that he just had a funny feeling about the way that Brenner had acted.

The Provost Marshal said, 'We have found the girl who was attacked last time and shown her a photo of the deceased but she says she knows nothing; everyone else down there has clammed up so tight that the silence is deafening. However, in my experience time tends to lead to careless talk and sooner or later we will have leads to follow.'

The Brigadier said, 'What sort of chap was he? Was he popular?'

John said, 'I can't say that he was, sir. He seemed to be very much a loner. When he was outside the camp he always went off on his own rather than sticking with the rest of the lads.' The Provost asked if there was anything else that he would like to tell them. John had thought things through the previous night; Brenner was now dead and thus he did not see any point in mentioning the whip he had found after tailing him to the disused buildings on the camp back in India. He said, in a measured and helpful tone, 'Nothing that I can think of, sir.'

The Provost said, 'Well, if anything does come to mind report it to your officer and he can radio the information back to us.' The Provost Marshal asked if anyone else had any questions, but as there were none the helpful private was dismissed.

The group then asked about the characters of Mckinley and the dead private. Bell gave John a very fulsome endorsement and told them that in the holding action in Burma he had taken command of the central defenders and that in his opinion he and sergeant Enderby should have been decorated for their valour. He was dismissive about Brenner saying: 'Always just the right side of being insubordinate! He was lucky not to have been court-martialled after he disobeyed a direct order when we escaped from the Japs.' He went on, 'He always caused problems. On shore leaves like these I always like to be near the men just to keep a lid on things if they get a bit too rowdy, but Brenner never stayed with the rest, he was always off on his own.'

The officers seemed reasonably content and Bell was dismissed. The Provost told the others that a girl was tied up and severely whipped several years ago, the last time this regiment was in port. 'I understand that another girl needed medical attention last night after what seems to be a very similar attack. We have not established who she was or which brothel she worked in yet, and I suspect she will have disappeared to another in Cairo or Alexandria by now. However, I do not intend to let things lie on the table. I consider it rather bad form to have one of our men killed and let the natives see that they can get away with it. For that very reason they will be enduring a lot of raids and bar closures over the next few months; it might just loosen a few tongues.'

In the SS *Corfu* word got round the men that Brenner had been killed somewhere in the downtown area. Most thought that he probably had it coming to him and really couldn't care less that he was gone. Bell said, 'It's a bit of a waste; if he was going to get it I would have liked him to have been shooting at the enemy at the time.' Montague was given the job of seeing to the details of the burial and writing home. A small honour guard was formed from the troop but apart from them, the officer, and a padre, no one else attended the small clean and very well kept British cemetery on the outskirts of the port, when the unloved private was laid to rest.

The ship had been re-provisioned and the captain was ordered to set off the next day. The destroyer that had occupied the next berth led off and they picked up two other cargo ships as they entered the Med and headed off towards Malta. They sailed straight past it, much to the regret of some of the crew, and eventually put into Gibraltar. After twenty-four hours in port, they were off again as part of a larger convoy bound for Southampton. Two days out, Mckinley was awoken by some sort of explosion and went up on deck. One of the oil tankers had been torpedoed. Fortunately, it was empty, but it had still caught fire and he could see the crew scrambling into the lifeboats.

A few minutes later a couple of destroyers were in the area and a few minutes after that he heard the crump of several explosions and shortly after that several more. He asked a deck hand if they were depth charging. The deckie replied that it was the new hedgehog. 'It shoots off a lot of charges in a pre-determined pattern. If any of 'em explode within fifty feet of the sub that will finish it; they are one of the reasons that we see so few attacks these days. I wouldn't like to be part of a U-Boat crew now, it's almost certain death with those charges set to blow at the right depths and with the new improved Asdic and the air cover.'

The *Corfu* sailed on with one destroyer still criss-crossing the area near the sinking tanker whilst the other picked up its survivors. An hour later it was daylight, and two aircraft appeared and started to circle the convoy in wide sweeps.

As they approached the final few hundred miles to the homeport, aircraft became more and more numerous. The deckie said, 'We won't see any more U-Boats now, it's plain sailing until we dock.'

The convoy chugged on through calm seas until they berthed in the safety of Southampton water. The sight around them was amazing; there were ships of various sizes everywhere. Mckinley had never seen any port so full of vessels. After they docked the troop was disembarked with rail warrants and a pass for fourteen days' leave.

They were to report back to Colchester in preparation for service in Europe on the fifth of August.

26

Mckinley and the Home Front

John and Quiller travelled homewards from the southern port in crowded third class carriages which were jam packed with civilians, privates and NCOs, seemingly from all over the planet. The two changed stations in South London due to some sort of diversion and got a succession of buses and tubes through the great city, moving towards King's Cross station. They made a point of travelling upstairs on the buses so that they could look at the sights of war in the streets they drove through. Occasionally Mckinley observed that two or three houses were missing from the ends or middles of neat terraces. Sometimes a whole row of them had been demolished.

Although the terror of the Blitz was long gone, a new flying bomb was apparently being used, but if you believed the propaganda those few that got through would likely as not explode on open land. Somehow, with the very evident bomb damage he could see, there was still an ominous sense of danger in the air.

It was just after six in the evening when they arrived at the station at the entrance to King's Cross. It was obvious to anyone with any sort of reasonably tuned antenna that the prostitutes were doing a roaring and apparently unmolested trade in the area. John said, drily, to Quiller, 'The girls are clearly doing their bit for the war effort.' They walked into the station and looked at the departures board. 'There's a train up to Donny at twenty to seven,' he said to Quill. 'We've just got time for a sandwich and a pint.' They walked into the station buffet, which was packed, and John said, 'I'll get on this side you go the other, it gives us a better chance of somebody noticing us.' The two slowly advanced towards the harassed girls who were serving the crowd as fast as they were able to. John noticed that if there was a choice they served those in uniform first.

After five minutes, Mckinley got his chance and caught the eye of an attractive redhead. 'Two pints and a couple of sandwiches, Red,' he called.

The girl smiled and in a rich Geordie accent said, 'Cheese or spam?'

John called back, smiling, 'Anything but spam.'

There was some mumbling either side of him from civilians who obviously thought he had been served before his turn. The girl busied herself pulling the pints and served up two thick slices of cheese in between two even thicker slices of bread and margarine. John winked and passed the money over and said, 'Keep the change, we're in a hurry.'

The two gobbled the food and washed it down with the beer. John made a point of saying loudly. 'That's my first pint in England for six years.' That seemed to have the effect of mollifying the mumblers.

'What do you think?' said Quiller.

'It's better than nothing,' John replied. 'If we get into Donny in time we might get the chance of a decent drink.'

A somewhat portly civilian in a rather old but well cut suit said: 'Where have you boys been serving?'

'Burma,' said Mckinley, sizing the man up and down. 'We've been sent back here for the job in France. We've just finished some Japs off at a place called Imphal; I don't suppose you've ever heard of it.'

The portly man exploded: 'Never heard of it! Everybody in Britain knows about Kohima and Imphal!' He said, 'Would you like another?'

John looked at the clock; it was twenty-five past the hour. He said: 'Yes, but we'll never get served in time.'

The man shouted out loudly in the direction of the bar. 'Mavis, get me four pint bottles of your best pale ale and hurry up, these blokes are just back from Imphal.' Everyone in the Buffet turned to look. Some gathered round and wanted to shake their hands, others were slapping them on the back, and one woman pressed a bar of chocolate into Quiller's hand. He accepted it without thinking, and the woman kissed his cheek. Mckinley, for once in his life, was taken aback and was lost for words.

The man asked: 'Which train are you on?' and was told it was the 6.40 to Doncaster. He said, 'You should make good time, it only stops at Peterborough on the way up.' He passed the pint bottles of beer across to the two men and said, 'Follow me, I'll get you a seat.'

He led them to the train and walked straight past the third and second-class carriages. He said, 'Have you got your travel warrants?' The two replied that they had but John wondered what was happening. It was soon revealed. The man pulled a tortoise-shell fountain pen from an inside pocket, took the warrants and signed them. He opened the first class carriage door and shouted to the steward, 'Henry! These two men have now got first class warrants on my authority. Make sure they are looked after and if food is available make sure they get the best of what you have.'

'Yes sir,' said Henry.

The portly man looked at the steward and said in a commanding voice, 'If there are comments from anyone you can tell them these men are here on the very highest authority and they can take it up with me if they want to pursue it.' He turned to the two and explained: 'All this is quite in order; the first class carriage is never fully occupied and I have full power to do this.' The two shook his hand, thanked him profusely, and clambered into the strange world of the first class compartment.

The steward saw that John and Quiller were comfortably seated at end seats in the dining car with a small table in between them. As they sat down Mckinley asked him: 'Who on earth was that? Was it the station master?'

Henry said, 'Oh no, much more senior than that, he is the railway company's general manager. Since his son was killed in Burma, it seems he has been here all the time, though he must get some sleep when things are quiet. He seems to be on a one-man mission to get the trains through and to make sure that everything works like clockwork. He wants to finish the war single-handed. They tell me he tried to join up after his son got killed but he was too old.'

He went on, 'There is no hot food but I can get you sandwiches and coffee.' He paused and said guiltily, like a choirboy at the confessional, 'It's real coffee! We have beef or ham sandwiches and smoked salmon. We don't often get it but yesterday we took a load of top brass and government types up north. After about two hours we dropped them off. It was an unscheduled stop at Grantham. I think they were off to one of the airfields.

'I heard one of 'em say something and saw a senior officer glare at him. They must really think we are very stupid; anyone who reads the Boy's Own knows about the V1. And I'm not going to drop Hitler a postcard telling him that someone here knows about it—I think he probably knows that already.'

All three laughed at the joke and the two settled back into their comfortable seats in the warm carriage. 'I wonder what the poor people are doing?' said Mckinley, grinning.

After a while, the steward re-appeared carrying a large plate with some beef sandwiches on it, and another with even more of smoked salmon. He produced a couple of half pint glasses. He said, 'For the beer. We are in First Class and I can't let you gentlemen be seen drinking out of bottles like some uncouth spiv down at the dog track. I'll bring you some coffee in a while; you'll need to get the food digested first.'

Henry made his way down the carriage, which was quite empty. A slim middle-aged woman wearing a fox fur was having tea and smoking using a cigarette holder a couple of tables down from the pair. She looked at them disapprovingly through gimlet eyes but said nothing. Her younger, harassed looking companion either had not noticed or just did not care. Mckinley clocked the older woman's expression and thought, 'She's looking at us as though we are a couple of Hottentots who have absolutely no right to be present in this compartment.' Ignoring the thinly disguised hostility to their presence, John and Quill ate and drank heartily as the train chugged up towards the north. It seemed to be making reasonable progress for a while but then slowed. They got into Peterborough just after nine, and John said: 'Not much chance of getting into Donny for the last one; it's going to be well after ten when we land.'

A couple of RAF officers boarded the train at the stop and gave the two some funny looks as they walked past. One of them in a rather officious manner said to Henry: 'Should those two be in here?' Henry, who was a past master in dealing with the bumptious, said, 'Oh yes, sir, the two ladies had valid first class tickets.'

'Not those,' exploded the Flight Lieutenant. 'The two privates!'

'Are you saying I don't know my job?' replied the steward, in a well-feigned and rather indignant tone. 'Their warrants are even more in order!' He went on in a very pained voice as though he was talking to a schoolboy, 'They are here on the highest possible authority. Those men are just back from Imphal and there is a war on, you know! As far as I have been informed our First Class seats are not just for officers.' He went on rapidly: 'I was given very explicit instructions by the managing director of this railway company concerning them and he told me if anyone has any query about it to refer them to him. He is a friend of Mr Brendan Bracken you know. He is frequently at the House of Commons on some sort of Rail Transport Committee and something to do with public information.'

The older officer leaned forward and said, 'Thank you steward, I am sure everything is in order.' The younger officer coloured up but fell silent. He had never seen privates, or any other member of the lower classes for that matter, in the first class carriages and it offended his sense of order. The older man said, 'Bracken is Minister of Information as you are undoubtedly aware, Anthony, and is apparently a close crony of Churchill's.' The younger man muttered something but what he said was lost in the noise of the train as it lurched forward on the last part of its journey.

After a while, a large man in a rather loud suit made his way into the dining car and sat at the table on the opposite side of the aisle from John and Quiller. 'Bloody freezing in those carriages, no heating on at all,' he roared. 'I can understand why you boys are in here.'

His accent was discernibly that of a Londoner and John said, 'We're here for the food, mainly.'

'Anything hot?' said the suit.

'No,' came the reply, 'but there were sandwiches earlier.' The steward made his way down to the two privates and put a pot of coffee down on their table with cream, sugar and two rather elegant coffee cups bearing the L.N.E.R. coat of arms.

The suit said, 'Any chance of a drink, squire, and something to eat?'

Henry turned and said, 'I will have to check.'

The suit leaned over. 'You boys will have one with me, won't you? I've had a bit of luck at the cards.'

The steward said: 'I will double check but I think we only have Guinness, will that be alright?'

The suit said: 'Fine,' and palmed Henry a ten-shilling note, winking, and said: 'Anything you can do in the food line will be very appreciated. Oh, and bring a few bottles of Guinness; I think these lads will be able to manage more than one.' Henry nodded and reappeared about five minutes later with a tray of beef sandwiches and half a dozen pint bottles of Guinness. 'Good man!' said the suit with another wink. He paid for the food and gave Henry another ten-shilling note saying: 'There's the other half, my old pal. That's what you get when you look after Jimmy Fox.'

Jimmy tucked into the sandwiches and poured a glass of the stout, saying, 'Good, it's nice and cool. I hate warm stout. Warm beer's bad enough but heat ruins Guinness, makes it taste like liquorice water.' Jimmy offered the two sandwiches but they had had enough food already. However, they were prepared to help him with the stout. The three sat drinking and chatting, with Jimmy doing most of the talking. He explained that he was a general dealer and had just missed the call up by being a few months past the maximum age. He said: 'Before it all kicked off I was scratching a living—a bit of commercial travelling, a bit of wheeler dealing here and there. I was just about getting by, but with the war it's been amazing, you wouldn't believe how many ways there are to make money now.' The train pulled past Newark on the last lap of their journey and he asked, 'Is it very far now?'

John said, 'No, we should be in Doncaster in less than forty minutes.'

Jimmy asked Henry if there was any more drink but he said, 'Sorry, sir. I can get you a tea if you like?'

The offer was refused and the conversation turned to Doncaster. John and Quiller were informed by their host that he was booked into a hotel called the Danum. 'Is it any good?' he said.

John replied, 'Poshest hotel in Doncaster, only about a ten-minute walk from the station.'

The general dealer seemed pleased about that and said, 'I'm seeing a contact about some tyres; you can't get 'em for love or money but he seems to know how to lay his hands on some, so I thought I would make the trip up north.'

The train pulled into the station at ten twenty-five. John said to Quiller, 'We might have to walk. I doubt if there is a bus this late.'

Jimmy leant across: 'Can't you get a taxi?'

John smiled and said, 'Very doubtful, this is Donny not Piccadilly.'

They made their way to the outside of the station; it was

deserted apart from a porter who was trundling a packing case towards a storage building. The older man said, 'Look, I was counting on a taxi to the hotel; if you lads walk me there I'll pay for a taxi home for you. It'll be in the middle of the blackout and its late and I really don't have a clue where I am, and if I know anything about hotel porters, if I wave enough money they can work miracles. He will get you transport of some sort back home.'

John looked at Quill and said, 'Well, we're not doing anything else, why not.'

The three emerged from the station and made their way through the dim streets towards the Hotel. Though Jimmy let Quill give him a hand with his suitcase, he kept very tight hold of a small valise he had with him. He also seemed nervous and looked over his shoulder several times as they traversed the now empty streets.

They arrived at the Danum just after eleven and the older man booked in and asked about transport for his two escorts. The initial response was negative but after money changed hands the night porter got on the phone. Jimmy said, 'You will be able to get us a drink, won't you. We'll sit in those leather armchairs in the foyer.' The porter rapidly produced three pint bottles of Double Diamond ale and three glasses; the three then sat back, drinking, whilst their host said, 'I can't thank you enough, lads. I'll explain it to you someday perhaps.'

Ten minutes later a man in a brown apron walked in and said, 'I'm here to give some lads a lift to Skellow.'

The three travelling companions shook hands and then John saw Jimmy press something into the driver's hand. The driver touched the peak of his cap very respectfully and led his two passengers outside. The conveyance was a greengrocer's lorry loaded with sacks of grain. The driver said, 'Hop in the cab lads, plenty of room for three. Chuck your kit bags at the front of the feed—they will be alright there.' The two did as they were instructed and got into the cab of the rather elderly wagon. The driver got it going and said, 'I'm off to a farm the other side of Campsall. We'll head up the A1 and I can turn down and drop you off on the way.' They set off, the lorry driver sticking to a steady twenty-five miles an hour, his route lit only by his shielded and dipped headlights. 'Much safer to drive slow in the blackout,' he said, 'and it's only six or seven miles; we'll be there in no time.' About twenty minutes later, he dropped them off at the end of their street and said, 'Cheerio.'

The two made arrangements to meet the following day and then Quiller walked down to Laurel Terrace and Mckinley marched cheerfully down Briar Road towards number thirty-nine. It was nearly midnight. As he was about half way down the road the air-raid siren started and after a minute or two he could hear doors opening as people scurried for the air-raid shelters.

He got to the gennel leading to 39 and 41 and waited as bodies came towards him in the dark. He followed them in to the low brick built structure and said: 'You won't mind if I sit the raid out with you?' It took a second to register. Mckinley had changed from youthfulness into full manhood but there was no mistaking his voice. They all realised at the same time who it was, returned at last after long years away.

His mother started sobbing with joy and relief but Cud was his usual excitable and animated self. Alice and Peggy grabbed him and hugged him and Bert just sat there smiling. After the excitement of greeting and reunion with them, they all settled down and sat back on the wooden benches in the shelter.

John asked about the raid. 'Do you get many?' he said.

'Nah,' said Cud. 'They are a rare event these days; they're probably strays on their way back from Sheffield. Lots of people don't even bother with the shelters now, but we do; you never know if one is headed your way.'

'Have you been bombed in the village?' John asked.

'No!' Cud said. 'Though one plane did drop some incendiaries on the pit tip; they were just allowed to burn out.'

'Anything much in Doncaster?' he asked.

Again, the answer was negative. 'The closest to us was a Dornier being chased by a Hurricane, jettisoning bombs near the Sun Inn by the Barnsley Road junction about three miles away. A girl stood at the bus stop got blown to bits, but apart from a hit near Pegler's Brass foundry and one near the Post office in Bentley we have hardly been touched.'

After another ten minutes, the all clear went and they made their way inside. Peggy said she'd make some tea and she put the kettle on the coal fire in the kitchen. John was surprised it was still so well up but Cud said, 'Bert and me were on late afters and did some overtime; we didn't get out of the pit till half-nine. We just had time for a couple of pints in our pit muck, stood in the bar at the Moon.' When the pit was sunk, the Moon Hotel had been strategically sited by the Samuel Smith's brewery on a site directly opposite the colliery entrance and consequently did a roaring trade, especially at the ends of the various daytime shifts.

Cud went over to the sideboard, rummaged in the cupboard above it, and returned with a small bottle of rum. He said, 'We can have a drink to John,' he faltered. 'You've no idea how glad we are to see you back, lad.' He poured rum out for all but Peggy who didn't like the taste. Alice didn't like it either but with a free and adventurous spirit she was not going to be left out. Margaret took a glass and poured it into her tea and said, 'With the shock of seeing you after all these years I need a drink. I haven't been like this since that telegram we got saying that you were missing in action.'

The family group sat round the fire chatting for half an hour with everyone wanting to know what John had been doing in Burma. He told them that there would be plenty of time for that in the morning. 'But there is one thing.' He reached into his kit bag and pulled out a small black elephant. It was rather crudely made and carved from mahogany. He gave it to his mother. John said: 'I got you this in the bazaar when I first got to India and it's been in my kit bag ever since.

434

I hope you like it.' He could see tears welling up again in Margaret's eyes—she didn't say anything but just hugged him for a long time. The elephant subsequently took pride of place amongst the small collection of ornaments on the old and rather battered sideboard that stood under the window in the living room.

In the morning, they all sat together eating fried bread with beans and powdered egg for breakfast. John handed his ration book to his mother and said, 'You will need this to get my rations until I leave. You might find these useful as well,' and passed three large tins of Spam and two very large tins of corned beef across to her along with a large bar of chocolate. He rummaged even deeper and pulled out five quarter pound packets of tea and a large tin of cheese.

She said, 'Are they from the army?'

'No,' said John. 'I did a trade with a cook on board the ship; the chocolate is from the NAAFI. There is one thing about being in action, they don't pay us much but you don't get many chances to spend it and people have been good to us on the way up. Quiller and me have hardly spent a penny since we got here. I had loads of back-pay after my adventures in the jungle.'

'What happened there?' said Cud. 'We were worried sick when we got the telegram.'

John made light of it. 'I just got cut off from my unit and it took a few weeks till I could re-join 'em and tell 'em I was OK.'

He asked how they were all going on for food and Margaret said, 'We're not going hungry. There's plenty of bread and potatoes and vegetables and fruit in the summer but the only bread you can get is brown; they're getting as much out of the wheat as they can. The things we are short of are meat, cheese, butter, lard and tea. You can get stuff like whale meat but it's pretty awful, and the Ministry of food keep pushing things like Woolton Pie; it's made of vegetables with no meat in it at all. It is filling but it's so bland I can't understand anybody ever wanting to be a vegetarian. We do get some eggs though;

Ida Morris next door keeps a few hens and we save our potato peelings and any waste for her to boil up and feed them.

'We get the odd can of something off that spiv that works as the bookie's runner, but it's twice the price that you pay in the shops; but everybody does it! I've never heard of anybody turning him down, even the local bobby. There's always beer but never any spirits, and you can always get cigarettes. Nearly everybody smokes now.'

'I don't,' said Peggy. 'They stink!'

'I've started,' said his mother. 'It sooths my nerves.'

John looked at her with surprise but said nothing.

Mckinley took stock and noticed how threadbare all their clothes were, especially his mother's pinnie. He said, 'What about clothes?'

Alice said, 'You can't get clothes for love nor money and it's the same with any sort of household goods. You can't get pots or pans and we are down to seven cups and mugs now. We have a few plates spare still, but I dread it when one gets broken, and we just have enough knives and forks. Sheets, blankets, all that sort of thing are so hard to get, it's almost impossible. In winter, I go to bed with an old cardigan on and with an old army greatcoat over my cover. Our one luxury is the wireless; it's pretty old now but my dad seems to manage to keep it working.'

Cud piped up: 'The other good thing is full-time working at the pit. Now you can have overtime every day and at week-ends, and we've just got that big pay rise.'

Mckinley had heard about the rise and said, 'About time too. I can remember talking to the union man before I left and he said the government had done a pay survey and out of one hundred industries, mining ranked eighty-first. It should always have been in the top five. I suppose it's because they are desperate for coal.' John continued: 'I've heard about the new conscripts for the pits, the "Bevin Boys", are they any good?'

Cud said, 'One or two are but most of 'em are next to use-less; they've got no "pit sense"! How can you expect a soft lad from London or the Home Counties to be anywhere near as good as a youth brought up hard in a pit village and working underground since he was fourteen years of age? Cud went on: 'I'm fifty-one now, but with the new coal cutting machines and other stuff they brought in just before the war I'm still on the face. If things had kept on like they were in the thirties I would have been moved back onto packing the roadways by now and my money would have dropped. You must have heard that we get free coal now and don't have to pick it out from the discards on the pit tip. I get ten tons a year and the house is always warm downstairs, but the kitchen is too hot in summer because we need the fire for the oven and the cooking and washing.'

John took stock of it all; it looked as though things were better at home than in the thirties. In this fairly isolated village they weren't being bombed, and they were getting enough to eat and were warm. He was aware that the miners were now given a yearly allowance of the 'black gold' that they produced due to a 'Cabinet Minute' dictated by Churchill in 1941; this was to the effect that 'the miners should have this perquisite in perpetuity due to their tremendous contribution to the war effort'. Though Mckinley was glad of it, he was also somewhat cynical and thought it might be just a ploy to get the mineworkers to work even harder. He also wondered if the great man had in part attempted to absolve himself from the Tonypandy incident, when he had sent troops in against Welsh Miners and against other trade unionists during the great strikes of 1910 and 1911.

The deaths of two dock workers as a result of being fired on by troops had entered trade union legend and hung around Churchill's neck like an albatross in respect of the union vote during every election he contested. No self-respecting trade unionist would ever vote for him. The one big exception to the general rule was the railway workers' union; though it contained some socialists, it was known that the majority of them probably voted conservative. Thus, in the mining communities they were generally despised as being gaffer's lads.

The following day, after a breakfast of Spam fritters and baked beans, John made his way to Arthur's parent's house, both to see them and to find out about his comrade's injured hand. Art's parents were delighted to see him and to find out that he was still in one piece. They told him that Art had just gone into hospital in Leeds for yet another operation on the hand and said that the surgeon was optimistic that he would regain full use of it. Art's old man said: 'He won't be back in uniform for at least six months, so it looks like you will have to finish the war on your own. Do you think you'll manage?'

Mckinley laughed at the old man's joke and said, 'It looks like I'll have to; Quiller will probably help a bit. If we get to Berlin first, we'll send you a bit of Hitler's moustache.'

The rest of the fortnight whizzed by with lots of drinking in the local boozers. John made a point of going to see old Bill at the Wellington Arms and was given an even warmer welcome than his previous one. John went through his various adventures and Bill said, 'You were lucky to get out of the jungle on your own lad. I heard of full squads going missing in it, with only one or two survivors getting out or sometimes none, when I was in the army.'

He was also interested in how the officers and NCOs behaved. He agreed with John that Enderby's actions should have merited a decoration such as being mentioned in despatches and said, 'It might have been some consolation to his relatives; but remember this, at the end of the day medals don't matter, what matters is staying alive!' And looking straight at him with a fierce look in his eyes, he said: 'Make sure that you do!' He went on: 'One of the problems with medals is that for every V.C. awarded, at least another dozen could have been given out if the heroics of the man concerned had been witnessed by an officer. At the end of the day you know what you did and what they did; if you can look yourself in the mirror with self-respect, that's the important thing.'

438

In respect of Ponsonby he said: 'That's the trouble with officers, some are clever, some are cunning, some are very brave, some are stupid and some should have never been allowed in a fighting man's army in the first place. It sounds as if your man was one of those last ones. It's a pity though, because if you'd had a really able officer, Enderby might still be alive; but that's how the cards get cut in wartime.'

Afterwards, John went down to the Bull to see Mae but was told that she was having a week in Blackpool. He left a note behind the bar and said to the barman, 'Make sure that Mae gets this; she will be hopping mad if she finds I've been on leave and haven't tried to see her.' After the flurry of visits and reunions, the leave ended all too soon and John and Quiller found themselves on the train heading to Colchester to join their new unit.

27

Mckinley and the War in Europe

The two arrived in the ancient barracks town late in the day on the fifth of August. They were allocated a bed each in a draughty dormitory and just had time to go to the mess for the evening meal before serving ended. They ran into Wild and a few of the others from the troop and asked the Hull man what was happening. He said, 'Everything seems confused; the troop aren't even in the same hut, they're all over the place. They are going to spend a few days sorting things out and getting everybody back off leave and then we are going to do some training with the Highland Light Infantry for a few days. They will give us updates on weapons and especially on anti-tank stuff and then they will ship us over to Normandy.'

John asked about Travis: 'Is he still a corporal? I thought he might get busted.'

'He nearly has been, twice,' said Wild. 'He's almost as much of a hot head as me but he's too good at the job—the officers don't want to take his stripes off him. If it wasn't war time he'd be back as a private.'

'I'm pleased to hear it,' said Mckinley.

Things took their usual bureaucratic course and it was the middle of August before the unit started to take shape. By then the troop were together in the same quarters and John was able to take stock. Of the original 1938 intake only four-teen remained; all the others were fresh new younger faces. He noted that Jerry Green and Tommy Jackson were looking older and tougher, and young Oldroyd was now no longer the youngest in the troop and was walking about with the swagger of a soldier who had seen some action.

He was pleased to see that Albert was still there. He said to the happy private, 'You seem to be getting even bigger.'

Albert replied, 'It's all this lovely army grub and exercise. I stayed here when we got back; there's nothing left now at home for me. They got me playing some rugby; they put me in the back row 'cos I can shove hard and I can pass a ball a long way. I never thought that I would be good at summat like that.' John smiled and wondered why he had not thought of it before; Arthur was obviously a natural for the sport due to his huge strength and those large hands that were ideal for catching the oval ball. He hoped that he would have a chance to develop his new interest in the game after the war.

An absentee from the troop was Burns who had been listed as absent without leave for a while. Eventually word came through that he had been hit by a motorcycle and killed while trying to escape a military police unit in London. It turned out that the civilian police were after him for glassing a youth very badly in a pub fight. John and the rest of the troop shared the same unsympathetic thoughts regarding the fate of the departed trooper. The general feeling was 'good riddance to bad rubbish.'

He was less pleased to find that most of the new intake of troops were totally green. They were all aged about nineteen and were just out of their basic training. He knew from the army and at the pit that lack of experience equated to a greater chance of death and injury until that invaluable commodity was gained and thus increased chances of survival. They were keen though, and asked lots of questions; some troopers tried to give helpful hints but Mckinley was terse with them and said: 'When it starts just keep your heads down, and when you hear an order jump to it, it might just save your life.'

The HLI was shaped into companies and battalions. The senior officers were briefed, and what they had been told trickled down in a filtered and rather rose-tinted form to the troops. None of the old hands took the slightest notice of it, but as time went on an independent and verifiable picture started to emerge. The infantry was being trained in the use of the PIAT anti-tank weapon; most thought it was a pig to load but word circulated from other units that it was effective at close quarters.

Other lectures were given about American units, uniforms, and equipment but it was made plain that the British and American armies would operate separately. Towards the end of August preparations seemed to be getting underway for embarkation and news came through that Paris had been liberated. John's first reaction was to get hold of an atlas from the education unit. He tore out the map of France and started to mark out the allied positions in the country. He was pleased with what he saw. Advances seemed to be occurring all over the place, including an invasion of the south of France called 'Operation Anvil'.

Jerry Green said, 'Do you think we'll get to see Paris then?'

Mckinley just raised his eyebrows.

Quiller said: 'You might see the bottom of a ditch! If you're really lucky you might get to sleep in a nice warm pig sty; the pigs'll just have to put up with it!'

In early September, the regiment shipped out from Southampton for the beachhead in Normandy. They were told that the Germans were defending the various key ports such as Dunkirk and Calais like grim death. The troop trundled forwards slowly from the beach, and by the middle of September they had reached their positions near the Belgian border and relieved units that had been in action since D-Day. They then started the slow slog of infantry warfare, with units clearing out German positions usually after heavy artillery bombardment and sometimes after bombing. It seemed very clear, even to the most hard-bitten cynic, that German air power was almost gone and that the Allies had more men and far more guns and tanks than the enemy.

During the weeks leading up to November, the troop lost two of its new recruits and one of the 1938 originals who was injured when they cleared a defended farmhouse. It was Wild, who was wounded while carrying the third man to safety. He had run in under machine-gun fire and dragged the man back. He had shouted for covering fire and everyone opened up at the farmhouse windows, but two SS troopers were concealed in a low shed with the intention of surprising the troop as it moved past them. One had thrown a stick grenade as Wild ran past with the wounded man on his shoulders. Rapid medical attention stopped him bleeding and saved his life, but with grenade fragments in his legs it looked as though his war was finished. Montague wrote it up and recommended a decoration, but apparently some admin type back in London classed what had happened as nothing exceptional.

Travis had then crawled up to the shed, lobbed a grenade into it, and then had run in firing his Sten gun. He came out with a grim look on his face. Mckinley learned later that the grenade had killed one of the Germans but another was just deafened and shaken up by the blast and had put his hands up and tried to surrender, but Travis had decided not to let him enjoy that privilege.

The deaths had the salutary effect of teaching the new recruits to be very wary and to be more alert. After that, the troop slogged on, sometimes in conjunction with larger formations but often alone. Several positions were cleared but each time it looked as though the Germans had left just previous to their arrival. The units had been told to beware of booby traps, as the intention of the enemy now seemed to be to delay the allied advance as long as possible by a mixture of shell and mortar fire combined with mines and traps as they slowly retreated towards a last major defensive position along the Rhine. On November 5th, a sniper picked one of the new men off as he stepped towards a window to look out to admire the view from a burnt-out farmhouse.

In late November the men were taken out of the line for

seventy-two hours rest and recuperation. The troop were glad of a chance to spend three days doing nothing apart from eating and drinking and to get hot baths and spend three nights sleeping on mattresses in what was a medium sized transit camp somewhere near Brussels.

Montague informed his unenthusiastic and weary men that they were not too far away from the site of the battle of Waterloo, and wondered if he could get transport if anybody would be interested in looking at the site. One wag called out from the back: 'Only if they've got a decent brothel, sir.' Montague smiled but was rather surprised at the lack of interest. Bell informed him that his men were just interested in resting and getting ready for the next period of hard slog through the winter as they moved towards Germany.

Mckinley picked up on news, both the official versions that he took with a huge pinch of salt, and that obtained from unofficial sources. Some was gleaned from gossip but the most useful stuff came first-hand from various troopers. He had a chat with a paratrooper who had been in action at a town called Arnhem. The trooper had spent several weeks dodging the Germans after the action there, had made it back to the camp about a week previously, and was hanging about waiting for transport back to his unit.

The trooper was morose and said, 'The blokes were fantastic; they fought the Germans tooth and nail taking out tanks at close quarters with PIATs and mortars. We were told that we had to take and hold the bridge for two or three days and then we would be relieved by Thirty Corps, and with the Guard's tanks at the front we expected that. We got there on 17th September but everything went wrong, most of us didn't get to the bridge, we were running into Germans everywhere.

'The officers interrogated some captured Germans and found out that we had virtually dropped on to their ninth and tenth panzers. They were in the local woods recuperating. What's more, I overheard a couple of our officers talking about it to a Dutch resistance type and it seems that our top brass knew all about it and knew where they were. They could have easily bombed the bloody woods where they had camped, but all we got was a bomber raid to take out anti-aircraft positions the day before we jumped. I ended up swimming the Rhine and after that I was cut off. I don't know how many were killed but it was a lot. I expect I'll find out when I get back to the regiment.'

John noted the information, marked out the positions on his map, and saw that the German border was getting closer and closer. He was pleased to see that a steady stream of troops, tanks, artillery units and other equipment was moving up, day by day, towards the front. By the middle of November, the troop was back in action but resistance seemed to be light. Lots of bombing was happening up ahead and twenty-five pounders and other guns could frequently be heard in the distance. The regiment was ordered to clear one hamlet after an artillery pounding and tank attack but all they found were dead and wounded Germans.

John then started to worry because things were getting a little too easy.

Four relatively uneventful weeks passed by with no casualties amongst the members of his unit and it seemed to John that they had been moving in a westerly direction towards the coast. In mid-December he could see that urgency was sweeping through the officer ranks—something big was obviously happening but no one was saying anything to the ordinary blokes.

The troop was pulled back towards headquarters and on Christmas Eve all were told that the Germans had attempted a counter attack through the Ardennes. The 6th SS and 5th Panzer Armies had spearheaded the German attack. It had foolishly pushed through on a narrow salient and was now being held. Hitler had named the operation 'Autumn Mist.' The attack had indeed depended partly on poor visibility, which would hamper Allied air attacks. However, the weather had now cleared and the Germans were being blown to bits.

Patton had started a counter attack from the south on 22nd December with the intention of relieving the 101st Airborne at a vital crossroads at Bastogne. Montgomery was in the process of gathering battle-hardened units for an attack from the north. The intention was to close 'the Bulge' that the enemy had created and to destroy those remaining in it.

The troop started to move into position early on the next day and took part in skirmishing actions to harass the enemy. Montgomery's main attack started on 3rd January and went like clockwork. The Germans had been pushed back to their starting points by 16th January and allied troops started to pour into Germany to the South West of the Rhine. On 5th January the troop was pulled out of the line for a couple of days and were delighted to be served with a belated Christmas dinner.

Beer was available; each trooper was to line up and be given two pint bottles. Nipper Smith, who was one of the troop's originals, did not drink and just sat there when the beer line was forming. John said, 'Get up and get your beer then slip it across to me and I'll give you some fags in exchange.' Nipper did as he was instructed and John and Quiller sat back in the mess hall near a roaring log fire and finished off their Christmas celebrations with three pints each. 'God,' said Mckinley. 'That tastes good, it's been weeks since I've had a drink. That is really one of the major pain-in-the-arse drawbacks about being in action. I'll make up for it when I get back home; you just watch me.'

'I will assist you in that noble endeavour,' replied Quiller.

The troop did not start to move into the forward positions until 10th January 1945. They saw their first action three days later when the whole company attacked a wood in which Germans were known to be positioned. The usual pattern of bombing, shelling and then mortaring followed by the infantry and tank attack moved forward. Two lead tanks were disabled by concealed German eighty-eights. This provoked a furious bombardment from a battery of twenty-five pounders.

The infantry probed the position and reported that the gun crews were dead and no one else seemed to be around.

The units moved slowly forward until they had secured the wood. Everyone had left in haste; there were dugouts and camouflaged huts and trenches and a good few bodies caused by the air and artillery attack. The order came through to secure the position and spend the night there. Mckinley and some of the others found an out of the way hut with a stove in it. As he entered the building he could smell chicken. A large steel pot was on top of the stove and the fire was still burning. Mckinley lifted the lid and poked around in the liquid with his bayonet and pulled out a piece of chicken. 'It's chicken stew, boys,' he shouted. 'We've captured their dinner.' The stew was shared out. One of the boys foraged in one of the cupboards and found some black bread and they all settled down to a large meal.

About half an hour later, one of the army catering corps arrived with a sack containing tins of bully beef and dry biscuits.

Quiller said, 'Thank you, my man, but we have dined already.'

John jumped in quickly and added, 'But you can leave the grub, we might get peckish in the night.'

After a while, he went round the back of their new billet to pee. He spotted a couple of very large wooden buckets apparently filled with snow. For some reason he pushed one over and was surprised at how heavy it was. As it tipped over, bottles of lager rolled out. Mckinley realised that he had stumbled on his enemy's iced Beer Keller. He scooped the bottles back up and struggled inside with the bucket. He shouted to his mates: 'Father Christmas has just arrived.' The bucket contained about twenty-five half litre bottles of the beverage. John said, 'There's another one round the back; you two can carry that one in,' pointing at two of the replacements. The other bucket came in and they surveyed the loot. There were eight troopers and forty-one bottles in total. John said, 'That's five each and one extra for the finder.'

They drank the lager with appreciation—it was the first time that any of them had tasted that beverage. Quill asked John what he thought of it as they settled down in the straw for the night. John said, 'It's not bad, it's far better than that sour red wine we've been sampling as we moved up through France.' They all settled down in a rosy relaxed mood, dreaming about home, girlfriends, and the end of the war.

Travis pushed his head through the door at about seven-thirty, and said, 'Get washed and shaved, grub's up at eight-thirty. They've found some bacon so it will be bacon and eggs this morning.'

Mckinley said, 'Real eggs?'

Travis said, 'Nah, don't be silly. You can't have everything.'

The mob made their way down to the makeshift mess and everyone got two large rashers of bacon each and a lump of the scrambled powdered egg.

John said to Quill: 'It's years since I had bacon like this; with the beer last night and food like this I am in danger of getting cheerful.'

Quill said, 'Knowing the army some almighty cock up must be heading our way. Let's just be grateful for small mercies.'

Intelligence thought that the enemy must have got out in a hurry with the SS eighty-eight crews being left behind to delay things. Orders came through that they were to hold the present position until reinforcements arrived with more tanks. They did so and it was almost the end of January before much more happened. Artillery could be heard in the distance and friendly aircraft seemed to be heading constantly towards the action. German aircraft, by contrast, were a rarity.

After a week, a film show was arranged in a large tent. A major came to the front before the show started and said: 'I have been asked to give you chaps a briefing. I can tell you that things are going well on all fronts. Our Russian allies are on the point of entering Germany from the east. We will advance towards the Rhine and expect to cross it within a month or two with little difficulty. In the Pacific, the Americans continue to capture islands and their aircraft are now regularly bombing the Japanese mainland. In Burma, our magnificent fourteenth army are advancing towards Mandalay. The end of the war is near and victory is absolutely assured, gentlemen.'

He asked for questions and was asked about the recent German attack towards Bastogne. He replied, 'I don't suppose they will shoot me for telling you this, but last night our intelligence corps came up with the assessment that Hitler had lost sixteen hundred aircraft and six hundred tanks during the attack. We think their battle casualties must number at least a hundred thousand. This really was the Fuhrer's last desperate throw of the dice. Although he has probably delayed final defeat by a few weeks he has thrown away his reserves.'

Back at their improvised billet, Nipper Smith remarked, 'With all these tanks and aircraft around I'm starting to believe all this bullshit about us winning the war.'

'Don't be silly,' came the jocular rejoinder.

The unit then started into Germany proper. The devastation was huge. Mckinley noted, though he was irreligious by temperament and upbringing, that amid all the ruined churches and other buildings the various large medieval crucifixes never seemed to have sustained damage.

The troop now very often had the luxury of being transported by lorries. However, in mid-February, one of them hit a mine. Mckinley realised that the lorry he was in had passed the place where the mine was located only a minute before. Two of the troop were killed, including Sergeant Bell. John reacted with annoyance that the gods of war had awarded such a fate to someone who had avoided death in action but succumbed to a stray mine. Several more were injured including Albert who had been thrown out of the conveyance and had severe concussion because of the fall.

Montague, who had just been promoted to captain, arrived white faced and in obvious pain. He had dislocated a shoulder and cracked a couple of ribs because of the blast. He took stock of the situation and said, 'I am promoting Corporal Travis to Sergeant and you, Mckinley, to Lance Corporal. I know you probably don't want it but you have the experience, you are one of the few left that does.'

John's heart dropped but he heard himself say, 'Yes sir.' The last thing he wanted was responsibility for others; he had enough on his plate looking after himself and Quiller. Montague handed the stripes over to the two men and told them to get them on as soon as they had a chance. The troop gathered themselves together and boarded another lorry along with the gear from the one that had hit the mine.

John said to Quill as they moved off: 'The bloody engineers were supposed to have cleared those roads.'

Travis joined in and said: 'That's the trouble with minefields, unless you sweep every inch you can always miss one. And they have some wooden mines that the detectors can't pick up.'

John turned things over in his mind; out of the original intake in 1938, only five now remained who had not been killed or injured. It was early March and the allied armies were getting near the Rhine. The British in Northern Germany were to cross the lower part of the river later that month; the war seemed to be at its last gasp.

The troop had seen some more light action; they had cleared villages against little or no resistance but were now usually greeted with white flags. Whenever they disembarked from the lorry and were ordered to dig in, John, as was his practice, dug his slit trench six inches deeper than anyone else. One night, some of the lads decided to sleep in an old timber framed barn. John was urged to join them but declined and collected a large bundle of straw from it and went back to his hole in the ground. It was a clear and starry night with a hint of frost in the air. He settled down to sleep in his hole in surprising comfort, snuggling down in the straw in his greatcoat and under a couple of blankets. He awoke just as it was getting light and took a swig from his canteen. Suddenly he heard the sound of incoming shell fire and ducked down and covered his ears. It seemed that a salvo of shells was bursting all around him, and when it finished the barn had been demolished and he was buried up to his neck in debris from the explosion.

Mckinley sat trapped in his hole for hours. He could see by the sun that it must now be near midday. All of a sudden, vehicles roared into the yard and there were troopers everywhere. The men looked around, with rifles at the ready, expecting trouble. John waited until one was close to him and said in a quiet voice: 'Hey Yank, would you mind getting me out of here?' The American nearly jumped out of his skin. John thought that his decision not to shout was the right one as the man was so nervy he might have opened up with his carbine in his direction if he had done so.

The GI shouted, 'It's one of ours, a Brit, buried up to his neck.' An officer ran forwards with seven or eight men and they started pulling debris from around him.

John said, 'Can you get into the barn? The rest of my troop are in there.'

The officer shouted again and about three dozen more men moved across and started to lift the timbers that comprised the remains of the roof. The officer got on the radio and within twenty minutes three ambulances had appeared with a mobile crane, a bulldozer, and two or three dozen more personnel. John said, 'You had better spread out; the Jerries seem to have spotted our position and shelled it.'

The GI captain said, 'Yes, and we spotted theirs after they opened up and shelled and bombed the crap out of those Kraut bastards.' John was pulled out of the trench soon afterwards and the officer said, 'You injured, buddy?'

John replied, 'No. Thank you, sir. Just a few cuts and bruises.' The officer seemed surprised to be addressed as 'sir'; it was as though he rarely heard it and just wasn't used to it.

The engineering officer who had arrived in a jeep with the crane rapidly took charge and John was amazed at how quickly the wreckage came away from the wrecked building.

John was sent to one of the ambulances. The officer said, 'The Doc will give you the once over, pal. We'd better make sure you are in one piece.' As he was having a cut sewn up, one of the GIs came across and said, 'We can hear voices, buddy. We'll soon have them out.'

The rescue took about an hour; afterwards the doctor came round and said: 'Two of your unit have been killed and all the rest are injured. One has lost a lot of blood but he's getting a transfusion now and should be OK. One or two have minor fractures but a couple have broken legs and one has a smashed pelvis. We are sending the lot of you to a field hospital about twenty miles back.'

Mckinley said, 'I ought to report to headquarters.'

The doctor said, 'We have already radioed the details through, but where's your officer?'

John told him that they were awaiting a replacement, or for Captain Montague to recover sufficiently to resume command.

'You are going to the hospital; you're suffering from shock, and its delayed effects might need hospital treatment.'

John got into the ambulance that was crammed with the walking wounded. He was delighted to see Quiller with his arm in a sling and learned that his pal had sustained a couple of bad cuts and had broken his wrist. He asked who had bought it, and was told it was a couple of the new lads. Quiller said: 'They were near the end of the barn that got hit. The rest of us had bedded down in the hay at the other end; it was falling beams and flying debris that caused most of the damage. Some stalls we were in took the weight of the main spars as they came down, otherwise we would all have been flattened. As it was it wasn't much fun being buried and in the dark listening to all those groans and moans.'

At the field hospital, they were all looked over again and a couple of the most badly injured were given more morphine. The doctor returned and told them: 'We are crawling with major casualties here so we are sending you all further back to one of the large British field hospitals to be treated.'

453

The ambulances trundled them back another twenty-five miles and the wounded were offloaded there. John's cuts were dressed and all were told that it would be a couple of weeks at the earliest before they would be returned to duty. The very seriously injured and those with broken limbs were transferred to a hospital train for transit back to England. Quiller was told that his wrist was a clean fracture but he would be out of action for weeks. News came through later that day that the Americans had captured a bridge over the Rhine at a place called Remagen and had crossed it and secured a lodgement area on the far bank. Shortly afterwards news came through that Montgomery had crossed the Rhine on 23rd March and that the Americans had pushed out of their lodgement two days later.

Montague visited the men and said, 'Those fit enough will be transferred to a holding camp and there the troop will be reinforced once again.' He could see no possibility of them being an effective fighting unit again before the middle of April at the earliest. He went on: 'I know you are as keen as I am to get back into action, but as things stand I cannot see it happening. Eisenhower apparently has eighty-six fully equipped divisions under his command; twenty-three of these are armoured and five are airborne. They are racing into Germany, sometimes doing fifty miles a day. The Germans now have only twenty-six under-strength divisions in the west. Their tanks and heavy guns are very severely depleted. We have absolute air superiority and thus they cannot move about in daylight. Thus, chaps, we are now into little more than a mopping up operation, with the enemy faced with total destruction or surrender.

'We expect that some of the SS regiments will choose destruction but the regular army generals will more than likely surrender when they grasp the hopelessness of their situation. Even when fully fit and reinforced it would probably be a week before we could get anywhere near the front. I am sorry to disappoint you chaps but I thought I should tell you directly rather than let you listen to the usual rumours.' He turned and left.

The men waited, just containing themselves until he was out of earshot, and the room then erupted with hoots of jubilation and celebration.

John reflected. It looked as though he had gotten through it all and would see home again. Out of all those he had joined up with in 1938, he was the only one of the troop who had not been either seriously injured or killed.

Soon afterwards, the remnants of the troop were transferred back to the regimental HQ in York and after that the war just seemed to peter out at a considerable distance. Quiller and Arthur had recovered from their respective injuries and had returned to duty and Montague eventually resumed command and started to re-form his troop. Those who had signed on as regulars in 1938 were left in barracks on light duties; it seemed that someone thought that they had done enough. All of them were due to end their service in a few months and it was thought better to move men who had a few years' service in front of them into Germany rather than use the old hands.

28

Mckinley and Victory

The allies had won the war, but in Britain it didn't seem much like it. John and everyone else had shared in the euphoria of hearing of Hitler's suicide and had celebrated VE day and VJ day, but he soon turned his thoughts to the future. Colonel Grimston had reached retirement age in 1943 but naturally had stayed until the end of hostilities and had thus been dined out of the Regiment almost as soon as he got back to England in 1945. Major Tasburgh was placed in command as a Lieutenant Colonel and set about rebuilding. He was keen to retain experienced troops, and the able and fit were approached to stay.

John was offered immediate promotion to sergeant if he would remain and Quiller was offered promotion to full corporal. Both declined the offers. John said he was going back into mining; he was polite but non-committal about his reasons. Actually, he felt it was far less dangerous than being in the infantry, and he knew that work opportunities and pay in mining had become much better. In addition, he had been away from his family for almost eight years and he wanted a more settled life. Travis had fully recovered and promotion to Sergeant Major was dangled in front of him, but he said he was going back on the trawlers with his mate Wild who had also made a good recovery from his wounds.

The only one who showed any interest was Arthur, who said to John: 'I might as well stay in, there's nothing left at home. If I sign up for the full whack I'll be out at the end with a pension. I might have been useless when I came in but I've learned a lot and I'm like you and Quiller. What with the victory medal, Burma and Germany and everything else, we've all got nine medals apiece. When I'm on parade I can see some of the young lads looking at me and they seem very impressed. I don't expect to get promoted but I enjoy being one of the mob. I like the army. I even like the food.' Mckinley shook his hand and wished him the very best of luck for the future.

The old barracks seemed almost unchanged. Some of the older NCOs were still about and Budd was now a Sergeant Major. Housley was still there and had been promoted to Warrant Officer. He told John, 'I must have had about the best war going. With thousands of conscripts passing through the place, my expertise in small arms suddenly seemed to become very important. I organised training, exercises, and the like, in charge of a small team of NCOs. The major just left me to it because he knew I was doing a bloody good job. They more or less had to promote me to top warrant officer because of it. I would never have got any further in the peace-time army and I should have been out in forty-two, but I've had an extra four years on higher pay and I'll be out on a warrant officer's pension.'

John smiled delightedly and said, 'Well, somebody had to come out of this smelling of roses. I'm glad it was you.'

Housley's expression changed and he said, 'I'm just sorry that first rate blokes like Enderby and Bell aren't back here to enjoy it with me.' When John said he wasn't staying in, he laughed and said, 'I thought not.'

The survivors went into York on their last night in the army and they all got pretty drunk, even young Oldroyd and Jerry Green, who since he had got back had seemed to want to shag all of the prostitutes in the town. Young Oldroyd said, 'I don't give a flying fuck about anything. I'm back here, I'm alive and I'm bloody well going to live!' Thus, they all staggered back to the barracks in high spirits and fell onto their iron bedsteads for a last night of rest courtesy of the Army. All woke bleary eyed, and after breakfast they presented themselves for their last pay parade.

Tasburgh made a short speech of thanks and spoke of the regiment's tremendous achievements and of lost comrades. Mckinley wasn't really listening, his mind now fixed firmly on what was to come. At the end of the speech, the parade was dismissed and all cheered as they broke ranks. They had received their war gratuities of fourteen pounds and sixteen shillings and a post-war credit of four pence a day for war service after 1941. The grand total was thirty pounds twelve shillings and four pence in John's case. All the men then went through stores and picked out a demob suit. Mckinley chose a durable looking dark-blue worsted two-piece, which was a remarkably good fit. He left his army uniform behind and walked out of the barracks carrying his kit bag with his other civilian gear inside it, and with his army greatcoat stuffed under his gear. Quiller had done the same. When the stores lance corporal asked about the coats the story was, 'They fell to bits. I was due for a new one.' No one in the stores gave a damn; it was discharge time and everyone was totally demob happy.

It was the Thursday after Easter. 'What next?' said his friend.

John replied, 'I've got a few people to see and then it's straight back to Bullcroft, if they'll have me.'

The two dropped off at the Pit office after catching the bus back from Doncaster train station. They were told by the new undermanager, 'Start Monday at six am; you'll be straight back on the face.'

'How's work?' John asked.

'We are working every hour we can,' was the reply. 'The country is desperate for coal and experienced blokes like you are just what we need.'

John got home just in time for some toast with a little jam

smeared on it. He handed his ration book over and said to his mother, 'I start back at the pit on Monday morning. What shifts are Bert and Cud on?'

Margaret said, 'They're on days.'

'That's a bit of luck,' said John. 'It means just one dinner when we get back, but we'll have to queue for the bath.'

Things slowly started to normalise in his mind—no need to salute, no need to hit the ground if he heard a loud bang, no need to get out of bed in the morning if he didn't want to. Best of all, a lie in every Sunday and then a trip to the club for a few pints before Sunday dinner. In the political sphere, the Labour party had achieved an amazing electoral victory in 1945, with a majority of one hundred and forty-six seats. Some feared revolution or the establishment of a totalitarian state, others were ecstatic that at last Labour had achieved a majority government, and still others were indifferent. What was clear though was that the old social order had changed forever.

Mckinley had attended a few of the discussions organised by the Army Bureau of Current Affairs in his last months in the service. He had come out shaking his head with amusement after one discussion on democracy, which had resulted in the question from one red headed socialist, who asked: 'Does that mean we will be able to read any newspaper we want?'

The bemused lieutenant, who had just come out of university with a third class honours in English said, 'Of course, surely you can do that now!' This produced roars of laughter, he could see no reason whatsoever for this outburst of hilarity. It was suggested afterwards to him by one of the NCOs that: 'Perhaps it's got something to do with the fact that the Colonel won't allow the Daily Herald on the camp—he thinks it's a communist inspired rag.'

'Surely he has no right to do that,' said the green young lieutenant.

'Hasn't he?' came the wry reply.

However, things were changing, peacetime life was resuming but there was a difference. Despite the rationing, which seemed to be worse than ever, and the drabness, there was a new spirit abroad in the village. The despair of the thirties had vanished and people seemed to have developed a sense of self-worth and individualism. The forelock touching pre-war days seemed to have gone forever; workers had rights and strong trade unions at their backs and the old fear of getting on the wrong side of the gaffers and being permanently unemployed seemed to have totally disappeared.

John had heard about a young, straw boater wearing, public school boy on a railway station who called out to a porter: 'My man!' The porter walked past him saying, 'Not any more, son, all that sort of thing has gone now.'

For the first time that John could remember, they were working full-time at the pit and there was as much overtime as you could cope with. There was plenty of money to be earned but very little to spend it on.

The normal rhythm of great sporting events was being resumed. During the summer weekends, people were swarming back to seaside resorts such as Blackpool, and at the August bank holiday the railways were so loaded that even with extra trains to try to meet the demand, they could hardly cope. Royal Ascot had resumed, to the total disinterest of most of the inhabitants of Doncaster. A local lad called Bruce Woodcock had won the British and Empire heavyweight boxing titles, to the delight and pride of almost the whole of the town.

In April 1946, the first post war Cup Final was fought out between Charlton Athletic and Derby County. The event was so emotionally important to the nation that even the king attended, wearing a grey overcoat. This was the first time for years that anyone had seen him at a public event not wearing a military uniform. Derby won the match 4-1 in extra time. Despite the socialist government, people still stood in cinemas and theatres at the end of the performances while the national anthem was being played, and it always terminated wireless broadcasting at the end of the day.

On John's first morning home, Cud pulled out an expensive looking envelope from behind an ornament on the mantelpiece over the kitchen fire. His stepfather said: 'This came for you about a week ago. It looks important; we didn't open it or send it on because we expected you to be home any day.'

John opened the letter. It contained a first class railway ticket to London and a letter, which read:

Dear John,

I understand that you are to be demobbed very shortly, and I should very much like to see you before you fully resume life at home. We can meet at your convenience and I can arrange for you to stay overnight if necessary. I feel I owe you a considerable debt of gratitude, please write or phone and I will arrange a car to pick you up at Kings Cross.

Yours very sincerely

Hugo.

John agonised over the missive for a couple of days. If its tone had been in any way patronising, or if he had been addressed as Mckinley, it would have been ignored. However, the tone of the letter seemed so warm and sincere, and he felt that if he accepted the invitation it might, in some way, help him to lay some of the ghosts which had arisen during the war. That evening he sat looking at the fire in the kitchen deep in thought. The coals next to the grate glowed a devilish red and slowly turned to white ash at the edges, while the couple of large cobbles, which he had thrown onto the fire before sitting down, puthered out streams of sulphurous smoke in small jets from fissures on their undersides.

The smoke kept catching light, burning with a yellow luminous flame for a few seconds, and then going out. This went on for several minutes until a wall of flame erupted from the undersides of the coals and started to consume the shiny black lumps at their edges. Eventually, he had thought things through and put together a letter arranging to meet Hugo in early May. As the appointed weekend approached he arranged to work early days at the pit on the Friday, and he didn't stay for overtime. He got an early night and, wearing his new demob suit and carrying an old gabardine Macintosh, he caught the earliest train possible down to London in order to meet his old acquaintance.

Outside Kings Cross a military staff car driven by a Wren awaited him and he was whisked off into the centre of London to an office in Whitehall. He was escorted through a maze of corridors and then through a large office crammed with desks, phones and various grades of military personnel. Most just ignored him, as though civilian visitors were a very normal occurrence in that particular establishment. He was taken through an anteroom and into a large and imposing office.

Brody-Bollers was standing looking out of a window, and Kirkwood was seated at a small desk looking through a file with a cigarette dangling from the corner of his mouth as usual. Bollers turned and rushing across the room he seized John's hand and said, 'My dear chap, delighted to see you again, and more importantly delighted that you have made it through it all in one piece.' He glanced towards Kirkwood, 'You remember Kirkwood, of course.' Kirkwood nodded sardonically in John's direction.

He continued: 'He's a Lieutenant now! I was faced with the choice of having him court-martialled for sarcasm or having him promoted. The officer class are prepared to tolerate sarcasm from a brother officer but not from a sergeant. The trouble is that he doesn't suffer fools gladly, but he's miles in front of most of 'em at this game and far too valuable to have me taking cipher codes to him to decode in the glasshouse.' Kirkwood's eyes glinted but he said nothing. Shortly afterwards he left and reappeared with a tray stacked with small pieces of cake and a jug of steaming coffee.

Hugo said, 'First things first. Do you intend to stay overnight? I can arrange that immediately. If not, we'll have coffee and a chat and then go off for lunch. I've arranged to meet my younger sister Rosalind. You'll like her; she is working for Ernest Bevin in the new Labour government. Always difficult to work people out, old boy,' he added. 'I always wondered if she would go off and be a nun or a missionary. She could have married and had a comfortable life, kids, cocktail parties, Bridge, Women's Institute, and that sort of thing, but she always had this streak of idealism. Dashed clever too, a dangerous quality in a female member of the upper classes.

'Apparently, she works all hours at the ministry and in addition on Saturdays she does voluntary work for the Workers Educational Association. She used to dutifully come home during the holidays to see father and attended the Sunday services with him. And, though a 'confirmed' atheist, she was charming and pleasant to the vicar. Did I ever mention that father was gassed at the second battle of Ypres? It left him rather frail and the damage caused probably contributed to his early death.

'Gossip about local families and talk of horses, county-shows, hunt meetings, left her bored stiff and she couldn't wait to get back to the centre of things. Her older sister did try some matchmaking when Rosalind was younger but seems to have given up on that. She doesn't mention it but there was a brief and intense relationship in her last year at university. He went into the RAF as a pilot and was killed in the Battle of Britain. Since then she seems to have had no interest in the male of the species.'

He turned back to events for the day. John told Hugo that his intentions were to get an early evening train back to Doncaster. Boller's said, 'We should have plenty of time to catch up, though.' He went on: 'I would like to get back into the tea business but I've been drawn into intelligence work, much against my will, really. I look like being stuck in it for some considerable time due to the nation's present needs which have been brought about by the unfolding threat of communism as presented by our former ally, comrade Stalin. But my dear chap you must tell me about yourself.'

John gave a modest thumbnail sketch of his later war service and Brody-Bollers sat back absorbing it all. At the end he said, 'I could really use someone like you in intelligence. I could find you a job as a courier or something similar. It would be a civil service grade with a pension. If you just want a change from the mines there are lots of positions on the estate. I could get you into a supervisory role in forestry or on the estate itself.' John started to reply but his host said: 'Don't turn it down flat, think about it whilst we are having lunch with my sister. She might also have some ideas.'

Hugo was called out for a few minutes and Kirkwood returned. John said, 'I noticed the Brigadier insignia; when did he get promoted?'

'About six months after D Day,' came the reply. 'You should have heard him curse.'

'What do you mean?' John said.

'Well, for a start,' said Kirkwood, 'rank or titles really don't mean a thing to him. He realises he has to have them so that the officers under him do as they are asked, and the idiot top brass he talks to take notice of what he says. You didn't hear him after his father and brothers died and he inherited the Baronetcy did you.'

'No,' said Mckinley.

'This time it was: "bloody Brigadier Sir bloody Brody-Bollers, bloody Bart, bollocks, bollocks, bollocks." He really cannot wait to get out of the army, but when things get less military I am pretty sure he will be prevailed on to join MI6 or one of the other Ms in some sort of very senior role. If they asked me I'd tell 'em to get stuffed and go off and get a job lecturing in Oriental languages, but he has this huge sense of duty.'

Hugo came back and said: 'I've arranged a car. We'll get off early for an extended luncheon at a place I know near the

465

theatres, and it's fairly close to Kings Cross, you could probably walk it there in twenty minutes if you needed to.'

As they departed Kirkwood said to John: 'All the very best for the future John. "Brave New World" out there; grasp it by the throat is my advice, suck it dry, kick it in the bollocks. Make sure you bend it your way and don't get bent or bowed by it.'

As they walked down the stairs, Hugo said, 'Amazing! That's by far the most emotional thing Kirkwood has ever said.'

When they reached the small and very exclusive restaurant, the two were ushered into a curtained booth and ordered drinks. John said he would like a pint. Hugo thought for a second and said, 'Make that two.' The waiter left and swiftly reappeared with two foaming glasses of cold and very palatable beer. His host said: 'It's not one of the London brews. One of our chaps is a son of a director of a Brewery in Burton-on-Trent; he gets it sent down periodically. I am not particularly a beer man but this stuff really is excellent.'

A couple of minutes later his sister Rosalind entered the booth. She was about five feet six with very pale red hair and a look that reminded John of the women painted by the Pre-Raphaelites. She was dressed in a two-piece suit that she carried immaculately, like a top model, despite the obvious Spartan utility of its manufacture. After introductions, they sat down to order. Brody-Bollers had told his sister all about John and the fact that he had saved his life on two occasions. Rosalind said, 'I also owe him a great debt, without him there would be no male members of our family left.'

They chatted and Rosalind spoke briefly about her socialist ideals and her work for Bevin. 'He really is amazing,' she said. 'He came up through the trade unions with virtually no education; he left school at twelve, and before that he was orphaned. Nevertheless, after a period leading the Dockers he formed the Transport and General Workers union. Throughout the war, his contribution in the War Cabinet as Minister of Labour was incalculable. What he achieved through innate

466

raw ability was staggering, often in the face of opposition from Oxbridge-educated Civil Service types who were telling him that what he wanted couldn't be done. Now he's been made Foreign Secretary and you should see the sods jump when he gives an order. It was rumoured that Dalton was going to get the job and that Bevin was to be Chancellor, but apparently Atlee changed his mind at the last minute and switched them round, which was an extremely shrewd move in my opinion.'

She then sat and listened in rapt attention as Mckinley described life in the mines and in Doncaster. He answered questions about the unions and local politics in his usual terse and intelligent manner and as the afternoon wore on she became more and more impressed. She had heard about miners and had read all of the production figures of the industry but this was the first time that she had actually met one of that mysterious race, face to face.

Rosalind did not normally drink but on this occasion allowed herself a small sherry.

Bollers ordered the meal, which was mulligatawny soup followed by roast leg of pork with all the trimmings and after a suitable gap, plum pie and custard. John was not aware of the fact but Kirkwood had been sent to obtain the large leg of pork in person the previous day; he had done so by rather nefarious means and had then delivered it to the restaurant in person, as Hugo didn't want the occasion spoiled by the usual food shortages.

Finally, at about three, Bollers said, 'You know what I feel, and I will keep the offers open should you wish to take them up.'

John paused for breath, looked down, and said: 'I really do appreciate it but I've thought it all through. It looks like coal will be in demand for a prolonged period, wages have gone up and it's getting safer.'

Rosalind interjected. 'Barely! Up to the start of the war over a thousand miners were killed each year underground, with tens of thousands injured. In 1940 and 1941 it was still over nine hundred a year. In 1945 it dropped to five hundred and fifty. Mining is still very dangerous and unhealthy.'

John continued: 'But Bullcroft isn't a gassy pit and has a low risk of a major disaster because of that, and if you know what you're doing, working on a coal face is a lot less risky than you think. It's a little like being an experienced infantryman. In addition, I have an arrangement with a girl up there and its where all my family and friends are. I am confident that I can carve a good life out for myself. The old misery of the thirties has lifted and everybody feels better about things, despite the rationing. It's strange,' he went on. 'Before it all, people were half-starved and felt ground down by the lack of work, but now they have a sense of themselves as individuals because of what they did in the war and they don't intend to take any nonsense and go back to how it was.'

Rosalind once again interjected: 'From my perspective it seems certain that Mining and Railways will be nationalised. It's not a question of socialist dogma; it's the only way that the country can get the money to re-equip these vital industries. There will undoubtedly be decline as older pits are worked out or those with unprofitable, narrow seams are closed. The strategists seem to think that coal production will become centred mainly on Yorkshire and the Midlands. I think in terms of employment you will be all right for many years. They are talking about electricity from nuclear power but the research will take decades as far as I can see. Oil may well come more and more into the picture as ships and trains convert to the far more efficient diesel engines, but this will be a gradual process through the fifties and sixties.'

She continued to give her privileged overview of British industry: 'The main problem at present is that, in simple terms, Britain is almost bankrupt. We owe, mainly to the Americans, a debt which is the equivalent of about two-hundred-and-fifty percent of our annual production. It will take years of austerity to pay it off.'

Mckinley said, 'What about Lend-Lease? I thought the

Yanks were giving us a lot of essential war materials; it was in their interest to keep us going wasn't it?'

She said, 'That applied to the Russians, they were given everything that they asked for without scrutiny. The only limit was our capacity to carry it to them. We in Britain had it from the US only if we could justify it and with restrictive conditions which have severely affected our ability to export now that the war is finished. The country will, in time, pay its debts and prosperity will return; we are a disciplined nation with a mature economy and institutions. However, it is goodbye to the Empire I am pleased to say; we can no longer justify the cost of colonial rule and the huge navy which that necessitates.'

John resumed once again: 'The other thing, of course, is class. I have no class prejudice or hatred personally, but I need to feel comfortable in my own skin. I have a distinct Yorkshire accent. That was OK in the West Yorks Regiment, almost all the lads had one, but I find it a pain in the neck down here when I open my mouth and the wife of some tuppenny ha-penny clerk in shabby clothes starts to look at me as though I've got a bone through my nose and acts as though she was the Queen.'

He went on, 'I know people like Bevin have clawed their way up and out of it, and in the pits you can get involved with the union or start up the long route to management. After you qualify as a pit deputy, you can take the second and then the first class certificate of competency in mine management, but it takes years and you study five nights a week in your own time. I don't want that. I want to work hard but I also want to live. The war has changed me at some sort of deep level. I am much more cynical and I seem to have lost interest in things such as poetry, which interested me before. On the other hand, I read some modern stuff on the boat coming back from India. It may be that the poetry has changed and not me. It was stuff by a bloke called Auden and some others. I could see it was very clever, very perceptive, but something seems to have been sucked out of it somehow.'

Rosalind went very quiet and Bollers looked somewhat sad. Finally he said, 'Well, is there anything at all that I can do for you?'

Mckinley looked him full in the face and said: 'As a matter of fact, there is. During a skirmish in Burma I took these off the body of a Japanese I killed, sort of spoils of war.' He produced the emeralds he had taken from the intelligence officer he had strangled.

Bollers held one up and looked at it carefully. 'Beautiful colour,' he said, 'and very clear and quite large.' He thought for a moment and said: 'Actually, I have a good contact in Hatton Gardens where all the diamond trade goes on, but they deal with other gems too. Would you like me to sell these for you?'

John said, 'Yes, I would, if you can do it without breaking some sort of regulation.'

Bollers said: 'Leave them with me. I will contact you as soon as I have the money.'

John stood up and said, 'It was really great to see you again and to meet your sister, but I really think I ought to be getting back.'

'I'll drop you off,' said Hugo.

'No, it's OK,' replied John. 'I'll walk up. I know the way and I'd like to see the centre of London. It is a novelty for people like me, and if I see some of the theatres like the Old Vic or famous buildings that I've never seen I will relate more to 'em when I hear them talked about on the BBC. It may be an awful long time before I come back down here.' They shook hands and he left to walk up to the station.

Bollers left with his sister in the staff car, and as they sped through the streets Hugo said: 'What did you think of him?'

Surprisingly, Rosalind snapped back with uncharacteristic irrationality: 'Just don't talk to me!' She then immediately said, 'I am sorry Hugo, but what a waste. With the advantages of a good education he could have done virtually anything. He obviously has far more talent than most of the group I work with. With the right background and a third in History from

Oxford you are on the gilded path for the rest of your damned superannuated life. The thing that amazes me is that the British proletariat did not follow the example of their Russian comrades. It makes me all the more determined to change things through my work at the ministry.'

Mckinley had a leisurely walk back through the great city, making a detour towards the Strand and then down Aldwych looking at the names of famous theatres and their current shows. He turned things over in his mind, thinking about the names that were frequently used in the papers and always with complete familiarity; it was done as though everyone in the country knew the places intimately when they were spoken about on the BBC and in the newsreels in the cinema. It was as though the broadcasters were located in some sort of large village in central London and as though everyone in the country was familiar with those places and had easy access to them.

He then detoured up Kingsway towards the British Museum. He had no time to go inside but at least he had seen the outside of the imposing edifice and in some respects he could now relate to it. After wandering through Bloomsbury, he made his way towards St Pancras and the adjacent Kings Cross station. As luck would have it, he was on a train in less than twenty minutes after finding his platform. He settled down into the comfortable first class seat in an empty carriage waiting for the train to set off.

A few minutes later, someone went by his window and then a moment later turned back and poked his head into the carriage. 'It's John, isn't it?' said a familiar voice. John looked up and saw the face of Jimmy Fox. The older man came into the carriage and laughingly said, 'Do you always travel first class?'

John smiled back and said, 'Second time; and somebody else is paying again.'

Jimmy sat down and said: 'I'm on my way up to Newcastle on business. We've just started a contract to scrap older warships, but first let me tell you the full story of my Doncaster trip and then we'll make our way to the dining car, and by the way, dinner's on me.' The older man explained that he had been contacted by a friend in the CID about a large-scale racket involving the theft of tyres and petrol from military bases. 'They wanted someone who was well known as a general dealer to buy some of the stolen gear so they could make arrests. They thought that if they used one of their own men they might be rumbled.

'So I set off for Doncaster with a briefcase full of money. I was escorted to the train and someone in the local CID was supposed to pick me up there, but when we got to the place there was no sign of anybody apart from a couple of the gang I was going to deal with. They had apparently decided to follow me from the station and try to get hold of the lolly; they could then have sold the hot goods to someone else. Apparently, the CID had gone to the Danum and not to the station; they were sat outside in a car when we got there.

'After the two thugs saw you and Quiller, they changed their minds. I saw them later with their boss as the money changed hands for a lorry load of tyres. Just after that, the CID jumped on them and they were not gentle. There was blood and teeth everywhere. If it hadn't been for you and your mate I would have been laid out in an alley somewhere, beaten to a pulp or worse.' They then heard the steward make his way down the train making the first call for dinner. Jimmy said, 'Let's get down there fast and beat the rush, we should have a good three hours or more before we hit Doncaster.'

The two made their way to the dining car, which was almost empty. Jimmy called the steward over and slipped him a ten-shilling note saying: 'You'll get the other half if we get well looked after,' and winked broadly. He asked what was on the menu, the steward said: 'Not much, we've got a corned beef hash, some steamed fish, and we do have steak and kidney pie but that's almost gone.'

'That'll do nicely,' said Jimmy, and can you bring us some beers?'

The steward said, 'We are OK for beer, sir, but we have no wine or spirits at all.'

'Wonderful,' said Jimmy. 'I don't drink wine or spirits. What kind is it?'

The steward said: 'It's Bass, blue label.'

Jimmy said, 'Marvellous, is it in pint bottles?'

'We have both pint and half pints, sir,' said the steward.

'Great,' came the response. 'Bring us half a dozen pint bottles in an ice bucket; I like it cold.'

The dining car had started to fill up by the time the steward came back with the beer. He asked if they would like soup to start with. 'What kind is it?' Jimmy enquired.

'Brown Windsor,' was the reply, with just enough of a look of discouragement for them to pass on it.

Jimmy said, 'No, we'll get straight on with the main course and after we'll have whatever pudding you've got.'

About ten minutes later the steward arrived with two large pieces of the pie and serving dishes containing ample supplies of mashed potato and mixed vegetables. 'Terrific,' said Jimmy, and the two started to tuck in with gusto. John listened to Jimmy, occasionally contributing to the conversation, but for the most part his loquacious host held forth about the business opportunities that post-war Britain was throwing his way. He said, 'Don't let them kid you that there's no money about. I've been raking it in on war surplus sales. I went to an auction to buy a Nissan hut. It was listed as "with contents". I looked in it and found it was crammed with about thirty filing cabinets in nearly new condition. Somebody had dumped some oil stoves in as well. They were saleable, and there were twenty packing cases there as well. I had a look inside and found that all of them contained parts of motorbikes, and when we assembled them later there were ten complete Norton two fifties, and they are like gold dust.

'I checked with the clerk and he said, "I don't care what's in the cases, the orders I've got invite bids for hut and contents, and they are mostly full of rubbish that nobody wants." So I made sure that I got hut number three. It cost me sixty quid; I was prepared to pay a lot more but everybody else got cold feet at about fifty quid.'

He went on: 'Then there's the ships; we are scrapping them all over the place. When we've done all the old ships that can be brought into port here, I have plans to bid for some of the wrecks beached on various islands in the North Sea and on Iceland. If you want a job at all, just ask me. The work is hard and in bloody cold weather and away from civilisation for months at a time, but it's damn well paid.'

Mckinley said, 'Thanks, but I've fixed a job up. It's down a nice warm pit and it's close to several boozers.'

Jimmy laughed and said, 'Probably very sensible to get a steady number. I can see us cutting ships up for a few years but they will eventually all be gone. What's more, some of the lads come back after months sleeping in old wartime huts with nothing to do but eat and booze with a fistful of money and they blow it on slow horses and fast women. After a few weeks they're knocking on my door asking to go back.'

He turned to the food: 'What did you think to the asparagus?'

'I suppose we were lucky to get it this time of year.' John replied. 'I wondered what it was; I've never had it before.'

'Never!' said Jimmy, in surprise.

'Never,' replied John. 'In the Army, it used to be cabbage, carrots, sprouts and turnips, or peas or butterbeans, and we had tinned tomatoes a lot. I've never had parsnips either; before the war it was always the cheapest veg we could get, so we followed the seasons and had tinned stuff when fresh veg wasn't cheap. My mother always thought that parsnips were a bit exotic and they didn't go very far compared to boiled cabbage.'

'Bloody hell,' said Jimmy. 'I never realised things were that bad up north; we were never really short of anything in London through the thirties.'

The steward eventually brought two dishes of bread and

butter pudding with custard. After they had finished the meal the two continued to drink until the train started to slow down for Doncaster.

Jimmy shook John's hand and said, 'I've enjoyed your company son. Here's my card with the phone number, if you ever want a job just ring.' Mckinley never met him again but in 1968 he saw a picture of Jimmy in one of the racing papers. He was described as, 'The millionaire race horse owner Mr James Anthony Fox.'

John's next urgent need was to try to see Bill and Mae. The old soldier was easy to track down but Mae seemed elusive and not around any of her old haunts. Bill, as usual, was delighted to see him and went through John's final campaign listening intently, nodding and saying things like 'good' or 'yes, I expected that.' He said, 'After the last show I didn't feel any animosity to the ordinary German soldier. I was doing my duty for King and country and they were doing likewise for Kaiser and country. I must admit though that after seeing them films about Belsen I wouldn't have batted an eyelid if they'd lined all the officers up and shot them out of hand. Never mind all this "I was only obeying orders" claptrap; if enough of them said no it wouldn't have happened.' John asked about Mae but Bill said that he hadn't seen her for months but he assumed she was alright as he had got a postcard from Blackpool saying she was enjoying herself.

A couple of months later Mckinley ran into Mae in Doncaster as she was coming out of a solicitor's office. She was wearing a fox fur, and was very expensively dressed. A small chap wearing horn-rimmed glasses who had his hair parted down the middle accompanied her. For some reason he reminded Mckinley of Jones minor, the character who appeared as the class sneak in the Billy Bunter comic strip cartoons. She greeted John formally and then turned to the little man and said, 'Cyril, go back to the hotel and wait for me. I have some other business which I need to see to. I will be an hour or two.' The little man said: 'Yes, dear,' and scurried off. Mae grabbed John by the arm and marched him into the Admiral Nelson pub just around the corner. She steered him into the small snug, which was empty due to the fact that it was early evening and also a weekday, and said: 'I could squeeze the life out of you, you big hunk. I was fighting to keep my hands off you outside but I needed to get rid of him.'

A waiter appeared and she ordered a gin and lime and a pint. She gave the man two half-crowns and said: 'Keep the change,' and with a salacious wink, 'Try to keep people out of here for half an hour.' The waiter reappeared rapidly with the drinks and then glided off. He reappeared after a couple of minutes and put a notice saying 'Private Party' on the door and then left once more.

Mae grabbed John, gave him a big wet kiss, and then said, 'Thank god you made it through in one piece.' John noticed that she was trembling with emotion, and until then did not realise how deeply Mae felt about him. He thought that he had better tread carefully. He asked what she had been doing and about Cyril, but she wanted to talk about John. He brushed it off, saying: 'Out of the army, back at the pit, living at home and earning a lot of money. That sums it all up in a sentence. I tried to contact you when I got back but Bill told me you were in Blackpool enjoying yourself, so that was fine. I dropped in at the Bull a few times but none of the girls really remembered me and there were quite a few new faces there.'

'Oh yes,' said Mae. 'It's amazing, a couple of the old pros moved down to London to get at all those lovely GIs. One of the girls fell in love with an NCO in the Black Watch and got married and moved up to Stirling in Scotland with him. I think she's a bloody fool, personally; she will be stuck up there doing housework, cooking Haggis and running round after kids. She left here with a bun in the oven but I think he can get married quarters straight away for some reason. Anyway, it's up to them; I have quite enough problems sorting my own life out.'

She looked at him again. Mckinley was the fittest he had

ever been. His shoulders seemed even broader than previously and with a few years on his back his looks had developed into the mature attractiveness that some men fortunately acquire, while others seem to go downhill every year after their twenty-first birthday.

The topic moved on to the little man. 'Oh him,' said Mae dismissively. 'He's a punter I picked up and have been seeing to regularly ever since. He has certain special needs which I supply and now he does exactly what I tell him to do without question; he has no choice!' she said, smiling as though enjoying some sort of private joke. 'We are in the middle of setting up a business partnership and buying a small hotel in Lytham St Annes. It's the posh little town just south of Blackpool. He has run a very successful boarding house here and has a couple of tobacconist's shops, and I have made an awful lot out of the war. I am keeping my flat here and renting it out, but he is selling up and I am putting nine-hundred of my money into the business. The idea is that he will do all the work and I will do a bit on reception and play the hostess in the evenings. I am good at that, and to be frank I am getting a little on the old side to make a lot on the game. This business should be ideal as a semi-retirement occupation and we can shut up shop between New Year and Easter and get about, maybe to London, or even abroad to get some sun.

'Of course, if he is a good boy and works very hard for me I will give him the sort of spanked bottom treats he likes,' she said, smiling again. She went on, 'I thought I'd seen it all; I've had the ones that shoot their load as soon as I take their pants down and those who can't come unless I wear silk panties or nylons and suspenders or high heels. I never thought that a hard spanking or caning would do it, but it does for Cyril. It's wonderful; it avoids all those messy rubbers and the douching afterwards. Moreover, to be frank, I've had more rubber up me than the A1, enough to last a lifetime. From now on, it will be a good show, a gin and tonic, and a cigarette. If I ever want sex it will be with someone just like you,' she said, with a look and intonation which told him exactly how she felt without putting him under any pressure.

She went on: 'He wants to marry me. What do you think?'

Mckinley thought a bit and then said, 'As long as everything is tied up legally in case you split, or one dies, why bother? You can always call yourself Mr and Mrs, who would know? If it's necessary, you can get him to change his name to yours by deed poll.'

'That's a good idea,' she said.

'Just make sure that your savings and investments stay in your name. If it works out long-term, fine, but you never know, do you?' said her younger advisor.

The waiter came back in and said, 'Can I get you anything else?' Mae told him that they would be leaving shortly and tipped him another half crown.

She then turned to John and said: 'By the way, one of the new girls is from your village. Do you know her at all? Name of Olive Bowden? None too bright. When she started on the batter she was nearly giving it away until a couple of the girls had words with her because she was ruining the market.'

Mckinley grinned and said, 'Oh! Olive. I've heard about her from the lads. She left school about five years after me. Attractive, nice legs. She went off to work at the big timber supplier in the next village. She was pretty basic by all accounts, her two priorities in life were sex and cigarettes, and she wasn't much bothered about the order she got 'em in as long as she got plenty of both.

'One of the local youths told a tale about when he was working at the same place, and this just about sums her up. Apparently, one day he was working out in the yard with her among the stacks of wood. It was dinner time and everybody else had gone to the canteen so he suggested that they might have a quickie seeing as no one was about. She was amenable, so he got her laid back on a pile of timber and got her knickers down and started to give her a good seeing to. He had been at it two or three minutes when she started to fumble in

478

her pockets. He kept at it, but then she asked him for a light! He whipped it out in disgust and buggered off to the canteen and told his mates what happened. Talk about insulting! The trouble is they told everybody else. Anybody else but Olive might have been embarrassed, but not her, she couldn't see anything wrong with indulging in both of her main pleasures in life at the same time. "I needed a fag," she told the other girls.'

Mae laughed and said, 'I wonder if she does that when she's entertaining the punters. I wouldn't think that they would be very impressed; the whole point of it is that while they are doing it you pretend that they are driving you wild. That makes 'em shoot pretty fast and encourages return visits. If she is going to look bored or wants to do her nails while they do her, they won't come back, unless they have a kink for that sort of thing of course. Anyway, it's up to her but I wouldn't predict a great future for her on the game; I hope she's not so stupid as to do it without rubbers.'

Mae looked at her wristwatch and said wistfully, 'Oh well, I suppose I had better get off, I don't want him getting into any mischief without me being there to supervise it. I have your address and as soon as we get the hotel up and running I will send you the details. Make damned sure that you keep in touch, big boy.' They walked out of the Nelson arm in arm towards the Danum. On the steps of that hotel Mae gave John a big hug and a last, long, lingering kiss. She then turned and walked up the marble stairs towards the imposing brass and glass doors. She did not look back, possibly because tears were streaming down her cheeks.

29

Mckinley and the Post War Paradise

John settled back into the routine at the pit and rapidly got into the swing of it again. He thought that the money was unbelievable compared to what he had been getting before the war.

Hugo sold the emeralds and arranged to meet him in Doncaster as he passed through it in transit to Scotland during one weekend. When they met, he told John, 'They were excellent quality, probably looted from a temple in Burma, but possession is nine points of the law and they are yours.' He went on: 'They raised just over fourteen hundred pounds.' Mckinley's jaw dropped, he had expected perhaps a hundred or two at best. Hugo said: 'I can pay the money into your Post Office or bank account but if you don't need it please let me invest it with my stock broker in the up and coming industries such as chemicals and electrical goods. You will find that the dividends are better than bank interest and what is more, John, I am so confident that they will do well that I personally will indemnify you against loss if their value drops below your initial investment.'

Mckinley was nonplussed as he knew nothing of stocks and shares and was naturally conservative like most other miners. Bollers was so enthusiastic and obviously trying to do him a favour that he eventually agreed. Hugo said, 'I will arrange an annual statement to be sent to you and a dividend cheque, but if you do not need the money please take my advice and let me reinvest it. If you do that, I think you will find that your capital will increases at a rate which is greater than the normal compound interest in a bank account. In addition, we must meet up from time to time, at least once a year, and Rosalind would like to see you to get some first-hand information about mining. After she met you she arranged a transfer and is now working for the new minister of fuel and power; he is called Shinwell, you must have heard of him. Her major project is work concerned with nationalisation of all the colliery companies. Apparently, they own coke works, brick works, engineering companies and all sorts of pieces of land. They employ almost eight-hundred-thousand people; the combined undertaking is huge and will take considerable effort to shape into a single entity.'

The two then spent some time reminiscing about India before Hugo departed for his meetings in Edinburgh.

Nineteen-forty-six dragged slowly into forty-seven. By now the small three bedroomed house in Briar Road was home to his mother and stepfather, his sister Alice, Bert, Lily and her two young boys. Lily's husband Fred increased the number, whenever he was on leave from the Navy. Peggy had been married in 1946 and went to live with her husband's parents just around the corner. The sleeping arrangements at number thirty-nine were: John and Bert in the smallest bedroom, his parents were in the middle room, and Lily and the kids with Alice in the largest room. The place felt crowded but it did not seem over-crowded, and the Shepherd family over the way were coping with three bedrooms and thirteen in the family.

The routine at home had rapidly re-established itself with Margaret cooking and cleaning. Lily was busy with her two young boys and grudgingly helping with the chores when she had to. At the same time, she never lost an opportunity to tell the men that she and her mother were 'working their fingers to the bone' with looking after the kids and all the cooking, cleaning and washing they were forced to do.

John turned to Bert after one such outburst and holding his hand up, said, in a very dry manner, 'Look at that, I've shovelled twenty tons every shift this week, I would have thought that the bones would have started to show by now.'

Lily coloured up, went into the parlour, lit a cigarette, and muttered to her mother, 'Men just don't understand.'

In other respects, things returned rapidly to normality but with much more money around than they had ever known. John and Bert went for a few pints at the Grange on most nights. On Saturdays, due to the new prosperity, the Grange always put on entertainment in the form of a comic or singer.

On those evenings, Cud escorted Margaret down to the club to catch the act the first time round. They both thought it was wonderful that after the years of poverty during the twenties and thirties, very often with barely enough to eat, finally they could afford some enjoyment and they had money in the Post Office as well. They were even thinking about having a week's holiday next year at a boarding house in Bridlington. Though they could now afford it, strangely they hesitated; the deterrent was the fact they had never previously had a full week's holiday and the experience would be alien to them.

Saturday nights always had a special air, which started off with Cud demanding silence and then settling down with a pencil next to the old and crackling wireless set, which he turned up to the highest volume possible.

After the pools had been completed, there was much rushing about as Bert and John got shaved; Bert always did it in the bathroom and John, wearing his vest, over the kitchen sink, using the small mirror that fronted the small metal cabinet that stood on the kitchen windowsill. He used shaving soap, mixed it to a thick lather using an old army shaving brush, and then removed his day's growth with careful and precise strokes using a Gillette safety razor.

They then changed into their best gear and left for the club early to pay their sweepstake money. John would meet Arthur and Quiller and have a drink with them in the Bullcroft Hotel until their girlfriends appeared at about eight. He would then leave them and walk down to the Moon Hotel for one or two and then to Carcroft Club to have words with people he needed to see about work.

Lily was usually left, sour faced, on her own, on those evenings at number thirty-nine, doing her bit as a dutiful mother. When Fred was on leave Alice was pressed willingly into service as a babysitter and paid with ten cigarettes. Fred always arrived back with as many as he could get hold of, because service men could get them tax free on board ship. Alice loved looking after her nephews and could not understand why Lily was so miserable when she was left on her own to look after the children to whom she had given birth.

During the week, many face workers poured out of the pit into the public bar of the Moon Hotel, which was just over the road from Bullcroft Colliery, immediately after finishing their shifts. There, they washed the coal dust out of their mouths with a couple of pints and sometimes more. The public bar was geared to cater for men in their pit clothes. The Pit Head baths had been promised for years for Bullcroft but they were not built until 1951. Thus, the men stood in the bar in their dirt, with faces black with coal dust and boots covered in the powdered dolomite that was now scattered down all the roadways to prevent dust explosions.

Through the week life rotated around the pit but for face men such as John and Bert this usually meant the day shift starting at 6 am so that they could shovel away the coal which had been brought down by the shot firing on the previous shift. A pit deputy, called Sam McGoldrick, was supposedly in charge of the day-to-day running of the face but it rapidly became apparent that it was John who was organising things to maximise how much coal was obtained and thus maximising pay for himself and his mates.

Occasionally, special jobs such as hewing out the two tunnels that advanced on either side of the two-hundred-yard-long face came up. The jobs were negotiated on a contract, which was paid depending on the rate of progress. John was always pulled off the face to do these jobs, negotiating the contracts and choosing the team to do them. He patiently explained the difficulties that would be encountered to Billy Burton, the new undermanager and put up with the bluster of the new official, who always tried to beat the contract price down. In John's estimation, he had about a tenth of Burkinshaw's brains and ability. Mckinley ran rings round him in the game of bluff and counter bluff that the negotiations involved. Early on in the game, Billy had tried the 'We can always get somebody else' gambit. John simply said: 'Fine,' and got up and walked out of his office and was halfway down the corridor when the undermanager's clerk came scurrying after him and said: 'Mr Burton thinks you've misunderstood what he was saying to you and wants you to come back.'

After a while it sunk in to Burton's head that although the contactors were earning a fair bit more than him, the rate of heading advance was always excellent, the job was always to a high standard and there were no foul ups or delays in getting materials out to the work. Most important of all, the Colliery Manager was very pleased with the way things were going on his face. Productivity was always very high, and there were no 'rag-up' strikes due to the stupidity of management coming up against a discontented work force. Much of this was down to Mckinley's shrewdness, and most of the face men looked to him as a natural leader.

The Manager who, unlike Burton, was no fool, was well aware of this and during his occasional forays underground made a point of always addressing John by his first name. It was always John who the manager seemed to ask about how things were going on the face. The information sought was always delivered in John's succinct and economical manner with no wasted words or embroidery. One of the younger colliers said, 'He always speaks to you, John. He's never said anything to me.' Another of the men said: 'He once spoke to me on the office steps. He said to me: "Get out of my way you bloody idiot!'" which raised the intended chorus of laughter. The undermanager would have done well to have adopted the same approach in the pit as his superior, or to take a leaf out of Burkinshaw's book.

The National Coal Board's Doncaster Area Director occasionally visited each of his Doncaster pits for progress reports on output, new face development, union problems and the like. The visits were always accompanied by much scurrying about by the office staff and other underlings. The Director liked to keep abreast of all matters including up and coming management talent. On one occasion, after looking at the productivity figures, he asked about Burton's potential for further promotion and was told by the Colliery Manager that he had gone as far as he was ever likely to get. The Director seemed surprised in view of the way the face was performing. The manager said laconically, 'Perhaps he's got a good team working on that face; if I moved him to another I don't think things would be as good.' The director raised an eyebrow and made a careful note of what was said to him.

Burton eventually left the pit and took his superannuation out of the manager's scheme to buy a post office. This occurred after he struck up a relationship with one of the women in the pit wages office who had a reputation for having a bit of a hot arse and who left her husband to live with him.

Peggy and Lily had put down applications for council houses with Adwick-le-Street Urban District Council but were told it would be a six or seven year wait at best before they got one, even with the extra preference points they had due to having kids, and a husband in the forces in Lily's case. She annoyed John by the occasional irrational outburst such as, 'I don't know why the government doesn't do something about the housing shortage.'

It was annoying for two reasons, the first being that she seemed to think that by expressing her indignation in the kitchen at number 39 that something would happen by magic and that her indignation would be transmitted in

486

some manner in the government's direction. The other reason was her steadfast determination to ignore the fact that bombing had destroyed over two-hundred thousand of Britain's houses and seriously damaged another five million. The house in Briar Road was always warm thanks to the ten tons of concessionary coal that Cud now qualified for. Fires were kept burning through the winter in both the kitchen and living room, and in the kitchen during the summer for hot water and cooking.

The food served at home was basic but adequate and nothing was wasted. If potatoes were left from dinner they were fried later to provide a supper, sometimes with an egg or a piece of thinly sliced Spam. Sometimes cabbage was left over with the potatoes and that was fried as bubble and squeak. The inventiveness with which Margaret produced meals out of virtually nothing was amazing. Beans on toast, tinned tomatoes and fried bread, cheese on toast, sardines on toast were other basic supper dishes. Sometimes she would get hold of a ham hock and roast it in the oven and make sandwiches and cook the rest with lentils and peas to make a thick ham flavoured broth. Sometimes it was just cheese and a chunk of bread. Cooking fats were always a problem and the fat from round roasted meat was always carefully saved and then used sparingly if things needed to be fried later.

If meat was obtained it was always one of the cheaper fatty cuts that could be made palatable by long roasting in the coal oven. The roasting also provided dripping which could be used for bread and dripping if there was absolutely nothing else available to eat. Fatty stewing meat was sometimes obtained and if any was left, it was reheated for supper and eaten with a couple of slices of bread. A tin of salmon was a rare treat, both because of its price and the five points needed from the ration card to obtain one.

With a ration for each adult, which was by 1947 just one ounce of bacon per week, that treat was reserved for the Sunday morning breakfast of bacon and eggs. It worked out at about one rasher each for the men and half a rasher each for the women. Tinned corned beef and Spam were available, often from illicit sources because of the government selling off war surpluses. Corned beef hash made from the thinly sliced meat with onions and sliced potatoes was usually the dinner served on Wednesday when the men got back from the pit. On Thursdays it was invariably liver and onions with mashed potatoes.

Sometimes a rabbit could be had from one of the lads working on the land or from one of the crew who used to go out poaching, and on those days rabbit stew resulted. A rabbit was expensive, but the miners had money and farm labourers did not, and it was thus a useful exchange for both. Occasionally a tin of stewing steak was obtained and it was usually eked out to the maximum extent as a meat and potato pie. Sometimes there was no meat left by the end of the week. Margaret dreaded those occasional days in the late forties when there was nothing to serve the men when they got home and they had to make do with boiled potatoes, peas and gravy made from cheap gravy browning.

By 1948 John had two nephews who were aged two and three and a half. They shared what was served to the adults but John noticed that Lily's priorities seemed to lie with her cigarettes and in wondering when Fred would come home. Then she could be taken out, as she deserved. She still lived in the fantasy world deriving from her time with the Naysmiths and when she was a Wren. She often made comments such as 'When I was at Leydene.' This meant little to anyone who heard it, as she never bothered to explain that she was talking about Leydene House that had been the wartime headquarters of the WRENs. Mckinley knew what it was and years later showed Alice a photograph of the place. Alice said, 'I always thought it must be a town somewhere near London!'

A year later John heard her describing to the eldest boy, now aged four, about how the WRENs had been trained to use gas masks in a shelter containing tear gas. At the end

488

of the session, the Petty Officer had given the order: masks off! She then described how they had all emerged from the place with eyes burning and noses streaming because of the gas. Her final remark amazed him; she said: 'You'll have to do that when you're grown up and they call you up for national service.'

He said to her later: 'Do you think you should be frightening a young kid with tales like that or the horrors of being bombed?'

Her shallow response was: 'Oh well, he'll have to learn!'

Mckinley said pointedly, 'Yes, but you should be saying things like that to him when he's a lot older.'

It just didn't seem to register, and Lily started to avoid John if possible. He became increasingly terse with her on the occasions when communication was needed. He was also less than impressed by the fact that someone who constantly wailed about never going out frequently managed to leave the kids with Alice so that she could visit the pictures with her mother or to go out for a drink at one of the local clubs. She usually did this by manipulating her good-natured and generous younger brother into taking her out for what she usually described as an hour; the hour usually extended into two or three.

For John, the last straw came in late 1949. His nephew was then four years old. As was its usual practice, the travelling Fair had arrived at Carcroft, a village about a mile up the road from where they lived. The tradition was that showmen gathered from all over the county for the huge funfair, which accompanied the St Leger, Race Week. After it finished they dispersed in all directions, in smaller groups, stopping at the various mining villages as they went on their ways. Some moved south towards Nottinghamshire or Lincolnshire, while others travelled up the Dearne valley towards Barnsley or Sheffield and others came north of the town heading for the West Yorkshire wool towns and cities.

The local dead-end kids turned up on the Saturday afternoon and asked if they could take David, her eldest, to the fair. Lily said, 'Well he is a bit young but I will let him go if you promise to look after him.' The oldest of the group was an eight-year old and he promised to do that. Having thus absolved herself of all parental responsibility she allowed the youngster to wander off with the group of five- to eight-year-olds and went back inside to put her feet up and enjoy a fag.

The kids wandered down the road in the warm late-September sun. Only one car passed them as they walked down towards the fair and a couple of horse drawn wagons also trundled past; one was carrying bales of straw, the other was a greengrocer's cart. The group arrived at the site and they wandered round looking at the strange sights of the sideshows and stalls. They paused to watch someone shooting at clay pipes and later stood looking as young men tried to knock coconuts off their perches with wooden balls. Others tried to land broad wooden rings over stands that had cheap looking watches on them.

They all stood fascinated, looking at another where the task was to hook wooden ducks as they whizzed by, with a goldfish as the prize. The group eventually wandered towards the centre of the fair where a large roundabout called the Noah's Ark, where brightly painted wooden elephants and horses and giraffes and other animals ran round and round. A deck like walkway structure surrounded the whirling beasts. However, there was a gap between it and the moving central portion. One adult was heard to say, 'Keep away from that edge; it's dangerous!'

The group of youngsters drifted up onto the walkway just as the contraption disgorged its latest set of riders. They watched as young adults, courting couples and parents with children climbed aboard. When it was full, the showman in charge pulled a lever and the animals started to rotate, slowly at first and then faster and faster. The walkway was still full and there was some jostling as people pushed through in order to get a good view and to be near the front for the next ride. Young David was pushed out of the group to the front of the crowd like a pea being squeezed out of a pod; then a woman screamed! He had fallen or been pushed, disappearing through the gap between the walkway and the rotating central portion of the contraption!

The showman leapt at the emergency brake and pulled it with all his strength and the apparatus juddered to a grinding halt. He then disappeared under the outer skirt of the roundabout and the youngster was carried out from amid the large gear wheels and shafts and cogs that comprised the drive mechanism of the machine. They sat him on the steps and the proprietor said, 'Are you alright, son?' The boy had been briefly aware of large cogs turning and shafts spinning near his head and then he had passed out. He said, 'My leg hurts!' The showman looked at the large bruise and broken skin below his knee on his left leg.

One of the adults from the village said: 'It looks bad to me. I would call an ambulance if I were you,' but no one did.

The showman wanted to get rid of the problem as fast as he could and start making money from the ride again. He said, 'Where do you live, son?'

One of the dead-end kids said: 'It's Briar Road, number thirty-nine.'

A woman standing near the roundabout steps said: 'I can push him there in the push chair; he'll be able to fit in it with the little one.' David was helped into the conveyance and the woman set off with her additional passenger who was moaning from time to time with the pain. At each moan, the woman pushed the conveyance a little faster. 'Don't worry, duck,' she said. 'I'll soon have you home.' But it seemed to be an age before they finally turned into the end of Briar Road.

Some of the group of dead end adventurers had run on ahead and taken the message to the house that David had been hurt at the Fair and someone was bringing him home in a pushchair. The response from Lily was: total inertia! She didn't seem to grasp what had happened, or want to grasp it. She made the kids describe what had transpired several times.

One of them came running down the jennel. 'They're coming now,' he said.

Lily got up still holding her cigarette, ran down the arched opening, and saw her son in the pushchair. She seemed frozen, not knowing what to say or do. The woman got the pushchair to the back door and then helped Lily to get her son inside and seated on one of the wooden chairs in the kitchen. She said: 'He fell into the workings of the Noah's Ark ride. He could have been really badly hurt; you can see that he's got a really bad bruise on his leg.' As she turned to leave she added: 'He's a bit young to be allowed to go running round fair grounds on his own don't you think, Mrs?'

Lily evaded the point and said, 'Oh, thank you, thank you for bringing him home. We'll look after him, and he'll be alright now.' She knelt and looked at the injury and said, 'Where does it hurt?'

The tearful response from her boy was 'All over!' The bruising now seemed darker and there was something not quite right with the leg. Lily looked and looked at it and then lit another cigarette and then looked even harder again at the injury as though in some miraculous way a solution would jump into her fear-frozen brain. Frozen, partly with concern about her son's obvious pain but mainly with fear of what might be said about her for letting the child go to the fair without supervision.

Shortly afterwards her mother came in from the shops. She knelt and looked at the leg and immediately said, 'We ought to get a doctor.'

Lily, who had been conditioned by her years in service and her time in the WRENs to obey and never to question authority, ran round in a flurry of indecision. Her voice became more and more clipped, almost as though she was trying to issue orders to herself. On the one hand, she did not want the doctor; he was old and very shrewd and might ask awkward questions about a four-year-old being at the fair without an adult. On the other hand, she realised that something must be done. Her first suggestion, which was received witheringly by her mother, was contained in the question: 'Do you think a cold-water bandage would do any good?'

Lily's eventual solution was not to do anything at all but to wait, saying, 'When the men come back from the pit, Cud will know what to do, he's a first aider.'

'But they won't be back for a while yet, we ought to call a doctor now,' said Margaret.

Lily's response was, 'He won't like being called out at this time of day. What will he say if it's just bad bruising? We will wait, they'll soon be here, it'll be alright; it doesn't seem to have gotten any worse.'

Margaret shook her head but reluctantly agreed to wait. She said, 'If he does get any worse I'm sending for a doctor straight away.'

The boy sat in the kitchen for over an hour with both women trying to comfort him and take his mind off the pain. Lily asked him if he would like anything to eat but the boy looked pale and said he felt sick and dizzy and could not eat a thing.

It was early dusk when Cud and John arrived back from Bullcroft Colliery. Lily had worked herself up into a hysterical state by then. All she could say repeatedly was, 'Thank god you're back, thank god you're back.'

Margaret calmly explained that David had been brought home over an hour ago and the kids had said he had fallen into the workings of a roundabout at the fair.

Cud knelt down immediately and examined the leg. 'It's broken,' he said.

'Are you sure? Are you sure?' wailed Lily.

Cud ignored her and said to John: 'Go down to the phone box and phone an ambulance. If you can't get one, phone George down at the pit first aid room and ask him to bring the pit ambulance.'

Mckinley ran out of the door carrying several pennies

and sprinted the three hundred yards down to the phone box on the main road. He inserted the coins and explained very tersely and precisely to the rather doubting voice at the other end of the phone what had occurred, ending with: 'The boy's in agony, if we don't get it sorted out fast he might lose the leg.' An ambulance was dispatched immediately.

Almost another half-hour passed before they heard the bell of the approaching vehicle. The ambulance men arrived with a young doctor inside it. The doctor said: 'I was told it was bad and decided to come out.' He examined the leg and said: 'We'll need an X-ray, but it's clearly broken, probably a compound fracture of the tibia and fibula. When did it happen?'

Cud replied, 'This afternoon at the fair. We sent for you as soon as we got back from the pit.'

The doctor said, 'But from the bruising it looks like it must have happened quite some time ago.'

Margaret said, 'Yes, they had to wheel him back home on a push chair. I said we should get a doctor straight away but his mother wanted to wait for Cud to get back; he's a St John's man, he's dealt with broken limbs in the war and at the pit.'

The young doctor bit his lip and then turned to his immediate professional concerns, saying, 'I need essential information. Has he had anything to eat or drink since he got back here?'

Lily, seizing the opportunity to demonstrate how dutiful she had been, said: 'We tried to get him to eat and drink but he didn't want anything; he hasn't had anything since breakfast.'

'Good,' said the doctor. 'He should be able to take an anaesthetic straight after the x-ray.' Lily's helpful smile faded.

The boy was rapidly stretchered out to the ambulance. Mckinley stood in front of the doctor, blocking his entry to the vehicle and said, 'Is there anything we can do from this end? I was thinking of maybe phoning ahead and telling them you've got an emergency coming in and to make sure you have a surgeon ready.'

The Doctor stood and thought for a moment and then

responded: 'Good point! Can you phone this number and say that Dr McBride says there is a bad fracture coming in and to call out Dr Laby, if he is not presently at the hospital.' He passed a card across to Mckinley with the number on it.

'When can we find out what has happened?' was John's next question.

McBride replied: 'After the assessment the leg will probably be set tonight. Phone tomorrow morning at about ten about his condition and about visiting times.'

He thanked the doctor and the ambulance raced off into the evening air with its bell ringing loudly. Mckinley trotted back down to the phone, relayed the message from McBride to the infirmary, and then walked slowly back down Briar Road to the entry between the houses, with a thunderously brooding expression on his face. Eventually, he got back to the kitchen at number thirty-nine. Cud was sat stony-faced looking into the fire. Lily seemed to be having what the Victorians would describe as 'a fit of the vapours' and was repeating, 'We thought it was for the best, we thought it was for the best, we didn't know what to do!' Cud had seen similar injuries during the Great War. Though no bones had penetrated through the skin of his grandson's leg, he had clearly seen the end of a fractured bone move under the bruising. He was well aware that there was a possibility that the boy may lose his leg if circulation had been seriously compromised.

When John walked back in Lily said, 'How was he, how was he when he left?'

'How did he look?' said John, icily.

'Oh! Oh! me bairn, me bairn,' said Lily lapsing into her usual defensive hysteria, and into an excitable Geordie accent which she had lost during her teen's after the family had moved south. 'Oh! Oh! me bairn, me bairn.' After a while, she said in a wailing voice, 'I thought that the ambulance men might ask me to go with them, after all I *am* his mother!'

'Yep,' retorted Mckinley, with venom. 'You're his mother alright!'

*

As it turned out, it was a compound fracture of the left leg. John's nephew returned home after a fortnight in the fracture ward with a pot on the leg and people at home fussed round him. A temporary bed had been moved downstairs and everything his grandparents could do to make him comfortable was done. A fire was kept burning in the living room so that the boy was warm and everyone seemed to want to bring him little treats, usually in the form of fruit. The family sweet ration was pooled and his grandmother made sure that he was given one of the large boiled sweets shaped like a fish every evening. A bottle of lemon barley water appeared from somewhere and the boy had his first taste of that diluted concentrate.

Lily had attended the hospital every day while her son was recovering. She was wonderfully attentive to every word the nurses had said to her about his condition, inquiring diligently and dutifully in the clipped and efficient voice she reserved for conversations with people in authority, about what she should do in respect of aftercare and convalescence. The nurses knew exactly what had happened, and gave her pretty short shrift. One of them said, 'I know we aren't supposed to say anything, but it's all very well her acting the role of a dutiful mother now. It makes me feel sick.'

At home the leg improved and it got awfully itchy in the pot due to the accumulation of dead skin. After several visits to the outpatients department, it was decided that the plaster of Paris should come off. What appeared to be huge, gleaming metal shears were produced, and the leg encasement was slowly and carefully slit open and pulled away.

After that, a final medical assessment was carried out. Lily was told that the leg had wasted somewhat due to lack of use but it would soon be back to normal and that the dry skin would be helped to disappear if the boy had a few hot baths. John had insisted on attending with Lily on the final visit. He had phoned ahead and asked to see Dr McBride. He had not told Lily about his intention, saying that he had to see one of his mates and that he would pay for a taxi back to Briar Road. McBride remembered John and said, 'Are you the boy's father?'

John replied, 'No, I'm his uncle. His dad joined the Fire Service after coming out of the navy and he's doing a four-week training course down at their place in Moreton-in-Marsh. I just want to make sure I have the full facts about David's aftercare. I'm afraid my sister is pretty useless.'

McBride thought for a second and pulled the X-rays of the fracture out of an envelope which was conveniently lying on the top of filing cabinet. He pointed to the images, explaining that the fracture was a bad one. 'It's a miracle that the boy did not have his leg torn off inside the fair-ground machine's workings. It was also very fortunate, very thoughtful actually, that you asked about ringing ahead; in another half-hour we may have been too late to save it.' He added, 'Make sure that the boy gets as much milk, cheese and eggs as you can manage. The ligaments will be stiff and when he has recovered sufficiently he should have some physiotherapy to enable them to stretch so he can bend properly. Even with that, you will find that when he is an adult the affected leg will be a half to three quarters of an inch shorter than the other one. However, everything should be fine now, and with reasonable diet he should be almost as good as new in a few months; but I do hope in future that the boy is properly supervised.'

Mckinley said drily, 'So do I.'

John thanked the doctor warmly and left to find Lily and his nephew.

Lily took her son on a couple of visits to outpatients after the pot was removed; it required two buses to get to the infirmary and several Woodbines. There the leg was prodded and bent and stretched and gentle questions were put to the youngster such as 'how did that feel?' and 'can you bend it a little further?' After the third visit, the doctor said, 'We can discharge your boy now, Mrs Etchell, he has made a good recovery. The bone has knitted together very well.' He went on:

'Physiotherapy is available and will improve the leg's flexibility; you should see your G.P. about that.' The woman nodded attentively, giving her Services impression of efficiency, and of maternal concern and competence. The doctor patted the boy on the head, gave him a boiled sweet for being such a brave little soldier, and waved the pair off.

A few months later John said casually to Lily over a family dinner: 'Shouldn't David be having some physio by now? After a break like that, he needs it; they used to have it in the army.'

Lily had thought about the several hours that the hospital visit would take out of her day and the fare for one adult and a child on the four buses needed in getting there and back. The cost would be more than a packet of cigarettes, and after all she had to have those! After weighing up all the pros and cons she had come to a decision; she was a mature adult after all and he was only a child and she had asked him how the leg felt and he had said it felt alright.

She replied vapidly, as though the matter under consideration was of extreme triviality: 'Oh, they said he *could* have that, but I decided he didn't need it!'

Mckinley glared at her, grinding his teeth in annoyance, but his furious look had no effect whatsoever. He got up from the table very abruptly and grabbed his coat.

Cud said in a voice that showed his surprise: 'Are you going out?'

'Yep, down to the club,' was the response as he pulled his coat on.

'It's a bit early,' said Cud, knowing that John would usually go down to the club much later.

John left the room muttering under his breath: 'If I stay here I bloody well might really tell her some home truths.' He walked down the street fuming with frustration. He wanted to tell her, she needed telling. However, they all needed to live under the same roof; best keep quiet for now, he thought. He knew he wouldn't even be able to work his frustration off by telling Quiller and Arthur; it was a family matter.

Mckinley could not work it out; it seemed his sister worked at some very superficial level in life. What should be important clearly was not, and trivialities, usually much unconnected to her families' needs and aspirations, clearly were. She would go on for ages about what the latest film star was doing or wearing or about the goings on of the local landed gentry and the Royal Family. It seemed as though her wasted words made her in some way a part of what she was talking about. He just could not see it.

They had come through the twenties and thirties, malnourished and with hardly more than the clothes they stood up in. All of them had got through the war in one piece. The house was warm but contained only a few sticks of old and basic furniture. At teatime crockery needed to be washed immediately after someone had finished with it so that all there could take their turns in enjoying a cup of tea more or less at the same time. Lily's children seemed in some strange way not to be connected with her or not to be her responsibility or of any particular or massive concern in respect of their health, education and general welfare. He was well aware that whatever maternal affection had come their way was from Alice, who was just the opposite of Lily in respect of those instincts and in respect of her deep concern she had for everyone in the family and for others around her.

The accident brought previous incidents into focus. He remembered one occasion the eldest was obviously hungry before bedtime and asked if there was anything to eat. Lily's response was not: 'I will find you something,' but 'what would you like?' The boy made a few suggestions such as some bread and jam. Lily said wistfully, 'Oh, we haven't any jam left.' David falteringly asked for bread and dripping and was told, 'Sorry there's just enough for tomorrow's dinner.' It was obvious that the last thing that she was going to do was to use her imagination and make a positive effort to think of something to feed her child with. It was almost as though she was playing some sort of clever game with him, expressing willingness but always bouncing the lack of a solution to the problem back onto the boy.

John stared in unbelief at the way she evaded her responsibilities by each time turning the need to make a decision back onto a small child. Eventually, he went to the kitchen and took out two plain biscuits he was going to take with his snap on the following morning's shift and poured out a glass of milk and took them to the boy. Lily jumped in when the food was handed to the lad, with the comment, 'Look what we've found for you, aren't you a lucky boy.'

Mckinley said nothing but absorbed everything and became increasingly disenchanted with his eldest half-sister. He had started to make moves to sort his own domestic situation out. He was spending more and more time visiting the nurse he had met back in Burma and became less and less engaged with life at number thirty-nine.

30

Mckinley and the Brave New World

On the first of January 1947, the coal industry was nationalised. The directors and owners were compensated, often comparatively generously, for undertakings that had seen little or no investment for a decade or more. That year was exceptionally cold, with heavy, late snows that melted in spring rains and then turned to floods. During the snows, one shift at the neighbouring colliery of Brodsworth was taken out of the pit to dig through ten feet drifts to the adjacent village of Pickburn. This enabled the villagers and farm labourers to get about, but far more importantly, it freed the roads up to Brodsworth Hall, which was the residence of the former mine owner's family.

On his first shift in the New Year, John asked Quiller and Arthur, who by now had returned to work, 'Does it feel any different now that "they" own the pits?' Both laughingly said that it felt exactly the same.

It was late into 1948 before John saw Hugo and Rosalind again.

He made the trip to London but this time insisted on paying for his own ticket. He had arranged to meet them at the small restaurant they had dined at previously. They all arrived just after midday and almost immediately Rosalind was asking him animatedly about the mines. She said, 'We took just under a thousand into public ownership with a work force of about seven-hundred thousand.'

Mckinley told her that working conditions had not changed much but they had been sent some metal friction props from Germany as part of the reparations. She asked if they were an improvement over the wooden ones. John replied, 'Yes and no; they are a swine to tighten but they clearly give more roof support than the wooden ones. However, the men don't like 'em because as the weight comes on with strata movement the wooden props creak and groan. They don't like the steel props because they don't talk to them, they just start to compress and go down all of a sudden without warning.'

Rosalind questioned him about morale. Mckinley said: 'It is good on the coal faces because of the higher wages and full time working, despite the dangers; but I will be glad when the program of pit-head bath building gets round to Bullcroft as the men are still having to go home in their pit clothes to bathe. When that comes in I think it will give the blokes a big boost. Another problem is that some of the younger men don't remember the thirties, so they often just turn up for three or four shifts every week because they were getting enough money from them to pay their way and to buy their beer and fags and have a bet. The older blokes mostly work every shift they can; some of the younger married ones do that as well.'

Rosalind, who seemed to have absorbed every statistic ever produced about the mining industry said: 'At least deaths in mining are dropping at last. It looks like there will be less than five-hundred this year for the first time this century. The last time it was anywhere near as low was in 1926. Five-hundred and seventy-seven were killed then, but that figure was heavily diluted due to most mine workers being on strike for seven months.'

She looked pointedly across at her brother who was now a civilian and working for a top-secret government department. He asked if John had changed his mind about working for him but the reply was, 'No thanks, I fit in there, I feel comfortable. But there is one thing. Over the last couple of years

I have managed to save over four-hundred pounds. I noticed from the statements that you sent me that the fourteen-hundred is now worth over two thousand. Can I ask you to add this to it, rather than it being in the Post Office?'

'Absolutely delighted, old chap,' said Hugo. 'It is almost a year since your last statement and during the last year with the huge drive to export, the stock market has been racing ahead. It is expected to have doubled its end of war value by the end of 1948. With the reinvestment of dividends and your four-hundred pounds, I expect you to be worth well over four thousand pounds. I can see you becoming a capitalist yet.'

This sparked off a few derogatory comments by his sister, but John rapidly went on, 'We get the newspapers, of course, but I never believe those as a result of what was written during the war. You are at the centre of things; how are things going?'

Rosalind launched into a thumbnail sketch of nationalisation: 'As you know we have now brought under public control virtually everything we promised to. Gas and electricity were largely in municipal control anyway and they were easy. The mines were harder, and we had to pay a hundred and sixty-four million in compensation to the owners, often for clapped out mines with clapped out equipment.'

She went on: 'Iron and Steel is proving really difficult. The Tories oppose it and they tabled over eight-hundred amendments to the Gas Nationalisation bill, most of them trivial, in order to delay it. For example, should nationalisation be spelt with an *s* or a *z*? Health presented similar difficulties, with the British Medical Association trying its best to make the scheme unworkable, but it finally got through.

'Aneurin Bevan bought out the privately-owned practices and is letting consultants treat private patients in NHS hospitals in pay beds. He recently described it to the Labour Party Conference as, "stopping their mouths with silver!" You will notice that if you have to call a doctor out now you won't get a bill.'

John said, 'Yes, my middle sister had one just before the

NHS started for fourteen shillings and sixpence. She was pregnant again and got morning sickness. He came out to see her and prescribed bicarbonate of soda. I could have told her to take that and wouldn't have charged a penny.'

John continued: 'The other big thing at home is that rationing is getting harder. We thought that after the war rationing would end but my mother came back from the shops a couple of weeks ago and made the comment: "How can you possibly feed a family for a week on this?" She said that for each of us it was down to: 1 ounce of bacon, 2 ounces of cheese, a shilling's worth of meat, 2 ounces of butter, 3 ounces of margarine, 1 ounce of cooking fat, 3 pounds of potatoes and a half a pound of bread a day, and we get a pound of jam a month to spread on it. We get two ounces of sweets a week. "Thank god cigarettes aren't rationed," she said, "or my nerves would go to shreds!" We are just about keeping clothed. Things like winter coats are very expensive, and shoes as well, and it takes forever to save the coupons to get a pair. My stepfather is still wearing the army boots he got when he was in the home guard, which they very generously allowed him to keep when it was wound up in 1944.'

Rosalind interjected, 'Yes, the civil service types wanted them to be handed in, after all there were nearly two million men in the home guard and they were government property. The men kept their boots apparently because of Churchill's personal intervention. Wonderful recognition for the hundreds of hours of vital voluntary service in each of those years they served since the call went out to form Local Defence Volunteer units.'

Bollers said: 'It may seem insensitive to say it but I must admit that with the estate farms we just don't feel the effects, but are you managing?'

John replied: 'People seem to forget that mining villages are mostly in the countryside and not in the towns, and we can get stuff that townies don't have access to. In the autumn you can get apples and the kids glean peas and spuds after harvesting, lots of 'em go picking peas and spuds as well. We get eggs from next door and we can get the occasional sack of spuds because, technically, they are controlled and not rationed and we can get other types of veg as well.

'Many of the blokes with allotments raise pigs and sell bacon and others sell things like cabbages or exchange 'em for tobacco. You can get the occasional chicken or bit of boiling bacon but they are expensive. There is under the counter trading at some shops. Our butcher raises his own beef; he seems to be able to squeeze in a few extras, and he often has offal for sale on Wednesday. If the fish shop is frying, you get a queue straight away, but other times you can get fish and there is tinned stuff about. We have just tried this new Snoek, it's a sort of poor man's mackerel; it's from the seas off South Africa. I read that we can afford to import it instead of Portuguese sardines because it's in the Sterling Area. You only need one point on your ration coupons to get it compared to five for a tin of salmon, but there is one major difficulty with it.'

'What's that?' said Rosalind innocently.

'It tastes bloody awful,' said John with a broad grin. 'More importantly, can you tell me how things are going in mining and in Britain? Do I need to think about emigrating?'

Rosalind replied: 'Though things are hard it will improve and quite rapidly. I think that when this decade is over mining will contract year by year and manpower will reduce due to more and more mechanisation on the coal faces. I think that you will find that rationing will diminish and probably cease as we move into the 1950s. I also think that in your location, in the South Yorkshire coal field, I would expect at least twenty years of stable, full employment.'

Hugo interjected: 'Have you thought of taking your capital and starting a business?'

John smiled and said, 'I know what I'm doing. It's very nice to have that at the back of me but I intend to get married soon and have a couple of kids and make a life in the village.'

Bollers said: 'I say, many congratulations old chap. How did you meet her?'

505

John told him how it started in the hospital in Burma. He said his fiancée was an RAF nurse who would be leaving the forces in a couple of months. He explained that they could rent a flat in Doncaster but he would apply for one of the colliery houses that were now owned by the NCB. He explained that the waiting list for them was shorter than for the council houses and they would be surrounded by people he knew.

Hugo said: 'I also have a young lady in tow and will be popping the question shortly. I do have a duty, I am told,' looking at Rosalind, 'to produce a son and heir in order to ensure the continuation of the baronetcy.'

Rosalind said, 'Can I ask you what the mood of the electorate is? Is the support for Labour much diminished from 1945?'

John replied: 'Not round us, but you can see how the Tory Press is weeviling away. A lot of working class people read the Daily Express and the Daily Mail and they are being drip fed a lot of insidious stuff about the hardships. That is creating dissatisfaction, especially among some women like my eldest sister, and the papers never lose an opportunity to go on at length about what a great man Churchill is and how much the nation owes him. The rationing is having an effect; it's been almost ten years now since it started and people are asking when it will end. Labour might get in next time but the big majority will be reduced. It all depends if people can remember how bad the thirties were; one major factor will be the new voters and what they remember.'

They parted company once more and again Mckinley walked back to King's Cross, wandering through London and drinking in the sights and sounds. There were far fewer uniforms about now and almost no foreign ones. There were far more cars though, and much less evidence of bomb damage. At Kings Cross he thought about travelling first class but eventually plumped for second. He had grabbed a meat pie and a couple of pints on the station in the hour he had spare before the train set off. He settled down in the corner of a crowded carriage lost in his own thoughts.

Occasionally his reverie was broken by a woman describing how terrible it had been on the two occasions that the small market town she lived near had been bombed. 'Yes, six houses flattened,' she said. 'And two people killed by a direct hit on a shelter.'

'Yes, it was very hard,' said another. 'All that time in uniform, and the paratrooper scares, and the drills and threats of invasion.'

'Which mob were you in?' asked a younger man.

'Oh, I was a sergeant in the home guard,' came the reply.

'I was in the RAF, ground crew,' said the youngster.

'Oh, did you see much action?' said the home guarder.

The ex-RAF type said: 'I got in just as it was finishing. I was hoping to be posted to Germany but I spent the whole time in Scotland, servicing and decommissioning some of the older bombers.' They both looked quizzically at John; he smiled but declined the invitation to join in the conversation.

He had made contact with Jenny a month after she returned home. She had obtained a job in one of the woollen mills near to the Frizinghall area of Bradford where her half-sister lived. She knew it would be a stopgap until she married; it paid more than nursing and was on a regular day shift.

John first went over on a bank holiday Friday evening and was to stay on Saturday and Sunday with Mary and Dennis in the three story Victorian house, which Mary had inherited. John was amazed at how spacious the rooms were. There were two roomy cellars downstairs and bedrooms on two floors above the spacious sitting room and living room, and the kitchen was about as big as the living room back at home. Dennis worked as a train driver on the newly Nationalised British Rail and had thus missed being in the forces due to his vital and 'reserved' occupation.

Jenny was totally no nonsense regarding her relationship to John. Her half-sister also had her feet firmly on the ground of the real world. His intended met him at the station and she showed him the route to the bus station and explained which busses would get him to her place of residence. She said, 'I have my own room on my own floor, above theirs. It's very roomy. I've got a big wardrobe, a dressing table, a wash-stand and a bed. It's a big double,' she said, looking him straight in the eye. She had explained to Mary that she and John would be getting married soon and that there was no need to make up a separate bed for him. Mary did not bat an eyelid. Jenny did not mention the fact that John, as yet, had not asked her.

On arrival at the house, there were cursory introductions and then Jenny said, 'Come upstairs. Mary and Denis are off into Bradford with the kids, and there are a few things I want to show you.' He rapidly discovered that she mainly wanted to show him a hot, wet and willing pussy, which had not been filled since the time she had been with him in the hospital in Burma. He found that her need exceeded his as she took him into her again and again, screaming at the top of her voice in ecstasy and relief as each long overdue orgasm wracked her body. The two spent the rest of the afternoon in the bedroom indulging their mutual desires and then resting and talking about the future.

The four adults got on like a house on fire and later went down to the nearby hostelry, the Black Swan, or the 'Mucky Duck' as the locals called it. The night developed into an impromptu engagement party.

Dennis, like John, had formed a somewhat low opinion of trade unions and politicians of all parties. He said, 'It would be fine if they stuck to the principles laid down by the founders, but a lot of 'em don't. For every idealist you seem to get two main chancers—usually very sharp, who have a lot of gob and get elected and then set out to use their positions for their own benefit. The number of times I've seen it at work. You can tell as soon as they open their mouths what they're angling for, and if they don't end up on the union or council you find 'em sooner or later on a Club Committee.'

He told John that a surprising number of the National

Union of Railwaymen seemed to favour the Conservative party. John told him that he was well aware of the differences between the Railway men and the Dockers, Steel workers and the Miners. He explained: 'We were treated like shit by the gaffers, and that breeds a militant attitude. The Railway companies were different, much more paternalistic with the workers very often coming from small market towns or agricultural areas, and they brought their forelock touching attitudes with 'em. If they'd had a few good rag-ups the gaffers would have treated 'em with a lot more respect. When you travel first class, with all the livery on the stewards and the crockery with the railway companies coat of arms on it, you can get the impression that you are in a stately home on wheels.'

John left Bradford with everything arranged. They would get married by special licence on the forthcoming pit holiday week and then on to Blackpool for a honeymoon. John would put his name down for a pit house as soon as they were wed. He would try to get a flat but knew that would be difficult. However, Mary and Dennis made it plain that Jenny and any kids that might arrive could stay with them until accommodation became available. For John, the main difficulty was the travelling. He needed to leave for Bradford after the Saturday morning shift and needed to return on Sunday afternoon to get ready for the day shift on the Monday.

Mckinley briefly considered realising some of his capital and buying a place. However, he was well aware of the small-minded dynamics that constrained life in a mining village. He knew very well that it would be a fundamental mistake to step outside the boundaries set by the herd. He knew very well that one good-looking lad at the pit had married a young lass whose dad had owned a semi up at the row of houses where Mona's dad had lived. These were inhabited almost exclusively by businessmen, local headmasters and bank managers and similar. The girl's dad had been a clerk on the council and she had inherited the house after he had died.

After that, it rapidly got round the pit that Kenny Weston had moved into a house on Nob's row up at the green and pleasant and posh end of the village. At snap time Kenny had started to get comments such as 'should I wipe the coal dust of this sleeper, my lord, so tha' can sit thee-sen down and have thee snap?'

In the village, he had liked to get out with his young wife on Saturday night to have a good drink and see the turn at the local working men's club. After a few deliberately loud comments from some of the wives, such as: 'Here comes lady muck and his lordship,' they had stopped going. Billy rapidly decided that he didn't want to be one of the lads any longer and took steps to qualify as a pit deputy. He passed the exams and became one of the officials in charge of shot firing. He started to attend the local colliery official's club instead of his former watering hole. It was much smaller than 'the Grange' and much quieter. He found it very boring compared to the very lively working men's club but there were social events held there and the beer was reasonably priced so he put up with it.

Mckinley didn't want that sort of difficulty disrupting the highly enjoyable social life which he had now become accustomed to, after those long periods in which he had found himself totally devoid of beer and any female company during the war. He turned the various options over in his mind but the conclusion he came to was always the same: others were putting up with overcrowded living conditions and so would he. Houses were starting to be built and they would get one in a few years. After all, they had managed during and after the war with not seeing each other for almost four years. However, the best laid schemes of mice and men, as one poet observed, 'gang aft a-gley'.

Back at the pit things continued as normal. John and Bert worked every bit of time they could and were making more money than they had ever thought was possible during the thirties. John organised small contracting gangs and alternated this activity with face work. Bert had developed from a small, fourteen-year old runt into a face worker who was short in stature but with shoulders like a bison. His work was confined to shovelling his 'stint' on the face, and he was paid accordingly. However, with the high rates of absenteeism colliers were frequently asked to tackle a double stint or to share an extra one between them. Bert was always one of the first to be asked and his earnings were always amongst the highest of those attained by the face men at Bullcroft. John's earnings usually topped those of Bert due to his contracting. By now, Cud had been moved off the face and was happily seeing out his last decade underground working as a packer, building up the walls of the various roadways that ran to and from the faces.

At home, things were improving. The clothes ration had become more generous and footwear was removed from the list of rationed items altogether. In March 1949, the meat ration was reduced again for some reason but that decrease was against a generally improving trend. At number thirty-nine there was great excitement in the late spring of that year when a van delivered a large cardboard box. Inside it was a brand-new rocking chair with a solid base and springs under the rockers to prevent it tipping. It was the first new item of furniture that Cud and Margaret had ever bought.

Major international events such as the 1948 Olympics had passed by with only moderate interest in the village. There were newspaper reports and items about the games on the radio, but for those far from the centre of things, horse racing and football were the two sports that captured almost universal interest.

A new and youngish deputy called Tony Watts had taken over on 22s face at the pit. He seemed a bit green to Mckinley but everybody thought that he would eventually be OK. On one Monday John's contracting team had arrived early and were moving props down into the heading while the deputy inspected the face, testing for gas with his Garforth lamp as he progressed along it. He emerged and said to the men that there was something a bit odd about ten yards down the face. John went back down with him to have a look. His heart sank when he got there as he could see that the problem was a roof void, and an unusually large one.

'What do we do?' said Tony.

Mckinley replied that the only way they could advance the face was to timber up in the void to avoid a major collapse, which meant they needed to climb into it and work under unsupported ground. By then the early face shift had started to arrive. John said to Tony, 'Don't touch anything! We'll bring the timbers in from the heading and get started; we will need to send off for some more props, we won't have enough.'

John knew the work under unsupported ground would be dangerous but it had to be done. He wished that Burkinshaw or some similarly very experienced and able official had been available to take charge, but the new man was all there was. John crawled back under the lip and out into the main roadway and started to organise things. He knew exactly what was needed. He told two old hands, Charlie Sims and Steve Woodward, to get back under and build a support using sleepers at the edge of the void, prior to them climbing into it to erect the necessary structure. A few minutes later, he heard a crunching sound and coal dust belched out of the face into the heading. He knew that there must have been a fall of some kind and was just bending under the 'lip' to crawl onto the face when Steve leapt through the gap and said: 'Tony's been buried!'

By then about a dozen men had arrived. They all scrambled onto the face to the site of the fall. Mckinley could see one boot sticking out from under the pile of coal. The whole party leapt forwards as though they were a single entity and started to tear the debris away, some with shovels and some just using their hands. It took about five minutes before they uncovered the buried man's face and chest. They splashed water on his mouth and face and tried to get him breathing again but to no avail. John looked closely and then realised that his protruding tongue and bulging eyes had an uncanny resemblance to those of the Japanese soldier he had throttled in the Burmese jungle several years previously. The sight made him feel sick.

A rescue team arrived and oxygen was applied along with more efforts to start respiration again. After about ten minutes the lead rescue man said, 'It's no good, there's no pulse; we'll stretcher him out and inform the manager and H.M.I.'s office.' Work grimly resumed on the face and the void was timbered up with little further difficulty.

Mckinley took one of the men he had sent in to one side and said, 'What happened? I told him not to touch anything.'

Charlie said, 'We'd got a cross piece and the props up just like you said. Tony stepped forward and shone his light up into the hole and then poked something with his Deputy's stick and then the whole lot poured down over him. It's a good job we got the props up or there might have been a hell of a lot more come down. I was buried up to my thighs with loose stuff and just managed to get out as you lot came charging down to dig him out.' John bit his lip in vexation, knowing very well that the mine had picked off another of the workforce due to his inexperience in that particular situation. If only the deputy had waited, he would have been all right.

On the way out of the pit, John said little. On the surface, he explained briefly to the manager what had happened. He was thanked and told the inspector might just want a word with him and with Sims and Watts. 'Can you ask them to call into the office on their way out of the pit after their next shift?' John confirmed that he would do that and then walked up the road in the direction of the Grange; he badly needed a drink. At the club, he had half a dozen pints. He could not get the sight of those bulging eyes and the protruding tongue out of his mind.

He got back to number thirty-nine almost two hours later than usual. Margaret was ready to explode with fury at the dried-up dinner that she had prepared and which had been waiting on the hot plate for him. He said to her, 'Don't start! Tony got killed this morning.' His mother stopped her intended attack in its tracks and served the food solicitously, drenching it with more gravy to try to make it palatable. Mckinley ate without enthusiasm and then went for his bath. After it, he said, 'I am off for a kip, give me a shout at about half five.' He went upstairs and managed a couple of nightmare filled hours before getting up and changing to go out. He wanted to get to the Grange at opening time; he wanted to get blotto, to get rid of the image of those staring eyes that kept on leaping up into his mind. The eyes of the buried deputy and those of the dead Jap had merged into one and just seemed to keep staring at him.

He got to the club at six and stood at the bar drinking steadily. Arthur joined him after eight and sat with him as he poured pint after pint down. Quiller came in to the club just before ten and the two discussed what to do. They had heard about the fatality and were surprised that John had reacted as he had. Fatalities occurred at the rate of one or two a year at the pit and they had all seen them and many others during the war.

By closing time, their friend was paralytic—far drunker than they had ever seen him at any other time. This was due to the combination of the booze taken before his dinner and the heavy overload of it taken afterwards. At closing time, they lifted him off the stool in the club and half carried him homewards between them. They got him to thirty-nine and then inside, and Margaret asked if they could manage him upstairs and onto the bed. They left him there in the small box room, fully dressed and covered with his old army great coat.

One of the effects of excess alcohol is a depression of the higher brain functions while the more basic ones continue to operate. Thus it was with Mckinley. He awoke at about nine with a shocking hangover and still, even then, befuddled by the beer. It took him some time to realise that the bed was sodden and the floor beneath it soaking wet because the sphincter controlling the release of urine from his bladder had relaxed, like that of an infant, due to his overwhelming need to pee.

His reaction was one of self-disgust. He tottered downstairs and cleaned himself up. He made a mug of tea that he drank and then went out and walked down to the park and sat on a bench, slowly collecting his thoughts together, looking at the clouds and trees and the park keeper cutting the grass round the beds of shrubs.

Back at thirty-nine, Lily was enjoying a fit of hysterical anger. She had been sniping at her mother for some time about the overcrowding at home, which was seriously affecting her sex life. 'There's me and Fred and the two bairns and Alice in the big bedroom and John and Bert in the small one. I don't see why John can't get digs at the miner's hostel in Bentley during the week; he goes to see Jenny at the weekend.' But now she was really having a go: 'All my efforts wasted—scrimping and saving—working my fingers to the bone—trying to feed the bairns, etc. etc.' Her mother sat in bemused silence, she was in a quandary. John had peed the bed and it had run through the floorboards and dripped through the ceiling into the pantry. Unfortunately, a tray of jam tarts, made from frugally saved flour, jam and margarine, which Lily had baked the day before, now lay in soggy ruin because of the unfortunate shower from above.

Lily demanded action; she could not live in a house where drunks periodically urinated through the ceiling. Margaret knew that there was far more to it than that and eventually talked it over with John, who kept the circumstances of the drunkenness pretty much to himself. He was not going to plead his case; either he was welcome in the house or he was not. 'In all the circumstances,' his mother said, 'it would be perhaps best if you moved out for a few weeks, into lodgings.' She made it clear that she would continue to do his washing and he was welcome round at any time.

Subsequently, Cud found out exactly what had happened and about the strangled enemy soldier. John had never mentioned it to anyone but the huge quantity of beer had prized the secret out from where it was locked, deep inside his brain, and he had told Arthur about how he kept seeing the staring eyes of both of the dead men. Cud told Margaret and she realised that she had made a terrible mistake. She went to see John but he said, 'Don't worry about it, mam. I'm comfortable enough through the week in the hostel. I've got my own locker and bed in a little cubicle and on Friday after work I'm off to Bradford anyway.' Lily, however, was inwardly triumphant. She just had to get rid of Bert or Alice now and it would be a whole bedroom just for her and Fred and the kids.

Alice solved the problem for her. She was livid at what had happened to John and walked in one Saturday afternoon to tell everyone that she had joined the RAF nursing service. She had talked it over with Jenny and would be reporting for duty at the start of next month. Alice was never unkind or devious in any way; her default setting was always one of concern for everyone. However, in Lily's case she could not refrain from saying pointedly to her: 'It will be a lot roomier for you now; won't it!' Her elder sister rapidly changed the subject of the conversation, to one which left her much less discomfited.

Soon after that, John and Jenny got married by special licence in Bradford. John invited Bert and Alice and explained that it would be a small affair with no celebrations apart from a drink and a sandwich afterwards at the 'mucky duck.'

31

Mckinley and the Drab Fifties

Mckinley maintained his commute to Bradford for over four years. While the spacious accommodation at her sister's suited Jenny, the absence of her husband during the week certainly did not. However, two kids came along and that gave her lots to do now that she had packed in working. The weekends were always extra special and they were in exactly the same boat as many others, it was just a question of waiting. John's earnings were very high and she put money in the Post Office every week out of her housekeeping in readiness for when they did get a place of their own.

Life had slipped into a tolerable routine and Mckinley was enjoying it. The only bit of strangeness he experienced was on the railway station in Bradford. Jenny had arranged to meet him so they could do some shopping before returning to her lodgings. Walking through the large foyer at the entrance to the station, they passed two women. One was about five feet tall and had a rather ugly and mannish appearance. The woman with her was built like a beanpole, about five feet ten and with a rather gormless expression on her face. The short woman obviously recognised Jenny and appeared to be about to say something but Jenny gave her an intensely withering look and swept John past the two. Mckinley, observant as ever said, 'What was all that about?'

'I'll tell you later when we are alone,' was the cryptic reply. At home, Jenny explained: 'Oh, those two, I met them when I started nursing. The dwarfish one was a staff nurse and always thoroughly unpleasant. I christened her Hop-toad; all the juniors thought it was very funny.'

'What about the one who looked like Olive Oyl?' asked John.

Jane explained: 'At work she was always the one favoured by the dwarf; I could never work out why. However, at a New Year's party at the nurses' home, they disappeared late on. I didn't know the place and was wandering round upstairs trying to find a loo as they were queuing at the downstairs one. I lost my way but could hear some sounds. I wandered along in an unused part of the building and found a door to a small dormitory right at the end of a corridor. I went in and saw those two.'

'What was going on?' he said.

'Well, I was stopped dead in my tracks,' she said. 'The tall one was partly undressed and she had been tied up with leather straps which fastened her wrists to her ankles in such a way that her legs were wide apart. She had also been gagged with what looked like a bandage and her own knickers. Hop-toad was knelt in front of her with her tongue deep in the woman's pussy. She was making grunting noises, the one on her back was moaning through the gag, and her eyes were rolling back, obviously in extreme pleasure. I thought about creeping away, but I lit a fag and then said loudly, "Either of you know if there's a lavvy up here?" Hop-toad jumped about five feet in the air and then started to try to say something, but I turned on my heel and left. After that, she left me strictly alone and I didn't get the worst duties dumped on me anymore. If ever I saw Olive Oyl she would colour up and rush past me to somewhere else. In addition, I never saw her in the presence of her lover again whilst on the ward. Soon after that, I was promoted to staff nurse. After a few months I joined the RAF, and then became a sister. The dwarf never got any further, even with the need for experienced nurses due to the war; apparently, she could never pass the sisters' exams. I could never stand the woman; she seemed to have a huge chip on her shoulder and obviously hated men.'

Mckinley said, 'I know all about lesbianism. I read it up years ago in a book by a German psychiatrist, but that's the first time I've ever met anybody who has seen it in action. Is there much of it about?'

'You'd be surprised, lover boy,' she replied, 'but fortunately for you the only thing I want anywhere near my pussy is your huge and throbbing dick.' She added in a voice dripping with eroticism and invitation: 'And that means now!' John had no choice but to acquiesce to the wanton's pressing needs.

John was also saving a lot of money and every couple of years he went to London and met up with Hugo and his sister. By now the Labour party was back in opposition and Rosalind had gone back to work at London University. She was also very active in the Fabian Society and preparing for the inevitable Labour victory at the next election in 1955 or 56. John always passed most of his surplus cash over to Hugo, who added it to Mckinley's share portfolio.

He explained to John how it worked: 'The stock market is essentially very simple, it works on greed and fear. When the market is booming, everybody wants a share and everyone buys. However, for various circumstances the market occasionally dives and when it does fear sets in and, irrationally, many people sell. People who follow that pattern get the worst of both worlds. We buy when the market falls and sell when it booms. The other thing, of course, is to have a wide range of shares and to avoid the tired and worn out industries such as cotton or ship building and to get into the up and coming stuff like chemicals, electricals and motors.'

Mckinley was highly impressed and could see that his funds had appreciated at a much faster rate than would have been the case at compound interest in a bank. As Bollers pointed out: 'Even if your shares halved in value due to some stupendous market crash you would still be well in front in terms of what you had actually put into the market.'

Other topics came up during the conversations. Rosalind

was endlessly interested in levels of support for the Labour party. She asked what people were spending their money on and about how they were entertaining themselves. John told her things were slowly easing with rationing coming off and less and less coupons needed to get consumer goods. He pointed out that finally you could get decent food if you had the money. 'Last Christmas we got hold of a chicken—it was the first time we had ever had one. Things like cars are out of the question for most people due to the huge amount of purchase tax on them and you spend a year or more on the waiting list even if you have the cash.' He explained that for most people entertainment was the pub or the cinema, or a football match on a Saturday afternoon if you were a man.

John enquired if they thought that this new-fangled television would go anywhere. Rosalind explained: 'Oh yes, look at what is happening in the States. There it is driven by market forces and starting to take off in a big way, but here vested interests are retarding its development.'

'In what way?' asked Mckinley.

'Well, for a start the big picture corporations are less than keen,' she replied. 'If people can see things at home they won't visit the cinema. Major sports promoters are opposed to it for the same reasons; they know it will affect attendance at football and boxing matches and the like. The sport shown on TV seems to be mainly the amateur stuff like the ABA boxing championships because of that embargo; people would far sooner see British title fights but the promoters block it. Top variety stars also rarely appear because the big agencies stop them. Another major deterrent, of course, is the price; a television set costs about a hundred pounds. For some people that is several months' worth of earnings. Even for the top earners the amount is substantial. However, people are keen to get hold of sets. I believe that at the end of 1949 over a hundred thousand TV licences had been issued.'

Mckinley now always treated himself to a first class return when he travelled down to London, and observed the types travelling in that section. It seemed that little had changed apart from the fact that there were far fewer military officers now using the trains. The first class carriages were for the upper middle and upper classes, business and civil service types, but always with a sprinkling of the vulgar moneyed classes. These were usually wide boys or bookmakers as well.

Occasionally he saw stout little mill owners accompanied by even stouter little wives, who dropped their aitches or added them inappropriately to a word. John smiled when he overheard one such pair travelling back from the opening of the Festival of Britain, hearing it described an 'Istoric Hoccassion.' More important were some of the snippets he heard. He gathered that there were problems in the mills and that it was difficult to get labour, at least at the wages that the mill owners were prepared to pay. One Bradford man had started to recruit workers from Pakistan. The little man said, 'If you go down to his mill, there are dozens of 'em there now.'

Things had improved to the extent that it was now possible to get a really good meal and have a good drink whilst travelling back. He enjoyed this and always followed Jimmy's practice of giving the steward ten bob when he came to take the order, knowing full well that for the rest of the trip if he caught the steward's eye the man would be straight there to ask what he wanted. He could see that the wide-boys, car traders, and the like always tipped generously but the middle classes did not. Unsurprisingly, the former group always got excellent attention but the latter group did not and usually resorted to complaining loudly about the appalling nature of the service. The stewards were past masters at ignoring or deflecting those comments.

On one occasion, he heard a steward apparently lose his temper when being upbraided by a particularly snotty woman because her soup had taken so long to come and was only lukewarm when she received it. The man launched into an anguished tirade, raising his voice so that the whole carriage could hear him. 'You don't know what it's like! I'm here on my own! Short staffed in the buffet car! We don't have the crockery! What on earth do you expect?' He finished off, Mckinley thought, with the beautiful remark: 'If it was left to people like you I'd be doing everything at the double and running up and down the carriage with a broom handle up my arse so that I could sweep the aisle as well!'

The woman was gasping with indignation at the end of it and demanded the steward's name so that she could complain to his superiors. The steward gave it to her and walked down the aisle towards John, wearing a broad grin. The woman got off the train at Newark and John said to the steward, 'I suppose you've got another job lined up then!'

The steward winked and said, 'Start next Monday! I've been losing my temper with such as her all week!'

Back home things continued much as before. The Pit Head Baths came into operation in 1951 and finally the men could go to work and then get out of their pit clothes and shower as they came out of the pit. Margaret was delighted that Bert and Cud no longer cluttered the bathroom up after each return from the mine.

In the world at large, the Korean War was now in progress, and grim bulletins came through from time to time. Mckinley noticed that the propaganda line in the papers and on the radio had changed from the War years' praise of 'The heroic efforts of our comrades in the Red Army,' to features about the insidious nature of the Communist state.

It was also obvious that the standard of living was slowly improving. At the start of 1952, Fred and Lily got a council house and John and Jenny got a house shortly afterwards. When Fred had come out of the Royal Navy in 1948, John and Bert had told him they could get him a job at the pit. Fred, who during the war had had some hairy experiences and had experienced attacks by bomber and submarine, was in no way prepared to countenance working underground. In the end, he had settled for the Fire Service. The job was low paid and then consisted of a shift system of twenty-four hours on and twenty-four off. Most of this, of course, was on standby with the men able to sleep in beds at the Fire Station during the nights.

This in turn enabled Fred to do what virtually all firemen did; he got casual work in his spare time. Some firemen worked as gardeners, others as pallbearers for the various funeral directors round Doncaster, others as cellar men or delivery drivers or as part-time builders. What was important was that the payments to them were cash in hand and with no question of paying tax on the additional earnings. Fred eventually put together a window-cleaning round with the principal aim of providing himself with cigarettes and beer money.

John observed everything in his usual taciturn manner but said nothing. One thing puzzled him, however, and that was the differences in his siblings. He could never work out how people with more or less the same upbringing could end up so different.

Bert was hard working and generous in spirit. He worked hard and played hard but, importantly, he saved hard and had a large amount in his Post Office account. Alice was even more generous in spirit and though never showing the slightest interest in religion showed those characteristics of human compassion of the very best sort of Christian. Peggy was plain looking, her front teeth were a little crooked, she was realistic about her prospects, and she had settled for a miner called Arnie who lived just round the corner. John knew of him from Bullcroft and had heard he was idle.

The mines bred a multitude of different characters. Some grafted very hard and spent it on their families, others did the same but spent it on booze, cigarettes and at the bookies. Some of the worst cases would go down to the bookmakers after being paid on Friday and could lose the lot before they went home. Anxious wives standing outside the pit gates on paydays to get their housekeeping before the bookies got it, sometimes made it obvious who the offenders were.

The worst case that Mckinley had heard about regarding a gambler was of the man at one of the Rotherham pits who had done just that and lost his week's wages plus two week's holiday pay. Rather than face his wife and kids, he had gone back up to the colliery and hopped over the barrier before the Banksman could stop him and jumped down the pit shaft.

Apart from the almost mandatory weekly sweepstake at his working men's club, John never gambled. Some miners drank whenever they could, others just drank at weekends or not at all. He found that these were the ones who usually made a point of having a week's holiday each year with their families. Some of the crowd smoked, drank and gambled, and these never had any money or very much in the way of clothes. John noted that they wore the same old jacket or threadbare suit all the year round. To them their behaviour seemed normal; it was the same as the behaviour of their dads back in the past.

To Mckinley's way of thinking the worst were those who just wouldn't have it at any price and who scraped by on just two or three shifts a week. Arnie was one of these. His priorities seemed to be cricket, cigarettes, beer, sex, and then finally his family. He came first in everything; his wife and family got what was left. He organised his life around the Test matches and would listen to the radio commentaries from start to finish when they were on. In those weeks, he would usually only get one or two shifts in. He did make a spurt at work when the Tests started to get televised, and then his pretty poorly furnished house always had one of the latest and largest screen models available, standing in pride of place in the centre of the living room in front of his chair.

Through the summer he would sit in silence, usually on his own, steadily smoking his Park Drives and devouring every over. In the evening, he would always make his way down to the club to fulfil his religious duty to drink four pints of John Smith's best bitter. Long suffering Peggy managed on what he could give her and on the family allowance for her and, by then, five kids, and on sacks of vegetables which he obtained by trading some of his coal concession to a brother who worked on the land. From what John could make out from his mother and sisters, Peggy's kids subsisted pretty much on chips and vegetable soup. When the kids eventually left, she adopted a policy of if he won't work, I won't either and would pack sandwiches and a flask and get out of the house on fine days and ride her bike into the countryside.

She also joined the church and busied herself with the choir, taking a leading part in it as an excellent contralto, and in church social activities. Arnie rapidly stopped asking the pointless question: 'Where's my dinner?' on those days, knowing that only on the occasions that he worked would it be on the table when he got home.

John occasionally saw Lily or Fred and their three boys but was less than impressed by what he saw. He could see that the top priority in the house was fags! He estimated that the pair got through about fifty a day between them. They seemed to think it was perfectly normal for about a third of Fred's fire service pay to be used to buy their cigarettes and that other things such as food and clothing should be regarded as secondary. Fred used almost all his window-cleaning earnings to finance his drinking. He would be across to the local, every night at eight, telling Lily, 'I am just off for a quick one.' The quick one usually consisted of four, five, or even six pints.

Mckinley had started taking his family each year to Butlins during the 'pit week' holiday as soon as the kids got old enough to appreciate being by the sea. He noticed that Lily and Fred never took their three boys on a week's holiday. Eventually Dave, then aged twenty-two and married, said to John, after taking his new family and himself off for a week's holiday in Bridlington: 'I always wondered what it would be like!' John sympathised, especially as he could see that his nephew shared his shrewdness.

John noticed other differences between the families. He had purchased a new television set as soon as they had moved into their new council house and they had all watched the Coronation, in 1953, on that small screen accompanied by lots of their neighbours and their families. The small box became a major source of home entertainment after commercial television started in 1956, mainly due to the light entertainment programs imported from the United States. Fred and Lily had finally managed a rental set in 1960; they were the last family on the street to get a TV.

One thing about miners' houses was the fact that they were warm due to the ten tons of concessionary coal, which they received each year. It was usually accepted that the Home Coal delivery drivers would keep one of the twenty sacks, which comprised each ton, and then sell it. Mckinley didn't particularly mind this as the delivery men were on the basic pit top day wage of about six pounds a week. Some of the greedier ones purloined two bags or even more from the unwary and sold them to the non-mining families.

Ironic comments were raised during the mid to late fifties, when cars started to become more easily available and it was pointed out that the only two groups in the village that seemed to be able to afford cars were the highly-paid face workers and the Home Coal men. Sackings occasionally occurred amongst them but it was reckoned that you had to be stupid to be caught. Arnie always stood and counted as each bag was dropped in his coal shed; he made absolutely sure that he always got the full twenty.

By now, Mckinley could easily have afforded a car; his earnings at the pit were the best they had ever been. Mining deaths were also dropping—in 1955 it was down to four-hundred and thirty-two and the year after it had dropped down to an unbelievable three-hundred and thirty-six. He saw some figures in the union office that informed him that in 1953 average earnings in the industry had topped eleven pounds a week. Contractors, such as himself, could easily earn three or four times that amount. In the thick seamed pits of the

Yorkshire coalfield, mechanisation was increasing and the pits were working with fewer and fewer men. The older collieries and those with the narrow seams were being closed with the miners either transferring to the large Yorkshire and Midland coalfields or taking redundancy and getting one of the very plentiful jobs that were available at that time.

At home, things were splendid, with two young and healthy kids and a brand new house built on a new estate at Scawthorpe. This was conveniently situated on major bus routes half way between Doncaster and the pit, about a quarter of an hour's journey in each direction. Rapid moves were made to build a Working Men's club there, and John was elected as the secretary of the embryo organisation. He knew very well how clubs worked; they were usually fine unless they elected a corrupt chairman or secretary and committee. In that case the balance sheet would show that the club made little annual profit despite being full most of the time and the place would eventually go bust and be turned into a factory or car sales lot. He had overheard the former secretary of one club, which had gone under, moaning to his mates in one of the underground headings: 'I had nothing out of that club—apart from a new car and a caravan!' All there thought it was funny but Mckinley smiled wryly and noted the incident and others like it.

When the club started looking for a brewery, reps started to arrive in order to persuade the committee to sign up for their particular beer on a tied house basis. Most clubs in and around Doncaster seemed to go for John Smiths; a few went for Sam Smiths and some for Barnsley Bitter. John realised that the approach involved sending a few very sharp operators out who would take the committee out for a slap-up lunch with plenty of beer thrown in. The venue chosen was always one of the upmarket hotels run by the brewery and the beer was always absolutely spot on.

After an afternoon of back slapping and joke telling, the sales team got on famously with the committee and rapidly got on first name terms with everyone and even started to talk about their wives on first name terms. One of the some-what bemused committee said to John after such a meeting, 'They were talking as though they had known us for years, it was almost as though they were family.' A few hazy details were discussed and then the committee were assured that they would be unable to get a better deal anywhere else. They would then be invited back to an even more slap-up lunch and more drinks a few weeks later and invited to sign the paper-work, which would lock them tightly in the Brewery's grasp.

Mckinley had asked around about what would happen and Bill had explained the ins and outs of the brewery trade to him saying, 'All of them will charge you pretty much the same price for their beer, with some discount if you do a big bar-relage, but whichever way you go there will only be a few quid in it for the members.' He continued: 'I know that local preju-dice about beer might be hard to get over but you might like to try one of the Newcastle breweries. They will give you a hell of a deal just to get a foothold in South Yorkshire. And there's one other thing, John,' he said. 'Those sales buggers are very sharp; I've talked to a lot of 'em, but they're not as sharp as you!'

Thus, Mckinley was prepared. He had briefed the commit-tee and they had several splendid lunches at the expense of the various local breweries. However, at the end of the day they signed up for Vaux ales. This meant that the new club could charge a penny a pint less than all the surrounding clubs and still make more profit. The new membership grum-bled a bit about the beer not being quite what they were used to but they soon got used to it, and the club always had a full bar every lunch time and during the evenings and the small concert room was always packed at the weekends. Fairly rap-idly the club had made so much profit that it was extended, with a huge new concert room added; the bar was enlarged to include a snooker table and part of the old concert room was converted into a very plushly-furnished snug.

John ran a tight ship with the committee being given their

small 'on duty' fees with a few extra beer tickets or bingo or raffle tickets thrown in. He paid himself strictly by the book but rapidly found that gaming machine salesmen were willing to use him as an agent to empty their machines and pay him a decent commission for doing it. There were other perfectly legitimate opportunities to gain income in the place that came his way as an exceptionally able club secretary, and he took advantage of all of them.

He thought back occasionally about his near starvation existence during the thirties. With the sixties approaching, the election slogan trotted out by Harold McMillan on behalf of the Tory party was: 'You've never had it so good.' Mckinley didn't know about anybody else but he had to concede that in respect of himself and his family the Prime Minister was spot on. In the 1959 election McMillan and the Conservatives returned to power with 365 seats to Labour's 258; the almost dead Liberal Party managed just 6 seats. Down in London Rosalind was beginning to think that Labour would never return to office.

32

Mckinley and the Swinging Sixties

It was hard to put his finger on exactly what it was, but as the sixties dawned Britain seemed to be gaining momentum and to be opening up in some ways. The fifties had still very much been dominated by the war and its aftermath and the slow struggle from near national bankruptcy. This had necessitated the continuation of rationing combined with high taxation for years but now more and more consumer goods were appearing. Although the bicycle and public transport were still the main means of getting to work around Doncaster, car ownership was increasing and each colliery now needed to build large car parks for the dozens of cars that were bringing workers to the pits. The manager at Bullcroft thought it was marvellous. If he now needed men quickly in an emergency or to deal with a breakdown or a roof fall or a fire underground, all he needed to do was to pick a phone up and the required personnel would be there within the hour.

Fashions were also changing, fewer and fewer men were wearing the Trilby or Homburg hats which the films of the thirties and forties had made popular. Cloth caps belonged very much to the older generation, and the younger colliers would not be seen dead in one. Hair styles were changing too. For a generation after the war most men stuck to the short back and sides that had been rigidly enforced during the war and during the years of national service after it. The teddy boys of the mid-fifties had struck the first blow against the rigid sartorial standards of their seniors by starting to wear long sideburns and longer, heavily Brylcreamed hair styles.

However, their hair was not as long as the shoulder length styles that arrived in the sixties. Perhaps it was something to do with the ending of National Service and that generation of NCOs who had the awesome power to tell new recruits to, 'Get your 'aircut you 'orrible little man.' John noted that usually the type of haircut sported by an individual could immediately enable him to distinguish between those who had done the compulsory two years in the armed forces and those who had not.

In the world at large, huge developments were occurring, with nuclear bombs seeming to get ever more powerful and the means to deliver them ever more deadly. John watched the Cuban missile crisis come and go but didn't lose any sleep over it; he felt that those in charge 'at long last' would be more severely affected by a nuclear war than the troops of working class lads they had sent off to fight the nation's wars in the past. He thus made the cynical calculation that despite all the sabre rattling and posturing, nuclear war was very unlikely to come about unless by some unfortunate accident or act of lunacy. The era of promise that had seemed to open when John F. Kennedy was elected as US president was rapidly ended by his assassination in 1963. The opening of BBC2 in 1964 was of far more interest to Mckinley than the remote possibility of nuclear obliteration or any other world event.

In that year, the Labour Party was returned to power after thirteen years in opposition. John thought that the parties were actually moving closer together in terms of policies but two things especially had assisted Labour's re-election. One of these was that a Government Minister called John Profumo had lied to Parliament about his affair with a good time girl called Christine Keeler. Unfortunately, Profumo was Minister for War at that time and Miss Keeler was also having an affair with a Russian diplomat. The other major factor was the feudal way in which the Prime Minister, Harold Macmillan, had handed the leadership of his party over to his successor who just happened to be the 14th Earl of Home. Everyone was amazed. Macmillan said he had 'taken soundings' both with colleagues and within the party but to everyone else it appeared that he had treated the Conservative Party as his personal fiefdom and passed the leadership to one who was very close to him in terms of class. After that, the Tories insisted that in future its leader would be chosen by an election in which all the sitting MPs would vote.

Labour won three-hundred and seventeen seats compared to the Tory's three-hundred and four, the liberals gained nine seats. It was a slim but workable majority and Labour once more took up the levers of power. At one of their increasingly less frequent meetings, John, Hugo and Rosalind discussed the new government.

John expected Rosalind to be ecstatic but could see that she had reservations about Harold Wilson, the new Prime Minister; after a couple of years, he could see why. He had seen mining change radically from coal faces manned by hundreds of men to now just a couple of dozen. From men working without helmets and going home black with coal dust to get bathed in a tin bath in front of the kitchen fire, to the sturdy safety helmets worn by all and the luxury of a hot shower in the pithead baths when they came out of the mine. From over a thousand mines the industry had reduced to less than three hundred as the markets for coal were slowly lost to oil powered locomotives, ships and power stations.

On the coal faces, instead of large teams of men shovelling ten or twenty tons each into the low steel tubs—with one shift being used for shot firing, another for maintenance and timbering up and the third for getting the coal—a mechanised system called Power Loading had arrived. Here, strips of coal were cut on the two-hundred-yard-long faces by a huge machine with rotating drums on which cutter picks were mounted.

A collier followed it and steered the machine, trying to

keep it level and cutting into the coal seam and not straying into the rock strata above and below it. The coal fell behind the cutter into flat steel structures called Line Pans and was carried down to the face end conveyors to be carried out of the pit. The coal was moved down the Line Pans by short steel bars, which were linked to each other with short lengths of heavy-duty chain. As the strips were sheared from the coalface, the cutter was advanced to cut the next one and behind it the whole panoply of equipment comprising the Armoured Face Conveyor, or Panzer as it was usually called due to its German origin, also moved forward.

Behind the Panzer, a system of hydraulic steel props was also advanced to support the roof as the AFC advanced. The props, or 'chocks' as everyone called them, consisted of a forward projection which supported the newly exposed roof, and two or three stout legs. The support was lowered and then advanced as the strips of coal were cut using these ingenious hydraulic mechanisms and then raised again to take the weight of the roof. Behind the face the strata was abandoned to collapse into the waste that had been left behind.

In the early days, after the first introduction of the new method of mining, errors had been made involving face advance. One of these came because of advancing through very good strata, where the roof remaining behind the advancing face held firm. The Doncaster Area photographer, who worked for the local Coal Board Scientific Department, told Mckinley of his experience at Frickley Colliery where the new face was advancing. It was possible to shine a light behind the chocks seemingly for hundreds of yards back into the void from where the coal had been extracted. As one deputy said, if it wasn't for the height, you could play a football match back there. Then, one day, the whole lot came down.

On the surface, in Frickley village, some people thought it was an earthquake. Fortunately, it was on a back shift and nobody was killed, but when the photographer got on the face he said the support legs had bowed and flowed under the huge

534

pressures giving them the appearance of almost melting. After that, the chocks were lowered, advanced, and then raised into the roof strata to crack it before advancing further. Following this procedure, the waste filled up rapidly, with material falling into it as the weight from the rock overburden exerted its inevitable downward pressure.

Mckinley and the older colliers who had worked with the old timber props could see advantages and disadvantages with the new methods. The days of having to shovel a ten-ton stint had gone, and the face teams were paid on the basis of the number of strips cut.

The effects of all these changes were not lost on the very clever men from the ministry and on their colleagues in the higher administrative levels of the National Coal Board. Mckinley, although having developed an early wariness of politics and union activity nevertheless was interested in the structures and systems that operated within the industry. He gleaned information about how things worked from various sources and found Rosalind an invaluable fountain of information regarding all these matters. Though one of only a few in the know at the lower levels in the industry, he realised that the NCB had been set up in 1947 on a very elitist basis. The key job of Mine Manager was not particularly highly regarded then in the corridors of Whitehall or at the NCB headquarters at Hobart House, which was located in the centre of London pretty close to Buckingham Palace.

In this world, a Colliery Manager who had left school at fourteen and then very slowly climbed the promotional ladder via evening classes could not possibly be equated to the young Classics and History graduates who had been recruited straight from university to fill the administrative posts at the centre of things. After all, these people would help determine policy and write briefs for ministers and the board members of this very large national organisation. They would be part of committee decisions about national mining strategy. How could a man from the working-class background from which almost all managers had come from up to then, possibly be equated with someone who frequently came into contact with the top flights of civil servants at the Ministry of Fuel and who spoke with the same accent. Managers dealt with the grubby day-to-day matters involved with getting the coal out of the ground, the higher echelons certainly did no such thing.

On the one hand, it had to be admitted that it was a big job. Managers were responsible for between a thousand and four thousand men working on three shifts in a mine that was operational in some respects twenty-four hours a day, three-hundred and sixty-five days a year. They bore the responsibility and the consequent pressure of meeting production targets and had full responsibility for deaths and injuries because of the various Mines and Quarries Acts.

All the other health and safety legislation made them legally responsible for all aspects of those matters within the huge curtilage of the colliery. On the other hand, of course, these people spoke with the same, rather odd, regional accents of all those around them. They knew little of the wider world and had only a limited and purely technical education. They could not read Euripides or Cicero in the original. Thus, how could they possibly expect to be paid a salary commensurate with that received by those at the centre of things?

The situation did cause some unease and Managers were provided with a largish house, usually with four or even five bedrooms, and a gardener was also made available, but in those early days pay was still determined by class and not by ability. Things came to a head soon after the new 'socialist' Prime Minister Harold Wilson was installed in Number 10. Mckinley then began to realise why Rosalind had her reservations about the man. He was very clever and reputedly had been given the highest marks ever achieved by an Oxford economics graduate. He saw the national picture certainly but he saw it in terms of numbers and not in terms of people and communities and the sacrifices they had made.

Thus, early in the mid-sixties, it was announced that a

536

new wage structure would be introduced for coalface workers. After all, they were now only an extension to the wonderful machinery that cut all the coal. It was also the case that with cheap heavy fuel oil now becoming available for the last main market that used coal, namely that of electricity generation, the pits were becoming less and less economic and less and less needed.

It was, of course, the case that, as far as any civil servant could envisage, this cheapness and abundance of supply from that marvellously stable and untroubled region known as the Middle East would continue for decades. Thus, after some opposition from the National Union of Mineworkers, it was agreed that the new arrangement known as the National Power Loading agreement would come into operation. The face workers would be paid well if they worked every shift available to them. The twenty-eight pounds a week they would get would equate to about the same as a teacher's annual salary.

It came as a considerable surprise to the very clever men from the ministry, but to absolutely no one in the mining industry, that face productivity dropped alarmingly. As mere cogs in the machine, the colliers now acted as mere cogs and did the specific job which was assigned to those cogs. If something now broke down, they sent for the fitters and sat around under the chocks waiting for them to arrive and fix the breakdown rather than helping them to fix it as rapidly as possible, as had been the case when production bonuses were paid.

Aspects of safety that had previously been ignored, if they interfered with earnings, were now given proper attention. If the water sprays which suppressed the dust on the face became damaged the machine stood until they were fixed. If the hydraulic oil had not been topped up in the chocks and they could not maintain adequate operational pressure it was no business of the men on the face, as mere cogs they got paid exactly the same if four strips of coal were cut or none, and the latter required a good deal less effort than the former. The motto of the organisation was now jokingly rewritten. NCB rapidly became 'No Cunt Bothered!' The situation could not be allowed to continue and very rapidly a cobbled together bonus payment was reintroduced. However, the colliery closure program, which had gone on ever since vesting day, was accelerated with production concentrated at the larger pits, with the peripheral coal fields in Wales, Scotland and the North East hit particularly severely.

In 1966 Mckinley was fifty and did some re-evaluating of his situation. In the past, men had been taken off the face, usually in their early forties, because they were too physically worn out to continue. With the new machinery, he could see himself as a high-earning face worker or contractor for at least another ten years. He had thought that the post nationalisation momentum in the industry would see him through to retirement but began to doubt it. The last thing he wanted was a return to the one and two day working of the thirties.

Rosalind reassured him, saying that 'the mechanised nature of mining requires high productivity from the newer pits with the thicker seams and, fortunately, you have these in your area. However, the industry generally can expect a marked decline through the last few decades of the century.' She did feel that a certain strategic minimum of perhaps a hundred million tons of coal a year would continue to be produced from deep mines in Britain, and this would come mainly from the Nottingham and Yorkshire coalfields.

She could not believe that the Civil Service and the politicians would be so mad as to place themselves entirely at the mercy of foreign energy imports. However, he was not so sure; he just did not trust any of those shifty bastards in politics, either locally or nationally, and from what he had gathered the Civil Servants seemed motivated only by a combination of their next promotion, their pension, and the possibility of eventually appearing in the honours list.

In terms of his own family, Cud had now retired, but Bert was still working underground and John's son had just started as a trainee miner much against his advice. Much to his relief, Lily's eldest had obtained a job with the Coal Board's scientific service. He was relieved because he knew that the youth had something of a wild reputation and had been getting into various scrapes, and he knew that if it had gone the wrong way the lad could have been in front of the courts.

Dave finished grammar school with a few O-levels but when he left there he had found a job as a labourer for White and Slack, Demolition and Excavation. John quizzed him about it, why he had packed it in and gone to the NCB, and young Dave had said, 'I just wanted some money and then I was off to join the army at eighteen, anything to get away from home. Most of the kids I left school with found jobs as trainee clerks or as engineering apprentices. At sixteen, they earned between two pounds and ten shillings and four pounds a week. I was working on a day wage basis but I got two pounds a day. Old man White started me on one pound and ten shillings but I showed him I could do the job just as well as any of the older blokes and he bumped me up to their rate. Therefore, I was keen to work for them, but things happen, don't they!'

The youth smiled and said, 'I know about some of the fixes you've been in, Uncle John; they make you think, don't they?' John invited more and the youngster said: 'It's like this: I'm eighteen now, nearly nineteen. The demolition was OK for money but the blokes running that firm are a pair of cowboys, they take a job on and then its brute force and ignorance; they don't have a clue about buildings, structures and how to take them down properly. As far as they are concerned its roof first and then work down. There is no health and safety or hard hats or boots or anything like that. If you want protective gloves, you buy 'em yourself.

'There were many small incidents, like when old man White stood on some boards, they gave way, and a nail sticking up went straight through his foot. We all get minor cuts and scrapes but there were some incidents that really made me think. One day a bloke was using a crow bar to take a wall down—he must have been about twenty-five feet up. He gave the bar a big tug but it sprung back and flipped him over the side. He fell on a pile of debris, but as luck would have it he landed on a discarded door and there was just enough give in the pile to break his fall, so he just walked away with bruises. He had to go home though; he couldn't carry on because of the shock. If the door hadn't been there, he would probably have been killed.

'Another incident was when old man Slack was using a chainsaw to cut through a big spar on a barn roof. White had taken his two lads, who were twins aged ten, out on site and they were sorting out some of the pipe-work for scrap. They used to do it for pocket money at the weekends and they used to wander all over the demolition site with no supervision. Anyway, that day they were stood under the end of the barn looking at Slacky sawing through this big horizontal spar and for some reason I told 'em to stand back out of the way. It must have been instinct. I said to 'em it'll probably be OK but you never know, so they moved back a few feet.

'About two minutes later Slack finished his cut and then leant back on his ladder, which luckily for him was against a main vertical support pillar, and then the whole bloody roof came down as a single piece. If the twins had been where they had been, they would have been crushed to death. Slack was left pale and shaking on his ladder and had to come down for a fag. Old man White clocked what had happened; he always seemed to want to give me as much work as he could after that and he always rounded the part hours I worked up to full-hours for me.

'The finisher was when we were taking down the old accommodation huts at Lindholme aerodrome. They were prefabricated type things and had been used as the sleeping quarters for the aircrews. One of them was full of debris, bits of reinforced concrete with steelwork sticking out and loads of broken glass and other nasty and very sharp stuff down below me. I was on a roof, which had had the outer skin taken off, and I needed to get up to the main ridge. It looked solid to me so I started to walk across it but it turned out to be thin plasterboard and I fell through. Luckily for me, by then I was about twelve stone of solid muscle and with quick reflexes, so I reached out as I went down and grabbed one of the steel cross girders.

'I can remember looking down at all these sharp things, about twenty feet underneath me as I hung by one arm from the girder before I pulled myself up and got off the roof. A few days later, I saw some adverts for Lab Assistants at the British Rail Regional Lab and at the Coal Board Area Lab, which was just up the road. I applied for jobs at both. I was lucky; they could not keep junior staff 'cos they all went off for better money to ICI or the CEGB labs.'

John looked surprised and said, 'What happened about the army? I had no idea that you were thinking about that.'

His nephew said: 'I was talking to a couple of kids from the Grammar who had gone in as boy soldiers at fifteen and they said it was OK. So at eighteen I turned up to the recruiting office in Donny and this sergeant, who was having a fag and reading the paper, gave me the impression that he really wasn't interested; he must have recruited his quota for that week. Anyway, because it was his job, I suppose, he asked me a few perfunctory questions and explained that the Army did not take just anybody these days. He asked me if I had any sort of criminal record and explained that if I had that would fail me right from the start, but I was OK there. He said the educational standards were higher and I would need to take some sort of test and he asked if I had any qualifications. I told him I had a few O-levels and he showed a flicker of interest.

'He then went on to ask if I did any sports. I left school as an undernourished sixteen-year old weighing nine and a half stone; at school I wasn't going to be made to do sports that I had no interest in, and that was all of them, apart from the athletics in the summer. However, after leaving and two years of decent food and with the hard work I was doing I was muscled like a shark and I had really taken an interest. I told him I did some running and discus throwing, swimming, boxing and judo. I could see he was keen by then and he took some forms out of a draw for me to fill in. He then asked me which Army unit I fancied joining and I said there was just one that really appealed and that outfit was the Paras! After that, he was just about slavering to get me signed up.

'He started to talk about the long training to get in the Parachute regiment and said something about pay scales. Finally, almost as a throwaway comment he said, "I don't suppose you have any medical complaint. You look pretty fit but even something minor like flat feet could keep you out." I said no, I can do fifty press-ups easily and then almost as an afterthought I said the only thing wrong with me is my lazy eye, but that doesn't affect me at all.

'The Sergeant's face fell and he said, "I'm sorry, son, but with something like that you will never get in today's army." I quizzed him and said it runs in the family and it didn't stop my granddad doing four years during the first war. He said: "But things have changed; then they were just cannon fodder, now they are very selective and you need to be A1; you just won't get in."'

Inwardly, Mckinley gave a sigh of relief that his nephew had managed to miss out on those wonderful experiences that had befallen him during his years in khaki.

Young Dave continued, 'After that I started to think about Australia, but about that time I went through the roof and after that I cashed my O-levels in, and now I look like being a scientist.' He went on: 'The money is crap but there is some overtime at weekends and you get day release. I've started an ONC in chemistry. It's a bit like an A-level in chemistry with subsidiary maths and physics and a strong practical bias, and after that I'll do the HNC and I can go on to get a degree after that because the Coal Board are dead keen on getting their blokes qualified. Mind you, I think a lot of that is because nobody wants to come from the universities into mining.

From what I can make out, apart from the mining engineers, a lot of the others, mainly the electrical and mechanical engineers, get qualified and then leave for a nine to five job on the same pay or better and with no crawling about underground.'

'What happened about the job with the railway scientific?' John asked.

'Oh! I got that and they gave me a start date, but I had to have a medical and their doctor didn't think I would be safe doing field work out on the track with the lazy eye.'

'But the Coal Board think you are OK to be wandering round underground with it,' said Mckinley, smiling. He mused for a second and then said, 'It's funny, if you're brought up to it you just don't think about it, but I can understand anybody wanting to get out of the industry. The only thing that's kept me in it is the money, and it's starting to look like that's not going to be as good in the future! Let me know how you get on, I can probably give you a tip or two if you start to do work underground—tell you how coal faces work and what dangers to look out for. I could even take you down to look round a few. You only really get to know about 'em by experience but that's sometimes after you've lost an arm or worse, so keep in touch.'

After that, when they met at family events or at holidays, John made a point of having a quiet word with his nephew and being updated on his progress. He was delighted to see that his nephew had suffered no long-term effects from the badly broken leg of his infancy.

A couple of years later the two had a further chat after a family funeral. John asked his nephew how things were going and received a wry smile in return. 'Well, I'm learning about it the hard way I suppose,' said the youngster. 'I've got through the HNC chemistry and that meant promotion and a fair bit more money. But being a big strong athletic looking lad I always seemed to be asked if I was OK to do field work, either up a Head-gear or out on some pit tip or underground. Pretty soon after I started there, I learned the lesson.'

'Which one?' said his uncle.

'Oh, you know, the main one about looking after yourself underground and never counting on anybody else,' came the reply. 'It made me realise what you and Granddad and Bert have had to cope with.'

He continued with the tale. He had been approached to go underground to calibrate a carbon monoxide monitor, which was located in a main return airway at Bentley Colliery. 'I pointed out that I hadn't done my underground training then, but was told: "Don't worry, you will be under Close Personal Supervision at all times. That means that the man accompanying you should never be more than two arms lengths away from you at any time."

'Anyway, I was kitted out and got the gear and went down with this Scottish bloke; he was something to do with the safety there, I think. He took me out to the district and then dropped this one on me: "It's like this, son: I've got to take some gas samples so I am giving you a choice. You can bring that gasbag and your tools with me. I am going to crawl down a face and then walk up and down a couple of roadways and then crawl down another face. We will be back here in about five hours and then you can do your job. But if you want you can walk up this drift, go round the corner, walk another hundred yards and then crawl under the conveyor and you will see your machine on the wall up a roadway. Then if you come back this way and walk down in that direction you can pick up the Paddy and get out; you will be out of the pit in a couple of hours." The bastard said, "It's up to you, son!"

'Well, what would you do! I had never been on a face before so I set off on my own. I found the UNOR, OK, calibrated it, and then set off to come back, but everything looked different in the reverse direction and I must have taken a wrong turn. I kept on walking and found myself in a tunnel. As I walked along I could see that the steel support rings were getting more and more distorted and that the roof was getting lower and lower because the rocks were starting to bulge through the meshing which was mounted between the rings to support the roof.

'Anyway, I kept on, with the roadway under foot getting worse and worse and the roof getting even lower. After a while my cap lamp started to flicker. I thought, *underground and lost with no lamp, that will be fun.* The lamp flickered a couple more times but then it seemed OK. I just kept walking, hoping that I wasn't going to get into old workings, especially if they were gas fast. It seemed ages but after a while, I saw a light ahead of me and as it got brighter, I found a door in the side of the tunnel. I went through it and it took me into a main roadway. About a hundred yards down it I could see the Paddy Station and a couple officials on the phone. When I got up to 'em, one of them said: "Are you the bloke from Scientific?" I said I was, and he said, "Thank god for that, because you had disappeared I was just getting on the phone to get search parties organised." I had words with my top boss when I got back to the lab about my escort, but nobody wanted to know.'

Mckinley could see his nephew had told the story in an amused manner and broke out into a wry laugh. 'You're realising what the rules are underground! The main one is watch your own back, especially in a strange pit. I just hope that the bloke who took you in got the bollocking he deserved. If the HMI had heard of it he would have been sacked.' He went on to give further advice, saying: 'Always do it by the book, never let them put you in the position where you make a decision which is against the regulations, because it will always bounce back on you.'

John could see that the lad was very like himself and was pleased that he had got a job on the Staff. He asked him about his plans. The youngster said, 'I can take the professional exams of the Royal Institute of Chemistry after the HNC. It's like a degree in analytical chemistry. I seem to be good at it, and after that I was thinking about signing up for this new Open University which is being proposed by Harold Wilson.

545

He's got Jenny Lee working on it at the moment. I understand that it should start round about 1970.'

John said, 'If you get a degree you will be the first in the family ever to do it; we will have a good drink on it when you get it. Don't forget all the rest of us left school at fourteen; apart from Cud of course—he left at twelve.'

In the wider world of the sixties, world events chugged on. The Americans had been sucked into a war in Vietnam and as far as Mckinley could tell by the end of the decade showed no sign of winning it despite a huge escalation in manpower and use of heavy bombers and horrendous new armaments. His one flicker of admiration for Wilson came from the fact that he had steadfastly refused to send British troops into that conflict. Lyndon Baines Johnson, the American President, would have loved to have even a token force there for reasons of legitimisation. He said plaintively to one of his aides: 'Just the Black Watch would have done,' but Wilson was having none of it. During that decade, the Beatles came and went, hairstyles got longer, and drug use increased.

Part of the madness, thought Mckinley, was when the registration scheme for heroin addicts was abolished. When this had been operational a heroin addict could register with a doctor and get their drugs on prescription. There were then only about 1800 addicts, about a third of these were from the medical professions, another third were Chinese and centred on Soho, and the remaining third were from various sources and distributed round the country.

The 'old woman' who was asked to compile the report on addiction expressed his 'serious concern' at the increase in numbers of addicts. Tabloids ran articles about how easy it was to fake the symptoms of addiction, then become a registered addict, and then sell the dope they were getting on prescription. None of them seemed to notice that all that any new addict had to do was register and then get their H free. The result was an end to the scheme and an effect exactly analogous to that, which resulted from prohibition in the states.

Two years after the registered addict scheme was ended, it was estimated that the number of heroin addicts had gone up from about two thousand to about seventy-five thousand and was rising rapidly.

Mckinley stood back and watched. It was all he could do—watch and look after his own. 1968 seemed to stand out from the ruck of years which were pressing him onwards. A moderate communist leader was elected in Czechoslovakia but when he tried to loosen state control the Warsaw Pact countries invaded and Dubcek was replaced by a hardliner. Martin Luther King and Robert Kennedy were assassinated. Students rioted in Paris and Charles de Gaulle vetoed Britain's application for membership of the Common Market.

The decade ended with Neil Armstrong being the first man on the moon. For some reason Mckinley found the experience uplifting. Did the achievement really herald some new era and in some way foreclose on the dismal trail of human events which had crowded his lifetime? He would have to wait and see.

33

Mckinley and the end of mining

The last time that Mckinley saw Bollers and Rosalind was in 1976. Bollers had virtually insisted on a meeting and had asked John if he would stay overnight at his expense as he had a lot to discuss with him. He arrived at the hotel in the mid afternoon and was met there by Rosalind. Hugo was to arrive later and join them for dinner. John found Hugo's sister in a strange mood; they discussed mining and the two strikes of the early seventies, which had been instrumental in bringing down the Tory government of Edward Heath.

Rosalind enquired about the industry in her usual animated way but John sensed that in certain respects she seemed to have lost interest. The old socialist fire had dimmed for some reason. It transpired that she still held firm to the ideals which had gripped her in the forties, but she felt that she was fighting a losing battle against the new breed that were coming into the party. John asked what was wrong with them and was told by the shrewd as ever Rosalind that they are just 'kids in suits' who have degrees from Oxbridge and have determined that a career in politics will bring in significant rewards. They have made the calculated decision that the Labour party will afford them the best chance of getting up the greasy pole of ministerial and post ministerial financial success. She said their choice is cynical; they would join the Tories if they thought their chances were better with that lot!

She smiled and said: '*The old order changeth.*'

Mckinley picked up the line and completed it: '—*yielding place to new, And God fulfils himself in many ways, Lest one good custom should corrupt the world.*'

Rosalind smiled again and gave him a strange look: 'I might have known that you would know that,' she said. 'Do you like the Idylls?'

John replied, 'I like Tennyson; I used to read him a lot as a kid. I love "In Memoriam", and "Maud" and some of the very lyrical shorter pieces. I must admit I found the "Idylls of the King" a bit dry. I can't quite bring to mind a word which describes what is wrong with it, but that bit from the passing of Arthur is very vivid and so I do remember it.'

He continued, 'But in the small pool that I operate in, I know just what you mean. I have less and less faith in the union. Before the war, we had part-time officials but now they are full-time and paid for by the levy that we all pay. I went through the seventy-two strike and the one in seventy-four without any difficulty. At the end of the day the outcome was very good for us but it was mostly accidental and no thanks to old Joe Gormley, the NUM president.'

'What were your feelings about him?' asked Rosalind.

John said, 'Well, anyone with half a brain could see that he had been massively got at by the establishment. Socialised here and asked on TV programs there, and with ministers appearing to listen very seriously to his views, and with him being slapped on the back and told what a responsible fellow he was in his leadership of his great union and in his service to the nation by virtue of it. The technique is as old as the hills but they can't seem to see it and he certainly didn't seem to. On the other hand, of course, Heath was worse. From the bits I saw on TV and read about, as Tory Prime Minister he had an analysis of the situation in mining that he was determined to stick to without budging. The interests of the mineworkers were going to be sacrificed in the interests of the greater economic good of the nation. He just didn't get it. With a bit of flexibility he could have had a settlement, especially with a weak union leader like Gormley and with the undoubted support of the tabloids urging the miners to accept.

'I can remember seeing old Joe on one TV program asking for an increase to the offer which had just been rejected by his union members. It was a much less than inflation increase of two pounds twelve shillings and sixpence. Gormley said: "I've got to have something to take back to the lads!" Even a further two and sixpence would have enabled him to put it to the ballot. He was being totally weak and spineless of course. He didn't seem to realise that his job was to try to get the maximum possible for his members and not the least that they would settle for. The rigid and white faced Heath would not bend an inch. The result of it, of course, was the seventy-four strike followed by the election, and Heath out of a job and the miners getting a rise of about eight quid.

'I take exception to the man personally, as well,' said Mckinley.

'Oh! Why is that?' asked Rosalind.

John said: 'Because of him, my nephew, the bright one, has gone and joined the Labour Party. I hope it's not too long before he realises he is wasting his time.'

'Was it Heath's general policies he was against,' she asked, 'or something specific?'

John explained: 'Well, the lad supports the Labour Party but he had never intended to join it until Heath brought his 'fair rents' scheme in for council house tenants.'

'Oh, I remember it well,' said Rosalind. 'As far as I can make out the policy was thought up by some creep in Tory Central Office or possibly by some creep in the civil service. The whole idea was to push up council house rents on a spurious accounting idea of notional fairness, based on market comparisons.'

John interjected: 'They seemed to miss the point, or perhaps they didn't, that in places like Doncaster rents were low but they were also fair, because those running the authority had borrowed money to build the houses when money was cheap. Thus, what was paid in rent fairly reflected the capital costs involved in building those houses and all other costs. The 'fair rent' policy has resulted in Dave's rent jumping by about forty per cent and he wants payback via Labour Party activity. The cynic might say that the policy is more about reducing the disposable incomes of a group of people who are predominantly Labour supporters.

'I suppose we have one thing to thank him for, though,' said John.

'Tell me,' said his hostess.

'Well, if he had been more flexible he would have probably stayed in office,' said John. 'But because he was kicked out we got Michael Foot in as the minister who was given the job of sorting out the mining problems, and thanks to him we not only got a bloody good rise but the new pension scheme which treats us like members of staff; it's absolutely terrific. The only people against it were some of the left wing NUM thickos. I heard one telling some of the lads to vote against the proposals and go for more money in the wage packet instead of the pension. I actually heard him say: "tha dun't need a pension from the Coal Board, the government gives thee one of them." It just did not seem to have sunk into his brain what the benefits of a state pension and a firm's pension could amount to in old age. The lads of course voted for the rise plus the pensions package and after Heath's U-turn and his return to Keynesianism I don't suppose that even the Tories would dare reverse it.

'The other major thing, which has loaded the dice in our favour, is the huge hike in the oil price, which followed the Arab-Israeli war in seventy-three. That really rattled the West. Fancy the Arabs daring to cut off supplies until the Israelis pulled out of the occupied territories. The NCB are working on a 'Plan for Coal' and intend to open a huge new coalfield near Selby to ensure supplies to power stations, which will now be coal burning instead of oil burning.'

It was obvious that Rosalind was fascinated by John's

erudite insights into mining and the culture that supported and surrounded it. She asked if he had seen the accident figures recently and Mckinley replied, 'Not for several years now; we don't seem to be getting many deaths though.'

Rosalind said, 'The one that struck me particularly was the fact that in 1970 deaths at the pits fell to below a hundred for the first time ever and for the next decade they look like being well below a thousand. Even as late as the fifties almost seven thousand miners were killed during the decade; it gives some indication of the true price of coal, doesn't it?'

At that moment, Bollers walked in and greeted both his guests warmly. He said, 'Do you mind if we eat straight away? I am rather famished and I have a lot of business I would like to transact.'

Rosalind looked somewhat concerned as they went in, thought Mckinley, and somewhat more solicitous of her brother's welfare than usual.

Hugo said, 'Do you mind if we just have the main course and perhaps something sweet to follow? The game pie here is rather good—I can thoroughly recommend it.'

John and he indulged themselves in large portions of the pie while Rosalind nibbled half-heartedly at some salmon. A youngish waiter had placed a rather small portion on John's plate and said solicitously, 'Is that enough, sir?' John had seen that sort of thing before, the waiter counting on natural politeness or on a desire not to seem greedy, and hoping to provoke a weak 'yes.'

Before John could say a word, Hugo roared out: 'Enough! Enough! That would not satisfy my hamster! We would like very large portions, young man, please see to it!' The startled waiter hurriedly obeyed and placed about four times as much as previously on both plates and then hovered in case more was required. 'Don't hover, man!' bellowed Bollers. 'Just leave the vegetables and get some more roast potatoes—I am rather partial to those.'

Suddenly the headwaiter appeared and took charge,

sending his junior hurrying back to the kitchen. 'I do apologise, Sir Hugo,' he said, with much emphasis on the Sir. 'We really can't get the staff these days—he thinks he's working in some sort of transport cafe. I will have words with him later.'

Bollers instantly reverted to his consummately polite persona, saying, 'I do apologise for raising my voice but I came in here famished after a very difficult day.' The headwaiter left and returned soon afterwards with an excellent Barolo and a pint of superb bitter for John.

Rosalind surprised both by accepting a glass of red wine; as long as John had known her, she had only ever taken rather abstemious sips of spring water or the occasional small sherry. After the meal, Bollers told the waiter that they would take coffee in the small private lounge at the rear of the premises and he was to see that they were not disturbed. The young man looked towards the headwaiter who said, 'Do you have a problem with that?' Adding imperiously, 'Serve coffee and check periodically to see if more drinks are required.'

The party adjourned to the lounge and Hugo sat back sipping the wine. 'Rather good, that,' he said. 'The Sommelier here really knows his business and we are not restricted to the usual, pretty dismal, French stuff.' He went on, 'Well, to business, my friend, and first things first, no point beating about the bush. I am seven years older than you are and in my sixties and must retire soon. In my case, it will be almost immediately. I have spent the last month winding down and briefing my successors. I will depart at the end of the month and retire to the estate. I will have a leisurely retirement and be able to spend much more time with my three boys and my darling wife. Being in the type of job I have I could have continued almost indefinitely if I had wanted to, but fate has rather taken the decision out of my hands.' Hugo looked at both of them, but especially at his sister and then said, 'No use beating about the bush. I have recently been diagnosed with prostate cancer!'

John was silent and looked at Rosalind who just sat with a

look of incredible sadness on her face.

Hugo went on, 'That is the bad news, but the good news is the medics are rather upbeat about it. Apparently, they can treat it. One eminent old Prof told me that these types of tumours are very slow growing things in any case and that something else will probably finish me off before this thing does.

'I take that with a pinch of salt, of course. It is amazing how many chaps I know who have been told that very same thing and who have eventually died of prostate cancer. I never trust the quacks. I have seen far too many diagnostic balls ups by them for that, but let us not be downcast, especially you Sis. I feel fine and anything that can be done will be done. I have easily enough funds to see to that, and as the poet said:

One moment in Annihilation's Waste,
One moment of the Well of Life to taste—
The stars are setting, and the Caravan
Starts for the Dawn of Nothing—Oh make haste!'

He looked towards John and said, 'You know the Rubaiyat?' He then answered his own question. 'Of course y'do, stupid of me to ask! If I dropped dead after finishing this bottle I couldn't complain; I have had an excellent and a very fulfilled life and have absolutely no qualms about a non-existent after life.

'Sorry to spoil the party, old boy, but I do have some very important updates on your financial situation. I have carefully watched over your investments and watched your original sum grow. With its periodic augmentations from you, I have built you up a considerable share portfolio spread over eighty or so of the top European companies. Very recently, I managed to increase our share-holdings substantially because of the last Arab-Israeli war. I had some advance notice through my contacts in the Middle East that the oil price would be quadrupled and realising that this would make the stock market dive I sold all our shares, then after a few months went back in, and bought the same stock at bargain basement prices.

'You have never taken any of the dividends that have accrued; they have all been reinvested. Thus, you now have a very, very substantial share portfolio. You could and should in my opinion retire immediately. I think you will find the dividends exceed your present earnings by quite an amount. I want you to sign some paperwork tomorrow which will transfer full control of your investments to you. I will give instructions to my stockbroker and he will look after you if you need to sell, or even if you should wish to buy. If you do, just stick to the greed-fear principle, which I explained to you many years ago. Remember, buy when everyone else is selling and stick to blue chip companies. If I were you I would just sit back and let the money roll in.'

Mckinley said, 'We must have been thinking along similar lines. I have just done the paperwork to take an early departure from mining; they are offering generous redundancy terms and an enhanced pension. Although I am still remarkably fit for my age, it is getting just a little bit too much for me. The other blokes on the face are starting to carry me and I'm not having that. They are happy to do it because I negotiate our contract for the work underground and it is always one of the best around. I can quite happily drift into retirement as secretary of my local club and find things to do with the kids and grandkids. I might even get round to reading some poetry again.

'I am a bit like you, Hugo. We have very different backgrounds but I have also had a *very* fulfilled life. It's been totally amazing when I think about the poverty and hardships of the thirties and the escapades that the war thrust my way. At the end of the day, we both came through them and many did not. As far as I am concerned, every day now is a bonus. I do not know how many more I will get but I don't really care. I did what was needed in my life and I feel happy about the way that things turned out. I know very well that if the fates had given me a different family background I could have gone to university and done well. However, some of those who did so from the village and who ended up as teachers or in local government have earned far less than I have and it looks like what you have done for me will make me a winner in respect of the size of our respective retirement incomes as well.

'To put it in mining terms, we are both heading for the end of the conveyor and at some time we must drop off the end of it; all we can do till then is seize each day. I can understand why *Carpe Diem* was a favourite Latin motto. If you want it more poetically, let me give you the quatrain in the Rubaiyat that comes immediately before the one you quoted:

Ah, fill the cup: what boots it to repeat
How time is slipping underneath our feet
Unborn to-morrow, *and dead* yesterday,
Why fret about them if to-day *be sweet.*

'I don't think I could put it better,' said John. 'Probably no-one could, apart from Shakespeare perhaps. It is also stated very well in Tennyson's *Ulysses*.'

They all remained silent for a while looking at the flames which licked up from the coals in the grate in the corner of the room.

Hugo said, 'We'll have more coffee and a celebratory brandy. I know it's not your sort of thing old chap, but please try one; I think you will enjoy it.' He asked Rosalind if she would join them.

She acquiesced, saying, 'I feel I need a stiff drink.'

Hugo rang for the wine waiter and said, 'A few years ago you still had some of that excellent forty-year-old Cognac, do you still have it?'

The waiter said: 'I believe we are down to the last two or three bottles. It's very expensive, sir.'

Bollers smiled and said: 'Better only make it triples, then. Please bring three.'

The trio sat round the fire in the plush surroundings of the small room savouring the wonderfully smooth liquid. Rosalind was still in pensive mood, thinking about what was and what might have been, of lost chances and those seized from life's maelstrom. Hugo sat back relaxing; he seemed very optimistic to John, who hoped he would be one of the lucky ones with the cancer. John also sat back relaxing, thinking he felt privileged to have met Hugo and his sister; it had markedly enriched his life. Although he did not know it, and nothing was ever said, Hugo and Rosalind felt exactly the same about him. He sat looking at the white ash dropping from the edge of the coals, thinking: life is what it is, you are dealt your cards and do your very best with your hand. It's no use moaning or asking for a new hand; at the end of the day it's up to you.

Eventually Rosalind looked at him and said, 'A penny for your thoughts?'

Mckinley smiled, pointed at the fire, and said, 'I was just wondering which pit this coal came from!'

Lightning Source UK Ltd.
Milton Keynes UK
UKOW08f1353020617

302524UK00001B/1/P